'The best of the all-o...

'The top original anthology.' *Locus*

'The best single exemplar yet of "the new British sf".' *The New York Review of Science Fiction*

Following the success of the first volume of ZENITH – half the contents of which were reprinted in various 'year's best' anthologies or became award nominees – ZENITH 2 presents another outstanding volume of the best new sf stories being written in Britain: inventive and entertaining, imaginative and exciting.

David S. Garnett is the author of science fiction novels such as THE STARSEEKERS and TIME IN ECLIPSE and award-nominated short stories such as 'Still Life' and 'The Only One'. He is also the editor of another sf anthology series, THE ORBIT SCIENCE FICTION YEARBOOK

Also edited by David S. Garnett and available from Orbit

# ZENITH 2
## The Best in New
## British Science Fiction

*Edited by*

David S. Garnett

ORBIT

AN ORBIT BOOK

First published in Great Britain in 1990 by
Sphere Books Ltd

ISBN 0 7474 0591 3

Photoset in North Wales by
Derek Doyle & Associates, Mold, Clwyd
Printed in Great Britain by
Cox & Wyman Ltd, Reading

Sphere Books Ltd
A Division of
Macdonald & Co (Publishers) Ltd
Orbit House
1 New Fetter Lane
London EC4A 1AR

A member of Maxwell Macmillan Pergamon Publishing Corporation

# CONTENTS

# ACKNOWLEDGEMENTS

The editor's thanks go to Martin Fletcher who originally commissioned this book, and to John Jarrold of Orbit Books who let me get on with it.

Most credit goes to my uncredited co-editor, Frances Jobling, for her valued assistance and invaluable advice. I didn't agree with all her suggestions, however, or else one or two of the following stories may not have been included ...

# INTRODUCING
# THE INTRODUCTION

*by*
*David Garnett*

Collections of short stories nearly always have an introduction.

There are two types of science fiction collection: those in which all the stories are by the same author; and those in which an editor compiles a collection of stories by different writers. This latter category is further divided into two sub-groups: the original anthology, such as *Zenith*, which consists of new stories; and the reprint anthology, consisting – as one might expect – of reprinted stories. Reprint anthologies usually have some kind of theme, such as the 'best' stories of the previous year ... for example, *The Orbit Science Fiction Yearbook*, which I also edit for Orbit books.

And the main purpose of the introduction to all of these is to say how great the contents are.

The stories in single author collections are usually reprints of ones that have been published previously, in the sf magazines or original anthologies; and the function of the book is to collect these together under one cover. It's probably not such a good idea for the author him/herself to write an introduction saying how wonderful the contents are. Instead, she/he will ask a friend – another writer, and most likely one with a more famous name – to comment upon the brilliance of the stories. Less modest authors will, of course, willingly say how magnificent their own fictions are.

I have been involved with all three types of short story collection. The first of these was *Cosmic Carousel* (1975, *long* out of print), which reprinted several of my own stories. I avoided the introduction problem by avoiding an introduction, although I did write the cover blurb. Suitably anonymous, I was able to say how great David Garnett's stories were.

9

For the first volume of *The Orbit Science Fiction Yearbook* (1988), I said, briefly, that here was my selection of the 'best' of the previous year's sf stories. There seemed no point repeating this for the second *Yearbook* (1989), so I hit on the idea of asking a famous author to say something about short fiction. Lucius Shepard wrote an excellent introduction. (And, as usual, Brian Aldiss contributed a perceptive afterword to the volume, while John Clute comprehensively covered the major novels of the year.)

That was the problem of the *Yearbook* introduction solved, but what about *Zenith*? In the first volume (1989), I concluded my preface with: 'In the end, the only reason for an editor to write an introduction to a collection such as this is to say: I enjoyed these stories, and I hope that you will. I did, and I do.'

But, no matter how true, there is a limit to the number of different ways of saying this. Neither do I really want to have to say it again now, and then next time, and …

This is probably why all the original anthologies that existed for any length of time soon dropped their introductions. The series which produced most volumes was *New Writings in SF*, a British collection edited by John Carnell. This published thirty volumes, by which time Ken Bulmer had taken over as editor. In America, Damon Knight's series *Orbit* (which has no connection with the *Orbit Yearbook*) reached volume 22. Terry Carr's *Universe* had published seventeen volumes by the time of the editor's death, but the series is continuing under the editorship of Robert Silverberg and Karen Haber. Silverberg's own *New Dimensions* series reached twelve volumes.

12, 17, 22, 30! Imagine having to write all those introductions …

The introduction is where the editor can say 'I' and maybe also prove that he made some real contribution to the book, that editing consists of more than simply sitting back and reading dozens/scores/hundreds of manuscripts, picking out the best and sending them off to the publisher.

It does.

But all the readers can know of the editor is what goes into these few pages at the beginning of the book; and that is perhaps how it should be.

Several of the reviews for the first volume of *Zenith* mentioned my introduction, which surprised me. What also surprised me was that in almost every case what I'd said was either misunderstood or misquoted or both.

Stories are meant to speak for themselves. But if the introduction – which is far more explicit – is misconstrued, what chance do the stories have?

One type of introduction is to write about the contents. Twelve stories, a paragraph each, that takes up a couple of pages.

The editor can also write about the authors, although I do that later. I could mention that four of the first six stories I accepted were by authors with doctorates, and I was considering the title *Zenith: the Educated Anthology*.

The first volume of *Zenith* appeared with a subtitle added by the publisher: *The Best in New British Science Fiction*. Once again, all the authors in this book are British. Lisa Tuttle was born in the USA, but after ten years here she considers herself a British author. Garry Kilworth and Jojo Bling live overseas at present, the former in Hong Kong and the latter on Vancouver Island. Perhaps from their different perspectives they are better placed as observers of the British scene than those who live here – but, no, wait until you read their stories, and all the others ...

# WINNING

*by*
*Ian McDonald*

Ian McDonald has been nominated for the John W. Campbell Award for best new author, the Nebula for best novelette and the Arthur C. Clarke Award for best novel. In 1989 he won the *Locus* 'Best First Novel' Award for *Desolation Road*. He still wonders what this award consists of, but hopes there's a 'best second novel' category for *Out on Blue Six*. He says he was 'briefly exposed to psychology at Queen's University in Belfast before they threw me out.' His story 'Gardenias' was in the first volume of *Zenith*; 'Vivaldi' was in the second *Orbit SF Yearbook*.

The beach is a white crescent of sand under the white crescent moon. Caught in the arms of the moon is a single bright star; a low-orbit manufactory. Below, the tourist hotels and beach-front restaurants show a scatter of lights. Tourists from Dahomey and Luzon and Costa Rica drink and dance and snort designer synTHC and stalk in sexual ambush among the pin-lasers and multi-layer video-shriek. It is many hours since they abandoned the casual nudity of the beach to the moon and the stars and Hammadi.

He slips under the loose wire by the irrigation channel outfall. The air is clean and cool, it has the crispness of autumn and the end of the season: after these tourists have checked out of their rooms and flown back to Dahomey and Luzon and Costa Rica, there will be no more. In the moonlight Hammadi limbers up using the isotonic flex routine the Company taught him. In twenty seconds he is ready. He slips out of the fleecy track suit. The repro-shops of Penang and Darwin produce good copies of professional bodysuits; skin-smooth, patterned with patches of bright primaries, sponsorship logos in all the right places. They look good, but Hammadi has worn both and knows the difference. A copy does not caress you, does not become one with you through eight thousand biomonitors and sensory systems and interfacers. It does not feel like a living skin. It feels like what it is: smooth stretch fabric made up in the immigrant sweatshops of Vancouver and Tananarive.

The wind is blowing off the mountains where snow has lain for weeks: Hammadi shivers, breathes it in, lets it blow through the hollow places of his body and soul. Tank-taught disciplines take over, tyrosine and norepinephrine levels in his bloodstream soar, pushing him into a state of amplified awareness. His senses are so finely honed he can count every grain of windblown sand against his cheek, hear the roll and surge of the blood around his bones, see the photons boiling from the lights of the tourist hotels and beach clubs. He gathers the energy surging within him into a tight cord, releases it. And he is running, past the hotels and beach-side clubs and closed down restaurants, down the long crescent of white sand. He is the Lion of God, the swift arrow of desire, he is the man Allah made fast so that he might delight to see him run.

It had always been his blessing and his curse, to have been specially gifted by God, for his father had used it as an excuse to exalt him above his brothers. At the dinner table, the only place where the lives of all the Al Bourhan family intersected, Al Bourhan Senior would bang the table and point at the inhumanly tall, inhumanly beautiful bodies of the professional athletes that moved with liquid grace and power on the wall-mounted Sony flatscreen. Mouth full of couscous, he would berate his four other sons for their uselessness. 'You think I don't hear, you think I am deaf, stupid, you think I am old and senile; that I don't hear you muttering how I am unfair, unjust, a bad father because I love Hammadi better than the rest of you? Well, I do not deny it. I love Hammadi the best, and you know why?' Crumbs of food would fly from his lips, he would stab his fingers at the figures drifting languidly around the track. 'That is why. Because God has given him the chance of bettering himself, because he can hope for a life that is more than just getting a job and marrying a good woman and raising a family, a life that is more than serving drinks on a silver tray in a hotel or selling brass tea-pots to tourists until you die. That is why.' When Al Bourhan spoke like this Hammadi would leave the room. He could not look at his father or his brothers. He had not asked to be gifted by Allah. The inhumanly tall, inhumanly beautiful figures of the athletes on the wallscreen kept drifting around the oval track beneath the tiered seats in the great stadium.

Jamila Al Bourhan was a woman who served God by serving men. She knew that men were stupid and vain creatures, capable of almost limitless stupidity in the name of their vanity, yet she married them, bore them, served them, even loved them, because she loved God more. Her work was her prayer, her kitchen her mosque. The law no longer required that women wear the veil, but some women can wear invisible veils all their lives. She watched Al Bourhan, the man God had made her to serve, wake Hammadi at five in the morning to train. She watched him take the boy out after his day at the garage to practise on the gritty, sweating streets. At night, when the cafes and bars were putting up the shutters, she watched him, on Haran's moped, pacing her son through the pools of hot green neon Arabic. She watched her family with the dispassionate detachment of Allah All Merciful, All Wise.

She was watching from the kitchen the day Al Bourhan presented the package at the dinner table. Everyone knew what it was, of course, but Hammadi pretended he did not as he opened the plastic wrap and held the brightly coloured bodysuit up against himself.

'It's only a copy,' Al Bourhan apologised, but she saw the look on his face that was at once shy and proud. She saw Hammadi duck his head to hide his embarrassment, she saw how her four sons ducked their heads to hide their disappointment and anger. That night Hammadi went running, brilliant as a bird beneath the glaring fluorescents, just like the professionals on the sports channels. His brothers sat around the table drinking mint tea and watching a Soviet metal band on a music channel beamed by satellite from Singapore.

That night, Jamila Al Bourhan spoke with the husband God had given her. 'You will drive your sons away from you; they see how you look at Hammadi and how you look at them and they feel unworthy, they feel they are not sons to you.'

'Wife,' said the husband Allah had willed to her, 'so many

times I am explaining this and still you will not understand. Hammadi has been touched by the hand of God, and God's gifts are not to be wasted. It would be as wrong for him not to run as it would be for me to kill a man. If I push him to train, if I push him to his limits, and beyond, if I make him hate me a little, I do it so that some day he will be the one standing there on that track with the world watching him. I do it only so that he may fulfil the will of God for him.'

'The will of Khedaffey Al Bourhan, you mean,' said the woman who loved Allah more than she loved men. 'It is an easy, and terrible, mistake to make, to think your will is God's will.'

But Al Bourhan was already shouting at his useless sons to switch off that decadent rubbish and tune the set back to IntRelay SattelSport. Hammadi's mother picked the discarded bodysuit off her son's bedroom floor. It felt like something a snake had left behind.

That Sunday night Al Bourhan took Hammadi by black and white moped-cab to a street corner where the palm-lined Boulevard of Heavenly Peace ran into the shanties where the refugees from the war in the south had been hidden by the government. There were a number of other boys already there, some in bodysuits like himself, some just in shorts and vests. There was a large crowd of spectators, people not just from squattertown, but from all parts of the city. Electric thin men kept this side of starvation by government food handouts stood only a bodyguard away from designer-muscled men and girls in paisley body-paint. Al Bourhan paid the entrance fee to a man sitting on an upturned tangerine crate. Hammadi went to warm up with the other runners. Excitement was a warm snake coiling in the pit of his belly. All the hours driving himself along those roads and pavements in those twilight hours, that chilly pre-dawn glow, in the weariness after hours of wrestling with the innards of buses and trucks, had been for this electric thrill of *competition*. He saw his father haggling with a small man in a crocheted hat who seemed to have a lot of money in his hand.

The starter called them to order. There were no blocks, no lanes, no electronic timing, no hovering cameras, but crouching under the yellow floodlights the government had put up to reveal the lives of the squattertown, Hammadi felt he was in that great silver dome with the eyes of the world watching. 'Fast as a cheetah,' he whispered. 'God's cheetah.' Then the gun went off and the spectators, rich and poor, rose as one with a roar, and Hammadi was burning along the boulevard under the tattered palm-trees, blood bursting in his veins, to feel the tape brush across his chest. He returned to his father, who was receiving a large amount of cash from the man in the crocheted hat, high on victory.

'Nine point nine seven,' said Al Bourhan. 'You can do better than that.'

Every weekend there was a street race somewhere in the city, or in one of the neighbouring cities. Al Bourhan's winnings from the man in the crocheted hat, who went to all the races, grew smaller and smaller as the odds against his son grew shorter and shorter. He still made quite a lot of money out of Hammadi, but it was not riches he wanted, it was success.

The season traditionally concluded with the big meeting in the capital, where the nation's youth met together in the Great Fellowship of Sport to have their endeavour rewarded with medals from the hand of the President. Medals from the hand of the President and the Great Fellowship of Sport were the furthest things from the minds of the athletes who travelled up to the capital: the talent scouts from the big corporations would be there with contracts in their thumb-lock impact-plastic cases.

The capital was an eight-hour bus journey distant. So that Hammadi might be fit and fresh, Al Bourhan booked them into a hotel close by the stadium. It was not a very expensive hotel, just grand enough to have prostitutes in the lobby bar. As Hammadi came down in the elevator for his evening run, they unfolded pneumatic thighs, smiled diamante smiles and surrounded him in a nimbus of synthetic allure from their wrist-mounted pheromone enhancers. They ran cooing, purring fingers over the firm contours of his bodysuit. Hammadi was half-hysterical with sexual confusion by the time his father shooed them away from his champion back to their stools by the bar. On his return, they clicked their tongues and pursed their lips and hitched their rubber micro-skirts to flash dark vees of pubic hair at him. Hammadi's sleep that night was prowled by soft, writhing, fleshtone dreams.

Entering the stadium from the competitors' tunnel, Hammadi was overcome by a sudden disorientation. He was a street-racer, a runner of the boulevards and the palm-lined avenues; surrounded by a curving wall of faces, tier upon tier upon tier of mothers fathers brothers sisters wives husbands lovers, he was reduced to a small and brilliantly coloured insect creeping upon the smooth red running track. He searched the banked seats for his father. Impossible to find the one face in the ten thousand that meant anything to him. He was anonymous. He was nothing. The other runners came out onto the track and he saw their spirits shrivel as his had done, and they were all the same, equally handicapped, all street-racers, night runners, poor boys on the round red track. Above the stadium blimp-borne laser projectors painted advertisements for the sponsoring companies across artificially generated clouds.

The starter called them to order. Hammadi prayed the prayer he always prayed before he ran; that God would make him fast today. All along the line the other runners completed their preparations physical and spiritual. The starter raised his gun. The flat crack filled the stadium one split second before the crowd rose in a wall of sound and Hammadi plunged from his blocks down the red tracks and across the line in one continuous thought.

He collected his medal from the President, who did not shake hands due to yet another public health scare, and took it to show his father.

'You show me that? A bit of metal on a string and you

20

think you have achieved something? Hammadi, meet Mr Larsby. He is from Toussaint Mantene.' A small white man in an expensive Penang suit shook Hammadi's hand for a full minute and said a lot of things, none of which Hammadi could later remember. He was high on winning. On the way back to the hotel in the taxi Hammadi's father kept hugging him and saying how this was the proudest day in his life. The small white man in the Penang suit was waiting for them in their room. With him was a taller, thinner man in a Nehru suit. He was scanning the walls with a small hand-held unit.

'Purely routine,' he said. 'You never know, they get everywhere.' He had the kind of voice Hammadi had only ever heard on the satellite channels. The small man opened his thumb-lock impact-plastic case and took out two thick sheaves of paper.

'Right here and here,' he said. The small man placed his signature under Hammadi's graceful Arabic, and Al Bourhan and the man in the Nehru suit witnessed.

'Congratulations,' said the small man, Larsby. 'Welcome to Toussaint Mantene.' Al Bourhan was sitting on the bed in tears. The realisation was only slowly penetrating Hammadi's victory high that he was not an amateur, a street-racer, a boulevard runner, any more. He was on the other side of the television now. He was one of the inhumanly tall inhumanly beautiful figures that drifted around the silver dome. He was a professional.

His father was ecstatic. His brothers unsuccessfully tried to hide their jealousy. His mother concealed her pride behind fear for his spiritual wellbeing. But they all came with him to the big airport in the capital where Larsby and the man in the Nehru suit would take him onward on a suborbital Sänger. The brothers watched the incredible shapes of the aerospacers moving in the heathaze. Al Bourhan shouted at them for not being appreciative of their brother's blessing. To Hammadi it was enough that they had come. His mother nervously watched the streamlined aircraft with the crescent moon and star of Islam on its tail approach the airdock. She took her son's face in her hands and in the intimacy of the gesture they abolished every other person in the departure lounge.

'God has given you a gift,' she said rapidly, for Larsby and the man in the Nehru suit were approaching through the aisles of seating. 'Never forget that it is not yours, it is only lent to you. Be true to the one who gave it to you. Honour Allah and He will honour you.'

Then Larsby and the man in the Nehru suit came and took him through emigration control into another country.

He has settled into his stride now. All the motor and sensory faculties of his body are operating at optimum. He is aware of the exact state and function of every muscle. He can hear, like gunfire in the hills, the crack and fire of his synapses, the seethe and surge of chemotransmitters along the neural pathways. He feels he can run at this pace forever. He knows this is just a phase, in time he will pass from it into the next when his body will begin to cry out in protest at what his brain is forcing it to do. The muscles will begin to burn, the lungs to strain for oxygen, the red dots will explode softly, noiselessly in his vision. He will want to give up; stop, give in to the pleading of the body. But he will keep on, along that beach, and he will find that suddenly the pain and the urge to give up will no longer matter, his spirit will have risen above them, above all things physical and psychological. He will perceive himself running on the crescent of white sand beneath the lights of the orbital factories with the eye of God. He calls this the 'Sufi State', after those men who whirled themselves out of the flesh into the spirit. Running is not merely a conquering of space and time by the body, but also by the soul.

He has left the lights of the beach-front cafes and tourist hotels behind, his run now takes him past the condominiums of the rich; the government officials, the police chiefs, the drug squirarchs. Their low white houses huddle behind triple-strand electrified wire and thermal imaging myotoxin dart throwers. A few lights burn on patios and by pool-sides. He can hear the cries of the women as they are tumbled naked into the swimming pools and the bull-laughter of the men who are tumbling them. The cool wind carries the smell of barbecuing meat and the sweet, glossy scent of synTHC. Close by the wire, dog eyes shine reflected long-red. The manufacturers of custom dogs supply implanted electronic surveillance systems as standard. Standard also the chips in their cerebral cortexes connected to a portable Behaviour Control Unit. Implanted compressed gas lances that can blow an intruder's intestines out through his mouth and anus are extra. They watch the running figure in their artificially enhanced vision. They do not bark, they never bark, their vocal chords have been removed. Behind the bio-beat and the *drastique* the cries of the women have taken on a new, insistent rhythm.

Hammadi runs on. His footprints in the damp sand by the sea edge slowly fill with black water.

They laughed when he asked where the windows were.

'It costs a billion apiece to build these things, you can't expect decoration,' said Larsby. Hammadi was disappointed. If he was going to the edge of space at least he wanted to see what it was like. Like a good Moslem he refused the hostess's offer of tranquilizers and was sick for the entire forty minutes suborbital flight.

The car from the airport had tinted windows, a bar, and an office unit. It drove along an ocean-front boulevard lined with ragged palms. There were tourist hotels and condominiums, there were street vendors and pedicab ranks, there were people running and people walking little dogs, there were beggars and security company prowl cars. There were holographic advertisements for cameras and computers and condoms and *cannabarillos*. The alphabet was different. The other difference was the immense truncated cone of a corporate arcology standing across the near horizon like God. Hammadi could not have said what part of the world he was in.

They gave him an apartment on the 55th floor with a verandah overlooking the ocean. The only thing he did not like about it was that he could not turn the television off. He went out onto the balcony to look at the ocean and saw that all the surrounding balconies were occupied by naked fat women lying on their backs in the sun. Toward evening a woman opened the door Larsby had told him only he could open. She was dressed in a leather pouch and paisley bodytint.

'Excuse me, can I help you?' Hammadi asked. The woman stood there a full minute, smiling at him in a way that was both pitying and relieved. She closed the door and he never saw her again. His training began the next day.

The first two weeks he did not run at all. He was measured, weighed, analysed, sectioned, taken apart and reassembled. He had electrodes connected to his skull and sat for hours in a darkened room telling synthetic voices which of two lights flashed first, he arranged shapes and matched up grids on holographic displays, he was lowered into sensdep tanks and exposed to different coloured lights, he was shot full of injections that made him feel angry or sleepy or horny or induced bizarre hallucinations or made him feel like crying continuously or that he had seen the face of God and forgotten what it looked like. The man in the Nehru suit made him sign a consent form and when he woke up from surgery he was thirty centimetres taller and had plastic parallel interface ports under his ears and at the back of his neck and along his spine and inner thighs. He stroked the soft plastic with his fingers. It made him want to cry.

Every day he asked Larsby when he was going to run.

'You'll be in full training soon enough,' Larsby said. 'Don't worry, this is all just to find out what we need to design a training programme specially for you that will bring you to your optimum performance peak. By the way, sign this.' It was another consent form.

'What is it for?'

'It's just a general consent for us to introduce performance enhancing agents into your food.'

'Wait please. Do you mean you want me to take drugs? Mr Larsby, Islam prohibits the abuse of drugs.'

Larsby pursed his lips.

'Well, they're not exactly drugs, in fact, they're not drugs at all, they're naturally occurring chemicals, well, synthetic copies of them, found in the body that stimulate muscle development, neural responses, and overall growth. Really, you shouldn't call them drugs at all.'

Hammadi signed the form. He could not tell when they started to put the performance enhancers in his meals. At the end of the two weeks of testing, Larsby sent Hammadi for five days of sun sand surf sleep and sex at a Company beach resort down the coast. When he returned having enjoyed all of these bar one, Larsby summoned him to his office.

'Got something for you.' A panel slid open in the wall. Hanging there, in this year's latest pastels and black, with all the logos in all the right places, was a Toussaint Mantene bodysuit. Hammadi tried it on in a small dressing room hidden behind another wooden panel in Larsby's office. As he sealed it shut he felt it move and settle around his contours, felt the temperature control mechanism adjust to his optimum heat-transfer pattern, felt the inbuilt film circuitry mesh with his parallel interfacers. Energy poured through him, burned up his spine, along his nerves and sinews. He had never experienced such a total, dynamic communion with his body before. He wanted to run and run and never stop. He looked at himself in the mirror, remembered the pride with which his father had presented him with the cheap Philippino copy.

The training began. Hammadi had thought he would be running every day with the other Company sponsored athletes. Again he was wrong. Most of the competitive races were run in computer simulation. The few others he did meet in out-of-training hours were mostly boys like himself, lifted from lives of disadvantage and insignificance by the hand of Toussaint Mantene. Different skin, different hair, different eyes, same lives. They had too much in common to be able to communicate. Hammadi trained alone, under the silver dome with its tiers upon tiers of flipped-up seats and the lights that were supposed to simulate sunlight but never quite did.

Larsby monitored the training sessions from a glass box that descended from the roof. It had not taken Hammadi long to realise that, despite the whispered comments on the speaker they had implanted in his mastoid bone, Larsby was his coach only in so far as he was the man who had speculated in buying up the contract of a promising street runner and invested his time and effort in bringing him to the point where he might someday win him and the Company a lot of money. He had heard from the other Toussaint Mantene athletes of the fortunes in shares and influence points that changed hands at the intercorporate athletics meets.

His real coach was the computer. It regulated his calorific, mineral, nutrient, trace and vitamin intake, it programmed his hours of sleep, it monitored his body functions and vital signs from the moment he pulled his bodysuit on in the morning to when he left it lying in a pile outside the personal hygiene cubicle at night, it produced optimum performance parameters for every action he made while running and programmed them into his muscles through the bodysuit interfacers, it compared his movements and responses with a holographic ideal synthesised from the performances of past champions, it checked Hammadi's real-time performance against his optimised model a thousand times a second and tightened up a neural firing curve here, flattened out a troublesome brainwave pattern there, adjusted the levels of alpha dopamines and K-endorphin groupings so that he was neither too happy or too sad, too much in pain or not feeling the burn enough.

He saw the other athletes flying off to competition every other week and asked Larsby when he could run for the Company.

'You've got a way to go yet, son,' Larsby said in his always reasonable, always right voice. 'Lot to learn, boy. Lot of mistakes to put right. But you'll get there, don't you worry about that.'

'When?'

'When I say so.'

Months passed, the passage of the anonymous seasons apparent only in secondary, human responses: the changing fashions of the girls who rollerskated along the palm-lined boulevards; the jet-surfers and powerskiers putting on colourful wet-suits, the fat peely women who sunbathed naked on their balconies resetting their apartment lighting to UVB and making appointments to have their melanomas frozen off. Hammadi sent letters and flat-light holograms of himself to his family. In the letters he received in reply his father would say how proud he was that the son of such a humble man could hope to rise so high. His mother would be constantly amazed at how tall he was growing, how broad, how strong, why she hardly knew him for the same Hammadi. She would always remind him that God honoured those who honoured Him. Hammadi looked at himself in the mirror in his personal hygiene cubicle, the long, deep look he had until now avoided. He saw what the radical replacement surgery, the growth factors, the daily physiotherapy, the muscular development hormones, the high-energy diet, the muscle-pattern optimisation treatment had done to him. He hardly recognised himself for the same Hammadi.

Now when he trained he was driven by a deep and dark energy. It seemed like determination. It was anger, anger that his father had always, only, loved him for what he could become, not what he was. Larsby noticed the new, driving energy. 'So, what's the secret then, boy?' he asked. 'The computer models never predicted you'd hit this kind of form at this stage in training.'

'I looked at myself in the mirror and saw that I was not what I thought I was.'

'You keep taking that look,' said Larsby. 'And keep liking what you're seeing. I think maybe we might try you at the next race meet.'

Hammadi was flown in another windowless 'plane to another arcology by another oceanside and another track under its silver dome and tiers upon tiers of seats and lighting that was meant to simulate daylight but never quite did.

'You're entered in the two hundred,' Larsby told him. They were walking the track, letting the real-time analysers in Hammadi's shoes produce a model of the running surface. 'Given the range of entrants, the computer assigned the highest probability of an optimum performance in that event. Friday. Twelve-thirty.'

Hammadi stopped walking.

'Could you not have entered me in an event that is not going to be run on a Friday?'

'You have some problem with Friday?' Hammadi had known Larsby long enough to read a full spectrum of expressions into his practised blandness.

'It's the Holy Day. I can't run on the Holy Day, it would be dishonouring to God.'

Larsby looked at Hammadi as he might some dead thing washed up on the beach from deep in the ocean.

'OK, so, I respect your religion, I respect every man who believes in something, but Hammadi: you say God's made you fast, that's the secret of your success, I can accept that, you have a remarkable talent, but answer this, which would honour God more, to use the gift he has given you to show a world which, frankly, does not believe, the strength of your belief, or let that light be hidden, so that no one will see what God can accomplish through you?'

'I don't know. I'll have to think about this. Give me time, will you?'

'Son, you take all the time you need.'

Hammadi went to his apartment. He sat on the balcony overlooking the palms and the ocean. He thought about what his mother said about God honouring those who honoured Him, and her accusations that his father had confused the will of Allah with his own will. He prayed. He waited on God but no finger of fire wrote blazing letters across the yellow tropical stormclouds that clung to the horizon.

He went back to Larsby and said, 'I'll run. If I am honouring God, He will bless me. If I am dishonouring God, I will not succeed.'

Friday. Race day. Hammadi's bloodstream had been boosted with synthetic haemoglobin assistors and doped with adenosine triphosphates. By race time his nervous system was boiling with artificially induced fury. He ran onto the track and as the trackside tech team ran final checks on his biological, physiological and informational systems the cameras looked on, hovering like blue flies on their silent ducted fans. Then the adenosine triphosphate kicked in fully and all he cared about, all he lived for, was to annihilate every other runner on that track. In the blocks, the pulser ticked in the corner of his field of vision, recording World, PanOlympic, Corporation and Personal records. The starter was a ringing blip in his ears and a flash of red across his vision. Cortical electrical activity peaked momentarily to multi-volt levels and sent him burning away from the blocks in a split-second of controlled epileptic spasm. The PCP pump in the base of his skull trickled 3-4-morphoatropine and tyrocine salicylate into his brainstem, he felt he was growing in size until he filled the entire stadium. He could complete the two hundred metres in a single stride. Larsby's voice in his ear spoke through a wash of mantras designed to erase everything unneedful from his attention except winning. He was running like a god, with the great easy strides Allah takes across Creation, galaxies in a single step. Yet, somehow, there were others in front of him. Under his bodysuit his muscles moved into new configurations as the interfacers fed new response patterns to the changing tactical situation.

It was begun and ended in less than ten seconds.

He had come third.

Larsby was ecstatic. 'Third! Third! In your first competition! Boy, you beat runners been competing for three, four, five years, runners who've won PanOlympic medals. I don't know what it was you did, boy, but you ran yourself right off our projections.'

Hammadi was disconsolate. Third. He felt he had failed father, God, Company. He had never felt the down after a PCP high before. He picked his way through the other crashed, shivering athletes for a place to hide and cry.

In his apartment there was a letter forwarded from his father. There was a photograph of what looked like several hundred people crammed into the front room of his old home, all cheering and waving. His mother was nowhere to be seen, presumably making mint tea for the men. He might have honoured everything else, but he had failed his mother.

He is beyond it now. Behind him lies the laughter of the condominiums and the dark, desperate pulsebeat of the tourist hotels. The city is a cluster of lights, soft as powder, at the end of the beach, like the jewelled hilt of a sword. He runs on into the night, under the moon and the orbiting factories, past the dark olive groves and fig orchards and the houses of the humble, the olive farmers, the sardine fishermen, people whose lives have been largely passed over by the twenty-first century, except for the satellite dishes on their roofs and the squatter camps of refugees from the war in the south in the shade of their grandfathers' olives. No lights here, these are a people who rise and set with the sun, but from the cardboard and plastic shanties Hammadi can hear the solar-charged televisions the government hands out. He wonders, do they recognise this running figure in its sleek primaries and corporate logos as the same man they cheered on to victory and national glory on those twenty-centimetre screens that were the only sources of light in the fetid, filthy shanties? The same sweet, glossy smell that haunts the condominiums carries to him from the shore-line squats. The condo people buy their highs with smartcards, the shanty people get them free, courtesy of the government as an exercise in social engineering, but they all end the same. Long-term synTHC users display symptoms similar to Alzheimer's. The government's generosity to its dispossessed gently shepherds the refugee problem to its own self-imposed final solution.

But Hammadi is the sufi, the dervish of Allah, translated into a purer, higher form of worship which gathers body mind emotion and spirit together in one living declaration of the power of God. This was the part of him the Company could never subcontract, the state of exaltation they could never simulate for all their chemicals and computers and conditioning, the part where divinity and humanity touched, the unknown fire that drove Hammadi Al Bourhan off their graphs and models and extrapolations.

Every other week he was flown to a competition against another company. Hammadi made steady progress up the ratings from also-ran and third to third and second to second and first. Larsby's wins on the credit and influence stakes grew smaller and smaller as the odds against Hammadi Al Bourhan grew shorter and shorter but Larsby's eyes were set on a greater horizon. In ten months it would be the PanOlympiad and the chance of glory against the gathered corporations. Hammadi saw that horizon also, but his immediate concern was with a man called Bradley Nullabiri. He had met him first in a training simulation, the man who was to become his closest and deadliest rival. Bradley Nullabiri, Bayer-Mainhoff GmBH, born December 21st 2002 Alice Springs Australia, one of the final generation of pure-bred Aboriginals: he studied that black man, ran and ran and ran that simulated two hundred metres against him until there was nothing about him as an athlete or as a human that he felt he did not know. Then he flew on a suborbital Sänger with Larsby and his twenty-person tech team to run against him in the flesh.

He lost. They met again, in the return meet, when it was Bradley Nullabiri's turn to fly in with his coach and tech-team. Hammadi lost. There was one more thing about Bradley Nullabiri that the files didn't cover: Bradley Nullabiri was also a man who had been touched by the hand of God, his gods, the stalking ones, the ancient ones, who had drawn his two hundred thousand year heritage behind them out of the Dreamtime. In every respect, they were the same. Except one, and that was the one that made Bradley Nullabiri unbeatable.

Bradley Nullabiri knew he was unbeatable.

'Question of attitude,' Larsby said. 'Nothing magical about it. You just got to believe you're more unbeatable than he is.'

Hammadi spent the three weeks until their next meeting in the company of the psychologists who never got round to explaining what their tests were for or how he had scored in them. Team Al Bourhan was loaded into an aerospacer and disgorged after the forty minute flight to do battle with Bradley Nullabiri. Media interest was by now so hyped they were charging two hundred thousand a minute for advertising. The race went to a freeze-frame finish. Hammadi lost by three hundredths of a second.

'Forget Bradley Nullabiri,' Larsby told a depressed Hammadi on the flight home. 'You got to concentrate on the PanOlympics. Every waking and sleeping moment, you're thinking of nothing but PanOlympic gold, PanOlympic gold, PanOlympic gold.'

'Bradley Nullabiri will be there.'

'So will Hammadi Al Bourhan. PanOlympics are different.'

His father, in his regular letters, gave the same advice: Allah would never permit the Godless to triumph over His Chosen, it was ordained that he would win gold at the PanOlympics and bring everlasting glory to Islam, his country, and the name of Al Bourhan. Incidentally, thanks to the money the Company put into a trust fund from his account, they had recently moved into a newer and bigger house, thank you son.

Hammadi no longer replied to his father's letters.

Twenty minutes into the flight, just before the aerospacer went into freefall at the apex of its orbit, Hammadi realised that either he hadn't asked, or hadn't been told, where they were going. The new diamond-fibre doped ceramoplastic ankle joints which enabled him to withstand even more acceleration away from the blocks ached dully in freefall. The anti-rejection drugs were ab-reacting with the freegee tranqs. He felt vast and vertiginous.

India. The room was the same, the television he could not turn off was the same, the balconies with the nude sunbathing women were the same (except that here they were fat and brown rather than fat and pink), the palm-fringed ocean with its cargo of jet-surfers and powerskiers and body-sailers was the same. But somewhere some geographical sense long abused by the mandatory uniformity of the world insisted this was *India*.

And this was the PanOlympiad. The youth of all nations gathered together in the Great Fellowship of Sport under the Eternal Flame and the Six Rings (one for each continent and one extra for the new orbital settlements). With the inevitable exceptions; some of the companies locked in take-over and merger battles were not sending teams, and T.S.A. Lagrange were boycotting the games as protest against the PanOlympic Council ruling that their technique of temporarily suspending their athletes' personalities through massive doses of PGCPE and ergominesterase and giving control of their bodies to the coaching computers was contrary to the PanOlympic tradition of sportsmanship.

Hammadi could not pronounce her name in her native language, but she told him it meant 'Swallow'. He translated that into his native language and she said she liked the sound of it very much. She had been assigned to him by the organising committee as his liaison and guide through the planetary party that was the PanOlympiad. He was mistrustful at first that she was a spy for a rival corporation; performance data was a highly merchantable commodity. He had no illusions that his training schedule had not been prepared with the help of black data. Larsby assured him of his hostess's impeccability.

'It's the PanOlympics, boy,' as he said twelve times a day every day. 'Only comes round every four years, enjoy it, make the most of it.' It was unnecessary for him to add that this might be Hammadi's only chance to enjoy it; Hammadi understood how short an athlete's professional life could be. In three years he expected to retire with at least one world record to a condominium on the coast and a life donating sperm to Toussaint Mantene's genetic engineering programme at a million a year. So when he came out from the closed training sessions he was glad to let Swallow whirl him through the colour and movement and gaudiness and loudness of the PanOlympic city. She was the perfect hostess; informative, spontaneous, with the intelligence to be a foil to Hammadi's curiosity, witty, pretty (he could not deny that) fun to be with. She never made him feel like a street-racing boy from the global boondocks. The anticipation of her company after training put an extra sparkle in his performance; with his probability models improving every day, Larsby was happy to accede when Hammadi asked if Swallow might be permitted into the sessions. She sat with Larsby in his glass booth and watched Hammadi pit himself against holographic enemies.

'You are so beautiful when you run,' she told him. 'So alive, so you. You are like a big, graceful cat. Like a hunting cheetah.'

Hammadi ducked his head and blushed as he had learned when he was a boy and his father praised him above his brothers. Within was a different heat altogether.

She slipped her tongue into his mouth for the first time in Vidjaywada Shambalaya's, immersed in ethnobeat and video-shriek of interior bio-scapes macro-projected from nano-cameras circling the bloodstreams of the club resident *drastique* dancers. Further radical replacement surgery had left Hammadi fifty centimetres taller and forty wider than Swallow; pulling her to him to taste her again, he understood how easily he could have snapped her like the bird from which she had taken her name. The *smell* of her enveloped him, erased the din of the club.

'You've never done anything like this before, have you?' she asked.

He shook his head, shyly.

'This is your first time.'

He nodded his head, shyly.

'Mine too.'

Larsby had a singular honour to bestow upon Hammadi. He was to carry the Company Banner in the Grand Parade of All Athletes. Swallow thought he looked most impressive in his specially designed team uniform in the Toussaint Mantene colours. Parading into the stadium at the head of Team Toussaint Mantene under the gaze of two hundred thousand spectators and fifty global sat-tel networks, he looked long at the place where she had told him she would be sitting.

Later, she said she was so proud of him.

He said it had been nothing. Duty to the Company.

She said she thought he was beautiful.

He said no, she was beautiful, beautiful Swallow.

She said she had never felt about any other man the way she felt about him.

He said he had never known a woman who could make him feel the way he did right now.

She said did he want to make love to her?

And his will said no but his body said yes, yes.

Of course he came too early, before she was even turned on. He was embarrassed but she told him it was all right, everything was all right, it was just inexperience, this was new territory for them both, they would explore together, as a team. They made love again and this time it was a slow attenuated coming together that had him roaring like a lion and whimpering like a dog and her growling guttural obscenities in the back of her throat. Afterwards he told her he loved her, he loved her, he loved her but she had fallen asleep like a small and graceful savannah cat. He woke her again with his penis to make love again. Outside in the sub-morning, blimps painted the clouds day-glo with holographic sponsorship messages and the never-ending world party coiled and uncoiled. The lights of the low orbitals, the new estate, rose to the ascendent and set.

He was too excited to sleep afterwards, though the two hundred metre heats were only two days away. He sat in a soliform chair and thought about Swallow and thought about God. Sexual impurity had been the most heinous of his mother's library of sins. Yet what he had experienced had been so good and so holy that it could only have been a gift from God. Only when he had run himself into a state of sublime awareness had he ever experienced anything as divinely thrilling. He felt no guilt; two adult, responsible humans had been attracted to each other, as Allah had created them, had come together, as Allah had created them, had made love, as Allah had created them. He had enjoyed the creation of God. He had committed no sin. He had not dishonoured God.

He crossed to the bed to look at her in the nakedness of sleep. He stroked her back, her thighs, her breasts, ran his fingers through her hair. His fingers stopped on the ridge of bone just behind her left ear.

Embossed in the flesh were three letters.

T.M.®

He knew those letters. He carried them himself, in the places where Toussaint Mantene had replaced his own bone and sinew with their diamond-fibre doped ceramoplastics.

He booked a ticket on a Sänger on the apartment unit. Team Toussaint Mantene Security came bursting in through the door they had told Hammadi only he could open to see just what the hell their prospective PanOlympic star thought he was doing, but he had already slipped away from them through the corridors and arcades. In the acceleration seat he thought about the prostitutes in the almost-grand hotel. The smile subtler, the costume less provocative, the enhanced pheromones less insistent, the approach less blatant. That was all.

He had told her that he loved her.

Despite the gee-shock tranqs, he still threw up. The hostess swiftly vacuumed up the floating globules of vomit before gravity returned.

He sat on the balcony and looked at the sea and waited for Larsby. He was not long coming. It gave Hammadi a dry satisfaction to see the bland carelessness discarded like the mask it was. He let the small man scream himself hoarse, then asked,

'Who was she?'

'Someone, anyone, no one, does it matter?'

'It matters.'

'Just a girl. From our Industrial Espionage Division. A Strength Through Joy girl. You would have recognised one of our own, so we had to do a little camouflaging surgery to, ah, fit her to the role.'

'Don't blame her. It was you got careless.'

Larsby grinned helplessly.

'Tell me why,' Hammadi said.

'Because you still didn't believe in yourself. Because there was still an area in your life where you believed you were a failure.'

'With women.'

'It's all there in your file. PyschCorps saw it the first day you walked in here. You have a massive self-confidence problem with women, you don't believe you can be successful sexually. While that self-doubt remained, you could never have beaten Bradley Nullabiri. So we set you up with a woman who would be irresistibly attracted to you, go to bed with you, tell you she loved you, so you would feel great enough about yourself ...'

'I know!' Hammadi shouted. Then, more gently, 'I

know …' He looked at Larsby. 'Did she ever, do you know, if, whether, she … felt anything?'

'Would it make a difference?'

'Not really.'

'We needed you to beat Bradley Nullabiri.'

'Winning is everything.'

'Yes,' said Larsby.

'You aren't even sorry,' Hammadi said. 'Well, it will just have to go down in history as one of the great unanswered questions in sport.' He handed Larsby an envelope.

'You don't want to do this, boy.'

'Oh yes I do.'

On the television you couldn't turn off, Bradley Nullabiri was running in the finals of the two hundred metres. He won. Hammadi did not feel a thing.

With regret the Company accepted Hammadi's resignation and took away his apartment with its view of the palms and the ocean and the naked sun-bathing women. It suspended use of his *plastique* card and payment to his account and his parents' trust fund. It stripped him of the pastel and black bodysuit in which he was to have beaten Bradley Nullabiri. It put him into surgery and took back the PCP pump in his brainstem. It removed the sensory amplifiers and implanted neurochips and the biotech interfacers. It took out the diffusers and the synaptic controllers and the bioassay monitors and the mastoid speaker and the subvocal mike and the parallel ports and the serial muscular triggers and the subdermal blood scrubbers and left him with himself. It took all this away because it was and always had been and always would be Company property, on loan to him under the terms of the sponsorship contract. That was what the man in the Nehru suit told him. The only thing the Company left him were the radical replacement ceramoplastic joints and shock absorbers. To have taken them away would have killed him. He stood two metres thirty in his skin and the weight of his new mortality bore down in him. He felt like an angel cast out of heaven.

The deductions the Company made from his account for the reclaimitive surgery left him just enough for a Sänger flight home. The seat-back flatscreen showed him the closing parade of All Athletes in the Great Fellowship of Sport in the silver stadium in Madras. Hammadi felt like he had died.

His father would not speak to him. Disowned him, disinherited him, ignored him, treated him as worse than dead. His brothers wanted to sympathise but were kept from doing so by fear of their father's wrath. His mother kept Al Bourhan from throwing Hammadi out of the house. She listened, long long hours in her mosque-kitchen as her son tried to explain why he had done what he had done. In the next room the television blared. His father's silence blared louder.

'I honoured them, but they would not honour me,' he said. 'They pretended they cared about me, that they respected me as a man, as a Moslem, but all they respected was winning, all they wanted was a piece of meat that could run around a track faster than the other pieces of meat. And to please them, I compromised myself, little by little. I became what they wanted me to be, not what God wanted me to be.'

'You did not compromise,' his mother said. 'Not when it really mattered. In the end, you honoured God.'

'And has God honoured me?'

Jobs were easy for anyone who had done time with the Companies, even a failed star. Hammadi settled quickly into his post at the tourist-bus company arranging transfers between airport and hotels for the people from Dahomey and Luzon and Costa Rica. His workmates soon learned not to question this over-tall, gangling freak about his racing days.

On his way home along the boulevards and palm-lined avenues he would be passed by street-racing boys, out practising. He could not look at them. His eyes were like lead. When he came home in these moods his mother would say, 'God made you fast, God still makes you fast. He still delights to see you run. He is not interested in whether you win or not, just that you run for His pleasure.'

It took many months for the truth of what she was saying to penetrate his sense of loss. But it was the truth, that in winning he lost, that in losing, he won. God had made him not to win, or to lose, but to run. Now when he saw the street runners, he would watch them, carefully noting, analysing, mentally commenting, correcting, coaching. One night he found his old, old bodysuit draped on the bed. Mothers' intuition. He stroked the silky stretch fabric, rubbed it against his cheek. He smiled at how ludicrously out-moded it was. In the privacy of his room, he stripped, slipped it on.

It was nothing like a real bodysuit, of course, and it hung oddly around his massively re-engineered frame, but it felt right. That night he found his way through the wiremesh onto the private part of the beach and began to run, slowly at first, but with gathering strength and speed, along the white crescent of sand, for the glory and delight of Allah.

It is nearly over now; the white crescent of sand is dwindling away between sea and stone to a horn, a sliver, to nothing. He has left the people far behind, their cities, their hotels and beach clubs and condominiums, their farms and squattertowns and satellite dishes and sardine boats. He is among the eternal things; sea, sand, stone, sky, stars; unchanging things, God-like things. At the end, where the beach peters out into jumbled rocks, he will stop, and then turn and jog slowly back beneath the moon and orbiting factories to the hole in the wire where he has left his tracksuit. But only at the end. Not before. He will run the race, he will go the distance. He glances at the fluorescent timer patch on the sleeve of his bodysuit. Not bad. Not what he would have hoped for, once. But not bad.

He is close now. The sand is running out beneath his feet, into the sea. He is tired, but it is a good tiredness. He is panting, but he still smiles. He is here. The end. The race is over. He stops, rests hands on thighs, bends over, breath steaming in the cool air. He looks around him, at the white crescent of sand, at the white crescent moon, at the sea, at the lights of the tourist hotels and the condominiums, almost all gone out now, at the eternal glow of the city.

And he leaps into the air. Arms spread, fists raised to heaven. A leap of triumph, a leap of joy. The leap of a man who knows that God has taken pleasure in seeing him run, for Him, just for Him, under the stars and the moon, along the deserted beach. The leap of a man who has won.

# THE TIME SHE BECAME

*by*
*Storm Constantine*

Storm Constantine claims that her educational qualifications are too embarrassing to discuss 'but at least woodwork isn't one of them.' She is the author of the *Wraeththu* trilogy; her fourth novel is *The Monstrous Regiment*, and her next book will be *May Tricks* and *Aleph*. She is a Libran, but wishes she had been born under the sign of Lucre. Her story 'The Pleasure Giver Taken' was in the first volume of *Zenith*.

We were sitting on the kerb edge of Celestial Alley just watching the night go by, when the girl out of time walked past, looking for a moment to keep.

'Well, lookit *that!*' Sax declared, thinking twice about handing me back the smoking-globe in the excitement of the moment. All I saw was a twitch of something not-quite-real swiftly skimming between the carcase-poles of the meat-traders, a buzzing brightness, whiter than the vine-bulbs. People stepped back and looked, traders and browsers alike, then leaned in to talk together about it. We'd all seen things like that before, but such events were hardly regular. The no-time people came to taste our hard world and swim in the tides of consecutive events. It was rumoured this was a danger sport in their reality, that they risked being trapped in the relentless time-stream, where they become solid and then grow old and die. We could not communicate too well with the visitors, but I had an envious admiration for their courage.

Sax got to his feet, shaking the alley dust from his hard toenails and twisting the smoke-globe until it shrank and fell in upon itself. I did not mind. Nearly all the smoke had gone anyway, but I still made a disgruntled noise out of habit. 'Tick tick,' said Sax, 'don't be wearing me thin, Zeeb, my stripling. Wet your tongue on the smoke of time, no less.' He had a habit of slipping into market-pole slang whenever he was smoke-steeped enough to get his tongue around it.

I shrugged. 'If you mean, follow the bright thing, it's been done,' I said, 'and no one has ever been any the wiser for it.' Trying to get close to one of those people was like trying to remember a fading dream. Always just out of reach, just a hint, just a fragment of memory. Sax would not be deterred.

'But we are on Celestial Alley, my loveling, bathing in the pretty moon,' he argued, 'and this is a night for timeless things. Come on.' We had nothing better to do and I'd been about to suggest we went for a walk to explore the alleys anyway, seeing how they always tended to twist into new patterns at such a rare moontime, so I stood up and went after him, into the caper of markets and yodelling street-rogues. He didn't even wait to take my hand.

It wasn't hard to follow her trail. There was a luminous, confused mist hanging around wondering what it should do with itself; fall to the ground or vanish gracefully. Passing through it put my teeth on edge. Already some of the more enterprising hawkers were catching it in bottles, which tomorrow would be on sale as 'measures of timeless vapour for those who seek euphoria'. I'm not sure whether what was experienced in the sizzling nothingness of that stuff could ever be termed euphoria – friends have told me about the stretch-writhe effect – but people like to buy expensive nonsense and the mist does sparkle so. I expect there are hundreds of bottles of it in hundreds of homes throughout Jubilee Garter town, just sitting on shelves as amusing ornaments, never to be opened or sniffed.

Sax skipped along the mist, squawking and high-stepping enough to make me embarrassed. I walked alongside, avoiding the glances of subtle whores and trying to look as if I had a destination. Spiky, black buildings, barnacled with balconies and walkways, towered into the night around us, silent and unlit above the melee of the market, the sky huge and majestic above them, the court of the pregnant moon. I wondered about those timeless people and whether they had a sky like ours where they came from. Did they have such things as skies at all? No one had ever been able to find out.

We followed the trail right out to the edge of town where everything declines into a tumbled wasteland of broken walls and discarded lives, the rubbish our advancing community drags behind it as it crawls across the land. Jubilee Garter is a voracious beast. In the last fifty moon-cycles the used and useless ground had increased beyond all proportion. Sax once joked about what would we do when we'd crawled all over the face of the world and ended up right where we started. I pointed out that must have happened a dozen times in our history. The world repaired itself eventually, but he rightly added that progress had speeded up in our lifetime. We might live to see the day Jubilee Garter met itself coming back. Would we then have to re-think our existance and pop away into the no-time place where the visitors came from? I hoped not. I liked the day and night of our reality.

There she was; a fizzing flame of uncertainty, wearing a familiar form that didn't look at all natural or comfortable, pacing carefully like a drunkard over the big stones of the Great Dead. What did she want here? Why had she come? Sax and I stood right on the edge of the town-life. If I moved my toes forward, I could feel the cold, the utter stasis of the Dead. It was not a shunned place however. Many people came here to pick over the past, looking for treasures that might have been left behind. Our shunned places were locked in the heart of Jubilee Garter and they were the centre of things always.

'Halloo!' Sax cried, waving his arms at the girl. He is such a fool. Most times, those people don't even seem to see us. I don't think he was expecting a response. It was simply a gesture to show me what a strong-blood he was, undaunted as the shadows, and worthy of my attention. Little did he know these were attributes I often doubted. Both of us sucked in our breath and made the Safe Sigh when the girl jerked like she'd been surprised and turned what could only be a face in our direction. She was like a picture on a scry-screen which wasn't tuned in too well. Something solid at the centre, yes, but wavery on the edges. Like all of her kind, she was wearing clothes that looked as if they were only holograms projected to cover the essential She. I don't know why I thought it was a girl. There is no way of knowing really if they have that kind of distinction. Perhaps because they are more 'Essence' than anything, they appear only as an assumption of elemental polarity; the she-ness of female, the he-ness of male. This may be something they can choose at whim. Do such creatures have whims? Sax clutched at my arm, panting with stimulating fear. 'Does she see us?'

Yes, she saw us. I have no doubt of that. I was looking through water it seemed, deep water, and she was struggling through it towards us, slipping to grasp at stone and splintered wood. Both Sax and I were stepping back. This was unforeseen.

'Maybe she's not one of them,' Sax whispered urgently. 'A trick. A game. Maybe.'

Maybe. She was close enough for me to see her smoky-white face, the dark bruise of eyes. We were not the followers now. I knew that. She had seen us and fixed on us and could not, would not break away. A fix. A point. A moment in time.

'What do you want?' I said because I truly did not want her, this thing, getting too close. The smoke-globe and Celestial Alley might never have happened now. This gave me a nano-glance of the concept of time itself, but it was too brief to be grasped at. The sting of a strange, sharp aroma made me blink. I saw her mouth working. It was black inside. It seemed she knew how to talk but had perhaps never actually done it.

'Here,' she said, as if invoking all the gods of everwhen and everhow, the greatest word of power. She raised her arms, leaving a scintillating stream of after-images behind them, saying, 'Now.'

How I fought with the urge to run, run, run, back into the living night of the Jubilee Garter, even though I knew one of the most important things in my life must be happening. I'm sure it was the same for Sax. I was thinking about how I would be changed forever after this meeting and the world would be a different place. It was hard to discern between excitement and instinctual terror at such a moment.

'Here? Now?' croaked Sax. Such simple harmless words. The girl from no-time had invested them with a power we'd never encountered before.

'*Is?*' she insisted and then made a wallowing, helpless gesture, lurching, stumbling backwards over the stones, as if we hadn't understood her. Of course, we hadn't – how could we? – and it must have been so important that we should. I was filled with a sharp sense of sympathy, of grief. In an instant I was seeing Profound Lostness – a religious experience rarely encountered outside of a moon-rite. *She* had given me that. I blundered forward.

'What is it? How can we help you?' She looked confused, failing, ephemeral, yet it was apparent, in hindsight, that she was becoming more real with every instant. She ignored me, peering close at the ground, this way and that, a maddening swirl of images and light vapour.

'Let's go!' Sax urged, pulling at my arm. Such a sentiment appalled me.

'There's something wrong,' I said. 'Can't you see that?'

'Nothing of ours to care to fret,' Sax replied in an unconvincing surly voice. He had wanted her to remain a ghost, a vision on the edge of vision, tantalising and mysterious, a moon-time transient pleasure. His phantom girl had become an animal, real and grubbing at the ground. I could see she was kneeling there now. I could see the flesh of her thighs through torn, thin fabric; dirty skin. She was crying, real enough. Light, wispy hair falling over her face like feather-down, the trembling, sharp shoulders of a bird. She kept patting the rocks around her, and then touching her face, smudging it with the grey, ash-like dust of the Great Dead. I pulled away from Sax and clambered through the ruins, just a little way, till I was standing right over her. No vapour out of time now. She was just an earthly creature.

'Who are you?' I asked, simply because I'd always wanted to know. 'Where have you *really* come from?' It is only assumed the ghostly visitors come from no-time. We do not know for sure, only that they have always been passing

49

through our world, creating legends. Some, who have the knowledge, glean information from deep-thought and say they have proof the visitors are exactly what the stories say they are. Perhaps they are right. It is more exciting to think so. Looking down on that girl, I was beginning to wonder whether her origins were not rather more mundane. Perhaps she was a snooper from a town travelling crossways to our own, spinning a vapour disguise about herself to see the ways of our lives. Perhaps it was all a lie and she came from a Shunned Place, existing only to deceive our senses. At that time, I did not consider she might be a victim of her own adventure, trapped in the time-stream she had wantonly dared to sample. I reached out to touch her shoulder and said, 'Will you answer me or not?'

'I *will*,' she said, setting her strange, bony face in an expression of courage, and at first I thought she meant to answer me, but it was a different kind of will she spoke of. 'I. *Will*,' she said again, and began to struggle to her feet, groping out to touch me for support. Her costume had fallen apart; she'd grown so quick she'd burst it. The nipples of her small breasts were tensed with cold but it did not seem to concern her; neither the temperature or the revelation of her body secrets. This person could only be human; female. She had become solid; a creature of space and time.

I think the trouble was we had too much time; it was haphazard, all over the place, in and out, fast and slow, sometimes looping just for fun – and, where she came from, they had none at all. Be too fast, too much and you get kind of used to it, part of it. It was a Wondering Moon we were in then, rare and beautiful, a lust-time of sensual pleasures; smoke-globe and skin-in-the-dust. It was a bad time for her to come. I led her to the crust of the town-life and could tell every step was pain and hurting to her. 'Cannot will,' she said miserably as our feet touched the warmth and she looked back over her shoulder at the Great Dead, a smokeless vista of worn-out living. In the distance everything turned into mountains, but it was a long way away and even in daylight no greening of vegetation could be seen in that direction. Jubilee Garter devours life in its forward creep, leaving very little behind, but it is only a temporary death.

We took her back to the room over Helot's Inn, where Sax and I lived our two-life, though Sax was grudging about having her there. I was thinking what a treasure she was, even soiled and torn. Much more of a treasure than a flask of sparkling vapour, though she no more sparkled than the dust of the Dead. I fed her soup, which she ate without sickness, though with little pleasure. Then I peeled off the rest of her ruined body-sheath, sponging down her skin with milk-water and a song. She touched her tired eyes, dragging her thin, white fingers over her face and asked. 'What?' in a bewildered voice, her eyes telling me she hadn't the words to explain what she really wanted to know. I told her she needed to sleep and lit a green lamp to help her. Sax had gone out onto the street again, waspish and ready to sting. I did not go after him because I feared my find would disappear if I turned my eyes away from her.

'You are my little ghost,' I told her as she began to drowse. '*I am*,' she murmured dismally in reply.

Nobody believed she was a no-time girl. Why should they? They thought I'd found a burned-out harlot and brought her home to fuss over. Sax's friends from the ore-shop where he worked came to stare and smile uncomfortably, hoping for a pretty distraction, finding something weirdly crippled that made them feel awkward. She did not look at them much. Me, I paid no heed to their words and brought her presents from the markets; beads to wear and scarves for skirts. She accepted these wistfully and filled my breast with love as she tried inexpertly to fix herself as decently dressed. I tried to tell her about myself, that I was a stone scryer. When I threw the stones for her, they fell in all the wrong places on my painted cloth, telling me nothing. I had not expected more really.

Gram'ma Pangelo, the big woman from the Inn below, to

whom we paid our gratitude for shelter, stopped me in the passage one day and said with a hand on my arm, 'That girl's got a sickness, Zeeb. She ain't a rightness that's for surely.'

'She's confused,' I answered patiently. 'She doesn't really feel comfortable in this world.'

'Poffle!' Pangelo spat, stamping in emphasis. 'World or no world, she's seen or been something that's knocked her head two spits left of her shoulders!' The Gram'ma didn't like my no-time girl being in the building, I could tell, but didn't go further than hints or gestures to make that known. The next day I saw her solemnly draping the barrels in the bar with benign ale-berry. Courting risk, I offered to help, but Pangelo only looked carefully at my hands before shaking her head.

Jubilee Garter was moving so fast at that time, we could hear the inn groaning in distress at night. I'm sure Sax suspected our visitor was somehow to blame, and perhaps she was, though I wouldn't admit it even to myself. Twice Pangelo came panting up our dull, narrow stairs, asking us to help her straighten the wall struts at ground level. She said she feared we'd have to abandon the building and find a new one to make into Helot's Inn. No wonder she was upset. Everyone knew Pangelo had grown fond of the angles and crannies of the existing Inn. I sympathised. It was a good place, and one which I felt sure had enough character to creep soundly forward for a long time to come. Some buildings were so weak and vapid they simply sighed into dust without anyone really noticing they'd gone. Helot's Inn wasn't like that, too full of life and merriment every evening to fade without struggle. Pangelo wasn't comforted by my reassurances. She merely looked wordlessly at the ground where backbones of earth flexed and wriggled, testament to her insecurity.

Even through such times of domestic panic, my visitor didn't take to speaking much, though one day she shouted, 'You *are!*' at Sax, which I guessed was some kind of insult in her reality. Sax kept teetering between interest in the girl and outright hostility. I suppose it was unfair I'd brought her to our nest, our one-place, where we were he and me and no one else, but it was beyond me to turn her out. She was so lost, so helpless and when I reminded Sax of this, he had to shrug and agree, though I suspect he harboured desires to steal her away and propel her into a Shunned Place so we'd be rid of her. He was wary of making the heart-signs in her presence, but even when we touched she didn't appear to notice. Flesh to flesh; it had no more impact on her than if Sax and I were just eating from the same plate. I can't say she was beautiful because she wasn't really like anything or anyone we set such standard by, but I enjoyed looking at her because she saw the world as perpetually new, unnamed and had no way to name it. I tried to teach her about how to live in our reality but she was revolted by it. I think the crudest, most animal, of human bodily functions were less sickening for her than making things real by defining them. What a horror our world was to her; huge and overpowering and rushing. She could not stand up for long without becoming dizzy and sometimes it overwhelmed her so much she cried out in pain and terror. I truly wanted to know her as a person but it was impossible. All I could do was hold her hands when she felt worse than usual and sing to her. I think she liked that, although even singing involves time because you have to begin and end it somewhere.

One day Sax said, 'Do you think she's dying?' which was more of a hope than a question. It would have been better for her if the answer had been yes, I'm sure, but I knew it wasn't. Her body had become human; she ate and slept and woke up again like anybody else, but the soul in her mind was in an alien place. She had the physical ability to adapt, I think, but not the acquired knowledge to do so. I lived in a cycle of time. I knew about changes, about how nothing remains the same and that things always have to begin and end. Even Helot's Inn would have to disappear eventually, no matter how strong it was now.

For a full turn of the moon, she stayed as a guest in our room, silent and undemanding. Daytime, I led her to my booth, a light, manoeuvrable construct I'd set up in a market alley close to the Inn. It was no bother to shuffle it about if necessary and I enjoyed rearranging things inside afterwards. My no-time girl would sit, shrinking against the canopy while I threw bright, polished stones for profit. I'd collected a sackful of glittering chips, rockeyes, bloodmarbles, moonstarmirror-straws and a host of others from the most scarred places of the Great Dead, all exciting to touch and full of the past. Often, I pressed a bagful of them into my visitor's hands, making her feel their hard, smooth or spiky heaviness. There was this dream in my head that one day, she'd lean forward to the table, cast the stones and pronounce some Marvel Scry. It would have seemed natural. Everyone would be surprised and respect her for the power she possessed. This never happened of course. She just sat there, blank-eyed as a moony-blind, her fingers lax and open, unimpelled to curl around the stones. People wondered why I didn't take her somewhere she could be cared for, out of my sight, estranged from my income and privacy. I never even tried to explain how I was waiting, just waiting, for a glimmer of light in her eyes telling me she had woken up in my world and was ready to live in it. I never stopped hoping.

One day, I took her to the prowling, forward edge of Jubilee Garter town, where the fingers of civilisation creep into the lush meadows of the future and people harvest the retreating fields. I jabbered on, as I always did, not telling her things exactly because I'd learned that was a fruitless exercise, but just making pictures with words to help ease her progress. She smiled at me sometimes and hung onto my arm like any ordinary girl. It lifted my heart. I thought we were friends at last and that she could understand me. When we reached the meadows, rolling strong and powerful to meet the far sky, she stopped abruptly, swayed, and gasped. Never had I seen her react so definitely.

'Like?' I asked. It was a question she'd quickly come to understand. Now she made a sweeping, urgent gesture with her arm.

'There!' she exclaimed proudly. I realised she'd grasped some concept or another. I shook my head and grinned. She was so lovely in her innocence. She bent down and pressed her hands against the first stone of the town and then the shrinking grass beyond it. She nodded to herself vigorously like a child at play, lost in some make-believe world. She stood up and touched my face lightly with her fingers.

'Zeeb,' she said tenderly, naming me utterly. I felt faint at the compliment. And then she was running, running out into the hazy meadow, past the gatherers who lifted their heads from their work as she scampered by. I called out and began to hurry after, but she was fast, so fast, a blur in time. I had no name to call. I'd never done that to her, stripped her of the last of her being and chained her to the earth; given her a word to be. So all I could do was shout.

'Here! Here!' She did not look back, just ran and ran into the future, speeding like a comet, faster and faster until she was all fire and steam. Soon I was running into a trail of sparkling vapour, knowing before she even blinked out of existence that I had lost her from my time, my space, my heart. Forever.

How could I grieve for long? How could I grieve for something, someone, who was essentially nothing in the nowness I occupied? Sax was sympathetic, stroking my skin with a satisfied grin on his face, full of a relief he was thankfully too polite to speak of. Now she had gone, I could name her. She became Ephemeralia, a wraith chained briefly by the heaviness of time. Sax laughed indulgently at this and eventually recovered enough to speak fondly of her memory, but he never followed such a visitor again. Now I stand at the future of the world, looking forward, and wonder, if we keep on moving faster, if we'll eventually stop moving and come to be in the world where there is no time at all.

# A JOURNEY
# TO THE KING PLANET

*by*

*S. M. Baxter*

S. M. Baxter's first book was *Angular Distribution Analysis in Acoustics* (1985). This began as the thesis for which he was awarded his Doctorate in Engineering by the University of Southampton. 'There aren't many jokes in it,' he says. His fiction has been published in *Interzone*, *Other Edens* and *Warhammer*. He was also a runner-up in a well known American science fiction competition which some authorities believe should not be mentioned. His first novel, *Raft*, will be published in 1991; this will be followed by his first collection of short stories. 'S.' is short for Steve, which is short for Stephen.

It was in the year 1882 that I reluctantly became one of the first men to leave the inner Solar System; and I find my keenest regret about the whole episode is that the launch of the liner 'Australia' from her yard in Antarctica was degraded from a spectacle into a bloody massacre.

I was to have been one of the great liner's most favoured passengers. I was met at the dock of Cape Adare by the ship's master himself; Captain Roberts was tall and resplendent in his Cunard dress uniform, and his space-tanned face, shielded from the polar breeze by a mass of black beard, creased into a professional smile. 'Professor Conseille? Welcome to the Pole.'

I stepped cautiously from the steamer's gangway and shook the Captain's hand. Roberts ordered a waiting steward to organise my luggage. The steward's name was Dart; he was a slight, solemn-looking fellow of about fifty. He scuttled on board the steamer. 'I hope your journey from France was comfortable,' said the Captain.

I grinned, remembering seasick days. 'I'm rather a – what is the English? – a landlubber, I'm afraid, Captain. Seafaring has been something of a theoretical science for me until now. And I suspect that at the age of forty-five I'm rather too old to adapt –'

Roberts smiled sympathetically. 'The ocean of space sails as smooth as an icerink, I can assure you.'

'I'm in your hands, Captain. And I'm enthralled at the prospect of converting another theoretical science to the practical – my speciality, celestial geology.'

'Of course. I read your popular monograph of last year on the Nix Olympica, Professor. And fascinating I found it too, if I may say so.'

I bowed my head.

'Professor,' Roberts went on, 'you may put your fourteen days at sea behind you; after only three days in space you will be aboard a Cunard airship sailing not fifty miles over that great volcano at Olympica.'

These words, simply delivered, sent a jolt of electricity through me. 'You know, it's scarcely believable that such things are possible. Are there no limits to what men can achieve with the power of anti-ice?'

'Oh, we've plenty of goals left, Professor Conseille.'

The Captain escorted me to a waiting railway carriage. Within minutes we were rolling smoothly across frozen earth, while, within the warmth of the carriage, Dart took our steaming overcoats and served us coffee. The crockery was china and inscribed with Cunard livery.

Soon the low wooden buildings of New Liverpool – mostly storehouses and other utilitarian constructions – slid past the iced windows. 'Professor,' Roberts said, 'a fine meal, a hot bath and a deep mattress are waiting for you a few miles further on in the heart of the town – but now we're approaching the shipyard and so I've asked the driver to slow.' He grinned proudly. 'I thought you might like an early glimpse of the great lady herself.'

As if on cue the train swept around a tight curve; and there, standing proud, was the 'Australia' herself.

The space liner was built around a pillar of ice not less than five hundred feet tall and a hundred feet thick. The pillar was engraved with deep flutings – for stability during the climb through Earth's atmosphere, I was told – and was capped with a cone of burnished iron. There was a stout construction strapped around the pillar about a hundred feet below the cap, like a boxy belt of wood; I recognised this from lithographs as the living quarters of passengers and crew. Precarious-looking elevators dangled from open hatchways in the belt. The ship was surrounded by a frame of wooden scaffolding over which shipwrights and workmen swarmed. The liner was the centre of a veritable village of huts, storehouses, dormitories and other buildings.

'Captain, she's magnificent,' I breathed.

Roberts nodded, his blue eyes fixed on his ship. 'She is, isn't she? Professor, would you care to postpone your bath and pause an hour?'

'Can we?'

'Of course,' Roberts smiled. 'I'll make the arrangements.'

And so I found myself striding across timber-carpeted ice towards the yard. Dart followed us quietly. Soon I stood in the shadow of the scaffolding, staring up at the bulk of the liner. The iron hood was hidden by the fluted perspective of her white-ice sides, and sunlight scattered highlights from the polished wood of the passenger compartment.

Captain Roberts pointed at the wall-like base of the ship. 'Look closely, Professor. What do you see?'

I made out a soft glow from within the ice itself. The glow had form, rather like the features of a face in shadow.

'That is the anti-ice motor,' explained the Captain, 'the agent of locomotion which propels this unlikely construction to the planets; and all embedded in the ice.'

'One would think it would require many tons of anti-ice to raise this monument from the ground.'

'Not at all,' said the Captain, 'and that is the most astonishing feature of the substance. Professor, this ship contains only a few ounces of anti-ice. And yet, such is its vigour of combination with ordinary matter, that tiny quantity will more than suffice to carry us all from Earth to Mars and back! – Yes, even poor Dart, who I can see has turned whiter than the ice.'

Roberts walked me slowly around the base of the ship. Navvies in frost-rimed coats of fur nodded curtly as we passed. Roberts went on, 'A powerful electromagnet generates a sphere of magnetism which stores the anti-ice, protecting it from instant annihilation by contact with the substance of the normal world. It is this antipathy the two forms of matter hold for each other that inspired the original savants, conducting their dangerous experiments, to assign the label "anti-ice".

'The slow destruction of the anti-ice, controlled by a series of magnets, liberates great quantities of heat. Every second one hundred and seventy pounds of ice is converted to steam. Over a flight of ten days fully half the ship would be consumed. The steam is expelled at some millions of knots from nozzles at the base of the ship; and so the liner is a kind of steam rocket.'

'Captain, this is an imposition, but I am longing to inspect the ship's interior. Is it possible …?'

Roberts hesitated. 'I'm afraid the crew compartment is deserted. Although the equipping and victualling of the ship is almost complete, my crew are engaged in final briefings. In fact I'm due to attend such a session myself in a short while –'

'You mustn't let me keep you from your work.'

He eyed me; then he grinned. 'I know quite how you feel. Dart!'

The spry steward was at our side immediately. 'Captain?'

'I've a little job for you. Escort the Professor up to the "Australia" for a brief tour, will you? Dart will see you on to your hotel later, Professor. And if you're sharpish, you'll catch the elevator that's about to raise over there. Ho!'

A navvy had just stepped into an elevator twenty yards from where we stood; at the Captain's call he started and turned. He was a thin, swarthy man; his eyes flicked over us. He clutched a heavy wrench against his coat of fur.

'You're ascending, fellow?' Roberts asked. 'Then be a good chap and take up two passengers.'

The navvy stared at me for a full second, unexpected hostility in his thin eyes. Then he nodded assent.

The cage of the elevator was an open box with walls no higher than my waist. The surly navvy pulled a lever and we rose from the frozen ground; Captain Roberts waved briefly, a grin splitting his upturned face.

The wind was sharp. We slid slowly past the white flank of the ship, dwarfed by its huge fluting. I resisted the temptation to clutch at the rim of our car. Dart stood staring at the sliding ropes that drew us into the sky, a sheen of perspiration covering his white cheeks.

'Are you all right, Dart?'

He managed a ghastly smile. 'Thank you, Professor. Despite my job, I'm no lover of heights.'

The navvy stood in one corner of the car, chilling eyes fixed on us.

The car glided upwards into a rectangular chamber about twenty feet long and ten wide. A metal lid was poised over our entrance. Garments of treated leather hung from the walls, and helmets of beaten copper were set on shelves, their glass plates staring like eyes. Canisters of what I guessed to be compressed air were stacked beside each helmet.

'This is the Wardrobe Chamber, sir,' Dart said. 'The suits are for excursions outside the ship.' Eyes averted from the four hundred feet drop below, he climbed stiffly over the wall of the car and offered me his arm.

'Men will actually leave the ship and enter space?'

'Only in emergencies, sir. For repairs and suchlike. This way, please.'

He led me to a heavy metal door set at one end of the compartment; our surly pilot had disappeared in the opposite direction. I stepped over the doorway sill and entered a chamber full of light. The inner wall curved around the ship and was coated with mirrors; the outer wall, which leaned inwards a little, was a copper latticework set with small glass slabs. I peered through a pane: a view of the Antarctic afternoon presented itself like a miniature painting. 'This is charming,' I said.

'We call this the Observatory, sir.'

'How many chambers are there?'

'Twelve, each about twenty feet in length, spaced around the liner like the divisions of a clock. To clockwise are passenger areas; to anticlockwise – the way that navvy set off – is the Bridge, and other crew areas. If you'll follow me, sir –'

I entered the next chamber to find it full of enclosed bunk-beds set out rather like a railway sleeper carriage. This Dormitory was warm and comfortable and included a small bathing area. The carpet was a rich crimson and soft as down, and there was a smell of freshly polished wood.

'Dart, I'm impressed.'

He flashed me a smile whose pride was reminiscent of that of the Captain. 'If you'll follow me into the Library –'

'A Library?'

And so the next chamber turned out to be. Oak-panelled walls were lined with books in uniform bindings, all stamped with the Cunard crest. The outer wall once more tilted inwards, so that a picture of an English hunting scene hung away from the wall. The floor also seemed to slope slightly. Electric globes fixed to the walls provided ample reading light. A leather-coated divan was placed between two desks, and seated at one of the desks, poring over a book of lithographs of outer-space scenes, was a small, bald man in morning dress. I judged him to be about fifty-five years old. He squinted up at me through thick spectacles and nodded, smiling.

'I'm sorry to have disturbed your reading,' I said.

'Not at all.'

'Let me introduce myself. My name is Conseille, of the University of Paris.'

'Ah! I noted your name on the manifest.' His smile broadened to reveal yellowed teeth. 'I've read of your work. I look forward to stimulating conversations during the fifty hours of our voyage to Mars.'

'You're also a passenger, sir?'

'Indeed.' He stood and offered me his hand; it was plump and warm. 'My name's Holden. No university, I'm afraid; I hail from London, where I scrape a living writing popular science articles for the newspapers.'

'Then you have a commission from some editor for this trip?'

He nodded, eyes swimming behind his glasses. 'At least for some of the fare. I'm afraid I've rather overstretched my finances in paying for the rest of it. But, you see –' He waved a hand at the open book on his desk. 'This voyage to another world will be my life's fulfilment.'

I nodded, warming to the odd little man.

'As you can see it's quite comfortable here,' Holden said. 'But there's no crew yet; I go dashed long intervals between cups of tea …'

'Allow me, gentlemen,' Dart said smoothly. 'I'll see if the Dining Room is open and –'

The ship shuddered. There was a sound of doors slamming.

Dart, halfway to the Library's far doors, gasped and turned. Holden took off his glasses and stood carefully.

'What the devil – Dart, is it an earthquake?'

The steward backed towards a wall, clutching at the spines of books. 'It sounded like launch procedures to me, sir. That slamming must have been the safety equipment closing external hatchways.'

'But that's impossible! Launch is five days away –'

Now a distant thunder rose from the heart of the ship. The carpet lurched upwards; the pictures rattled softly against the walls.

Holden stood before me, stolid, round and grim-faced. 'Impossible or not, Professor, I suggest we determine what is happening. Steward! Take us to the Bridge.'

Poor Dart's mouth gaped like a fish's. 'I – yes, sir. This way.'

We returned to the Observatory. Panes set low in the wall gave a panoramic view of the ground. A bank of vapour surged from the base of the ship, evoking steam from the polar earth and forcing men to flee – but to no avail.

They went down writhing.

I thought I saw the tall figure of Captain Roberts battle

valiantly towards his ship; but soon he, too, was lost, wrapped in live steam.

'Dear God,' I breathed. 'They're utterly unprepared. It's a slaughter.'

The deck slammed upwards once more. The ship sloughed away its scaffolding surround. I saw workmen, shipwrights and navvies all tumbling in the air, hurled loose as a dog shakes off fleas. The ground fell away, sliding sideways. The land turned to a cap of ice, human suffering lost in the scale of it all, and for the first time in my life I saw the curvature of the Earth.

'We've launched,' Dart sobbed, his face pressed to the windows. 'Holy Mother of God.'

A breeze whistled through the Observatory. 'But – how can it be, Holden? There are no crew, no engineers –' I recalled Roberts' statement that the crew of the liner were engaged in briefings away from the ship.

Holden spoke bleakly, clinging to the frame of the glass wall. 'There are no engineers during the flight. The anti-ice chamber is inimical to life. The engines are worked from the Bridge by an arrangement of current-bearing wires. Professor, one man could fly this ship.'

And yet, despite this ease of theft, the shift had been left unguarded. Not for the first time in my life I reflected sourly on the overweaning confidence of these English that surely no one would dare impede their designs.

Well, if the scene beyond the windows was unreal, more immediate concerns soon crowded in on me, hard and sharp. I was shivering. My chest ached; suddenly I seemed to be sucking at drained air. I gasped to Holden, 'My God, the hull must be breached!'

'The cause is not hard to find.' Holden pointed to a quartet of smashed panes. 'This has been done deliberately – no doubt to seal us off from the Bridge, which lies beyond that far door.'

A wrench with jaws the size of my fist lay on the floor beside the damage, the obvious instrument of this violence. I remembered the shifting-eyed crewman who had accompanied myself and Dart into the ship. Was he the sole pirate? 'Then we must break down the door and apprehend the villain –' I stopped, coughing. My limbs felt heavy as lead; black spots crossed my vision.

Dart was tugging at my sleeve. 'There's no time, Professor! Within minutes the air will be gone and the acceleration of the engines will crush us. We have to return to the Dormitory.'

'But the Bridge –'

'The steward's right, man,' Holden panted. Leaning heavily against the wall he made his way back towards the sleeping chamber. 'Let's make sure we survive this launch. Then we can think about wresting back control of the ship.'

So we returned to the Dormitory; Dart pulled closed the heavy door and air sighed into my lungs. I climbed cautiously into a bunk and was soon pressed into the mattress by the joint action of Earth's gravity and the locomotive power of the anti-ice rocket.

The whistle of atmosphere faded. The fatigue of my astonishing day crept over me, and after a few minutes I was surprised to find my eyes sliding closed.

There was a discreet cough. I opened my eyes. Dart stood beside my bed. His stance was composed but the hands clutched before him showed white at the knuckles.

The noise of the launch was gone now. I heard and felt only a distant, solemn vibration; it was like being aboard a large ocean-going liner, and the soft scents of furniture polish and bed linen added to the impression of normality.

I sat up, rubbing my eyes. 'How long did I sleep?'

'About two and a half hours, sir. Mr Holden asked me to wake you; he says you might be interested in the view.'

I swung my legs from the bunk and stood cautiously. I might have been standing in my own study. 'Dart,' I asked, in sudden, confused hope, 'surely we haven't landed?'

Dart raised an eyebrow. 'I fear not, sir. The weight you

feel is caused by the "Australia's" steady acceleration away from Earth, at the – at the mercy of whoever is on the Bridge.'

The catch in his voice moved me. I touched his arm. 'Do you have a family, Dart?'

'I – Yes, sir. Two grandchildren.'

'Well, don't lose hope of seeing them again, man. We're not finished yet.'

We walked through the Library: Holden's book of lithographs lay open on the desk, and I noticed that the paintings now hung flat against the exterior wall. We entered a chamber I had not previously visited. 'The Saloon, sir,' Dart announced.

Once again this chamber was about twenty feet in length. Tapestries and some small paintings adorned the inner wall. Couches and small tables studded the carpet, and on a number of stands around the room rested glass cases fastened with copper rivets. The cases contained models of notable Cunard vessels, both of sea and of space, their every fixture beautifully crafted.

The outer wall was composed of oak panels punctuated by a series of small windows. At one of these Holden stood, hands compressed behind his back. A stark light slanted through the window and crossed his grim countenance. He turned at my entrance. 'Professor Conseille – forgive me for having the steward wake you. The viewing conditions aren't ideal here, but we must make do now that the Observatory is open to vacuum.'

I pressed my face close to a window. At first I saw only stars, precise and unflickering – and then a tranche of light slid into view from the left. I made out a light-grey surface mottled by splashes of darkness and crater rings.

It was the Moon, of course. It looked close enough to touch.

'As luck has it,' Holden said, 'our unplanned flight has swept us to within a few thousand miles of the lunar surface. A grand view, you'll agree.'

The brilliant sphere slid to the right and out of my vision. After less than a minute the ship's evident rotation returned the sister world to my view – but she was a little diminished; we were obviously receding dramatically. 'Why are we rotating?'

'For stability,' Holden said briskly. 'A spinning object is more likely to retain its orientation. It's all designed in, Professor; you may have noticed – on Earth – an odd tilt to the chambers, tapestries hanging away from the walls, and so on. Now that we're in flight the rotation adjusts our perception, so that the floor appears level, the walls vertical.'

Once again the glory of the Moon danced past my eyes. 'But this is impossible. Have I truly slept for only three hours?'

Holden smiled sadly. 'Professor, with every second that passes we pick up an extra twenty knots. At present I judge we are travelling at around one hundred and seventy thousand knots –'

I gasped.

'– and so we have reached the Moon as if it were no more than a brisk morning's walk away. And, of course, we are still accelerating. Who knows when it will end?'

I shook my head. 'Mr Holden, I am scarcely a man of action. But clearly we must act.'

'How?'

'We should reach the Bridge and take it from whoever has commandeered the liner.' I began to think it through. 'Now, the Observatory is a barrier of vacuum. But since the habitable compartment is circular, we can travel around the ship and approach the Bridge from the far side.'

The steward was shaking his head. 'I'm afraid that's impossible, sir.'

'You see, Conseille, while you slept Dart conducted me on a tour of the rest of the ship. Beyond this chamber lies a Dining Room; then comes a galley and a forecastle followed by an equipment station, a supply area which includes air reservoirs, and finally a cargo hold. Beyond the hold lies the

Bridge. The hold contains material for our planned excursion into the Martian atmosphere, including airships folded neatly away; but I'm afraid those airships will never fly.'

'What do you mean?'

'The hold is open to space, its walls blown outwards, its contents shredded. The Observatory on one side, the hold on the other; our unknown pilot has surrounded his Bridge with a fence of vacuum.'

'And so we plummet into open space, further and faster – and utterly helpless.'

Holden nodded grimly.

Dart shook like a leaf, his face coated with a thin sweat. He noticed my eyes on him. 'I'm sorry,' he said.

'Dart, you didn't sign up for this kind of escapade, did you?'

'Hardly, sir.'

'We'll just have to make the best of the situation. Now then, I've heard mention of a galley. Is it functioning and provisioned?'

'It is, sir.'

Holden clapped the steward on the back. 'Dart, how's your cooking?'

Dart smiled faintly. 'I'm hardly an expert, but I dare say I could rustle up a respectable omelette.'

'Omelettes it is, then,' I said. 'And we'll eat in the Dining Room.'

'Yes, sir. And,' he asked, a twinkle in his eye, 'will a cloth laid for two be appropriate?'

'Yes, thank you,' I said with a smile. 'Entirely appropriate.'

And so we settled into a parody of civilisation, punctuated by the clink of wine glasses over Dart's modest meals, and by the companionship of Holden over cigars in the saloon. It was a dreamlike interlude during which I found it easy to forget that I was hurtling away from Earth – that even the comforting solidity of my own weight was a sign that the thrust of the runaway ship was unwavering.

Holden and I debated the nature of our captors. 'Heaven knows,' Holden reflected, puffing out cigar smoke, 'we Britons have plenty of enemies in the modern world. I sometimes think the mechanical revolution fuelled by anti-ice has been a curse rather than a blessing – even for Britain herself.'

'That's a surprising viewpoint. Surely the development of your great cities, the wonderful machines which ply the skies of Britain, Europe and beyond –'

'But consider the uses to which we've put these marvellous machines. It was in 1842 that our explorer Ross traced Australian legends to their source in Antarctica, to the cache of anti-ice locked safely into its fold in Earth's magnetic field. By 1850 our engineers had constructed the first simple devices to extract and exploit the anti-ice – and by 1860 our flying bombs were dropping into Paris, Berlin and Boston.'

I sipped at my port. 'I suppose I speak as a victim of Britain's expansion. But your Pax Britannica is less severe than many regimes I could envisage. And Britain was on her way to establishing a dominant position in world affairs even without the anti-ice.'

'But not nearly as dominant as she is,' Holden said sourly. 'And the supply of anti-ice is not infinite. Ross found about a ton of the stuff. Although tiny amounts will power the hugest machines, nevertheless we are finding ever more ingenious ways to use it up. What happens when our flying machines are grounded? How will our "trading partners" look on us then?'

I thought it over. 'That's a gloomy prospect for us all. How do you think it might relate to our present predicament?'

'I assume some enemy of Britain has seized the Bridge in order to damage the country's prestige and power. Our fate depends on this hypothetical person's further intentions. I see two possibilities. Perhaps he intends to land the ship in some other country. We will ride into space for some period, then turn around and return to Earth.'

'Then,' I said, sudden hope stirring, 'we will have a chance of escape after landing.'

Holden took the three-quarter-full bottle of port, leaned forward and refreshed both our glasses. 'But the pirate's plans may be simpler. Perhaps he does not intend to return to Earth at all. Perhaps he merely intends to waste his own life, and ours – and a few ounces of anti-ice into the bargain.'

I frowned as the bleak prospect unfolded. 'So we would fly on into interstellar space, on without destination, until our food, warmth and air expired.'

Holden said quietly: 'The longer we continue to accelerate outwards, the more the latter course becomes likely.'

And so the hours wore on, as we waited for the steady thrumming of the engines to die, for the great ship to turn in space and head once more for Earth.

But the thrust never wavered and my agitation increased.

A day and a half into the flight we completed yet another of Dart's bland meals. Holden checked his watch. 'You may like to know,' he announced, 'that we have just passed the orbit of Mars. My limited astronomical knowledge informs me that the planet of war is far from our present position –'

I thumped a fist into the table. Crockery rattled and Dart jumped like a startled rabbit. 'Damn this uncertainty!' I said. 'Holden, surely our pilot has no intention of returning to Earth.'

'I fear you are right.' Holden sipped at his wine, mulled it over his tongue. 'And so we must face our deaths.'

'Mr Holden,' I said grimly, 'I don't intend to go down without a fight.'

Holden nodded. He set down his wine glass and turned to face me, a sparkle in his eyes. 'What do you suggest?'

I stood, paced around the Dining Room. 'Let's take it a

step at a time. We need to halt the ship. Dart, is there any place other than the Bridge from which the craft can be controlled?'

'No, sir.'

'Very well. Then we must reach the Bridge.'

'But vacuum surrounds it,' Holden said.

'Then we must cross the vacuum. The ship holds suits to allow men to work outside the air.'

'True, sir,' Dart said, 'but those suits are all stored in the Wardrobe Chamber to which you and I rode in the elevator – and that chamber is itself cut off by the airless Observatory.'

'So,' I said doggedly, 'one of us will have to brave the vacuum unprotected.'

'I fear that courageous volunteer will die without result,' Holden said sombrely.

'Will he? Holden, I can hold my breath for a good half-minute. Why could I not survive the vacuum for as long?'

Holden hesitated. 'You know,' he said at length, 'I'm not sure if you're so wrong. Although you might be better advised to enter the void with your mouth open. Retained air would expand to fill the vacuum – and rupture your lungs in the process. So – yes, keep your mouth open.'

Your mouth …

A silent understanding was growing in the room: the mission was devolving to me.

My breath grew shallow, as if in anticipation of the vacuum. Could I undertake such a task?

I considered my companions: the steward pale and wavering, the journalist overweight, ageing and patently unfit.

It was clear there was no alternative. Therefore I did not address the question further.

'So I'm outside the air. What next?'

Dart said, 'The entrances to the Bridge from the Wardrobe Chamber and the hold will undoubtedly be locked.'

'Then I'll take an axe.'

'Axe-wielding in the vacuum, Conseille?' Holden said. 'You'll be lucky to get in one good blow. And besides, the

73

doors are of plate steel.'

'Then we must find another door. Dart?'

'Well,' the steward said doubtfully, 'there are emergency access points …'

'Can they be opened from outside?'

'Oh, yes, sir. That is their purpose.'

'Then lead me to them,' I whispered.

'Now, Conseille?'

'I see no advantage in hesitation, Mr Holden. And besides,' I admitted, 'I'm not certain how long my courage will last.'

Holden touched my shoulder. 'Then let's be at it,' he said softly.


We walked around the ship to the air supply chamber. The copper reservoirs of air were each taller than a man. They were girdled about by bands of steel, and their spherical forms were obscured by pipes that snaked into the walls and ceiling.

There was a ladder leading to a hatch in the roof. I climbed the ladder and found myself in a plain metal box, barely large enough to stand upright. This was an 'air capture chamber', Dart explained. Its air could be withdrawn. And the door from the chamber, operated by a wheel, led to space.

Holden popped his head through the hatch. He handed me the end of a series of knotted tablecloths. 'Around your waist, Professor,' he said briskly. 'If you reach the Bridge dip the ship's lights. If we do not receive your signal within sixty seconds Dart and I will open the hatch and start hauling you back.'

I nodded, my neck muscles stiff as ropes.

Holden reached up and handed me the heavy wrench the saboteur had used to smash the Observatory. 'You might need this.' He reached up to shake my hand. 'Godspeed, Conseille. Now remember: mouth open.' He ducked down through the hatch and closed the metal lid.

I heard the wheel lock close. The scrape of metal on metal was final; I fought for some seconds with the temptation to cry for readmission.

At last, with an effort, I turned to the doorway. I laid my hands on the ice-cold metal wheel, took as firm a grip as I could, and turned the wheel anticlockwise.

The door opened a fraction of an inch. Air hissed – and there was a whir of electric pumps, a stab of pain in my ears. I opened my mouth wide and felt air rush past my drying tongue.

Sound died.

The door slid open and I stepped out of the air capture chamber.

I stood on the roof of the passenger compartment, a wooden path that snaked like a mountain road around the curving wall of ice to my right. To my left was – nothing. An infinite drop with a backdrop of unflickering stars which rotated grandly.

Needles of pain thrust at my eyes; I clenched them shut, allowing myself only the occasional squint through tight lids. I reached to the right and found the cold wall. Then, trailing my fingers over the fluted ice, I hurried around the roof, my footfalls eerily silent.

After some forty feet – perhaps fifteen seconds into vacuum – my cautious glimpses showed me another air capture compartment. This, I knew, was the entrance to the Bridge.

Mouth gaping, the need to suck in a breath mounting in me, I grabbed at the door wheel and twisted. It gave; shreds of air puffed out around my face.

I untied my knotted cloths and entered the chamber, pulling the hatch behind me. Air sighed into the chamber and sound returned in a rush. I fell to my knees, gasping; I found blood flecks at my mouth, ears and nose.

When the pain in my lungs had dulled enough to let me think I bent to the hatch set in the floor. I hefted the wrench in my right hand and with my left hand turned the wheel.

The hatch fell open easily. I obtained a sudden impression of the Bridge – of a mosaic of dials and needles set around a circular, midnight blue table – and of a single, swarthy face looking up at me in shock. It was indeed the navvy who had accompanied me and Dart in the elevator.

Surprise was my only ally. I half-leapt down the ladder to the deck; I gathered the muscles of my right arm and swung the wrench in a wide arc. The jaws hit his left temple; he crumpled to the floor.

A hasty scan told me that he had indeed been alone; other than Bridge equipment and fixtures there were only the remains of a packet of food, a cask of water and some improvised toilet arrangements. It was a matter of a few seconds to find a way to dim the lights of the main compartment, and so to signal to my waiting companions that my extraordinary mission had been successful.

And then it was over. I stumbled against a bank of instruments and felt the universe whirl around me; my every muscle trembled as if drained, and I wished passionately that I were safely back in my book-lined study in Paris.

When I had recovered my composure I bound up my kidnapper with his own jacket. He stirred briefly to consciousness, fixed me with eyes whose despair was jarring, and collapsed once more.

I found that the Wardrobe Chamber, adjacent to the Bridge, was still pressurised. The deck hatch had closed over the gondola Dart and I had taken up to the ship less than two days earlier; its remains jutted from the metal frame. I donned one of the clumsy vacuum suits and entered the airless Observatory. I used the material of spare suits to block up the smashed panes of glass. At last air hissed once more into the chamber and I was able to doff my suffocating helmet.

I threw open the door to my waiting companions. I allowed them to remove my vacuum suit and put up with their effusive expressions of thanks. Holden took my wrench and returned to the Bridge; I allowed Dart to make me some coffee, stretched out on a couch in the Saloon, and slept for three hours.

On waking I washed myself and gargled for some minutes in the Dormitory's small bathroom, attempting to relieve the vacuum pain of my throat and chest; then I straightened my tie and walked through to the Bridge.

Dart was surveying banks of dials and switches. I recognised manometers and thermometers, among much else. The steward doubtfully compared readings against diagrams in a fat, leather-bound manual. I noticed he carried the wrench tucked into the belt of his trousers.

'Professor!' Holden had his jacket off and was bent over the circular table I had noticed earlier. 'I trust you're recovered.'

It was difficult to speak. 'I'm fine, thank you, Mr Holden.'

The renegade I had overcome lay propped against one wall. His arms and legs were firmly bound by strips of tablecloth and his dark head was down, his chin against his chest. I dropped to my haunches before him. At length he raised his bloodied head and met my gaze. His thin face, covered by three days' dirt and growth of beard, had a dark, almost Latin complexion. He looked less than twenty-five.

'I hope I didn't hurt you,' I said stiffly.

'I live,' he said – in French. 'My name is Michelet.'

A shock passed through me at the sound of my native language. 'So we're countrymen,' I replied in the same tongue. 'But I don't understand –'

'And I don't understand why you walked through vacuum to help these pigs.' His accent, full of bitterness and contempt, bore soft traces of the south – perhaps of Marseilles.

I noticed the Englishmen glance around uneasily at this flow of high-speed French, but I ignored them. 'How could you fly the ship alone?' I asked.

He sneered. 'It was not difficult. The ship is directed by a set of controls simple enough for the English monkeys to operate. Despite my appearance I have some technical education; of course no English would suspect a lowly "Frenchie" of such capability. I got myself assigned to the bridge and simply observed their training routines.'

'Why did you take the ship? You were trying to destroy it, weren't you? And yourself in the process. Why?'

'Because,' he said as if to a child, 'I wanted to hurt the English. I wanted to take away their prestigious space liner. I wanted to waste a little more of their damned anti-ice, against the day when it is all used up and we are free.'

'Damn it, man, the war is a generation ago. History. We have to live in the world as is. Why so much hate?'

'Because of the Declaration of the Rights of Man,' he said. 'Banned from the streets of Paris since the day the English bombs flew from Kent. Now do you understand?' And he dropped his head, as if dismissing me.

Shaken, I turned to Holden. The journalist still worked at the blue table. 'And how is progress here?'

'The steward seems to be making a good job of checking the ship's systems. And I have been puzzling out this remarkable gadget.' His cheeks were flushed with a kind of pleasurable excitement.

I stepped forward and studied the midnight-blue table. It was some five feet across. Eight concentric rings, each separately moveable, surrounded a globe of yellow glass. Each ring bore a marble-sized globe of its own. The context made the meaning clear. 'This is undoubtedly an orrery,' I said, 'showing the sun and all eight of its planets, out to the furthest, Neptune.'

'An arrangement of cogs and gears beneath the surface makes the models track across this wooden sky. And that's not all – notice the fine perforations covering the tabletop, Professor; and see these flags thrust through the perforations.'

The little metal flags marked a line, nearly straight, that swept outwards from the third marble – from blue Earth.

'This is our course?'

'That's right. The orrery is a navigation aid, a mechanically maintained image of our trajectory. I imagine it works by inertial means. There must be a series of gyroscopes buried in the table, capable of detecting changes to the ship's orientation or acceleration.'

'Ingenious. But can it tell us how to return to Earth?'

Holden grinned. His hair stood in an excited fringe around a flushed scalp. 'Ah, Conseille; it tells us that – and a lot more besides. Look.' We bent over the line of metal flags. 'Here we are. At present we are flashing away from home at some three million knots, and we are still accelerating. We must subdue the ship's engines –'

'Can we do that?'

'Yes, it's quite a simple matter,' Holden said testily. 'After all ignition was easy enough, as our unkempt companion over there will verify. Let us suppose that takes another six hours. Next we turn the ship over, so that we're flying along backside first. There are small rockets fitted to the nose and tail of the ship for just that purpose. That takes, let us say, twenty-four more hours. Then we relight the engines and begin a steady deceleration. It will have taken us over three days to reach our top speed; we will be about here –' he pointed to the orrery '– and it will take as long again before we glide to rest. And then we will start to build our velocity once more for another week's journey home.'

'We will come to rest twice as far from Earth as at the midpoint. We will be – about – here.' My finger rested on the fifth ring from the Sun; a fat, pink marble lay beneath my nail.

'That's right,' Holden breathed. 'We will lie some five hundred million miles from the Sun. We will have flown further and faster than any human before. And look where your finger lies, Conseille. That globe is the fifth planet. The king world, Jupiter! An adjustment of just a few degrees to our trajectory – easily achieved with the controls laid out in this Bridge – and we can sail past the Jovian moons.

Professor, we must take this opportunity. We owe it to ourselves – to science!'

Fired by his enthusiasm I could only agree. Even Dart eyed the orrery with interest.

So our journey was transformed from a helpless fall into terror to a voyage of wonder – and yet …

And yet I found it impossible to put aside the words of my compatriot.

I walked up to Michelet. He raised his face, a look of faint scorn about his mouth. 'Listen to me,' I said in our common language. 'You have made your gesture.'

He snorted. 'All I have achieved is to deliver to these English another world upon which to plant their ugly flag.'

'But,' I persisted, 'you would agree that further damage is futile.'

I waited for his reply. At length he nodded.

'All right. I propose to cut your bonds and take you out of here. I will watch your every moment. And I will have Dart, the steward, keep that wrench in his belt. But you will have some freedom of movement.'

He studied me distrustfully. 'Why are you doing this?'

'When we return home I will deliver you to the proper authorities. But until then you are a fellow human, one of just four in this immense void. I would rather you did not suffer.'

At length he held up his bound arms; I freed him and, leaving Dart and Holden to continue their inspection of the ship, I escorted Michelet through the ship to the Dining Room. And so, at a table set with silver cutlery and the finest china, a Professor of the University of Paris set a meal before a round-eyed boy from Marseilles, the whole tableau hurtling tens of thousands of miles every second through interplanetary space.

A gong sounded through the ship. The vibration of the great engines faded and weight disappeared from my shoulders. Dart and Holden, our impromptu crew, worked on the

Bridge, while we two Frenchmen remained in the Saloon and Library, clinging cautiously to the furniture. Now more subtleties of the ship's design became apparent: each piece of furniture was attached to the floor or wall, either by screws or by lengths of elastic, and within each divan were concealed belts which could pin one reassuringly into place.

I took a bottle of wine and attempted to fill a glass. To my surprise the liquid emerged in small, wobbling spheres. Michelet and I poked at them until they combined into a single planet of wine; we pierced its meniscus with straws and took sips of the stuff, watching the globe shrink as we did so.

Michelet laughed. When he did so he looked very young.

After some hours of this the gong sounded again, telling us that the turnover manoeuvre was complete. The huge motors inside the ice shuddered to life, and weight settled on us again.

Three days and ten hours past the mid-point, the steward summoned us to the Observatory. I stood before the glass wall and wonder surged through me.

Jupiter hung before us. Its pinkish clouds were swirls of watercolour paint. We were slightly above the equator so that one pole was tilted towards us, and a crescent slice of the sphere lay in the sun's shadow. One moon showed as a clear disc, off to the right; the sharp shadow of another tracked slowly across the cloud tops.

The four of us stood in a mute row, our faces bathed in salmon light. 'Professor,' Holden said, his shirt open at the collar, his voice strained, 'this is a sight never before granted to human eye. Was the trip worth the trouble?'

'Oh, I think so, Mr Holden. Don't you?'

The liner's slow rotation brought another moon into view. This had been made irregular by a series of monstrous craters.

'Which moon is that?'

Holden shrugged. 'It is only a mile across. Far too small

to see from Earth. It is our discovery. Ours to name and claim.' He grinned. 'Not much of a territory, mind you; it looks as if truly severe explosions have taken place on that surface.

'Now then, Dart, Professor, I suggest we return to the Bridge and begin our observations. We have barely a day before we begin our rush back to Earth.'

And so the three of us reluctantly turned from the window …

The three of us?

The door to the Wardrobe Chamber was closed. Holden studied it, as if puzzled.

'Michelet,' I breathed. 'But he gave me his word.'

Holden whirled, eyes blazing. 'Has that damn Frenchie gone ape again? I knew we shouldn't have trusted him. Is he going to destroy us without giving us a chance to take all this home to humanity?'

Dart coughed sadly. 'I don't believe he betrayed your trust, in fact, Professor. Look.'

We turned back to the windows. A figure, stiff and immobile, drifted over our heads and away from the liner.

Michelet's eyes were closed.

I sighed. 'He must have stepped out of the air capture chamber over the Bridge.' And he let the air spill from his lungs and stepped over that infinite cliff –

'That's a damn fool thing to do,' Holden murmured. 'What's that he's got in his hand?'

It was a fragment of multicoloured cloth. 'I believe it is the Tricolor.'

'The what?'

The body arced towards the battered moon, caught in its feeble gravity field.

– and a flash like noon sunlight slammed into the Observatory. The ship lurched, rocked, stabilised.

There was a new crater on the moon, glowing still.

Dart crossed himself. 'Dear God. Was that the Frenchie?'

'It was.' Holden turned to me, eyes narrow and glittering

82

in the Jovian light. 'You know what this means, don't you, Conseille?'

I thought it over. And I feared I did understand.

'No simple impact could cause a bang like that,' Holden said. 'There's anti-ice down there. Maybe the whole damn moon – cubic miles –

'Just think of it! No longer will we have to fear the exhaustion of our cache in Antarctica. I picture fleets of magnetised freighters plying to and fro from Earth – of course we'll have to work out vacuum mining techniques –' His words came faster, higher-pitched. 'Perhaps anti-ice is scattered throughout the Solar System and beyond, waiting to be claimed by British explorers. The shadow of the Union Flag will stretch out across the centuries and the stars, vast and unassailable! Come, gentlemen. We're at a turning point in human affairs. Let's retire to the Saloon and drink a toast to the future.'

I lingered for some seconds, staring at the crater made by the boy from Marseilles. Then I followed the Englishmen.

# X-CALIBRE

*by*
*Garry Kilworth*

Garry Kilworth left school at fourteen, but they allowed him back over a quarter of a century later to take an honours degree in English at King's College, London. In between, he served in the RAF, worked for Cable and Wireless – and wrote the first of his sixty published stories and twenty books. He now lives in Hong Kong. When he returned to Britain in 1989 for the publication of his bestselling novel *Hunter's Moon*, he was homesick and ate at a Chinese restaurant. His next novel will be *Midnight's Sun*, his next collection *Dark Hills and Hollow Clocks*. His story 'White Noise' was in the first volume of *Zenith*; 'Murderers Walk' was in the first *Orbit SF Yearbook*.

## The Dark Age

A dark age has fallen upon the ancient halls of
Whorestraete. Men gather in groups, heavy-eyed, hollow-
eyed, whispering from gaunt faces. Others stand alone, in
the washrooms, staring into mirrors which appear to have no
finite depth. There are those who have plunged from high
places, some figuratively, some even physically.

Whorestraete was once a flourishing stronghold, its floors
sounding with the soles of expensive shoes, its walls ringing
with the shouts of dealers. Its noble houses seemed
indestructible, its stockbroker lords immortal. Now and then
one might fall prey to the temptation of insider dealing, and
be struck off the lists of the mighty families, or destroy itself
from within, but these had hitherto been isolated
misfortunes. The oligarchies whose vaults had once seemed
invincible had now been shown the index finger. Since the
crash fortunes have been lost overnight. Out of this darkness
has come widespread corruption, as men try to save
themselves from the pit. The red figure of bankruptcy stalks
the kingdom: he prowls through halls, offices and corridors,
and gathers men to him in a harvest of broken dreams.

In the house of Utha, prayers are muttered before vdus,
murmured into telephones: prayers for a saviour, who might
deliver them from chaos and restore confidence in the
market once again.

## The Legend

Amongst the rubble of fallen firms, in the basements of
crumbling companies, it has long been whispered that a

Hero strong enough to restore order and sanity to the kingdom will arise. It is said that this man will come from the family of an aristocratic firm of stockbrokers, will be of inherited wealth, but by necessity will have been raised in ignorance of the vagaries and vicissitudes of the market. Thus he will be pure of spirit, untarnished by the sordid dealings of the Dark Ages and able to operate with a clear conscience.

He was expected to be, like all great stock market heroes, a man of great wisdom, without fear; ruthless but with an impeccable integrity. He would no doubt continue the practice of worshipping Chance, the god of Whorestraete, but with a clean mind, capable of restoring the treasure house to its former respectability and glory. Security would be his watchword and all would yield to his advice.

## The New King

And a Hero does emerge from the mists, fresh from the College of Business Administration, but her name is Gwenyth, and being a woman the remnants of the Old Families of Bankers and Stockbrokers refuse to accept her. Never before has a female warrior stood at the head of their armies, led them into battle against their foes.

There is a split amongst the nobles, and some leave with her half-brother Morton, a man dedicated to corruption, and some remain with Gwenyth who forms a New Company. Gwenyth is elected the President of the new company, which she calls The Avalon Group. She insists that all the board members have an equal vote, and that there shall be no lobbying and no yes-men, and the board table shall be *round*, to emphasise the fact that it is a *group* effort and no single member is more important than another. Gwenyth is aware that internal petty jealousies can be more devastating than any damage an outsider may inflict.

88

## The Magic Weapon

Gwenyth knows she needs a symbol of authority to give her the strength to rid Whorestraete of the damned Morton, who has already covered his arrears with gold and silver. Gwenyth has a childhood sweetheart by the name of Merle, who is an electronics wizard. Merle invents for her a computer the like of which has never been seen before. The magic of Merle is not only in the system, which is able to accommodate any software program in the known world, but in the flexibility of its disc drive slot, which will expand and contract to accept any kind of disc that was ever forged on the anvils of computersmiths. Thus a disc from any region of the earth can be inserted and its information assessed immediately. In Whorestraete, fractions of seconds count, and fortunes are made by the quick, leaving competitors dead. In Merle's computer, Gwenyth has her taliswoman.

$$x = Slot\ vol,\ where\ x\ is\ l \times b \times h\ of\ disc$$

Merle explains that $x$ equals the calibre of the disc drive slot when $x$ is the size of any given disc. Gwenyth bestows upon her magic weapon the access code '$x$-calibre'.

## Right-hand Man

Gwenyth discovers that great heroes also require a friend and adviser, a trouble-shooter who will go through fire. Although she trusts those around the board table, she needs a consultant with unshakable loyalty. This person must have impeccable credentials, be afraid of nothing, be pure of spirit. She asks her secretary to search the lists for one who is not afraid to joust with dark market forces.

Such a person sweeps into her office one day. She has travelled from a distant land called Lundun, and has knowledge of Hung Gung and Toakio stock markets. She is the ex-vice-president of French and French Inc., a family business famous for its integrity and morals. The woman's name is Lily. She states that private domestic misfortunes caused her departure from F&F Inc., that she has heard of Gwenyth, and now wishes to serve The Avalon Group in any capacity.

Gwenyth is overjoyed. With Merle's x-calibre computer in her hands and an ex-inc vip for an ally, she is convinced that Morton will soon need more than heavy metals to protect his assets. Her half-brother is casting a slick shadow over Whorestraete, and brokers go in fear of him, for he has destroyed many of their options in his greed for power. His self-interest is boundless. Now Gwenyth has the means to meet him on the battlefield in a final confrontation. She begins to make her plans.

There is some jealousy in the Avalon camp because Gwenyth shows a marked preference for the views of Lily and favours her new companion with more time than she gives others. The Company President is aware of this dissatisfaction, but considers there are more important things with which to concern herself.

## *The Unknown Factor*

Illicit love will penetrate the strongest armour with its barbed and wicked arrows. Until Lily arrived at Whorestraete, Merle and Gwenyth had an understanding, a close relationship of the shared kind. Gwenyth possessed a high retreat to which they escaped from time to time, but when they could not they played bondage games behind the gates of their office citadel, finding great excitement in locking each other in Gwenyth's personal stocks.

Now that the great battle is almost upon her, however, Gwenyth has to work late. She cannot meet with Merle in her high tower, nor does she have time for manacled love in the shadowed recesses of her office fortress. She tells Lily she would appreciate it if her right-hand man would keep Merle company of an evening, explaining that though Merle is magic with electronic equipment he bores the socks off most people with his interest in computers.

## Suspicion and Envy

There is talk behind closed doors in the House of Avalon, of how Lily is having an affaire with Gwenyth's lover. Noble lords and ladies mutter through gritted teeth that 'the woman must go' for she has committed the cardinal sin of monopolising all sexual intrigue, and is driving everyone mad with envy and suspicion.

They all add their own dark misgivings, at the same time craving similar liaisons with Lily, Merle and each other, but not daring to make the first move for fear of rejection. Lust is in every noble's mind. It eats away at the very mortar of their foundations, it gnaws at the bastions and keeps, and the company begins to crumble.

Gwenyth will hear nothing against her friend, nor against her lover, both of whom she would trust with her bank balance. When Merle and Lily run away together, to Akapulko, Gwenyth falls into deep despair and neglects the management of the kingdom.

## Regrets and Betrayal

Lily dispatches a message to Gwenyth from Akapulko, repenting of her deeds, and stating that before she left Whorestraete she had uncovered treachery. Lily's note tells Gwenyth that the user manuals Merle wrote for the $x$-calibre system have been stolen, lock, stock and barrel, by Gwenyth's secretary, who is an agent for the Morton Group.

Without Merle to advise her on the system, the user instructions for *x*-calibre are essential, and Gwenyth sends her knights out, to seek the traitorous secretary. They are in the field for many weeks, some of them never return from their quest. They are lost out in the wildernesses of concrete and brick. Some fall prey to higher offers from other giants and dragons of the business world. Others do battle with terrible bulls and savage bears, occasionally making a killing, but more often than not going under. Those that do return are empty-handed, dispirited and unable to assist her in the final fight for the controlling shares of key companies.

At the fateful hour of the battle with Morton, *x*-calibre goes down. Merle, her electronics wizard is somewhere else, humping her right-hand man.

Gwenyth stands in the fray with the remnants of her army, teeth gritted and with blood in her eyes, but without her magic weapon. She is still determined to destroy Morton for good and all. She has right on her side, and she prays that her god will see her triumph over her half-brother.

The carnage that follows is awful to witness. Holdings are lost, trusts destroyed, bondsmen are driven back and forth, stockades fall, shares are forged into weapons on the fires of wrath. Votes are cast and the air is thick with oaths. Finally, just before the market closes only Morton and Gwenyth stand head to head trading blows. At the height of single combat, the swaying Whorestraete god finally settles his support on the corrupt Morton. Chance is amoral and distributes his favours by whim. Gwenyth is forced to yield and crawls away at the end of the day, hollow and defeated.

### The Aftermath

Gwenyth never recovers from this last betrayal. She is found sitting before a blank screen, punching at random keys in a daze, and is finally prised from *x*-calibre. To her credit, her last quotation is spirited and full of venom.

'Throw the fucking thing in the lake!'

Gwenyth has not failed because she is pure, nor because she put her faith in the wrong kind of people, nor because $x$-calibre went down at a crucial time. She has not fallen from grace because love has no place in a board room, nor even because her secretary was a spy for the Morton Group.

She failed because she chose a fickle god.

# A PASSION FOR
# LORD PIERROT

*by*
*Colin Greenland*

Colin Greenland, D.Phil. Sci-Fi (Oxon.) won the University of California's Eaton Award for science fiction criticism in 1985, for his book, *The Entropy Exhibition*, on Michael Moorcock and *New Worlds*. He is also the author of four novels, including the space opera *Take Back Plenty*. Why is it so entitled? 'Read it and see,' says the author. But he would, wouldn't he? His story 'The Traveller' was in the first volume of *Zenith*.

In the land of Anise, on the planet of Triax, it is the hour after dinner. Lord Pierrot sits alone in his apartment, playing the accordion. He reclines on a couch and plays a slow, sad tango. A melancholy fit is upon him, for he remembers the past, the years before he came into his inheritance.

He is thinking of other nights, nights of gaiety when he sauntered with his comrades through yellow gardens on the moon, the same moon that now shines on the lake, turning it the colour of fine honey. On those nights he had not a care to his name, and the songs he sang were merry. He was young then, Lord Pierrot, and now he is old, as they reckon such things on the planet of Triax.

Lord Pierrot's whole apartment is most sumptuously appointed. The furnishings are made of velvet, the floor of glossy yellow hardwood imported all the way from Peru, on Earth. Splendid specimens of the local wildlife decorate the walls, represented by their severed heads. But tonight Lord Pierrot is not comforted by luxuries, nor by the trophies of his skill in the slaughter. Tonight there will be no comfort for him but in the arms of his paramour, Daphne Dolores.

He will go to her now, this minute. He rises and tucks the accordion under his arm, to entertain her, later, with some music. With this thought he steps from his chamber into the shaft and goes down, out of the front door into the stifling night.

Lord Pierrot crosses the lake by means of his little rowing boat. The moon is bright. Tomorrow night, he thinks, it will be full. Across the water he sees a light in the window of the lodge that stands upon the other shore. Moon or no moon, that is his beacon, his guiding star.

He moors below the lodge, in the lee of a black rock that shelves out like a parapet over the water. The rock was brought back from the Horsehead Nebula by Lord Pierrot's father, at a time when society admired such actions. Lord Pierrot climbs upon it now and stands gazing at the moonlit lodge. A languid breeze toys with his pale hair.

In the silence he hears the door of the lodge open, and then he sees her, sees Daphne Dolores, running to greet him.

'Daphne Dolores!' cries Lord Pierrot, and he springs from the rock. At once she is in his arms. He holds her very tightly, though not inconsiderately. He feels the beating of her heart, that splendid organ. Its rhythm betrays only a slight sign of exertion – or is that passion, passion for Lord Pierrot?

'Daphne Dolores,' murmurs Lord Pierrot ardently. 'My love.'

'My darling,' Daphne Dolores replies, in rapture.

Daphne Dolores is slight and becomingly small of stature. She looks up at Lord Pierrot and presses the palm of her hand to his breast in a way that he finds irresistible. Her blue eyes sparkle in the moonlight. At this moment he would do anything for her, anything she asked. At this moment he would give up his wife, his house, his lands, his laboratories, and take her away on a journey to another star, a journey to last a lifetime.

Fortunately, Daphne Dolores does not ask him to do so. She does not ask him for anything. It is not in her nature to ask for things.

The most she will ever ask is: 'Are you pleased to see me?'

Lord Pierrot is inflamed with love for her. He kisses her fiercely, bearing down on her in his hunger for her lips.

She returns his kiss as avidly as he gives it her, Daphne Dolores.

Thus they remain, a minute or more, as they reckon these things on Triax.

Then they enter the lodge, and close the door upon the night.

Lord Pierrot bids his darling extinguish the lamp that

guided him across the lake. He prefers darkness for these meetings. He does not like to let Daphne Dolores see his face too clearly, for it will remind her that he is old, and remind him too of what she is.

She is a young woman, Daphne Dolores.

She obeys him in this request, as in all things, and returns to him at once.

Lord Pierrot is solicitous. He pays full attention to the woman in his arms. He must not waste an instant of her company. He kisses her again, hungrily, as if he could somehow suck new youth from her mouth.

Daphne Dolores makes a small noise in her throat. Her hand presses the back of his neck as they kiss.

Her love for him is complete and true. Lord Pierrot knows that of her. He knows it so well that he no longer reflects on it. It is not in her nature to love a man and afterwards, cease from loving him.

Lord Pierrot rolls up his ruffled sleeves, pushing them back from his long, slender wrists. His hands are narrow, his fingers taper. He wears a ring with a large, square, black stone. He wears it at all times, and never takes it off, not even with a woman. He has excused it to them, to Daphne Dolores and to all those who came before her, as a sentimental attachment, a betrothal gift from his wife.

Lord Pierrot begins to undress Daphne Dolores.

She stands quietly on the rug as he reveals her body to the night.

Daphne Dolores is white and slim as a boy. Her hair is cut short, and layered as closely to her head as the fur of an otter. Lord Pierrot runs his hands over her hair and kisses her throat. She shuts her eyes and lifts her chin with pleasure.

Her shoulders and hips are narrow, Daphne Dolores, her stomach flat. She has no breasts to speak of. Her nipples look like wounds in the dim light. It is scarcely conceivable now, but thus his wife, Lady Dove, used to be, ah, long ago, in the first days of their marriage. Lord Pierrot goes down on one knee to remove her stockings. With his lips he brushes her pubic hair. He is consumed with desire for her.

Rising, Lord Pierrot pulls at the buttons of his gown. Beneath it he wears neither shirt nor undergarment. His chest is narrow and hairless. He kisses Daphne Dolores as he tugs his arms from the sleeves and forces down his baggy trousers.

His penis is slender, and elegantly curved. It lifts in the dark like some strange nocturnal plant of Triax, seeking for the moon.

Lord Pierrot directs Daphne Dolores to take hold of it, and she does. He gasps in pleasure.

Later, when pleasure has had its fill, Lord Pierrot lies back against the pillows with Daphne Dolores nestling in the crook of his arm. She lies lightly upon him, for which he is grateful, for the night is very hot, and they are both somewhat sticky.

Up in the rafters, something catches Lord Pierrot's eye: a small mass darker than the darkness. It is sure to be a nest of skylings, which persist in infesting his eaves. Every year at this time it is necessary to send an automaton to pluck out the nests of the skylings and cast them into the lake. These nights Lord Pierrot shares with Daphne Dolores are numbered; they are precious and few. The squawking of baby birds must not be permitted to disturb the making of love.

'You're very quiet, my love,' says Daphne Dolores.

Lord Pierrot kisses the top of her head.

'What are you thinking of?' she asks him.

'I'm thinking of you, my delight,' he tells her. His voice is high, and quavers. It seems to lose all its virile resonance after lovemaking. Lord Pierrot has remarked it before, and wondered whether anything can be done about it. 'I'm thinking of you,' he says. 'And how perfect you are.'

It is a lame, trite answer, he knows. Nor is it altogether true. Lord Pierrot is in fact thinking of his wife, Lady Dove, and wishing she were away from home. But what a gross error of tact it would be even to mention this to his mistress, as they lie together in the afterglow of passion. Lord Pierrot is nothing if not fastidious. It embarrasses him to utter falsehoods and platitudes, though Daphne Dolores has an inexhaustible capacity to receive them. She rejects nothing, not if Lord Pierrot gives it.

He gets out of bed, leaving her lying there. He finds his accordion on the floor and, dusting it reverently with the palm of his hand, remembers his plan to delight Daphne Dolores with a serenade or two. He opens the door and sits there, on the step, looking out at the night.

Now that he has drained the cup of passion dry, the melancholy fit is upon him again. Lord Pierrot plays once more the slow, sad tango.

'What a mournful tune, my love!' exclaims Daphne Dolores.

Lord Pierrot looks round at her, seeing only a dark shape in the dark house, out of reach of the moonlight. The lodge is full of the musky scent of her. Lord Pierrot lays his accordion aside.

'Would you have me always happy?' he asks her.

'For my sake,' she tells him.

'Ah, that I might do everything for your sake,' he muses, sorrowfully. 'Then would you be mistress indeed.'

Lord Pierrot wishes his wife might be sent away, just for a while, before the end of summer. He has an aunt, in the north-west. She and Lady Dove have always got on wonderfully well together. They play bezique, and compare their illnesses.

While the accordion finishes its tango Lord Pierrot cups his chin in his hands and watches the golden moon of Triax climb above the trees along the lake shore. The heat blurs the sky about it to the violet of a fresh bruise.

The moonlight creeps through the open door, finding Daphne Dolores where she reclines, naked and pale on the tousled sheets. When the instrument falls silent, Lord Pierrot speaks in Latin, telling her that his melancholy is but natural, under the circumstances. '*Post coitum*,' says Lord Pierrot, '*omne animal triste est.*'

'You have said that to me before,' says Daphne Dolores. 'I remember it. I wish I could be learned, and know such things.'

'So you could, my dear,' replies Lord Pierrot, 'so you could, if you would first grow to my age.'

'Oh, now you will complain of your years, and talk of decline and the inadequacy of flesh,' says Daphne Dolores at once, protesting, though in gentle merriment. 'I shall not allow you to remain in this mood,' she declares, and she rises from the bed and comes to him where he sits in the doorway. Stooping, she embraces him from behind, stroking his cooling flesh and kissing his ear and his neck until he begins to rouse again.

'No, Daphne Dolores,' says Lord Pierrot then, and with a touch he deters her, disengaging her arms from about his neck. He nods his long head in the direction of the lake. 'It is time I returned to my lady.'

At that Daphne Dolores casts herself upon him and clasps him to her once again. 'Stay with me tonight,' she pleads. She twists her fine fingers into his soft white hair.

Lord Pierrot is surprised at her forwardness, though flattered as any man would be. Usually she is more modest. He felicitates himself for having roused a new passion in her tonight. Her love for him, which he would have sworn was complete, is growing yet.

He detaches her hand from his hair and brings it to his lips. 'Alas,' he says. 'I may not. Women,' he tells her, 'are creatures of the heart; but men must bend the knee to duty.'

The truth is, that Lord Pierrot is grown old, as they reckon these things on Triax, and amorous exertion, especially in the season of heat, leaves him not only melancholy but also exhausted. But this is neither the place nor the time for truth; only for the voice of regret, in words of parting.

Bidding Daphne Dolores a gallant farewell, Lord Pierrot

closes the door of the lodge, straightens his cuffs, and steps carefully in the dark, down past the black rock to the sandy margin of the lake. He goes to board the little boat that will take him back to the shore.

It is a boon, Lord Pierrot's little boat, a device of his own invention quite indispensable for these nocturnal trysts. As it rows itself noiselessly across the honey-coloured water, Lord Pierrot is able to take his ease and recoup some of his dissipated energies. He looks around at the torpid, sultry night. In the reeds not a lizardfish, not a dabchick is stirring. The whole world, it seems, is still; still as if all Triax were barren, and the secret ways of life not yet pieced together there.

Lord Pierrot congratulates himself on the satisfactory conclusion of another night's dalliance.

Back indoors, Lord Pierrot sheds his clothes and hands them to a waiting automaton, which trundles away to launder them. They will be fresh and dry by morning. Belting a poplin robe about him, he steps into the shaft and allows it to carry him up past the dining hall, past the libraries and laboratories, to the upper floor where both he and his wife have their apartments.

He looks in on his wife, the Lady Dove. She is still awake. She lies propped on a great many pillows, reading a volume of the collected correspondence of a grande dame of another age. Here, on this benighted outpost of the empire where the Pierrots keep their family seat, few letters reach them, and Lady Dove must make do with these printed relics.

She looks at him over her glasses. 'What time is it, Pierre?'

She has her bedside console, and need only ask the house intelligence; but she prefers to ask him. Lord Pierrot stifles his irritation, making an effort to construe this habit of his wife's as deference due to his authority in the household. He tells her it is half-past eleven, or a quarter to one, however they reckon these things on Triax. 'Time you were asleep, my dear,' he tells her, and pats her on the shoulder. Lady Dove needs a great deal of sleep. She has grown colossally fat since he found it expedient to remove her ovaries. The slightest exercise fatigues her.

'And you, Pierre, are you not going to bed?' she asks.

'Directly, my angel,' says Lord Pierrot; but first he will stay and converse with her awhile, as is only mannerly. He looks around for a chair, but they are all laden with clothing, books and female impedimenta that Lady Dove has been too weary to put away. Lord Pierrot averts his eyes from a pile of her enormous underwear. He sits gingerly on the narrow margin of the bed that is not occupied by the flesh of Lady Dove.

'I have been taking a stroll in the grounds,' he tells her, 'by the light of the moon.'

'Moonlight is not good for the brain,' declares his wife at once. 'The radiance of the moon is unsettling. It tends to unbalance one.'

Lord Pierrot strokes her great hand consolingly. 'I find it more calming these days than the heat of the sun,' he tells her mildly.

Lady Dove is full of opinions on what is and is not healthy. Her capacity for them has grown as her bulk has swelled, and as her own vitality has declined. This stricture against moonlight is typical, mere feminine superstition. As a scientist, Lord Pierrot would like to dispute it, but as long as he allows her to remain in error, he can be sure Lady Dove will leave him to pursue his nocturnal excursions uninterrupted, for fear of moonlight.

And Daphne Dolores knows never to come near the house. So all is well.

He embarks on a trivial anecdote, the story of an amusing but entirely logical error made by his automatic lepidopteron, which has been unable to grasp the subtleties of Triacian taxonomy. 'There it sat, solemnly mounting and labelling an entire drawer of bluebottles!'

Lady Dove lies like a torpid hippopotamus, breathing

hoarsely through her open mouth. Her heavy eyes never leave Lord Pierrot's countenance, though he does not assume she is attending to his anecdote. She is simply watching his mouth move. Meanwhile, covertly, he is studying her. Unintentionally, automatically, he compares her cumbersome flesh, her stale and suffocating bosom and lank hair with the fragrant delights he has tasted so recently in the arms of Daphne Dolores.

He remembers when he first set eyes on Lady Dove, at a gala concert on Artemisia to celebrate the opening of the new Trans-Galactic Passage. She was a delicate flower then, a rose in bud adorning the arm of her papa, Lord Panteleone, while he himself was but a subaltern in the ranks of science, a rising young buck of some promise in the Innovation Corps. Now he is Lord Pierrot, master of the tango and the heavy night, yearning madly for the moon.

'You seem tired tonight, Pierre,' says his wife. 'You drive yourself too strenuously.'

Lord Pierrot looks sharply at her. It would be unlike her, unworthy of her, to resort to innuendo.

'Science is a hard taskmaster,' he replies, blandly.

'I hope you are not overdoing it,' she says. 'You will make yourself ill.' He thinks she sounds a trifle disgruntled, but Lady Dove has returned her attention to her book. Lord Pierrot bids her politely good night. He kisses her pendulous cheek, quickly, and goes to his own room.

As he bids the intelligence turn out the light, a second poignant memory occurs to him, unsought, of that time when Dove and he made a foursome with Gerard Pomeroy and Mona Twisk to sample the innocent pleasures of the gardens of the moon. Those golden days. Behind the marshmallow kiosk his Dove had unbuttoned her glove and, almost unprompted, relieved him of an importunate erection. His astonishment and pleasure were alloyed, a little, with alarm at her expertise. How could his dainty treasure be so knowledgeable about the male organ? How did she know what to do? Not, thinks Lord Pierrot to himself, that she had to do very much. In acts of venery, he commends himself as he falls asleep, he has always been prompt, very prompt.

Next morning, when Lord Pierrot awakes, he directs an automaton to throw open the window. The green land of Anise lies veiled in haze. This day promises to be just as hot as all its immediate predecessors. The heat can affect a man, playing upon his blood. Lord Pierrot thinks again of his memory of Dove, of her unexpected dexterity. It is bitter to him now. When did he and his wife last enjoy the pleasures of concupiscence? How many years is it since he has seen beneath that billowing nightgown?

Lord Pierrot winces inwardly and turns away from these unhappy reflections. Already he is suffused with longing for his paramour, for Daphne Dolores. He must meet her again tonight. He orders breakfast in the Magenta Room, with the french windows open onto the terrace.

It is nearly an hour before Lady Dove makes her ponderous appearance. She drops, panting, into her reinforced chair. Lord Pierrot is courteous, even solicitous. He waves away the butler hovering with its scalpel extended and cuts Lady Dove's grapefruit himself.

'My poor precious,' he murmurs, 'how was your night? Was it comfortable at all?'

'Not a bit,' answers Lady Dove, and proceeds with a catalogue of symptoms and grievances so anatomically detailed that Lord Pierrot's disciplined scientific objectivity is almost overborne. Swiftly passing beyond sympathy into squeamishness, he withdraws his attention, and recovers equilibrium only by most meticulously buttering a muffin.

'I was thinking you might visit Aunt Penthesilea, my darling,' says Lord Pierrot, 'in the north-west. It is cooler there.'

'Your aunt is on a cruise,' says Lady Dove. 'To Percival's Star. She has gone to take the waters on Syringa. I told you so. You never listen to me, never.'

She mashes her grapefruit clumsily with a spoon.

Lord Pierrot looks at her in rising anger. His wife is being petulant. She believes she is the one who should have been taken on a restorative cruise to Syringa, as if that or any other fanciful 'therapy' might make a dent in the arsenal of her ailments.

Lord Pierrot regards his wife, her wet lips drooping over her breakfast dish. He is on the point of retorting that he too could wish her halfway across the galaxy; but he maintains his dignity.

'What a shame,' he says, and finishes his muffin in three quick bites. Slender as he is, Lord Pierrot has always had a robust appetite.

He attempts a new, neutral subject. 'The skylings will be hatching any day now,' he observes.

Suddenly, for no apparent reason, Lady Dove drops her spoon. It falls from her fingers and clatters among the crockery. She gives a small, convulsive quiver, but no sound.

To his horror, Lord Pierrot sees that she has begun to cry. There she sits, silent and still as a great bolster, while tears well up in her tiny eyes and slither down her mountainous face.

Embarrassed by this unprovoked effusion, Lord Pierrot blots his lips hurriedly with his napkin and flees the table, leaving his kedgeree almost untouched.

He spends the day in the laboratories, where his privacy is guaranteed. While the brilliant primary of Triax moves pane by pane across the stained glass windows, dappling the apparatus with rainbows, Lord Pierrot tends his vats. They are coming along very nicely. Suspended in their rich brown soup of nutrients, the fibrous lengths of pale pink matter slowly twist and thicken.

In his laboratory Lord Pierrot is accustomed to be happy. He will talk to his specimens, and fancies they reply, mutely, waving their rosy fronds. He will sing to them: no melancholy tangos here, but snatches of songs of love.

His homunculi gather chirping and chuckling around Lord Pierrot's feet. They like to fetch him the curious, wriggling things they trap behind the wainscot at night. On any other day one might find them skipping along after as he glides from vat to vat with flasks of concentrate and slips of litmus paper.

Alas, today his mood is quite ruined by this disgraceful display of his wife's. To break down! at the breakfast table! And for no reason at all.

Sensing their master's displeasure, the homunculi retreat, cowering beneath the cabinets. Lord Pierrot slumps on the couch, fingering his black ring.

At dinner that evening Lord Pierrot is relieved to find the table laid for one. Lady Dove, the intelligence informs him, is indisposed. She will dine in her room. There will be no need for him to attempt polite conversation, to conduct relations with his wife as though her shameful outburst of the morning had never happened. Instead he can concentrate on the pleasures of the palette, a fitting preliminary to the pleasures of other senses, other organs, he will shortly be enjoying in the company of Daphne Dolores.

Night falls swiftly in the land of Anise, on the planet of Triax. The moon rises and blesses the park with its golden glaze. The heat does not subside. It grows, if anything, more oppressive. Thick clouds begin to mass in the sky.

Lord Pierrot lingers a moment on the terrace, breathing deeply of the rich scents of hibiscus and false phlox. It is night, and the melancholy fit is upon him. He gazes into space, remembering other nights on other worlds, fresh, piquant worlds at the frontier of science.

On his way through the hot gardens, Lord Pierrot composes a poem on themes of ripeness and decay. Once he looks back towards the house, and sees the light at his wife's bedroom window. He sighs.

A blundering sourmoth flies into his face, battering him with its dusty great wings. Lord Pierrot brushes it aside without anger. Tonight, nothing can disturb his mood. He is feeling acquiescent, resigned to his age and the passing of time, accepting his place in the grand scheme of Nature. He can afford to be magnanimous, to his poor, suffering wife, and to the ignorant little creatures of the dark and stifling night. He puts the sourmoth into his poem.

Arrived, at last, at the lake, he summons his little boat and rides out across the gilded water. He sees the light burning in the window of the lodge, and yearns towards it. How he envies the simple life that Daphne Dolores leads there. That, he decides, is all one really wants: a lantern and a humble wooden bed; a loaf of bread and an accordion. What need has an old man of more? He could let all the rest go, the great house, the laboratories and libraries with all their oppressive weight of ambition and responsibility, history and posterity. True peace is to live simply, in a little house by the water.

Lord Pierrot lands and climbs on his father's rock. He stands with arms akimbo, looking towards the door of the lodge. He waits for his paramour, Daphne Dolores. She always hears his boat and comes running. He waits; but she does not come.

Something is wrong. Perhaps she is ill. Perhaps she has been stolen away.

Lord Pierrot climbs down again from the rock. He goes to the lodge and stands outside, listening at the door. Should he knock? At the door of his own property? What if he does, and alerts some brigand, some beast of prey lurking within, poised with fell intent over the swooning form of his beloved?

Courageously Lord Pierrot reaches for the door and flings it open.

The lamp is burning, and she is there, Daphne Dolores, lying naked on the bed. She is, as always, alone.

She smiles at him, a fetching smile. 'Welcome to my house, Lord Pierrot,' she says.

'Daphne Dolores!'

She reaches out her arms.

'Come to me,' she commands him.

Moving like one in a dream, he crosses to the bed and

embraces her. She clutches him in a grip of desire. How urgently she caresses him. He hears her breathing shallow and quick. He feels her heart pounding in her breast as if with an emotion too large for that narrow cage.

'Daphne Dolores, my treasure!'

Lord Pierrot wonders if she is unwell.

Daphne Dolores laughs. 'Do you like my surprise?'

'But you are naked,' he says. He feels a twinge of annoyance at this: she knows it is always his pleasure to undress her when they meet.

She sets him at arm's length and looks into his eyes.

'I am pretending this is my house,' she says. 'I am mistress here. And you are *my* suitor.'

Her manner is intense, Daphne Dolores, her eyes amused at his discomfiture. Lord Pierrot has never seen her like this before.

'I want you,' she says. Her voice is deep, suddenly, and thick with passion. 'Now.'

She tears at his clothes, straining seams, snapping buttons from their threads.

Lord Pierrot is alarmed. He tries to restrain her hands, but desire lends her strength. She fights him, attacks his gown again. He falls sprawling across the bed, laughing feebly. But he is not amused. He is an old man, and not accustomed to such violent handling. And from a woman! One of his women!

'Gently, my pet!' he cries. 'Gently!'

She takes no notice. She lunges at him, throwing herself on top of him and kissing him fiercely.

Something must be wrong with her. The heat has unhinged her. They are such sensitive creatures.

Lord Pierrot pushes weakly at her, at Daphne Dolores, striving to rise; but she pushes him in return, turning him over on his back and clambering upon him. She grasps his baggy trousers, dragging them off and hurling them into a corner.

This is not love, that sweet, sad, tender enchantment,

Lord Pierrot thinks to himself as she tears off his gown; this is brute lust! What can he do? With all his women he has always been able to retain control, even in the giddy toils of desire. Daphne Dolores seems to have gone quite mad. Mad, it is true, with passion for him, for Lord Pierrot; but mad nonetheless.

He is almost unmanned by dread, repelled by her undignified abandon. Pinned beneath her writhing body, Lord Pierrot closes his eyes and thinks of her as she has always been before: soft, tender, yielding.

Daphne Dolores fastens her teeth on his nipple. Lord Pierrot cries out in protest. But she laughs and twists around above him, seeking every moment a new and more gratifying position.

Lord Pierrot thumbs his ring.

She sees him.

At once she rises up, straddling him in a way that makes him catch his breath. She seizes his hand, and tugs at the ring.

'My dear!' gasps Lord Pierrot.

'Off!' she cries. 'Off with it!'

'No!' He covers the ring with his hand.

Daphne Dolores pauses, looking down at him with a wrathful gaze. 'I hate it. I hate everything that reminds me of her,' says Daphne Dolores.

'It was never hers,' Lord Pierrot says at once. 'What I told you was untrue.'

Daphne Dolores arches her brows. Her curiosity is piqued. She keeps hold of his hand. She requires an explanation.

Glad of the respite from these exertions, Lord Pierrot gives her one.

'The ring was never a gift from Lady Dove,' he says, somewhat hoarsely. 'It is a family heirloom. A device of my great-great-grandfather's. He was a man of many enemies.'

With a flick of the secret hinge he shows her, concealed beneath the square black stone, a needle steeped in a swift and fatal poison. Concocted by the first wearer, that poison has been improved by his subsequent heirs. Against it there is no appeal.

Lord Pierrot tells her of the apprehensions he suffered outside her door. 'One sweep of my hand, my love, and there he would lie, your assailant, paralysed and dying at your feet!'

Daphne Dolores examines the ring, the needle beneath the stone.

'And have you ever made use of it?' she asks, speaking low.

'Experimentally,' he tells her. 'On suitable local creatures.'

She laughs again. In her present mood such macabre prospects amuse her. She flips shut the ring and, before he can prevent her, ducks her head and lightly kisses the square black stone.

She looks at him from under lowered brows, her lips still touching the ring.

'On suitable creatures,' she repeats.

Then she is upon him once more, and there is nothing he can do while she has her way with him.

Lord Pierrot senses at last the stirring of desire. There is something splendid, he recalls, about a woman towering over him thus, in an access of hunger and power. Unnatural? Is it truly so? There may be many things in Nature, he thinks; many hidden things. And did not Lady Dove excite him thus when they were wed?

She reminds him, Daphne Dolores, of his wife when she was young. They all do, all his women. He is prone, Lord Pierrot, to such sentiments.

He thrusts into her with rekindled appetite. The old voluptuary is not defeated yet.

But even while she grinds and rocks upon him, yelping and growling like an animal in rut, the scientist in him considers: was there no warning of this last night? No sign, no prior indication of this unprecedented frenzy?

Lord Pierrot has always prided himself on the accuracy and good order of his memory. Even as they rise together towards their climax he recalls how Daphne Dolores disparaged his serenade, and opposed him when he made reference to the melancholy matter of his age. And yes, he remembers now how she revealed her hatred for Lady Dove, trying to keep him from his lawful place beside his invalid wife. She clutched him by the hair! And he thought nothing of it!

It was love, Lord Pierrot understands as Daphne Dolores falls upon him in her sensuous spasm. Love, that delusive, obliterating passion: only love could make so experienced, so wise a man so blind.

Daphne Dolores lies lathered and gasping on his chest. But Lord Pierrot, he is not yet spent. He heaves at her, stroking distractedly at her hair.

She lifts her head, Daphne Dolores, from under his hand. She lifts her hips, and withdraws.

'My love!' cries Lord Pierrot, aghast.

She kneels up once more, straddling him, toying with him. Her eyes are languid now, her movements satiated.

Yet he is not done, Lord Pierrot.

And nor, it seems, is she, Daphne Dolores.

She speaks. 'Take me up to the house,' she says.

'But my sweet!'

She ignores his protest.

'Take me to the house,' she says again. 'Let me be mistress there.'

Lord Pierrot is astounded. This is absolutely counter to the first rule, that she must never interfere in his domestic arrangements. Daphne Dolores has abandoned all sense of place and propriety.

Then he smiles.

Is his spirit dead, his blood quite cold? Is he not still Lord Pierrot, the libertine of Fomalhaut, the rakehell of the Innovators? And is she not Daphne Dolores, creature of his passion?

He flings his arms about her slender waist. 'Yes, my love, you are right. Let us be wild! Let us be free of trammelling checks and consciences! Let us go where love bids!' He chortles. 'Oh, my darling, my *mistress*, I must say: how cunningly you teach me!'

Together the lovers scramble from the bed and out into the clouded night. Barefoot and naked they run down to the rock where the dependable little boat has moored itself. They climb aboard, Lord Pierrot sitting astern with Daphne Dolores sprawled between his shrunken thighs. He gives the command to steer for the shore.

As they ride, Lord Pierrot looks behind them. The moon is still hidden, and all the stars.

He strokes the short, soft hair of Daphne Dolores. Perhaps she will be calmer now, more docile since slaking her lust. No – she turns energetically in his arms, nuzzling forcefully at him, almost upsetting the little boat.

'Will you take me to the house?' she asks again.

'To the very heart of the house,' he promises.

They cross the lake. Lord Pierrot passes by the boathouse and puts ashore at the abandoned grotto. Leading Daphne Dolores by the hand he scales the bank, and slips between the statues of the Astral Graces, each of which wears his mother's face. Along crazed paths, between straggling rhododendrons the couple hasten, circumventing the garden by an obscure route that brings them out at last on the croquet lawn. The east wing looms ahead, its windows glittering darkly.

Suddenly Daphne Dolores stops. Lord Pierrot knows she remembers his instruction, that she is never to come near the house itself. She stands naked and panting on the croquet lawn, seeking her lover's face in frenzied, mute appeal.

'Come, my darling,' Lord Pierrot bids her in a secretive tone. 'Let us within. We shall baffle Lady Dove with our boldness.'

All at once he hears a dreadful sound.

*'Pierre! Pi-erre!'*

It is his wife. It is Lady Dove, materialising as if at the

*114*

merest mention of her name. She has left her bed and come blundering into the garden in her nightgown. Lord Pierrot hears her now smashing towards them through the undergrowth, bellowing for him like a panic-stricken heifer.

Does she suspect? Has she seen them? Or is she sick, and roaming in her sleep? Perhaps, of all things, her premonition has come true: the full moon has unsettled her brain. It is a night for the madness of women.

Lady Dove is coming nearer. Lord Pierrot sees her monstrous shape bobbing in the darkness beneath the shade trees.

Silently giving thanks for the iron self-discipline, the blood and breeding of the Pierrots that enable him to keep his head even through the ordeal of such a night, Lord Pierrot puts his fingers to the moist lips of Daphne Dolores, commanding her to silence. He points across the croquet lawn to the flowerbeds. They will confuse Lady Dove. She will not think to seek them that way.

Daphne Dolores drops Lord Pierrot's hand. She sprints away across the Triacian grass, Lord Pierrot panting after.

Trampling the blooms so carefully laid out by Lord Pierrot's horticultron, they burst into the arbour leaving Lady Dove behind, still stumbling through the shrubbery. Arriving at the door of the conservatory they hear a faint, disconsolate moo, a distant sound of breaking branches.

Inside, the house begins, without asking, to raise the lights. Lord Pierrot countermands it. Daphne Dolores does not notice. She hardly pauses to admire the glories of the Sirian frescoes. She kisses Lord Pierrot vigorously and pulls him into the gloomy passageway and along the hall, where the butler rolls out to greet them.

It scans them with a brief burst of invisible light. '*Good evening, sir and madam,*' it says, in its buzzing voice. '*May I take your coats?*'

Daphne Dolores laughs uproariously, heedlessly. Her laughter echoes in the rafters.

'Let us go up, my love,' Lord Pierrot bids her.' 'To my chamber.'

Again she contradicts him, her blue eyes shining with joyous anticipation. 'No, dear heart,' she insists, 'to your laboratory! Did you not tell me that Lady Dove never sets foot there?'

With a private, wistful smile, Lord Pierrot congratulates her on her stratagem. 'An excellent choice, my precious!'

Ignoring the attentive automaton, they jump into the shaft and float up to the level of the laboratories.

Here too Daphne Dolores strides ahead, as if she knows the way. She was here once before; perhaps, unconsciously, in some infant part of her brain, she remembers it. She sweeps through the catalogue room, where all knowledge lies sleeping in banks of deep cold drawers. In the mechanatory, beneath the great bleached skeletons of Lord Pierrot's first automata, she runs her white hand carelessly across the rack of obsolete implements, the tarnished rods and serried claws that recall his years of service in the Innovation Corps. She does not spare a glance for the cabinets of the *salon zoologique* with their stiff, staring specimens of every kind of fauna, natural and otherwise, as they reckon these things on the planet Triax.

Lord Pierrot is pleased to follow her. Her haste gladdens his old and disappointed heart. He is grateful that, in the dark, she fails to notice the lines of mannequins above her head, encased in glass along the wall. Each is clad in some cast-off of the younger, slimmer Lady Dove; yes, even back to the yellow sundress and matching gloves that she wore on their trip to the moon. It would not do to let Daphne Dolores see those clothes; nor the figures that wear them. They might disturb her.

'Ah!' cries Daphne Dolores then. She has reached the last laboratory. She stands amid the vats, gazing about in wonder and delight.

Behind her, Lord Pierrot slips into the curtained alcove for a gown. As he plucks one from the hook and wraps it around his nakedness, the homunculi stir in their nest of rags. Lord Pierrot hastily silences their querulous cheeping, dropping a cloak over them. He steps back into the laboratory.

The stained glass windows are black and opaque in the occluded night. The only light in the cluttered chamber is a faint glow of phosphorescence from the things in the vats. It highlights the slick bubbles of alembics and retorts, the dusty brass barrel of a giant microscope. There is a lingering scent of formaldehyde and rotting orange peel.

Lord Pierrot sees Daphne Dolores padding barefoot from vat to vat, trying to discern what each holds. Some are mere seeds yet, little spatters of darkness in the broth. Others are burgeoning, dendritic: a tubular stem with floppy branches above and below. Daphne Dolores has reached one so far grown as to be spinning a slick integument about itself, like a protective cocoon. Its members are well defined.

The largest tank stands alone in the corner beneath a sagging bank of shelves. The waters of that one, Lord Pierrot knows, are empty.

As Daphne Dolores goes to peer into its slimy depths, the moon of Triax suddenly heaves itself from behind a bulwark of cloud and sheds light into the laboratory. All the coloured panes flare up at once like a curtain of cold jewels.

Daphne Dolores turns about. She catches sight of Lord Pierrot standing there in his white gown, and cries out in pleasure.

'My love!' calls Daphne Dolores. 'You have become a very harlequin!'

Lord Pierrot looks down at himself and chuckles. He is illuminated, as if by the rainbow-coloured primary of an unknown world, daubed from head to toe with carmine and gold and viridian. All down his gown the smears of acids and enzymes show up as harshly as though they were stains of rust or blood.

From beneath the coloured window comes a cry. *'Pierre!'*

Lord Pierrot crosses the floor and cautiously peeps out. Lady Dove is there, still tangled in the bushes, swiping blindly at the moonlight with her huge arms.

Daphne Dolores laughs.

'Will you not take care of her?' she asks.

'Take care of her?' repeats Lord Pierrot.

'Release her from her misery.'

She nods at his hand, at the fatal ring.

Lord Pierrot looks at his ring as if he has never seen it before. He marvels at the audacity of Daphne Dolores, at the daring and ambition she has concealed from him all this while. Her spirit is a match for his own.

He sighs.

He opens the ring, inspects the reservoir. 'Let us be sure,' he says. 'I should not wish her to suffer even a moment.' He closes his eyes, suppressing a shudder of emotion, of potent memory; and opens them again.

'I have some fresh distilled. On that shelf up there, in the corner.'

Daphne Dolores turns to look at the shadowy ranks of vials and flasks that have bowed the shelves. Lord Pierrot, feeling behind the couch, fetches out a slender staff of glass a yard long, with a brass ferrule. A homunculus scrabbles briefly from under the valance. He shoos it back out of sight.

Daphne Dolores leans across the vat, stretching up to the bottles. She cannot reach. She lifts herself up and puts one knee carefully on the rim. The coloured light streaks her tiny buttocks.

'Oh, I can't get it,' she complains. 'Come and help me.'

Lord Pierrot comes and stands behind her. He puts one long, thin arm around her naked waist, hugging her body to him as if to steady her on her precarious perch. Her flesh is warm in his embrace. With the other arm he reaches over her shoulder for the flask. Their faces are very close together. Daphne Dolores turns her head and kisses Lord Pierrot on the lips.

'*Pi-erre!*' moans the stricken woman beneath the window.

Daphne Dolores gives a little laugh and slips her tongue between her lover's teeth.

Lord Pierrot thrusts forward with his shoulder.

Daphne Dolores is small and slight, like all his women.

With a cry and a splash, she topples into the tank.

The questionable fluid at once froths pink, surging high and closing avidly about her delectable limbs. It spatters Lord Pierrot's motley gown, and he steps quickly backwards.

In the spume he catches a final glimpse of Daphne Dolores, bobbing up: her startled eyes, her open mouth. He raises his glass staff, plants its brass tip between her breasts, and thrusts her down.

From her little ears, her nose, her perfect lips, bubbles flurry. Lord Pierrot waits patiently until they cease.

Whispering, the homunculi scuttle from their corners and come to stand around him in a flock, holding hands and craning their necks. They lift one another up to the glass.

Lord Pierrot does not rebuke them. The moment is too solemn. Wiping the staff on his sleeve, he turns away and opens the window, admitting a wave of hot, dank air.

Lord Pierrot sighs. The melancholy fit is upon him once again, as always when he has made the great renunciation. One by one he raises them; and one by one they become unstable, unreasonable, and have to be stilled. Must it be ever thus?

He gazes out of the window into the thick and tangled garden. By the light of the yellow moon of Triax he sees his wife, Lady Dove, standing below, her nightdress in tatters, twigs and leaves in her hair. She looks up and recognises him. A scowl crosses her bloated face. '*Pierre!*' she shouts.

Fatigued, unhappy, Lord Pierrot orders the intelligence to send his taxidermatron. Then he goes out through the salon, passing beneath the line of his daughters, going to seek forgiveness once again of Lady Dove.

# THE DEATH OF
# CASSANDRA QUEBEC

*by*
*Eric Brown*

Eric Brown left school at 14 to go to Australia. Having served his sentence, he is now back in Britain. He lives in Haworth, Yorkshire, which is apparently famous for something. The majority of his short stories have been published in *Interzone*, and he was the winner of that magazine's first annual reader's poll. The winning story is the title of his first book, *The Time-Lapsed Man*, a collection published the same month as this anthology.

I came to Sapphire Oasis in search of experience, or so I thought at the time. I had made my home on Nova Français for almost two decades, the last few years a repetition of cafe-life, parties and second-rate exhibitions where even my best crystals failed to sell. I was getting old and lonely and my work was suffering, and some vague desperation drove me to Earth to experience that which I might synthesise, through my skill, into art.

The famous crystal *The Death of Cassandra Quebec* was being exhibited for the first time in ten years, and I made this my excuse to revisit the planet of my birth. I took a bigship through the interstellar telemass portal to Timbuktu and caught the mono-train north to Sapphire Oasis.

I had seen many a lavish illustration of the colony – had even admired Tyrone's famous hologram of '37 – and as a result I was overcome with a sense of *déjà vu* at first sight. The oval oasis, perhaps a kilometre from end to end, was surrounded by a great leaning series of golden scimitars, their hilts planted in the sand of the desert, their arching blades supporting the pendant globes that comprised living quarters and spacious studios with views across the artificial lake. It was like a mirage, or a shimmering scene from a surrealistic dream.

That first night I dined alone in the revolving restaurant on the island at the centre of the oasis. I ate synthetic gazelle and yam, with chutney and Moroccan wine. The view was magnificent: beyond the illuminated orbs of the individual domes, and the fringe of surrounding palm trees, the desert extended in dark and sultry swathes the size of Europe. Across the dunes to the south stood the telemass portal. As tall as a mountain, its blank interface was braced in a

123

glowing frame like a hexagon of colossal fluorescents.

It was through this portal that I and a thousand other tourists had journeyed today from Nova Français, and tomorrow it would be open to the world of Henderson's Fall, 61 Cygni B. The talk in the dining room was of nothing else but Nathaniel Maltravers, and his arrival tomorrow evening at Sapphire Oasis.

I ordered a second bottle of wine.

As I drank I thought about another famous artist, a woman this time. Cassandra Quebec had inspired more women than just myself to seek expression through the medium of fused crystal. After Lin Chakra, she was the artist who had shown the world her soul, who had taken the fledgling form and proved it as a legitimate means of self-expression. At the height of her career she was the world's most celebrated artist. Then she spoiled it all by announcing her betrothal – I was young; I wept when I found out – to the minor laser-sculptor Nathaniel Maltravers. A year later she was dead.

I finished the second bottle and contemplated a third. I had known when I booked the bigship to Earth that Maltravers – who was indirectly responsible for his wife's death, after all – had decided to return to Sapphire Oasis for the twentieth anniversary commemoration of her passing, but I had not let it put me off the idea of making the trip. Tomorrow, I would visit the Museum of Modern Art and request a private viewing of the Maltravers/Quebec crystal.

I retired early and lay on my bed, staring at the stars through the dome. A party was in progress on the lawn beside the lake, one of the interminable *soirées* that gave the place more the air of a luxury resort than that of an artists' retreat. Artists, their rich patrons and guests, mixed with a social ease I found enviable; snatches of cultured conversation drifted to me through an open vent in the dome.

Unable to sleep, and reluctant to join the gathering below, I took refuge in a memory-tape. I placed the crown – more like a skull-cap – on my head and selected a tape. As I shed my own identity and slipped into the programmed persona, I could not help feeling a twinge of guilt at my escape. Memory-tapes were a spin-off from a device known as mem-erase, illegal on Earth for almost two decades. Mem-erase – the process of self-selected amnesia to which I had once been addicted – had been proven to have certain adverse psychological side-effects. Not only had their private use been proscribed, but even law enforcement agencies, who had used mem-erase to access the minds of suspected criminals, had been denied its advantages. As a result of the ban, the simulated scenarios of memory-tapes were viewed in some circles with a certain stigma.

I selected the erstaz memories of a fictitious vid-star, lay back and for the next hour lived a life of success, fame and love.

I awoke early the following morning, booked some time alone with the crystal and strolled along the palm-lined boulevard to the museum.

On the few occasions when the crystal had been exhibited in the past, I had been loath to experience it – the mere fact of Cassandra Quebec's death had been painful enough, without subjecting myself to the emotional reality of it. But twenty years had passed since the incident; I was older and perhaps wiser now, and I considered myself ready to have the experience.

Not that I was without misgivings. I held, perhaps irrationally, a fierce dislike for the man who had married Quebec and who was ultimately responsible for the accident that killed her. Added to which, Maltravers' production of the crystal had elevated him from the minor artisan he was to the status of a world celebrity. Perhaps what had prevented me from experiencing the crystal before now, quite apart from the emotional trauma I would have to undergo, was the thought that I would be participating in the metaphorical aggrandisement of man at the expense of woman.

That morning at breakfast in the revolving restaurant I had been invited to the table of a group of Hoppers – rich artisans and their hangers-on, who skipped the globe from one artists' colony to the next. They were shrill and opinioned, and I sought the protection of silence, offering nothing to the debate about Maltravers and the reason for his return. I heard one claim that he was returning to seek artistic rejuvenation from the locale of his wife's horrific death; another, that he intended to end his life here, as befits the artistic temperament.

The truth, I suspected, was neither. It was my guess that Nathaniel Maltravers was staging the spectacle of his return for no other reason than that, in the years since Cassandra Quebec's death, his own artistic and popular success had floundered. The dozen or so 'major' works he had released upon the universe had flopped abysmally. His return was probably nothing more than a cheap ruse to gain publicity.

*The Death of Cassandra Quebec* remained his first and last great work.

The museum, which housed the crystal and a thousand other works of art, was an onyx cathedral raised above the desert on flying cantilevers and approached along a sweep of gently ascending steps. It was cool and hushed within, and I took my time and strolled towards the crystal wing. I paused at the arched entrance, showed my pass to the security guard and stepped inside. The chamber was empty; I was quite alone. Before me, in pride of place in the centre of the room, was the crystal – in fact a thousand alien stones fused into one faceted, centimetre-thick disc perhaps two metres across. Visually, it was a mere swirl of colour, a coruscating vortex of argent and indigo. Only to the touch would the crystal discharge the stored emotions of its creators.

I must have heard a hundred different reports about Cassandra Quebec's death, and staged and re-staged the tragedy in the theatre of my mind. I was on Nova Français when I first read about the accident; the article was in a journal almost two years old, and the shock of the news was compounded by the fact that I had learned about it so late.

Her arrival at Sapphire Oasis, with her husband and new-born baby, made world news. It was her first public appearance since the birth of her daughter; the film of their approach in an open-top vintage Mercedes, smiling parents and babe-in-arms, is famous – a scene imprinted on the collective consciousness by the tragedy of the events to come. The fact that the instrument of her death was travelling with them makes the short clip all the more grotesque. As a wedding present, Quebec had bought her husband a bird-like alien known as a Pterosaur from a newly-discovered planet in the Serendipity Cluster. It was an ugly, featherless creature, had a beak like a scythe and was reputedly empathic – a suitably bizarre pet for the world's most famous couple. It could be seen perched on the back seat, maintaining its balance with edgy adjustments of its vast, leathery wingspan as the automobile swept through the gates of the colony.

Like most couples in their first year of marriage, Quebec and Maltravers argued. It was reported that their differences of opinion, because they were artists, were all the more vituperative. Maltravers, the rumour went, was jealous of his wife's talent and success; Quebec, for her part, despaired that her husband's constant envy would prevent him from ever attaining greatness for himself.

The one known truth of their relationship was that, however violent their arguments, their *rapprochements* were just as intense. They were hailed, in media hyperbole, as the planet's greatest lovers – how jealous I felt when I read this! – and as evidence the news-media offered up the fact that, as well as sharing a bed, they also shared a studio.

It was in this studio, three days after her arrival at Sapphire Oasis, that Cassandra Quebec met her end.

They had argued. Quebec was part-way through a crystal that would stand as testimony to their love, and as such it had to contain *everything*, their imperfections and flaws of character as well as their strengths. Maltravers was loath to subject himself to so public a scrutiny, and his protestations which began their final argument were overheard by their daughter's nurse.

They were in the studio, facing each other across the sun-lit chamber. The volume of their recriminations was noted by several other artists, who paid no heed as this was nothing new between the husband and wife. The nurse reported that she had glimpsed the alien pet, flapping in agitation beside Maltravers, before she departed to attend the crying child in another part of the living quarters.

According to Maltravers, they had reached an impasse in their disagreement, a temporary cease-fire, and Cassandra remained staring at him from across the work-strewn room. Maltravers admitted to feelings of anger, and it was this anger, experts testified at the inquest, that the Pterosaur must have picked up.

Before Maltravers could move to stop it, the Pterosaur left its perch, swooped across the room and attacked his wife with claws like sickles. Maltravers fought it off, but so savage was the attack that within seconds Quebec was lacerated beyond recognition. He realised – he said later in sworn testimony – that his wife was dying and that nothing, not even the latest surgical techniques, could save her.

The events that followed were bizarre to say the least.

Beside Quebec was the fused crystal, empty but for touches of her love for Maltravers. What he did then, in his grief and regret and overwhelming sense of loss, was to lift his wife and place her on the slab as if it were a catafalque, and then lay his brow against its faceted surface and impress upon it his turbulent emotions. She died in his arms minutes later, and the crystal recorded the moment for eternity.

For three days the world's media vilified Maltravers as a monster, until the coroner reported at the inquest that nothing could have saved Quebec. Then his agent released the crystal, and over the next year or so public opinion swung in Maltravers' favour – the vilification turned to sympathy and appreciation.

In the silence of the Museum I steeled myself, stepped forward and laid my palms on the crystal's surface. Warmth ran up my arms, the warmth of Quebec's love for her husband, with which she had begun the work. This joy lasted only seconds, though, for as I moved my hands from the edge of the piece towards its centre, pain swamped me, physical pain – the scream of every nerve slit through and through again. Beyond this, on some deeper sub-strata of the crystal, was Quebec's bewilderment, and then her sudden comprehension as she realised what was happening, that life was ebbing from her, that everything she had ever experienced, the hate and the joy and the everyday miracle of existence, was draining away, becoming faint as she approached the terrible point of total annihilation. Her end was a crescendo scream of terror as oblivion descended.

Then my touch encountered Maltravers' pain at his loss. The howl of desolation that communicated itself from his soul to the crystal, and then to my senses, was almost more unbearable than the pain of Quebec's death – for it continued long after her dying, a lament of grief for his wife, a scream of despair at the realisation of his existence without her.

Unable to take any more I tore myself away, and the sudden cessation of pain was an exquisite relief. I had no idea how long I had been standing before the crystal, so captivated had I been by the raw human emotions. I realised then that I was in tears.

As I made my way slowly from the Museum, I knew that I no longer resented Maltravers. The act of creating the crystal had been instinctive, born of pain and the need to share his grief, and not the opportunistic bid for fame I had assumed for so long.

Within a week of his wife's death, Maltravers took his daughter and sought refuge on the colony world of Henderson's Fall, as if by doing so he might distance himself from the pain of the tragedy.

And tonight he was returning to the source of that pain.

* * *

That evening I attended the party thrown by the President of Mali to welcome Nathaniel Maltravers to Sapphire Oasis. It was held in the President's own dome – he dabbled in photo-montage – with a view across the desert to the telemass portal, through which Maltravers was due to arrive at midnight. The dome was packed with eager guests: I recognised the two dozen or so serious artists who made up the nucleus of the Sapphire colony, faces familiar from Earth to the furthest settled world. Also present were the flamboyant Hoppers, attendant sycophants, and sombre-suited officials from the countries of Northern Africa and Europe.

I drank by myself beside the alcohol dispenser and thought about returning to my own dome. There was an atmosphere of excitement and expectation about the gathering that smacked of voyeurism. I was on my fourth drink when I admitted that the only reason *I* was here was to see for myself how the passage of years had treated Maltravers, and perhaps learn the real reason for his return.

At twelve, we spilled out onto the balcony and marvelled at the exhibition of interstellar *son et lumière* enacted to the south.

Until its activation, the portal was nothing more than an illuminated hexagonal frame, through which could be seen a continuation of the starlit African sky. Within minutes all that had changed. The frame flickered, as if affected by a power-drain; then a thunderous report rolled across the desert, and the scene through the portal was transformed. The guests gasped and applauded as an alien landscape appeared: a busy spaceport, distant blue mountains, and binary suns in a pink sky. As we watched, a bull-nosed bigship eased its way through the interface and entered the atmosphere of Earth. The ship came to rest on the apron of the spaceport at the foot of the portal.

We returned inside. As the flier carrying Maltravers raced across the desert towards the oasis, the conversation in the dome had about it a charged expectancy. I kept to myself by the dispenser; around me, guests quipped, exchanged stories and looked frequently to the gates as if at any second Maltravers might arrive.

I was thinking about my experience with the crystal that morning when a sudden hush fell upon the company. I stared through the diaphanous, curvilinear wall of the room as the flier slipped through the gates and settled beside the lake.

Two figures climbed out, were met by the President and his entourage and disappeared into the scimitar shaft that supported the dome. The conversation started up again, self-consciously, all eyes on the entrance. Seconds later the door opened and applause rippled through the room.

I can recall very little about Nathaniel Maltravers as he made his entry – I was too intent on watching the person who entered with him. While the guests flocked to congratulate Maltravers on his return, I had eyes only for his daughter.

Corrinda Maltravers surprised me on two counts. The first was that I had never thought of her as a young woman – if I thought of her at all, it was as a babe-in-arms, a cypher in the tragedy, untouched by the passage of time. The second was that she was as beautiful as her mother.

Maltravers moved from one group of guests to the next, and his daughter followed in his wake. This was the first time she had returned to Earth since the tragedy, and she appeared shy and bewildered at the reception. She was small, slim, wore a black tube dress that left her shoulders bare, hugged her hips and finished just above the knees. I caught only a glimpse of her large green eyes and isosceles face – *so* painfully like her mother's – before she disappeared into an admiring throng of guests. I wondered how long it would be before she found herself waking up beside the next self-professed Picasso.

My reverie was interrupted by the arrival at my side of Maltravers and the President of Mali. They sipped their drinks and the President regaled Maltravers with a short history of his country.

Nathaniel Maltravers was in his middle-fifties, tall and

silver-haired, with the well-groomed, distinguished appearance of someone who has foregone the life of an artist for that of a sybarite. I could not reconcile the man beside me with the artist who had suffered the anguish of his wife's death and communicated it so harrowingly.

Then I noticed the distant, blitzed look in his grey eyes. I recalled the report that, during his self-imposed exile on Henderson's Fall, Maltravers had taken the easy way out. Before the possession of mem-erase became an offence, he had duly self-administered the process of wiping from his memory the entirety of his stay at Sapphire Oasis. His only knowledge of the tragic event was what he read in factual accounts, stripped of all emotion and pain.

Now he glanced my way, his eyes measuring me for size in the places he thought important. His gaze was less lecherous than professional, as if he were seriously considering me as a prospective model.

'Aren't you Eva Hovana?' he asked. 'The creator of the *Persephone* crystal?'

I admitted that I was; it was an early piece and not one of my best.

'If I may say so –' he smiled '– I have always found your work rather derivative.'

I was quick with the riposte, and immediately regretted it. 'At least I don't get other people to do my work for me, however derivative it might be.' It was a reference to the fact that he had achieved acclaim only with the aid of his dying wife – and he didn't like the dig.

He moved off instantly. 'As I mentioned earlier,' he said to the President of Mali, 'my next piece will be influenced by my obsession with symmetry.'

The President hurried him across the room. 'Ahh … meet my friends from the Council of Europe …'

I escaped onto the balcony.

I gazed out over the body of water, glittering in the moonlight, and wondered what was keeping me at Sapphire Oasis. After all, I had experienced the crystal I had come to see. I was contemplating a trip to Europe when I sensed someone beside me. I felt a hand on my arm, and turned.

Corrinda Maltravers stood before me, even shorter than she had seemed in the room, almost childlike. She had quickly withdrawn her hand when I started, and now regarded me uncertainly.

'I'm *so* sorry. My father ... he –' She gestured.

I smiled. With her shock of sun-bleached hair, her green eyes, she was so much like the picture of her mother I had kept at my bedside during my uncertain youth.

She smiled in return, relieved at my acceptance. 'My father *hates* women and artists. It's bad luck if you happen to be both.' She had the habit of emphasising certain words as her mother had done.

I shrugged. 'I can live with the hatred of men,' I told her, and cursed myself for being so obvious.

She regarded me shyly. There was a diffident look in her eyes that could *not* be what I believed it to be. 'I think your best work is the *Goddess of Lesbos*,' she whispered.

My stomach fluttered. 'You do ...?'

There were a thousand questions I wanted to ask her, about herself, about her mother ... but I was frightened of being seen to be too forward, too eager.

Maltravers called her name and Corrinda almost winced.

'I *must* go. I'll see you again?' She smiled shyly. 'I really meant what I said about your work.'

She slipped through the sliding door with a small wave and disappeared into the crowd.

I decided to remain at Sapphire Oasis for a while.


Over the next few days I saw Corrinda on a number of occasions; but she was always with her father and it was obvious that she felt she could not leave him to join me although, I thought, she gave the distinct impression of *wanting* to do so. Or was I kidding myself? I was pushing forty and desperate, still searching for that which most people have either found at my age, or have given up hope of ever finding. Besides, I had to admit that it wasn't Corrinda I was attracted to; rather, I was obsessed with Cassandra Quebec and the tragedy of her death.

However much I tried I could not bring myself to start work. I had brought with me several small crystals in various stages of completion, with the notion of dabbling with them should no new project inspire me. Not only did nothing come to mind, but I found it impossible to complete the crystals already begun. My thoughts were too occupied with Maltravers, his daughter and the death of Cassandra Quebec. I was afraid of corrupting the unfinished work with my turbulent and unresolved emotions, and reluctant to begin a fresh crystal, perhaps on the subject of Quebec, for fear of being unoriginal. It had all been done before, and how might I bring some new and stimulating insight to the drama?

I spent more and more time beside the sparkling oasis, sipping long drinks and wondering whether my assumption the other night as to Corrinda's preferences had been nothing more than a drunken fantasy. Certainly, she did not join me as I sat in full view with my drink. But then, I told myself, perhaps this was because her father was in evidence so much of the time.

Maltravers spent a few hours each morning in his studio. Around noon he would emerge, showered and suited, and hold court in the bar. He had found himself lionised by the clique of Hoppers, and had proved himself a competitive drinker and an able raconteur. From my lounger by the water, I took the opportunity to watch him as he drank and illustrated his spiel with expansive gestures. I recalled the way he had eyed my body at our first meeting, and during the course of the next few days I realised that he was likewise sizing up the women in his crowd.

He soon found what he was looking for. Within a week of his arrival he was escorting a willowy Nigerian Princess, a laser-sculptress with a penchant for scarlet gowns that emphasised the absolute ebony of her flesh. They spent the mornings in his studio, afternoons in the bar and the evenings partying at various other oases scattered about the desert. I heard one rumour that they were creating a crystal together, another that they were producing a sculpture.

As much as I disliked seeing a beautiful and talented artist used by him, it did have the advantage of keeping Maltravers occupied and out of the way. I lived in hope that Corrinda might take the opportunity to seek my company.

Then one evening as I watched the sun set and the moon rise, and was contemplating whether to go to the bar for another drink or to return to my dome, a shadow fell across my outstretched legs.

Corrinda smiled uncertainly. 'Miss Hovana?'

'Eva, please. Won't you sit down?'

She perched herself on the edge of the chair across the table from me, and gave a shy smile in lieu of words. She wore a spacer's silversuit, chopped at shoulders and thighs. I could not help but notice, on the tanned flesh of her limbs, white scars like tribal striations.

In mutual nervousness we both began speaking at once. We stopped, and I said, 'Please, you first.'

She shrugged, reddened. She seemed younger than when we first met. 'I just ... I wanted to *apologise* for not meeting you sooner. I was working.'

I reached across the table and took her hand. 'Working?'

She reacted to my touch with characteristic nervousness. 'Didn't I tell you that I'm an artist?' she whispered.

'An artist?' I was surprised and delighted.

'Shh! Not so *loud* – if it ever got back to my father ... You see, he hates women and artists. What do you think it's like being his daughter?'

I made a small sound of commiseration.

She looked up from our hands. 'That's what I wanted to see you about – my art. I've just finished a piece. I ... I was wondering, *would* you like to see it?' She watched me with eyes so soft it seemed they could be bruised by rejection.

I said that I'd like nothing more, and she led me around

135

the curve of the oasis, talking earnestly by my side in relief at my acquiescence. She took me through the lounge of her father's hanging dome and into her bedroom.

'I must keep it in here,' she explained, hardly able to meet my gaze, 'so that father doesn't find out. There's no telling what he'd do.'

She stood beside an angular object covered by a silken sheet, and unveiled it so shyly that she might have been uncovering her own nakedness. 'What do you think? *Honestly?*'

I approached it slowly, aware of some choking emotion in my throat. It was a sculpture in some kind of glowing, off-world wood; perhaps half life-sized, it was of a naked woman seated on the ground, hugging her shins.

Corrinda was watching me. 'It's you,' she said in a small voice.

I touched the wood, caressed it. I wanted to cry, and yet did not want Corrinda to see me doing so – which was ridiculous. I wanted to cry because Corrinda had produced in the carved representation of myself all my loneliness, all my desire to want someone who wanted me.

The invitation was obvious, but I was too scared to trust her. She was so young, I told myself, while another voice asked what did age matter beside the fact of her compassion.

I bit my lip in a bid to stop the tears, turned to her. 'And your father would put an end to this?'

'He's ruled by his hatred. Success makes him jealous.'

'You should leave him!'

'He wanted me with him when he returned. He said that by returning here he could come to terms with what happened – then I *will* leave.'

'You must hate him,' I said.

Corrinda looked away.

In the silence that followed, I heard a sound from beyond the open door: the leathery creak and swoop of wings. I recognised the shape that flapped across the lounge and alighted on the back of the chesterfield.

I screamed.

Corrinda took my arm. 'It's okay, Eva. It's not the same one, and anyway it's quite tame.'

'But even so!'

'I know. It's sick. But, you see, my father is quite insane.'

She reached out and pushed the door shut. 'We'll be alone for the rest of the night,' she said, her eyes downcast.

For the next week, at every available opportunity, Corrinda would leave her father's dome and visit me, and we would make love on my bed beneath the arching dome. I blessed each minute that Maltravers spent in the company of the Nigerian, creating his work of art.

The day before the twentieth anniversary of her mother's death, Corrinda sat cross-legged beside me on the bed. I stared at her naked body, her torso a sun-browned canvass on which a pattern of pale striations had been inscribed. Some incisions were more recent than others, and the tracery of mutilation was too symmetrical to be the result of an accident. I wondered what had driven her to this masochism that masqueraded as art.

I stared through the dome at the clear blue sky. It was as if all week our love-making had been a rehearsal for what we had just shared. I had gone as far as I could, taken carnal knowledge towards an intimacy beyond which only a verbal declaration of love remained. Perhaps my circumspection, my refusal to match with words the physical commitment I had shown, communicated itself to Corrinda.

She traced a scar on her thigh, and said, 'Do you love me, Eva?'

I made some tired remark to the effect that we hardly knew each other, and that when she was my age she would come to doubt if anything such as love existed.

'I'm sorry – that's cynical. I like you a lot, Corrinda. Perhaps in time ...'

For so long I had hero-worshipped Cassandra Quebec that, having her daughter, I could not be sure if the girl I wanted to love was no more than an illusion of my fantasies, a substitution for the love that was impossible.

'I love you,' she whispered.

I kissed her projecting knee. I wanted to tell her that she longed for a mother, and as I was both the right age and an artist ... I glanced across the room at the statue, now installed in my bedroom, and convinced myself that even this was her subconscious grieving for her mother's absence, with myself as the transferred subject.

Ours was a union born of tragedy, and I kept asking myself how such a union might succeed.

I changed the subject. 'Tomorrow we could visit the Museum of Modern Art. We could experience your parents' crystal.'

Corrinda regarded me with a shocked expression. 'My father would never allow it.'

'Why are you so imprisoned by your father's wishes?' I asked harshly.

Corrinda just shrugged, ignored the question. 'I've read about the crystal, Eva. I *want* to experience it, to understand what my father went through. Then I might come to understand what makes him like he is. I might even be able to sympathise with him, instead of hating him.'

'Then come with me tomorrow.'

She shook her head. 'He wouldn't like it.'

In the silence that followed I realised that it was because of her father that Corrinda was so pathetically shy, her experience so circumscribed.

Then it was her turn to change the subject. She leaned over me and stared into my eyes. She could see, in my distant, shattered pupils, the tell-tale sign of addiction.

'You've used mem-erase!' she declared.

I told her that I had used it often in my twenties.

She shrugged. 'But why? What did you need to erase?'

'Oh ... I suspect periods of unhappiness, old lovers ... Of course, I can't remember.'

'But didn't you know it was dangerous?'

I shrugged. 'Not at the time,' I told her. Mem-erase was withdrawn from sale only when it was discovered that memories could never be truly erased. They were just blanked from the conscious, pushed into the subconscious, and could resurface at any time as trauma, psychosis.

'Have you ever thought of *replaying* those memories, reliving those affairs?'

'No, I haven't. I always thought that if they were sufficiently terrible for me to erase in the first place, then perhaps I shouldn't relive them. Then again, perhaps I was mistaken. How can I claim to be an artist if I can't face my past and make something of it?'

Corrinda smiled timidly. 'Would you erase *me* from your memory?' she asked.

I pulled her to me. 'Of course not,' I said, and I wondered how many times I had made that promise in the past.

I touched the scars that covered her body. 'You still haven't told me, Corrinda.'

'Please, Eva,' she said, and would say no more.

That evening, as the sun sank beyond the dunes of the Sahara and a cool night breeze tempered the heat of the day, the entire colony turned out to witness the ceremonial unveiling of Maltravers' latest work of art. There was a full moon shining, and above our heads the bulb of his studio hung like a replica of the ivory satellite. There was no sign of the great work, and I was not alone in wondering just what form it might take. Corrinda had chosen not to join me; she said that she *absolutely hated* her father's latest production, but had refused to tell me why.

There was a patter of applause as Maltravers appeared on the balcony, resplendent in white suit and cravat, and gave a short speech. His latest creation, he claimed, represented living evidence of his contention that all art attempted to attain the symmetry of nature. I found the monologue vain and pretentious, but I had to admit that it did have the desired effect of creating a considerable air of anticipation.

He came to the end of his speech and gave a slight bow, the minimal courtesy suggesting a certain contempt for his audience. The Nigerian joined him on the balcony. She wore a vermilion gown, fastened at the throat and gathered at the crotch to form a pair of voluminous pantaloons.

Maltravers kissed her hand and, as we gazed up in expectation, he stepped behind the woman and unfastened the choker at her neck. The gown whispered down the black curves of her body to reveal her terrible nakedness.

She struck a demure, Junoesque pose and the crowd gasped.

Her flesh had been sliced and flensed, the incisions opened, pulled back and pinned to reveal the inner organs in their precise, geometrical arrangement; the kidneys were displayed in positional harmony, the lungs likewise. The muscle of her abdomen had been turned back to form an elliptical orifice, through which could be seen the opalescent coils of her intestines. Her arms and legs had also undergone the depredations of Maltravers' scalpel: the ebony skin was scored and folded in a baroque series of curlicues and scrolls, repeating the motif of red on black.

But Maltravers' ultimate abomination – or master-stroke, depending on one's point of view – was the woman's heart. It perched between the orchids of her segmented breasts and throbbed like some grotesque alien polyp.

I recalled the scars on Corrinda's body and almost retched.

Maltravers stepped forward and took the woman's hand. She twirled. 'The Symmetrical Goddess,' he announced.

The stunned silence extended itself for several seconds, and then someone whooped and clapped, and immediately the acclamation was taken up by the rest of the crowd. Maltravers and his model disappeared into the dome; minutes later they strode out across the lawn, and there was a mad scramble to be the first to congratulate the pair.

I took refuge on the patio outside the bar and anaesthetised myself with alcohol. I alone seemed to understand that Maltravers' macabre violation of the woman's body had its source not so much in his desire to create new and outrageous art, but in some deep-seated psychological need known only to himself.

It was not long before my thoughts returned to Corrinda. I recalled her scarred body – her diffidence, which amounted almost to shame, at my insensitive questioning – and her refusal to attend the exhibition. I pushed myself unsteadily to my feet. I wanted suddenly to find her, to comfort her as best I could.

A party was raging in Maltravers' dome. The guests filled the various levels with a buzz of conversation, debate as to the man's genius and the occasional burst of laughter. I pushed through the groups of drinkers and searched for Corrinda, my desire to be with her increasing with every passing minute. I felt a surge of panic take hold of me, as if fearing that Corrinda, provoked by the extent of her father's latest perversion, might take it into her head to do something stupid. I wondered how much she hated Maltravers.

I found myself on a small, railed gallery overlooking a sunken bunker of loungers, which in turn overlooked the darkened desert. The mutilated Nigerian stood on a coffee table in the hub of the bunker, striking a series of extravagant poses. Light flashed off her exposed internal organs. 'He took my heart,' she was saying drunkenly to a posse of admirers, 'and did with it that which no man has ever done.'

I was overcome with revulsion and hurried around the circular gallery. The only place I had not yet looked for Corrinda was in her bedroom. I was about to make my way there when, across the lounge, I saw a door swing open and Maltravers stagger from his studio. His sudden appearance silenced the gathered drinkers; he became the focus of attention as, in evident distress, he pushed his way through the crowd. He paused at the rail, breathing heavily, saw his model and hurried down the steps into the bunker. He grabbed the woman by the arm, dragged her from the pedestal and pushed her across to the outer membrane of the dome. The circle of admirers hastily evacuated the bunker; already, a crowd had gathered along the gallery rail opposite me. I stood directly above Maltravers and the woman, and I alone overheard what followed.

'Where is it?' Maltravers sounded all the more menacing for the low pitch of his question. He still gripped the woman's patterned arm, and she grimaced at the pressure and raised a hand, palm outwards, as if to protect herself from a blow.

'I have no idea what you're talking about!'

I noticed that, for all the violent intimacy of the assault, Maltravers could not bring himself to regard the woman. Her organs were highlighted, the line of liver and kidney duplicating the overhead fluorescents – but Maltravers stared past her at the desert outside, as if ashamed of his creation.

'You were the only person in the studio when I opened the locker.' He was shaking with rage. 'Where is it?'

Pinned inelegantly to the wall of the dome, the woman nevertheless affected disdain. 'Where is *what*, exactly?'

Then he brought himself to regard her. He hissed something too low for me to hear, and the woman looked shocked. I could guess, from my knowledge of his past, from his haunted eyes, the reason for his secrecy.

I pushed myself from the rail and hurried through the dome to Corrinda's room. I opened the door without knocking and slipped quickly inside.

She was curled on her bed in the foetal position.

I paused by the door. 'Your father still uses –' I began.

She looked up and stared at me through her tears. 'After every session with the Nigerian and me,' she whispered. 'He didn't want to remember how much he enjoyed cutting us up.'

I could barely make out her words. She seemed traumatised, present only in body. Her eyes stared through me.

Then I saw the mem-erase crown beside her on the bed.

'Corrinda …'

'I had to!' she said. 'I had to know what it was that made

him do these things. I knew he was ill, but I didn't know *why*.' She struggled into a sitting position, picked up the crown and held it out to me. 'So I took this and accessed his past.'

I accepted the crown. The access slide was set at its very first programme. I looked at her.

'I replayed his memory of the death of my mother.' She began to cry. 'Take it! Access it for yourself!'

From another part of the dome I heard Maltravers, calling his daughter. Corrinda looked up at me and smiled a terrible smile. I quickly kissed her and hurried from the room, at once eager to learn the reason for Corrinda's horror and yet dreading what I might find. I left the dome as dawn touched the desert sky. The party was breaking up, the revellers leaving and making their way around the curve of the oasis.

In my own dome I poured myself a stiff drink, and then another. I sat down, picked up the mem-erase crown and re-checked the setting. I placed the crown on my head, connected the probes and pushed the slide to activate the programme.

Instantly, I was inside his head. I saw what Maltravers had seen that day, experienced everything he'd heard and said. But his thoughts, as they were not my own, remained in the background, blurred and indistinct, full of nebulous anger.

He was in the studio, facing his wife – oh, so much like Corrinda! – across a floor littered with slabs of crystal, frames and crystal-cutters. The Pterosaur, hunched and menacing, regarded him down the length of its scythe-like bill.

Cassandra stood in shirt-sleeves next to her fused crystal, sunlight falling on her golden hair. 'I don't understand your objection,' she was saying. 'The crystal will show my *love* for you. I want you to collaborate.'

'I want no part of it. It's your crystal, not mine.'

'But you're part of me. How can the crystal be anything other than *both* of us?' She stared at him. 'Are you frightened? Is that it, Nathaniel? You don't want the world to see you as you really are.'

Maltravers turned at a sound from the door, and the nurse hurried away to tend the crying baby before he could find the words to censure her.

He slammed the door and turned to his wife.

'How can you talk of love like that, after what you've been doing?'

Cassandra stared at him, stricken. 'What do you mean?' It was barely a whisper.

Maltravers tried to laugh, but the sound he made was desperate. 'How did you think you could keep it from me?'

She was staring at him, shaking her head.

'How long has it been going on? Before we came here?'

Cassandra was silent for a second, then said, 'Two days – no more. I met her here. But she means nothing to me.'

(Paralysed, on the edge of consciousness, I screamed.)

'Then why have an affair with her?' Maltravers cried. 'It isn't even as if … as if she's a good artist. Christ, the woman's third-rate. She isn't even as good as me!'

(I wanted to hit the release stud, retreat into the safety of ignorance; but some other part of me, fascinated and appalled by this vision of the past, would not allow me so easy an exit.)

'Oh, Eva's much better than you, Nathaniel. That's what attracted me – her talent. But, please believe me – I don't love her. It was only a physical thing, an infatuation.'

Maltravers' anger welled; I could feel it massing in my head like a thundercloud.

'Then if you think she's so good, why don't you stay with her!'

The Pterosaur hopped from foot to foot in agitation. At any second, I thought, it would swoop across the room and tear Quebec to shreds.

'Because I love you!' Cassandra yelled through her tears.

'I don't want your love – I want your respect for the artist I am.'

She broke; the walls of her reserve crumbled and she was no longer able to lie. She bent almost double and screamed at him.

'But, Nathaniel – *you are no artist!*'

His anger exploded, rocking me.

I knew, then, what was about to happen, I suddenly understood the reason for Corrinda's terrible smile.

The Pterosaur remained on its perch.

Maltravers rushed at his wife.

He lifted a crystal-cutter and in a blind rage attacked, slashed at her again and again as she stood before him and offered no resistance.

(I tried to shut out the vision as Cassandra Quebec was transformed before my eyes into a lacerated carcass – but the image played on in my head.)

Then Maltravers ceased his attack and Cassandra slipped to the floor, and realising what he'd done he fell to his knees, and his remorse swamped me. He saw the crystal, and something – perhaps some insane idea that this was the only way to immortalise his wife *and* her talent – moved him to lift her and lay her to rest on the slab of crystal. She died and gave her dying to the world, and Maltravers was overcome with a weight of guilt and regret that I was slowly coming to realise was my burden also.

I hit the release, tore the crown from my head and sat staring through the dome, weeping at the new order of reality revealed to me. Then I realised what day it was – the twentieth anniversary of Cassandra Quebec's passing – and something, some vague and disturbing premonition, reminded me of Nathaniel Maltravers' obsession with the symmetry of art. I could see, across the oasis in Maltravers' studio, the evil flapping form of the Pterosaur. I pulled myself upright and staggered from the lounge.

I crossed the lawn in a daze of disbelief. I seemed to take an age to reach Maltravers' studio, aware of the terrible fact that my affair with Cassandra Quebec had brought tragedy upon two generations.

Just as I, denied the emotion of grief by my use of mem-erase all those years ago, had been brought here by my subconscious for motives of its own – to empathise with Quebec's death on its anniversary, to fall in love again with her through the medium of her daughter? – Maltravers too had been delivered here by his subconscious for its own sinister reasons. He hated women and artists and – as Corrinda happened to be both, as well as a substitute figure for his wife – what greater act of artistic symmetry might there be than a *second* celebrated Nathaniel Maltravers' crystal, twenty years on?

I came to the scimitar support of Maltravers' dome and, sobbing with desperation, hauled open the door. I ran inside and up the escalator, numbed by the knowledge of what I might find.

I was crossing the lounge when I heard Corrinda's scream from the direction of the studio, and my relief that she was still alive was tempered by the knowledge that soon, if her father had his way, she would not be. I heard Maltravers' curse, and the din of things being overturned from within the room. I reached the communicating door and tried to yank it open – but it was locked. Corrinda yelled my name, pleading with me to hurry, and I called in return that I was coming. Through the frosted glass I could make out two indistinct figures circling each other with extreme wariness, and above them the Pterosaur in flight.

I scanned the lounge for something with which to smash the door when I heard another cry: Maltravers, this time – though whether in victory or defeat I could not tell. Then silence. I hefted a carved statue, pitched it through the glass and stepped in after it.

The scene that greeted my eyes was a grotesque tableau, the aftermath of tragic events played out to their conclusion. Maltravers lay on his back on a slab of crystal, his throat slit and his torso, from gullet to abdomen, opened to his spine. Beside him, Corrinda braced herself against the faceted crystal, as if in exhaustion or in silent prayer.

*146*

Still gripping the crystal-cutter, she stared at me with eyes burning like emeralds.

'He attacked me,' she whispered. 'He had it all planned, the crystal set up …'

Only then did I notice the rip in her one-piece and the bloody gash across her stomach. She stared at the cutter as if seeing it for the first time, then dropped it and reached out to me. 'Eva …'

'After all I've done?' I said.

'I *need* you!'

As I took her in my arms, the Pterosaur swooped through the air, alighted on Maltravers' corpse and began picking at the bloody remains.

Corrinda looked at me and, together, we reached out to the crystal and experienced Maltravers' death. We shared his initial shock at the realisation of his end, and then his profound relief that his jealousy and guilt were drawing to a close. We experienced his macabre satisfaction in the symmetry – not quite that which he had planned – that the crystal would come to represent.

Then, in a subtle underlay of emotion, I became aware of Corrinda's contribution to the crystal. I felt her joy that at last she was free, her delight in the irony of creating a work of art at her father's expense.

I came to Sapphire Oasis in search of experience, or so I thought at the time.

# THE PILL

*by*
*Jojo Bling*

Jojo Bling lives in Canada, but drinks in Britain, and 'responding to the call of arborealart' has personally installed over one million trees in the future forests of British Columbia without receiving an Arts Council grant – 'green rectangles of tree skin' – for services to literature. The author admits to once being a winner of a Kellogg's 'Design a Car of the Future' competition and confesses to having never published any science fiction until now.

I ... I, I ... I, I, I ...

I've seriously considered taking The Pill ever since ... ...
ever since experiencing the eye of my stormy youth, I
suppose. Funny thing is, before The Pill came onto the
scene I'd always thought myself to have particularly strong
Whacko tendencies. I realise now, being one of a dwindling
minority of Evolvers (or Revolvers, as the Whackos know
us), just how far off the mark I was.

Of course it's well recognised that everyone whose
synoptic awareness has been temporarily expanded beyond
the set limits of its conventional receptivity, considers
themselves to have come into possession of some esoteric
intelligence, some dark compelling insight, some suddenly
vital comprehension of the manifest world.

The fleeting encounter with this secret lore is acquired
with, and even portended by, exceedingly potent feelings.
Everything at this moment has become not only irrevocably
Right (there is nothing left to have right to), but also
seminally On.

First sneered at as Wow Cows, the proto-whackos' habit
of inspirational thigh-slapping eventually lent the final shape
to their name.

Thus these heightened sensibilities transcend the
ideation to the point that now every concept becomes
impressed in direct proportion to the intensity of the
accompanying feelings, i.e. wowings: thus Archimedes'
ecstatic 'Eureka!' (not to suggest for one moment that the
venerable Greek was stoned).

However, upon re-entry into the linear progressions of
straight-narrow-and-true Evolver space, the volatile content
of the experience rapidly dissipates leaving just the sole

survivor, general impact, as the vouchsafing officer for the integrity of the vapid revelation. A kind of touchstone, the General might express himself through the proto-whacko in what the Evolver could only describe as 'transcentric behaviour'. Nevertheless, the type of condoned conduct normally bracketing the young, the infirm, the old, was severely censured in the potential Whacko.

But now The Pill has arrived to herald the legitimisation of the wow, and to enfold society's carnivalisation of revelation deep into the indigestible roly-poly troughs of now-then.

And as I sit here sucking in contemplation, nowing the then, I cannot deny that The Pill has come to alter a retentive perception of the parameters of consciousness. Yet within this spectacular arena, practicable individual experimentation by members of the fringe was previously deadlocked.

The sounding off of social alarms over the 'dependency' issue, arose from the necessity of repeated doses of pilot brain chemicals in brave attempts to flatten out society's 'mountainous mundanity'. Moreover, the push for a sustained 'high' through these various 'parameter jerks' became defamed throughout Evolverdom because of the focused attention on the early heavy casualties of those plucky Whacko pioneers.

But The Pill has come amongst us, making all psychic boosters obsolete, regenerating the degenerate, transforming the dependency question into the 'deep tendency' solution. For what The Pill purports to offer is an expansion of consciousness that through want of any plausible comparison can only be said to promote, yes – total mind distension.

You may ask then, why I sit here sucking a molevision tube, an activity dating back to the earliest pioneers, when The Pill could hold me up beyond the pale of decay, and set me soaring.

Let me explain: the mole in her tunnel can always sense the eagle high above, but the soaring bird can only saw.

I need to be straight.

You see, the quality of my high is ultimately dependent upon the grudging corroboration of my ground level low.

High-low, high-low, is I believe, from particle-wave quantum through to expansion-contraction cosmic, the primal greeting extended to all of us by the Multiverse itself.

Hi-lo, hi-lo, is what is going on here.

If social dynamics could have accomodated the many prodigious complications arising from this straight-whacko-straight, see-saw, evolver-revolver, hi-lo – goodbye fluctuation (the straight unknowingly bending unto the helix of its paraform – but ever the incalculable curve of all interdependencies), then perhaps The Pill might have been staved off for an indefinite period, and mankind flourished in her evolved revolving condition, forever experiencing the rush of Becoming, that transitive perpetuity of Almost Being.

Unfortunately, the administrators of primitive Evolverdom were the most hopeless of all addicts themselves.

Whereas The Pill takers were well beyond the entrapment of addiction, Evolvers were dependent in such an absolute fashion that their web of excuses eventually constituted an entire branch of science – now as redundant as metempsycho-siology: viz. politonics, econoconcoctics, behavioural accountancy, theofiscality, doshology, and so on. This narcotic which they had been shovelling into their veins by way of their pockets since the very dawn of Evolver Man, was, in its most seminal state, Money.

In a pure base form money could be cut into multiple lines of credit producing any number of desirable sensations. Taken in small quantities, the mild euphoria known as consumerism was experienced, but soon trailed off as the drug was spent. Medium doses produced the thrilling pal-pitations associated with higher purchases, affording far more impact and without the lingering after-effects of lower-dose installments. In very large wads the twin hallucinatory conditions of power and security might be aroused; however, the drawbacks were said to be terrible – loneliness, paranoia, depravity, although some contend that these were rumours put about to limit demand whenever procurement of the drug became especially heavy.

The term Evolver was first coined during this frantic era, as the burgeoning drug philosophy contrived to explain the naturalness of money in ever more devious convolutions of thought. And by degrees, the sum of human knowledge became adjusted to incorporate this single denominator common to all.

An astonishing levity came to replace old Newtonian gravity: Money makes the world go round.

Those few scattered souls not yet flung from the planet's surface through their ignorance of this pervasive bond were not to last long. Systematically rooted out from their primitive existence by fanatical proselytising addicts operating through megalithic corporations (drug syndicates ballooning on 'controlled inflation' principles), they were first forcibly loaned massive doses – and then, without pity, left to beg, borrow and eventually steal like everyone else for more.

Perhaps a word of explanation is necessary to clarify this concept of stealing. Evolvers readily admitted that 'All addicts eventually steal to support their addiction.' Unable to recognise themselves as addicts of the first order – money-addicts, Evolvers sanctioned the massive scale of their own thefts through the invention of an expedient they termed generally 'enterprise', and more specifically 'capitalism', thereby fundamentally condoning the cavalier expropriation of the drug on a world wide scale.

Ironically, their order of drug enslavement became termed The Free World.

It hardly seems credible now that these drug-crazed barons of the mass habituation of mankind to money, with all its evident fallout in the form of harrowing human casualties, not to mention the insensate pillage of the planet to produce ever greater quantities of the drug, actually viewed the activities of the brain chemical pioneers as constituting an invasion of their righteous moral order. More realistically, these early psychic materials, subversively passed from hand to mouth, evaded the vast tax superstructure (an inspired concept by the money-peddlars to wrest some of the drug back from their clients in order to resell it to them, thus generating more of the same). So enraged became these dosh-dealers that even death penalties were shrilly invoked to effect the cure of such 'duty-dodging junkie slime'.

But the illicit trickle of brain chemicals continued, soon to become a dodgy flood, with The Pill finally emerging, some say from the Money Establishment's very own Institute of Psychosecurity.

Through the tenacity of the early Pill Martyrs, the opportunity for massive insolvency solidarity was at last made available on the street. Whackos were here, and now to stay.

It was at this point that tottering Evolverdom threw itself recklessly into the sham of its frenzied Final Crusade: God's gotten out of debt, but Satan's still whacko!

Statistics, albeit Evolver statistics (Whackos consider stats to be merely an addict's exploitation of mathematical form to justify a craved solution), indicate that the proportion of Whackos to Evolvers is roughly equivalent to that of water to land. The Whackos now know our planet as Aquaria; Evolvers call it The Terra Bank. Most coastal areas and islands have gone Whacko. Evolver communities occupy for the most part suburban sprawls, and of course their main area of influence is still the Unified Spenders of Avarice.

Evolver enforcement of nine-tenths law amounts lately to hardly more than impulsive but sporadic Whacko-bashing. Coercive rehabilitation under macroeconomic powers led to the inevitable investigation of global Pill terrorism, and the incremental infiltration of what was claimed to be 'a vast maggoty network bent on sucking the lifeblood from our treasuries'. But shortly thereafter the paramilitary arm of CRUMP appeared to disintegrate as a coherent force of repression. Some cynics said that half of them had suddenly become immensely wealthy, and that the other half were probably already Whacko before they'd gone in.

Entrenchment is at present buying us Evolvers a short breathing space, time in which to come to terms with the horrifying legacy of money-addiction, time in which to understand our Whacko neighbours, time to plan the restructuring of the remnants of our diseased society. But time is running out. Anyone can now gain access to The Pill by money order through the mail.

It is unsettling to think how the world seemingly took this Other Revolution so much in its stride, as if the orgies of money-addiction were mere zits on the face of boyish mankind. Not yet Whacko, possibly a last generation Evolver, I feel I have a viewpoint to offer which is somewhere between Evolver credit-laced-debt credulity, and impenetrable Whacko awe.

I write 'viewpoint to offer' and yet upon reflection I realise what a pompous statement that really is: I doubt if any Whacko will ever read these words (the World is for reading, words are for believing, but believing is seeing); money-addicts might, if only I knew how to sell it to them; and hi-lo Evolvers are all too busy penning their own.

And yet the compulsion persists, to shed light on these recent unexpected twists in human destiny. As for my metaphorical inclination, I blame the pips that I swallowed during the behaviour modification of my childhood, especially in such fruity routines as the picture-letter game which, properly, constitutes the basic cash-creationist initiation of all Evolver-kinder: A for Adam, B for Bank, C for Credit, D for Debit, E for Earning, F for Financing, G for God, H for Heaven, I for I, II, III …

For many years Whackos lived surreptitious lives within Evolver communities, often keeping up orthodox appearances so successfully that not until the onset of the Final Crusade with its subsequent Whackohunt (triggered incidentally when the Pope publicly confessed to Whacko fallibility), did Evolvers comprehend the magnitude and full implications of the slogan 'Beware, there lurks a Whacko within!'

Wives suddenly looked with suspicion at their husbands, and husbands back at their wives; and neighbours at neighbours, and strangers at strangers; and children at pets. What was it to be Whacko? Evolvers could only wager.

Intending to sharpen the wits of Evolver-kinder, television networks offered large cash prizes for 'spotting the Whacko, at any time, on any show'. Response was like an avalanche. Soon cartoons came to replace all live media personnel.

The Whackohunt spread like money-lust. Politicians gave over their seats to insurance company directors. Judges and architects freely surrendered. The medical profession broke up voluntarily.

Figures indicate world population is continuing its sharp decline. But even though Whackos are known to accept death as ecstatically as they embrace life (Death is Life without life), they appear to be on the verge of an important compromise. When the first publicised Whacko birth took place recently, the eyes of Evolverdom were on it: could it survive? How would it behave?

Its beaming mother, in front of an assembly of stern Evolver observers, as if attempting to make some unutterable statement, resolutely dropped the baby onto the floor. Everyone gasped. The infant, somewhat dazed, shook itself, looked up at the gathering – and smiled.

Some Evolvers now claim to have Whackos around the house as pets, although I suspect that Whackos might see this relationship from an entirely different perspective.

It's a bad bet that imperial money-business will ever attain its former gloriously profane proportions. Most terminal addicts have long headed off to the heartlands of US, where dreadful massacres (involuntary foreclosures) of the residual Whacko population caused such a point-of-order flurry.

The flotation of the Coastal Waters Bill, ostensibly to raise diminished tax-based revenues to bolster security forces so that they might better protect the passage of the bill (and which, incidentally, led to Whacko verification of land mass heartlands as 'self-isolated tubs of synthetic evolver lolly-lotion'), called for the issue of millions of fair shares. Those evolvers formerly involved in this equitable distribution have recently turned to operating an expanding mail-order empire. The world's skeletal postal system is still surprisingly efficient: for the most part, Whackos have kept it going. For them it appears to be a ritual of unrivalled significance. They seem to conduct themselves as midwives when delivering the mail, to the extent of opening envelope or package at the door and carefully birthing its contents into the addressee's cupped hands.

Thus an overview of The Pill crisis here on Earth would at present indicate a gradual easing of tensions. The work of informants, telecast blacklists of suspected Whackos, and even restrictions on public 'beaming' have all but ceased. This nascent tolerance of Whackos, initially generated out of a sense of business pragmatism I suspect, has coincided with the current promotion of two well-publicised rumours – both equally astounding.

The first is that the money habit can be kicked: unfortunately, the lengthy treatment is said to be prohibitively expensive. The second is that whackoism may after all be reversible, and that the antidote, when made available, will be free.

Long before the circulation of such transparent rumours, my partner persuaded me to enter into a pact with him. We'd discussed Pillory on numerous occasions. He thought that if we took The Pill together it would be a way of perfecting our Evolver relationship, freezing it in its prime, and would signal the new beginning of a recombination of our still young and forward-looking lives.

I had held back, arguing that our devotion to one another was yet to climax; reasoning that our past would eventually recombine in our future Evolver years, continually enhancing and refining our meta-relationship beyond all imaginable bounds.

He riposted that my ego had always been the cutting edge

of my tongue, and that without Pill Therapy I would continue to display both the evasive and unyielding tendencies of the degenerate addict.

On the contrary, I countered, it is you who crave The Pill, yes, The Pill, a narcotic's narcotic which your neuroses have invented in a desperate bid to avoid detection.

He scowled. If these neuroses of mine are playing such cloak and dagger games with my mind, then The Pill may very well provide just the sort of primal auditing my memory banks are in need of.

His reasoning was as cute as a bookie's ledger.

It was of course simply a battle of wills, and in the end my ego won the day through a display of its superior flexibility: I gave in. But with one condition.

I suggested we substitute one of the two pills with an identical dummy. This was to allow one of us to remain in the Evolver continuum, however briefly we saw fit, in order to document the Whacko perspective. That done, the documentor, either he or I, would then join the other in permanently blissful Whackoland. It was the most responsible gift I could think of to bequeath the shrinking Evolver dimension I was about to desert.

I made him pledge that if it was I who chose the Real Pill he must at least make an attempt at a record before joining me. He made the solemn vow as he came during our final act of intercourse on shrinking Terra Bank: I'll write! I'll write! he rasped, as if on the very brink of some immutable change of address.

Together we threw straws and the I Ching (predictably) gave us its blessing.

We were naked, on our knees, crouching opposite each other, staring intently at the two little pills between us.

Don't be afraid, he had reassured me, don't make comparisons. Just regard it as the one essential piece of nourishment you will ever require.

Having ostensible freedom of choice, the strange-attractor surfaced: we selected, then swallowed our pills.

159

Mine had no taste. I was the first to blink. My mind was in turmoil. I had the nagging thought that somehow I was taking part in an execution: it's just the Evolver in me clawing for air, I reasoned. I was expecting the blade of darkness to descend with a screeching terror, and then a blindfold to loosen, revealing the kaleidoscopic radiance of the Whacko world before me.

But it was he who had selected The Pill.

At length, his mouth stretched, and stretched, stretching into a great beaming smile, fixing upon his features an absurd but dazzling expression I had never thought him capable of before. I felt shabby and humbled, surrounded as I was by his glorious, magnifying presence.

I rose abruptly, hurriedly dressed, rummaged for sunglasses, and snatched up pen and paper.

Darling, I think it's working – on you I mean, I whispered foolishly: tell me what's going on in there. His aura was becoming so brilliant I found myself fainting with fear for his safety. But he remained crouching there, beaming, the surface of his body shimmering and rippling as if it were no more solid than liquid light.

Then his jaw slowly dropped. And still maintaining that awesome smile, he wheezed, I … I, I … I, I, I …

He, well, existed with me for a time. My pet Whacko. I decided I wanted a baby from him, before I could complete my side of the bargain, but all his languid flesh ever seemed to exude was impalpable streams of limpid luminescence.

I'd ask myself: is this Evolver habit of mine really too deep-rooted to be overcome? This habit, so superficially diagnosed as money-addiction; but rampant materialism is still too flaccid a term to define intrinsic evolver status. One thing is certain: it grips us through the realm of the senses, becalms the surface of consciousness, invades the very core of our physicality.

The history of Evolver Man has hitherto been a predication of self-justifying, mostly violent actions within the ever contracting arena of our perceptible space. It has been characterised by an absence of significant truth, an abundance of self-praise and a particularly glaring avoidance of as-it-happens analysis. But this same account of the pathetic procession of creditors to the bank of human misery, this tawdry catalogue of the eventuation of raw material immanence, this is the very pinhead on which I dance crazy, and most of all fear falling from.

The fundamental revolving nature of Evolver culture holds me rapt and gyred. I need to know more than anything else how our committed addicts can defend their dependency on the hallucinations of substantive matter.

This puts into context some graffiti I once took account of, scrawled across a 'Prohibited' notice at the edge of a deserted pebble beach. It read: Evolver is to stone as Whacko is to wave.

Of the future – of everything, I am uncertain. And the Uncertainty Principle has it that we can neither detect nor measure fundamental units – without altering them. This then is the very core of the Evolver drive mechanism, and the ghost in our machine is simply a compulsion to disturb …

It is this account of The Pill before you now which has become that pledge I made to my partner, the pledge to document the equation of land's interface with water. Maybe everything I ever attempt will be mere prevarication, putting off until tomorrow that little pill I should be swallowing today. This reassures my essential Evolver nature, my sense of belonging through the rage of addiction.

'All addicts eventually steal to support their addiction.' And thus I steal time, so my story may never end.

# THE FURNITURE
# OF LIFE'S AMBITION

*by*
*Brian Stableford*

Brian Stableford recently resigned from the Sociology Department of the University of Reading to write full time. His many and various works include *The Third Millennium*, a history of the next thousand years written in collaboration with David Langford, and *The Empire of Fear*, an alternative history novel in which Richard the Lionheart meets Vlad the Impaler. He has webbed toes but cannot swim. Dr Stableford wrote his own introduction, except for this sentence.

'Jesus, Jude,' complained William Morris to his wife one night, as they lay cuddling in bed, 'I've got to get out. I've just got to.'

Judy Morris strangled the sigh which rose unbidden to her lips, as it did every time William had one of his moods. She loved him dearly, but he could be *very* tiresome. She opened her cornflower-blue eyes and passed a tired hand through her silken blonde hair.

'You don't mean that, dear,' she said. 'You've just had a bad day, that's all.'

'Bad day!' said William. '*Bad day!* Jude, we're on the threshold of a whole new scientific revolution here. Our entire technological repertoire stands to be transformed in the space of a single lifetime – *my* lifetime. But all Plasmotech care about is meeting consumer demand! You know what they want me to work on now? Fish, that's what! I've been summoned to see Curtis and Wilberforce tomorrow, and I know exactly what they're going to say. They're going to talk about cod fillets and caviar, and make stupid jokes about Moby Dick. It'll be kids' stuff, Jude – a five-year-old could do it. It's just one bloody supermarket novelty after another. Is this the future, Jude? I mean, Jude, *Jesus!*'

Judy knew that she must at all costs avoid making jokes about loaves and fishes. William, as his finely-chiselled, delicately pre-Raphaelite features implied, was rather over-sensitive, and prone to overreact to any slight. As a child he had been spoiled dreadfully because of his marvellous intelligence and stunning good looks, and in adult life he remained petulant, horribly jealous and prone to outrageous tantrums. Those who loved him had to learn to handle him very delicately.

Most people were willing to learn. After all, one has to make allowances for genius, and William was certainly a genius – possibly the best geneswitcher in the entire world. His employers at Plasmotech were aware of this, and were careful to pay him a very handsome salary. Judy knew it too, and she adored him as much for his fine and reckless mind as for his remarkably beautiful features and lissom body. William was absolutely certain of it, and saw himself as a combination of Albert Einstein and Thomas Alva Edison, without peer as theoretical scientist or practical man.

Plasmotech dealt in factory-produced food: meat and dairy products manufactured biotechnologically, without the aid of animals. Geneticists of an earlier generation than William's had figured out how the genes in an animal egg-cell provided the blueprint for the structure of a mature animal, and how genes were selectively switched off in different kinds of specialised cells to produce organs and tissues. These discoveries had opened up a scientific Klondyke for the geneswitchers whose business it was to design useful organic structures and then to control the switching of genes in developing embryos so as to produce those structures.

It was no longer necessary to allow a cow's fertilised egg-cell to develop into another cow, which would have to graze for years in open fields in order to produce milk or beef. Technical control of the geneswitching process meant that a cow's egg could be instructed to develop into a gargantuan milk-making organ or a single huge muscle. Such entities could easily be kept alive in nutrient baths, fed on an organic cocktail of carbohydrates, proteins and trace compounds which was manufactured in bulk by genetically-engineered fungi.

The earliest food-producing entities had been limited in size. Tissue-cultures, like organisms, age and die; cells cannot keep dividing forever, and as they become more specialised they age more rapidly. At one time, therefore, a cow's ovum could only be induced to develop into a lump of solid muscle approximately the same size as an actual cow. William Morris's first breakthrough had been to find a way to overcome this limitation. He had discovered how to 'neotenise' the developing tissue-culture, so that the onset of specialisation could be delayed. The early phase of the development of the quasi-embryo could then be extended to produce a huge spherical 'superblastula' before the switching of genes need actually begin. This allowed the growth of very large tissue-cultures. The meat-producing ones were quickly nicknamed skyscraper steaks, while the ones which produced milk attracted less dignified titles.

William's second discovery had been just as dramatic. Plasmotech had had profitable meat-producers and milk-producers even before William joined the company, but they had failed to develop a really efficient substitute for actual chickens as producers of eggs. Co-ordination of the different kinds of specialised cells involved in egg-making was very problematic if the egg-making apparatus was not situated within a greater organism equipped with built-in control mechanisms: a nervous system and a hormonal system. William, working with general-purpose silicon chips and standard organo-metallic synapses developed for medical purposes, managed to fit simple multi-tissue entities with appropriately simple inorganic 'brains', adding just sufficient control to allow the entities to function. He was thus able to design an egg-producer the size of a family car, fuelled by a mammoth drip-feed, which could spew out four hundred standard eggs an hour. William called it his 'Heavyside Layer'.

With achievements like this to his credit many a lesser man than William would have been contented, but William's imagination was the kind which loved to reach out into vast vistas of half-glimpsed possibility; he had dreams and ambitions, and he felt that his job was becoming a kind of strait jacket preventing him from fulfilling his true destiny. He was not a happy man, and Judy had often to listen to the outpourings of his anguish.

'Well dear,' she said, judiciously, 'Plasmotech are a food company. It's an important job, discovering new ways to make cheap food. There are still two billion people in the world who don't have enough to eat. You used to find the job exciting.'

William groaned. 'That's because there used to be problems to be solved. Important problems, like superblastularisation and silicon-organic integration. Do you have any idea how useful those techniques might be, once their true range of application is explored? Skyscraper steaks and the Heavyside Layer are just scratching the surface ... but Curtis can't see any farther than the next bloody delicacy! A thousand other geneswitchers will be picking up the threads of my discoveries and doing really interesting things, while I'm supposed to fart about with fish.

'The stupid thing is that Plasmotech will make billions in spite of their blindness, because they own the goddam patents. *My* patents, Jude! I won't make as much out of it as Wilberforce and Curtis, and I bet they won't even give me a Nobel Prize, because I'm just a vulgar commercial engineer. Jesus, Jude, I've got to get out. Somehow, I've got to go solo, work for myself. I've *got to*.'

'Well dear,' said Judy, caressing him soothingly with her gentle hands, in her own peculiarly distinctive fashion, 'I think that's a wonderful idea, but you've said before that it would be very difficult. All that equipment you work with – the DNA-thingumajigs and the advanced electronic doodads. It's such a heavy investment just to get started.'

'I know that,' said William, who was beginning to wind down under the palliative pressure of Judy's stroking, gradually becoming plaintive instead of angry. 'But I've got a first class record, second to none. God knows, I've done enough to show my worth. If I lived in America, big-dollar men would be queuing up to finance me – I've got American biotech firms headhunting me all the time, though Plasmotech try their level best to keep them away from me.

I'd need six or seven million to start up – ten at the most. That's petty cash in the City. *Somebody* should be willing to finance me.'

Judy didn't like the idea of moving to America. She was part of a big, close family, and had an enjoyable job of her own at the BBC. She was also genuinely devoted to England's countryside and sense of history. Her heart sank at the prospect of giving it all up.

'We did a financial documentary last week,' she said, pensively. 'There was a rather charming man on it – very striking red hair. Name of Marshall. He's part of a firm of investment managers and financial consultants. He talked about multi-million dollar deals as if he fixed them up every morning before breakfast. I've got his card at the office. Shall I bring it home?'

The stroking was by now having such an effect that William was beginning to relax. He seemed ready to forget the whole matter for the time being, and was evidently prepared to turn his attention to a more pleasant occupation.

Judy permitted herself a sigh of relief, and abandoned herself to passion.

'The trouble is,' said Peter Peregrine Marshall of Marshall & Faulkner, leaning back in his fancy swivelling chair and flicking cigar-ash on to the shag-pile carpet, 'that you haven't really thought this through.'

William was not in the least disturbed by the other man's casual *savoir faire*. He stared into Marshall's brilliant blue eyes, noting how like in colour they were to his wife's. 'Actually,' he said, 'I think I'm the only person in the world – or at least the only person in Britain – who has thought it through. I've just explained to you that these techniques are the basis for a whole new industrial revolution. Do you know how many scientific breakthroughs have been made here, then blocked and mishandled by the obtuseness of the financiers, so that the Americans and Japanese stole all the thunder?'

'That's an old story, Dr Morris,' Marshall replied, 'and you'd be surprised how many people try to tell it to me. Don't mistake my meaning. Marshall & Faulkner do have access to the kind of money you need, and would be happy to put it into the kind of industrial enterprise that you're talking about. When I say that you haven't thought it through, I don't mean that you lack vision – far from it; you can see the far horizons very clearly indeed. What you can't quite see, it seems to me, is the road that will take us there.

'You've said yourself that the difficulty with this kind of research and development is the high cost of the equipment you require. DNA manipulation is so difficult and so delicate that the technology which Plasmotech have laid on for you is phenomenally expensive to purchase and run. You may be able to work miracles, Dr Morris, but you need a very costly magic wand. Plasmotech may seem narrow and unimaginative in the range of applications to which they put your discoveries, but in order to generate the income they need to sustain your research they must have products which they can sell on a very large scale.

'You've talked to me about some amazing possibilities – kinds of organic machines that you might be able to build *one day*. You've talked about new kinds of houses, new methods of mining, new transport-systems. I don't doubt that in the fullness of time you might make those dreams come true, but you can't move to those levels of complexity in the short term. In order to keep your project going for thirty or forty years you have to make it show a return in two or three years – four at the most. I can understand why you want to work for yourself, and why you're contemptuous of the idea of using your talent to make cheaper fish fingers, but you can't really afford that kind of contempt. If you're to start a new company, you need a *product*, and it must be a product which you can start to manufacture quickly and sell to a mass market. That won't be easy, especially as Plasmotech hold the patents on your research work; they won't let you set up in competition to them without a very hard fight, which means that the food market is effectively closed to us. So what can you make, Dr Morris ... not in twenty years time, but *tomorrow?*'

William smiled. He had not been taken by surprise by the line of argument. He was, after all, a genius, and he understood something of the wicked ways of the Capitalist world.

'Furniture,' he said.

'Furniture?' Marshall echoed.

'Chairs, couches ... that sort of thing.'

Marshall raised a quizzical copper-coloured eyebrow, assuming an annoyingly contemptuous expression which made William writhe inwardly with resentment.

William had previously decided that he would not much like P. P. Marshall; he knew that the man was deemed by some to be a genius in his own field – Marshall was known in the City as the 'copper-crowned certainty' – but William could not bring himself to admit that there could be geniuses in the field of finance. He detested casual smoothness and polish, and despised people who made fortunes by playing games with other people's money. He knew full well, though, that he *needed* Marshall, and that he could only win his scientific independence by tying himself to a man of this kind.

'We don't just get beef from cattle,' William explained, patiently. 'I've been looking at the price of leather. The Americans have begun producing it in sheets for the clothing and furnishing industries, the way they produce furs. They've helped to sustain the fashionability of leather upholstery. But their leather-upholstered furniture is just ordinary furniture with a biotechnologically-produced covering. It's not so cheap, despite the cheapness of the leather, and it's crude. I can design a superblastula that will mature into a single armchair or couch, with its own leather skin. An elementary silicon chip connected to a primitive nervous and circulatory system – simpler than the ones in my chicken substitute – would allow the chair to alter its

171

shape to accommodate a particular sitter, to recline as desired, and vary its softness and its temperature. The ultimate in home comfort: adaptable furniture with inbuilt central heating.'

William could see that P. P. Marshall was impressed. He was pleased with himself for keeping this trump card up his sleeve, and felt that he had chosen the right psychological moment to play it.

'This would use existing technology?' Marshall queried.

'Elementary,' William assured him. 'But the application is sufficiently novel for us to be able to establish a new set of patents. Plasmotech couldn't touch me. Only I know my methods well enough to do it. We'd have six or eight years clear start on any possible opposition.'

'These things would need nutrition.'

'Minimal. Once-a-month injection.'

'I don't want to be a wet blanket,' said Marshall, 'but I have to take the part of devil's advocate. Is the world really ready for living furniture? Mightn't it make people uneasy? A whale-sized piece of meat in a factory is one thing – all the consumer sees is the same old package on the supermarket shelf, and she doesn't have to think about superblastulas any more than her mother had to think about abattoirs. But to have something like this in your living room, to sit on … that might be scary.'

'If it's properly marketed,' said William, firmly, 'it won't be. If we have an ad agency with imagination, we can put it across. My furniture would have a lot of selling points. The ultimate in comfort, utterly safe. Do you know how many people still have furniture stuffed with foam which gives off toxic gases, because they begrudge the expense of replacing it?'

Marshall looked at him ruminatively. 'How expensive would this stuff be?'

William shrugged. 'To develop … well, you've already looked closely at the cost of equipment, sites, manufacturing capacity. To produce, once the groundwork is done … I can do for the price of chairs what the Heavyside Layer did for the price of eggs.'

The russet eyebrows ascended again toward the remarkable fringe. '*That* cheap?' said P. P. Marshall. He had the air of one who had scented a proposition as copper-bottomed as he was copper-crowned, and William knew that he was hooked. Marshall fingered the arm-rest of his own high-tech executive chair, speculatively. 'Everyone sits on chairs,' he mused.

'First the chair,' said William. 'In time, the entire environment. Do I get my twenty million?'

P. P. Marshall stubbed out the butt of his cigar.

'I think I can arrange that, Dr Morris,' he replied. 'In fact, I'm certain that you and I can do business.' He stood up and offered his hand. William rose, too, and reached out to clasp it.

Thus began one of the most remarkable partnerships ever forged between scientific and financial genius.

Even as the two men looked one another so frankly in the eye, though, it was plain that the relationship would never develop into a genuine friendship. In some ways, they were too different, and in others, too similar. William despised the financier for his cupidity, but he already suspected that Marshall despised him equally for his unworldliness. Marshall was one of the few men in the world who was almost as handsome as he was, and one of the few who was every bit as competitive and ambitious. On one level, William knew that he would *hate* working with Marshall, but on another level, he was rather looking forward to finding out which of them would triumph in their personal struggle to be top dog.

The firm of Morris, Marshall & Faulkner (Furniture Manufacturers) started small, but grew very considerably. P. P. Marshall's anxiety as to whether the public was ready for superblastular entities in the home proved to be fortunately unfounded. The world, with a little help from an ad agency with imagination, proved quite willing to welcome the new biotechnology into the inner sanctum of the home.

The new Morris chair passed quickly through the classic stages of product evolution. At first it was a novelty. Soon it became a status symbol (not of wealth-status, because it was so cheap, but of cultural with-it-ness, of biotech chic, of futurist foresight). In remarkably quick time it became a standard fitment. It so caught the popular imagination that it seemed to be a perfect embodiment of the spirit of the age. With the arrival of the Morris chair, biotechnology crossed the threshold of social intimacy. The move from factory to salon was one small step for a chair, one giant leap for superblastulakind.

William Morris became his own boss, the steersman of his own researches, and revelled in his self-appointed status as an unfettered pioneer. His name had become, in a literal sense, a household word. The public delighted in the for-tuitous combination of circumstances which allowed him to echo, on so dramatically amplified a scale, the achievement of that earlier William Morris, who had also lent his name to an adaptable chair. That earlier Morris, it was recalled, had been a Utopian, who had brought *News from Nowhere* of a finer and happier world to come. The new William Morris, it was widely said, was a Utopian in a more impressive sense, who was actually bringing a finer and happier world into being.

William became rich. Then he became very rich. It was rumoured that it would only be a matter of time before he received his knighthood. His phenomenally handsome face grew even more finely-chiselled with age, and was to be found on magazine covers everywhere. The snatched snapshots of the *paparazzi* showed him often in the company of his equally handsome wife, who was perennially pestered for the 'secrets' of her milky complexion and silky, honey-blonde hair.

Despite the closeness of their financial relationship, though, William was rarely seen in the company of Peter Peregrine Marshall, the flame-haired golden boy of the City.

Marshall was just as famous as William; he was fêted as the entrepreneur extraordinary, and was universally regarded as

England's most eligible bachelor, not even excluding the princes of the realm. But William always considered Marshall's fame to be undeserved, because it was essentially parasitic upon his own. He was resentful (though never in public) of the fact that Marshall often seemed to enjoy more of the limelight than he did, because he had to spend so much time in his laboratory, while Marshall was always abroad in the world.

William loved celebrity, after his fashion. So did Judy. P. P. Marshall pretended not to, but he didn't fool anyone.

William did not allow celebrity to distract him from his work. Indeed, he threw himself into his researches with ever-greater zeal. A lesser man granted his success might have rested on his laurels, but William had always had greater aims in mind. He wanted to be the Isaac Newton of genetic science – the man whose efforts paved the way for the building of a new world. He was fearful that his intellectual prime would not last forever, and was determined to exploit it to the full before the inevitable decline set in.

While the Morris chair went through the phases of its success, therefore, William worked longer and longer hours on more advanced techniques of genetic manipulation. Morris, Marshall & Faulkner hired dozens of brilliant young men to work out commercial applications for the basic techniques derived from his patents, while he operated on an entirely different level, paying no heed to issues of immediate applicability. William was committed boldly to do what no man had done before in the usurpation of godlike power.

'A century ago,' William told a reporter, in one of his many interviews, 'men looked at the wonders of nature, and were awed by the power of the hypothetical being who might have wrought such marvels. Now, the intelligent man can only wonder at the poverty and narrowness of that Creation, and must reserve his awe for contemplation of the things that *men* will make, given their mastery of DNA.' William never actually claimed, when he indulged in such reveries, that DNA had no other master as virtuous, as adept or as ingenious as himself, but no one who heard him speak doubted that it was true.

And yet, in spite of everything, William was not altogether happy. Resentment and dissatisfaction had not been banished from his everyday existence.

'Jesus, Jude,' complained William one night, as they lay side-by-side in bed, 'I've got to get out. I've got to.'

'You don't mean that, dear,' said Judy, stifling that same old sigh. 'You've just had a bad day.'

'Bad day!' William retorted. 'I'll say I've had a *bad day!* You wouldn't believe the way they keep trying to drown me in paperwork. They want me in on *everything*: planning committees, product development, public relations, foreign buyers, franchises. I mean, for Christ's sake, what does a man have to do to get rid of that kind of crap? What the hell is Marshall supposed to be for, if not to keep that stuff out of my hair? What's the point of being the boss if the pressure from underneath is even greater than the pressure from on top used to be? I'm trying to run a bloody scientific revolution here, and I keep getting tangled in red tape. It's all around me, tying my hands and strangling me. I lock the door … I don't even have a phone in the inner sanctum … but they lie in wait for me outside the door like a flock of vultures. I mean, Jude, *Jesus!*'

Judy knew that she had to refrain from making jokes about disciples and the hazards of being worshipped, and must at all costs refrain from colourful word-play featuring crucifixion or other styles of martyrdom. William was as sensitive as ever, and reacted badly if he suspected that she was not taking his anguish sufficiently seriously. If anything, success had made him even more of a prima donna. He had recently taken to making camera-smashing assaults upon the *paparazzi* – a well-known badge of unstable temperament.

'Well, dear,' she said, 'it is your company, and everyone in it does rely to such an extent on your methods and your ideas. They depend on you, and you can't blame them for wanting to consult you when you get so angry if they do anything wrong, or anything you don't like. You do have a responsibility to them, you know.'

'Responsibility!' groaned William. 'If Prometheus had as much to cope with as I have, the fire of the gods would still be in Heaven. Marshall, who ought to protect me from the flak, is the biggest battery firing at me. I've made that red-haired bastard a multi-millionaire, but he thinks he has a mortgage on my bloody brain, and he always takes first place in the pestering line. Jesus, Jude, sometimes I think I ought to get out of Morris, Marshall & Faulkner and set up a nice little research establishment in the middle of the Arizona desert. I've got the money, you know. I could do it.'

This was an idea of which Judy disapproved very strongly. She would still quote all the old reasons for wanting to stay in England – family ties, her work in broadcasting, her sense of belonging – but nowadays there was more to it than that.

She had done everything possible to conceal it from William, whom she still loved very dearly, but she had come to treasure exactly what he had come to loathe: the attentions of Peter Peregrine Marshall. Marshall and she had been enjoying a passionate love affair for some years, aided and abetted by the nobility of commitment which kept William out of the way in his laboratory for such long hours.

In consequence of the strain which keeping this secret placed on Judy, her patience was not quite as endless as it once had been. Their sex-life had lost something of its old magic, but whenever she began to stroke him in her own distinctive fashions with her uniquely gentle hands, William's anxieties still ebbed gradually away.

She stroked him now, to soothe away his pain. There was something a bit mechanical about the way her hands moved, but she was certain that William was too wrapped up in himself to notice. The tokens of her love for him had become matters of routine, which no longer engaged her full consciousness, and no longer carried the meaning they once had had, but he would surely never know the difference, even if he *was* a genius.

'You mustn't worry so much, dear,' she told him, as she worked on him with her clever fingers. 'I'll speak to Peter for you, if you like. I'll explain to him how desperately important it is that you shouldn't be bothered while you're working. But you mustn't fret, because that's hurting you just as much as all the pressures on your time.'

'The trouble is,' said Marshall, leaning back against a workbench in William's laboratory suite, 'that you haven't really thought this through.'

William stared into those frank blue eyes, reflecting on the incompetence of nature, which allowed such an innocent expression to mask chicanery and double-dealing. Here, he thought, was a man who could betray his best friend without a flicker of conscience. His private detective had handed in a very full report, and William had read every word of it several times over.

'Actually, Peter,' he said, 'I've thought it through very carefully. I want to retire from this kind of life, so that I can concentrate entirely on pure research. No more chairs, no more waste-disposal units, no more living-light systems, no more biotech batteries. In fact, no more *products* at all. No more rat race. I shall continue to work for the scientific revolution in my laboratories, but I shall no longer man the barricades.'

Marshall spread his hands wide, as if he were about to embrace his colleague in a spirit of pure cameraderie, and favoured him with a look which had melted many a heart.

'Billy,' he said, 'I understand how you feel. Believe me, I do. I know that your eyes have always fixed on those far horizons. I know how the everyday business of Morris, Marshall & Faulkner gets you down, how sordid it all seems to you. I do my best to protect you, far more than you can possibly realise. I've kept a lot of weight off your back, shielded you from so much hassle, stood in for you in every way that I could, though I don't really understand the nuts and bolts of biotech at all.

'I know you're a genius, Billy, and I also know that because you're not like ordinary men you don't really know what's good for you, what you really need. Judy knows, Billy, and we've talked about it. Trust her, Billy. Trust *me*. We can take care of things for you, and together we can bring about this fabulous revolution of yours. Side by side, each with our part to play. Together we can do it, but apart ... each of us amounts to less than we'd like to think. We're not as young as we once were, you know – both of us past our best. All the City whizzkids I started out with have burned out, and all the geneswitching geniuses of your day are on the downhill side now. We still have a great thing going, here, Billy, if we can just keep it on the rails, but it needs work. Trust me.'

'Well,' said William, carefully, 'I've trusted you for a long time, Peter. I know how much I owe you; I really do. And to show you how much I appreciate all we've meant to one another, I've got something I'd like you to look at, which will demonstrate to you exactly where I'm up to right now ... to make it clearer what I've been working on, and what the fruit of my labours has been. It's in my inner sanctum.'

This was the very heart of William's private empire, inviolate even to his most intimate co-workers. Marshall had never been inside, and William knew how much it would surprise him to be invited now. Surely even P. P. Marshall would deign to feel a little bit proud as he stepped across this strange threshold, with William following behind.

The inner sanctum was quite cramped, because of the vast quantity of equipment which had been crammed into it over the years. William knew that to Marshall, as to Judy, it was simply an array of 'DNA-thingumajigs' and 'electronic doodads'.

In the middle of the room was a Morris chair.

'Sit down, Peter,' said William, amiably.

Marshall sat, relaxing into the chair. It was warm and (of

course) supremely comfortable. Like almost everyone else in the world, Marshall loved Morris chairs. William watched while Marshall's fingers ran appreciatively over the armrests. The chair accommodated itself to its occupant's shape, moulding itself snugly to his contours.

'Nice texture,' he commented. 'New, isn't it?' He continued to stroke it with his fingertips, testing its quality. 'It's got a really nice feel to it – could do well as next year's model. How long have you been hoarding it away in here?'

'Oh, it's new all right,' William told him blandly. 'I only made it this week. Entirely new design – tricky, in its way, though I'd practised the techniques a lot. Programming the chip wasn't too difficult, but any manufacturing process is delicate when you use new raw material for the first time.'

'New material?' queried Marshall, interestedly. 'It's not grown from a cowball, then?'

William had never liked the way that Marshall referred to superblastulas as cowballs. 'I didn't grow it at all,' he said. 'You see, I've progressed quite a bit in the matter of making superblastulas. I've found a method of producing them, as it were, the other way round. I can now switch *on* the genes of specialised cells, neotenising a mature tissue by reducing its cells to the undifferentiated embryonic stage. A superblastula made from a mature organism doesn't have quite the same capacity to grow, of course, but it can be redifferentiated into an entirely different structure.'

'My God!' said Marshall. 'You mean that you made this thing from a mature cow? You reduced an actual carcase to protoplasm and then reshaped it?'

'Oh no!' said William, permitting himself a tiny smile. 'I didn't use a cow.'

'Good,' said Marshall, shifting his position slightly. 'That would have been rather too macabre. Another chair, then?'

'It wasn't a chair,' William told him, calmly. 'It was Judy.'

William watched those familiar ruddy eyebrows lift, as the alarmed realisation dawned on Marshall that this might not be a joke. Marshall tried to stand up, but found that the chair, which had so conveniently modified itself to accommodate him, was actually folded about him rather tightly. He began to struggle, but the more he struggled the tighter the grip of the chair became. His arms gripped the rests more tightly, and William watched his face change as he realised that the chair's colour was the delicate hue of Judy's wonderful complexion, and that the tiny silken hairs with which it was covered were honey-blonde in colour.

William waited calmly for P. P. Marshall to stop writhing, and to start remembering Judy's embraces, and the special texture of her flesh.

Eventually, Marshall was forced to accept that he was not to be allowed to rise to his feet, and he looked up at William, with horrific questions trembling on his tongue.

William smiled, angelically.

'This is a very advanced Morris chair,' he said, quietly. 'If you attend very closely, you might be able to discern a slight pulse. This is a chair with a *heart*. It has a more complex nervous system than the standard model, better circulation, and – as you've probably realised – much better musculature. But the chip, oh, my dear Peter, you can't *imagine* the cleverness of that tiny, tiny brain!'

William took a small gadget from a nearby drawer. It looked rather like the kind of remote-control device issued with TV sets and other automata. William began pressing the buttons, and the chair began to grow hands. One pair grew by Marshall's wrists, and promptly gripped them; two pairs grew on either side of his torso and began to run their fingers lightly over his ribs and belly; a further pair grasped his calves and more fingers began groping about in his crotch. William could see, though his prisoner could not, that more hands were emerging beside Marshall's head.

P. P. Marshall, golden boy of the City, wet his pants.

'Don't worry about that, Peter,' said William, lightly. 'The chair can take care of it.'

The hands set about undressing Marshall, and being many, made light work of it. He was soon stark naked.

'I understand that you have frequently benefitted from my wife's caresses,' remarked William, in a strangely abstracted tone of voice. 'I always felt that her touch had its own quite distinctive quality. No doubt you agree. I treasured that talent of hers, and I assume that you did too. We two are the only connoisseurs, I think – the only people in the world who would appreciate this particular Morris chair. What wonderful opportunities this new Judy presents, don't you think? I've tried her out, and found her really quite exquisite. An experience to be savoured. I think you're going to find this a real privilege, don't you?'

Marshall made no reply to this. In fact, if appearances could be trusted, he was feeling rather sick when the chair began its foreplay, making love to him with all the mechanical tenderness of which it was capable.

P. P. Marshall, flame-haired darling of the media, began to scream.

Nobody could hear him. William's inner sanctum was soundproof. After a minute or so the screams began to distress William, so he directed one of the hands to clamp itself tightly over Marshall's mouth. Marshall resisted this stifling clutch fiercely, biting at the hand and making it bleed terribly. But the chair had no mouth or throat, and could not cry out in pain; it could only quiver. It continued, though, with its insistent caresses and its lascivious appreciation of the naked body which it held captive.

William watched the orgy for some time, with mixed feelings. He was glad that his victim didn't seem to be enjoying himself much, though Marshall did manage eventually to demonstrate that he was the last man in the world who needed to worry about the humiliations of impotence.

'Can you see the product potential, Peter?' asked William, earnestly. 'Can you see the kind of market that this opens up? We have the seed of a sexual revolution here, you know.'

P. P. Marshall was unfortunately past the stage where he could give this line of thought his full attention. He was sobbing desperately, presumably suffering from a rather extreme case of post-coital *triste*.

William's delicate fingers brushed the buttons of his remote-control device once again, and the hands relaxed their grip on Marshall. The one that had clamped shut his mouth withdrew, throwing off blood and saliva with a contemptuous flick of its fingers.

'Damn you, Morris,' grated the copper-crowned certainty, retreating into cliché as if he were an actor in some tired old sci-fi movie. 'You'll never get away with this!'

Marshall was right, of course – as he usually was. William didn't get away with it.

People of the social standing of Peter Peregrine Marshall and Judy Morris cannot simply disappear without questions being asked. When it came to the consideration of motive and opportunity, it did not require a Sherlock Holmes to figure out who was responsible. Eventually, the police obtained a search warrant and invaded William's inner sanctum, where they found sufficient evidence to prosecute.

The Crown versus William Morris became one of the longest and most confused criminal trials on record, bogged down by unprecedented problems of definition as the jury struggled to decide whether his victims were legally dead. In the end, William was convicted, but only of Grievous Bodily Harm – a verdict which many observers thought eccentric. Cynics concluded that the jury (which included eight women) had been swayed by the defendant's amazing good looks, and had sympathised with his jealousy. Optimists pointed out that the light sentence he received would allow him to resume in a matter of months the researches which might easily lead to future benefits for all mankind.

When it was all over, though, the Crown found itself faced with an altogether unprecedented problem: what to do with Exhibit A.

Exhibit A was an entirely new design of Morris chair, resembling two armchairs facing in different directions but intimately fused together – a 'love-seat'. Half of it was decorated most gloriously with silken blonde hair, the other half upholstered in a remarkable shade of coppery red.

And somewhere deep inside it were two hearts, beating as one.

# DEAD TELEVISION

*by*
*Lisa Tuttle*

Lisa Tuttle took a degree in journalism at Syracuse University. That's in New York, not Greece. She is probably the most famous Texan sf author living in Britain. Author, interviewer and TV star, she has recently turned to editing. Her first anthology, *Skin of the Soul*, is a book of horror stories by women. Her story 'In Translation' was in the first volume of *Zenith*; 'The Wound' was in the first *Orbit SF Yearbook*.

Personally, I blame Thomas Alva Edison. I know most people hold Marcus Vandergaard responsible, but Marcus, though he could never admit it, was only the dead inventor's tool. Yes, of course I'm prejudiced – I can't deny that I loved Marcus – but I'm also *right*.

Check this, from Edison's 1920 diary: 'If what we call personality exists after death, and that personality is anxious to communicate with those of us who are still in the flesh on this earth, there are two or three kinds of apparatus which should make communication very easy. I am engaged in the construction of one such apparatus now, and I hope to be able to finish it before very many months pass.'

Marcus always liked being compared to Edison. He, too, was a brilliant, eccentric maverick with a wide-ranging, startlingly creative intelligence and a talent for making money. He was too easily bored and too quirky to make a good team-worker, and he couldn't limit himself enough to be a specialist. He liked to follow his ideas wherever they took him, and to go there by himself.

But unlike Edison, Marcus had no mystical leanings. He was a solid, sceptical materialist, and I'm sure he had no sympathy with Edison's weird theory about memory consisting of subparticles which travelled through space and lodged, in swarms, in human brains, creating intelligence. After death, Edison thought, the swarm might disperse, or stay together until they found a new host for the original personality. I'm certain Marcus never believed in reincarnation, nor in the survival of the personality after death – until, of course, we all *had* to believe it. So why should his genius lead him in that direction?

I am no scientist. But I have my own talent – I might even

say genius, if that didn't sound immodest. But others have called me genius, and surely not *all* the critical acclaim can be put down to the novelty value of a serious composer and orchestral conductor who is also a fairly attractive young woman. The work survives. At least, I hope it will. Anyway, having my own talent, I understand what drove Marcus. Even without understanding what he did, I know how the work can take over, demanding expression. Maybe, for Marcus, dead television began as a joke, or as something else entirely. Maybe it was unintentional. I once sat down to write a song for my niece's birthday; three weeks later it was a chamber opera.

I used to think I was most myself when I was composing, which may seem odd because there is also the sense at those times of being *taken over* by inspiration, of being inhabited by some other force, greater than oneself. It can't be forced or willed, that divine gift, that possession. I miss it, sometimes, but I won't let it happen again. The possible results are too terrifying.

Composing isn't just a matter of inspiration, of course. There's the work that follows. The construction. The fooling around. The hard slog. The mistakes. The testing and discarding, the reluctant compromises, the agony, frustration, dreariness, boredom and depression of writing music, leading to the ultimate, always qualified and partial, satisfaction. And I miss the work just as much as I miss the divine gift. Neither means anything alone – they have to go together. It was Edison (again!) who composed the formula my high school music teacher used to write on the blackboard: 'Genius is one per cent inspiration, and ninety-nine per cent perspiration.'

What I'm saying is, that one per cent in Marcus Vandergaard may have been Edison, swarming around the cosmos for years as a disincarnate entity, desperate for a chance to make himself real again.

Everybody remembers where they were when it first happened, and I am no exception. I was the second person in the world to have the experience. Naturally, I didn't understand what it meant at the time.

I'd just come back from a two-week tour with the orchestra. The air in the house was stale and dusty and it felt deserted, but when I saw all the cups and coffee mugs – every single one in the house – piled unwashed in the sink, and the empty McDonald's and Kentucky Fried wrappers spilling out of the bin, I suspected I'd find Marcus out back in his workshop. As I passed through the living room again I noticed that the TV was missing, but because the VCR and CD were still in place I suspected Marcus rather than a burglar.

I was right. He was in his workshop, watching television.

'Hello, darling,' I said. 'Working hard?'

He gave me a brief, distracted glance. 'Isn't it amazing?'

I stood beside him and looked at the screen. On it was an actor dressed in a 1920s-style, three-piece, cream-coloured suit, lecturing vigorously about the uselessness of the public school system. The actor looked like the elderly Thomas Edison but the picture – in colour – was obviously not a film. It was either live television or good quality tape, and the reception was clear and vivid, much better than I'd ever seen on that particular set. 'You fixed the picture?' I guessed.

Marcus was too absorbed to reply. To be polite, and because I had missed him, I went on watching for a few minutes more in silence. But it was a remarkably boring production. The actor just went on and on in a crotchety, opinionated sort of way about teachers, the school system, and kids today. It was probably an accurate representation of Edison, I thought, but who cared? And there was nothing else, no setting, just a black backcloth behind him. Finally I got tired of waiting for Marcus to explain what was so interesting about it.

'Are you picking this up on the dish, or is it local?'

'It's Edison.'

'I can see that, but what's the play? Who's doing it?'

Finally he looked at me. 'Oh, you're back. Aren't you

early?'

'No, it's been two weeks.'

'Oh. Well, I'm glad you're back.' He didn't ask about the tour, which was usual, or kiss me, which wasn't. His attention was still on the screen, and that struck me as strange. This was a man who never watched television: his boredom threshold was too low, his other interests too demanding. It had to be something technical that interested him – was the reception really that remarkable?

'Can't you switch it to something better?' I asked.

'There's only the one channel. I suppose somebody else might come through later, but Edison is just who I was hoping to see. It couldn't be better.'

'What do you mean? Marcus, what *is* this?'

'It's Thomas Alva Edison. Out of the flesh. I've invented dead television.'

If *I* had ever thought of trying to construct an 'apparatus' for communicating with the dead it would surely have been a telephone, not television. A telephone implies reciprocity, two-way communication, individuals taking turns talking and listening. With television, the message travels one way only, and the viewer is forced into the role of passive receiver. You don't *have* to listen; you can turn it off, or switch to something else, but talking back to your television set is a futile exercise. So many of the modern dead – including Edison – have been preserved on film and tape that it can't have been the desire simply to see and hear his heroes that led Marcus to convert our television set for their use. He acted on Edison's inspiration, but he had his own reasons and his own methods.

Television and not telephone because he didn't want to talk to the dead – Marcus found it enough of a chore talking to the living. Once I began living with him it became my responsibility to maintain the few non-professional relationships in his life. He seldom answered the phone, or even listened to the messages that piled up on the answering machine tape, which meant – since he never made phone calls unless they involved some absolutely vital transfer of information – that whenever I was away from home I was effectively cut off from him.

I'm sure it was psychologically easier for him to construct a receiver which might never receive than attempt to initiate a conversation with the dead. It seems impossible now, but Marcus didn't believe in existence after death. He offered the dead a channel like some cable-TV magnate giving one free to a minority group as a tax write-off – but never expected them actually to use it.

Marcus himself never knew why he did it – the idea simply took him over, as others had done before – but it was certainly no reflection of his personal belief. Quite the contrary. And it was his very lack of belief which allowed him to succeed; which made his success so deadly.

The dead have always had their channels to the living. Psychics, mediums, 'channellers', priests, shamans, all the different names for the possessed believers. Because in the past, belief was a necessary component. If you didn't believe in them, the dead wouldn't speak to you – they couldn't. What Marcus did, by his very lack of belief, was to remove belief as a necessary factor. He gave them technology, which works whether you believe in it or not. Once they had converted from spiritual to electronic power, there was no stopping them.

For a genius, Marcus could be awfully stupid. It never occurred to him that what he was doing might be undesirable, even dangerous.

To be fair to him, even if he had thought of it, why should it have seemed a bad thing? It is hard to believe now, but there was a time not long ago when people thought communication with the dead was too good rather than too bad to be true.

At first, the dead appeared only on sets which Marcus specially converted, and at first they were all scientists. Thomas Edison would talk for hours, without stumble or pause, but when he faltered he would flicker and vanish from the screen, replaced immediately by some other chatty spirit. I recall Alexander Graham Bell, Michael Faraday, Albert Einstein, Rosalind Franklin, Enrico Fermi and Marie Curie, but there were plenty more who were unrecognisable, and many who did not speak English.

News of 'the Vandergaard effect', or dead television, spread rapidly, of course. Even when reporters sneered and punned, news-readers twitched ironic eyebrows, or frankly disbelieved, they still reported 'the news', and taped the dead speakers off the small screen of our television set, allowing satellite technology to transmit the information, with sound and pictures, all across the world. A lot of people didn't believe it, of course; they called it hoax, or mass hysteria. But belief was no longer the issue, as I have said. It didn't make any difference whether or not you believed the dead could speak as long as you saw them posturing or heard their weirdly uninflected voices on the evening news.

Within a matter of weeks the dead were appearing on television sets throughout the world; on ordinary television sets unconverted by Marcus. And it wasn't only dead scientists who could come back. Information was the key now, not belief, and anyone who knew the dead could appear on television might turn on the set and discover their late, great-grandmother on screen reciting her recipe for sweet potato pie, or see Marilyn Monroe pouting sadly and whispering breathily. For the most part, the apparitions were relatives or ancestors or famous dead people with whom the viewers felt some affinity. For example, artists appeared to artists and art-lovers; dead presidents, kings and queens appeared to historians, chief executives and habitual readers of popular biography; and dead film stars were absolutely everywhere. If natives deep in the Brazilian jungle weren't haunted by the dead it was only because they hadn't heard the news yet because they didn't have the technology.

I mention Brazil because I'm pretty sure that's where Marcus went when he disappeared. I imagine him in the middle of whatever few acres are left of the Brazilian rain forest, beyond the reach of the information network which his obsessive tinkering took away from us, the living, and delivered into the power of the dead. Is there such a place left in the world? If so, I think it won't be safe for very long.

Poor Marcus. He was as much a victim as the rest of us. He didn't know what he was unleashing. How could he know that the dead would prove not passive consumers, content with their one channel, but even more greedy and expansionist than the living?

There are so many of them, you see. And they all have something to say, and they all want to say it – to everybody.

They may be dead, but they're not stupid or slow. Once they had the use of technology they used it in a big way, until there was nothing left for the rest of us.

Not just one channel, but all channels. Not just television, but radio. And then they managed to tap into telephone lines. At first they broke in on conversations, a babble of unknown, distorted voices erupting into any pause. Then they learned direct dialling, and all over the world telephones began ringing, unceasingly. Nobody else could get through; only the dead had the time and the numbers to overload every line.

My first phone call was from Ethel Smyth. I thought this was unlucky, because, although I was bound to feel a certain sympathy for her as one of the very few women who ever managed to make her name as a composer, I have never thought much of her music, and I knew from my reading that she had been notoriously deaf and egotistical and a non-stop talker, even in life. As in life, so in death: I couldn't get a word in edgewise, and when, finally, in desperation, I hung up, she rang back immediately and went ranting on about the general lack of appreciation for her music.

The next caller was Erik Satie, which thrilled me. But although I do speak French, and had always imagined we would have a lot to say to each other, it was soon obvious that he couldn't hear a word I said. It was like listening to someone talking in his sleep. Whatever I said made no difference, and what he said only occasionally made sense.

I soon realised that, for the dead, the telephone was no different from television or radio. It was a one-way system, a means for transmission, not reception, and maybe that was the way they wanted it. After so many years of listening to our broadcasts and our lives, unable to participate, they had finally found a way to interrupt, to erupt back into the living world, and a little would never be enough.

At first, they came at us through the electronic media – remote, distorted, unreal, irritating but ignorable. They couldn't stand being ignored; they insisted upon being heard, and sought other ways of imposing their voices on us. Once the first barrier was breached, how quickly they all crumbled!

New films, tapes, recordings of any kind could not be made without the faces and voices of the dead appearing, overwhelming and replacing those of the living. Their words burst through and conquered ours in new books, magazines and newspapers as computers and electronic typesetters responded to their impulses. As for old-fashioned means of communication, like pen and paper – well, the dead, too, had their old-fashioned instruments: people.

Some count it an honour to be possessed, to let another soul speak through them, to live in reflected glory. If they have nothing original to contribute themselves they might welcome the chance to make it possible for Rembrandt or Picasso to paint another picture, for Colette or Dickens to write another novel, for Beethoven to compose another symphony. But the dead are insatiable. There can never be enough willing victims. And so, as belief was no longer necessary, willingness was no longer a requirement.

We are all in danger of being taken over by the dead. It's not just an audience they want, but hosts.

I'm having dead people's dreams now – Kafka and Strindberg, at a guess. Or am I over-reacting and imagining things? It's difficult to know where influence stops and possession begins.

I've had to give up composing. I no longer know where

the music in my head comes from, I can't trust any inspiration as my own. I hardly know who I am anymore, but I know I want to do my own work, or nothing. I won't let the dead compose their music through me.

Is it horribly selfish, even precious, of me to worry about something like that in this time of crisis and destruction, when civilisation has broken down around us? Even if I dared try to compose, I don't have the leisure: all my time is spent on just getting by, on survival. Even if I did manage to write something new, who, besides myself, would care? Who would even know? How could I transmit it? Would it ever be performed?

In the long, dark hours I think a lot about Marcus – at least I know those memories are my own – and I wonder what he's doing now. How is life in his distant jungle? Is he still tinkering, still managing to invent things in a stone age culture?

As soon as he disappeared the rumours began that Marcus was dead, but I know that can't be true. If he were dead I would have heard from him by now. And not just me. If he were dead he'd be everywhere, seen and heard by millions. After all, there could hardly be a more famous dead person in the world today than Marcus Vandergaard. Fame is what immortality is all about.

Edison explained his concept of personality as memories, and it appears that the dead have a chance of survival only if they are remembered by the living. I wonder what happened to the anonymous legions of dead who never did anything when they were alive, not even produce a descendent to remember them and give them another shot at life – did their subparticles disperse? Were they absorbed by their more powerful companions? Did they simply wink out of existence, or linger to combine with other subparticles until they gradually reached critical mass and could be reborn as a wholly new personality?

Maybe that's what I am, someone wholly original, able, therefore, to bring more new creations into the world ... if only I had the chance.

It's so unfair. I've lost everything that made life worth living – everything, indeed, that made me myself. The mere struggle for existence isn't life. What is life without the chance to create?

Maybe it is time to go over to the other side. Not to give up, but to desert the living and join the winners. Dead, I might have a better chance of survival.

My name is still known. I have some small measure of fame as a musician; more, the notoriety of being the woman who lived with Marcus Vandergaard.

The living have no time or space for music anymore. As time passes, I'll be forgotten. If no one remembers me, I won't be able to come back. The dead have shown us the importance of fame. Memory is the only immortality there is. I'm not going to miss my chance. If I can't live this life, I'll have another.

I'm looking forward to talking to Marcus. There is so much I want to say to him.

# INSIGHT

*by*
*John Gribbin*

John Gribbin has a Cambridge doctorate in Theoretical Astrophysics, was the first British recipient of the Gravity Research Foundation prize (Stephen Hawking was a later winner), is the author of around fifty books and hundreds of magazine and newspaper articles, but for some reason wants to be a science fiction author when he grows up. The co-author of three sf novels (*Sixth Winter* and *Brother Esau* with Douglas Orgill, *Double Planet* with Marcus Chown), his first solo novel *Father to the Man* was published in 1989.

Leaning on the rail, he watched Hawk trying to set fire to the ship, while Captain Bryon ostentatiously kept out of the way below decks, making it clear that he had nothing to do with this madness. The Navigator asked himself, not for the first time, just how he had arrived in this insane position. Fire on board a ship at sea! To think he had lived to see this. Rantor glanced up at the almost cloudless sky, with the Sun, as always, at the zenith. In an habitual gesture that had become automatic, he mopped at his forehead and the back of his neck with a large, red kerchief. He shifted position slightly, to take benefit from the modest amount of shade offered by the sail, barely drawing in the light wind, and leaned forward again to watch the antics going on in the waist of the ship.

There were enough volunteers ready to participate in any crazy task that the Hawk might set them – you had to be half crazy in any case, to volunteer for this voyage into the unknown, sailing far beyond sight of land. Students, half of them, granted leave of absence by the priests who ran the college, back in the Archipelago. And you could be sure that anyone the priests granted leave of absence to was someone they were glad to have out of their hair. A sprinkling of good sailors, of course – men who would follow their Captain anywhere.

As for Captain Bryon himself, he was here because he trusted the Navigator, the man in charge of this expedition. But why was Rantor here? He asked himself the same question every day, and had yet to find a satisfactory answer. The *un*satisfactory answer was that he was here because he had faith in what most people thought of as the strangest man ever to live on the Islands (a thought usually qualified by the comment that, after all, he *was* an outsider, from some remote atoll far across the Archipelago).

A couple of nervous sailors were tending a brazier of hot charcoal, under the supervision of a little man, naked to the waist and smeared with soot until he looked like a devil. This was Hawk, so named (half mockingly) because of his visionary view of the world. What other men regarded as mundane, the Hawk's far-seeing eyes found strange; what he seemed to think was normal, most men found incomprehensible. And yet, enough of his curious ideas had born fruit to tempt the Navigator into following where Hawk pointed, ostensibly in the hope of finding wealth and fame, in reality because – well, because it felt good to do something out of the ordinary himself.

Only the Hawk could have persuaded the Navigator to allow a fire to be lit while the precious *Far Trader* was in the open sea, even under conditions as calm as this. Only under the direct orders of the Navigator would Captain Bryon, responsible for running the ship and for the safety of his crew, have allowed such insanity. In a wooden vessel, out of sight of land, with the Sun beating down, fire was the sailors' greatest dread – but Hawk said it was important. The damnable thing was, Hawk needed calm conditions for his experimenting, and calm conditions meant that it was infernally hot, with sails and cordage ready to flare like tinder at the touch of a spark. In eight fivedays of voyaging, this was the worst possible time to be lighting fires.

Just what was important about the way sparks flew up into the air from a fire, Rantor could not comprehend. Everyone knew that sparks flew upward – that was why, unbidden, half a dozen crew members had manned the rigging, watching out for any errant specks of fire from the Hawk's activities, and snuffing them out before they could alight on the dry sails. Sparks, though, scarcely seemed to be good enough for Hawk. Scraps of cloth, of various sizes, were consigned to the glowing brazier, and wafted up from it as they writhed and burned. There were even some sheets of precious paper, which the Hawk seemed particularly interested in, but these were the greatest cause of concern to the sailors. As the paper floated upwards it was still on fire, in the process of being consumed into charcoal wafers that drifted up and eventually span away from the ship, under the watchful gaze of the crew.

Watching the sparks rising above the brazier, Rantor caught sight of the Sun, and shivered, in spite of the heat. Hawk's latest crazy notion could not possibly hold truth, could it? But if it were true, sparks were to blame. Sparks, of a different kind, were responsible for them being here, so far from home. The Hawk's strange signalling device, the morphic resonator, had faithfully reproduced its little flashes of artificial lightning every dawn, in response to the action of the large lightning generator installed in the topmost tower of the castle of Lord Kyper, at home in the Three Islands. Rantor remembered the demonstration of the morphic effect, back in the castle: how the banks of electric storage jars, discharging across a gap between two metal rods, had produced the lightning and the thunder, with an acrid smell, like that of Hell itself; and how, at the far end of the long gallery, the miniature replica of the lightning machine had produced its own feeble sparks in tune with the flash of lightning and crash of thunder, although it was untouched by any human operator. For all Hawk's fine talk of the scientific principles of morphic resonance – the law of similarities which required that like objects must behave in similar fashion, in tune with each other even when separated by great distances – it still seemed like magic, and not entirely white magic, to the Navigator. He remembered too well the tales from his childhood, in the village where, it was said, Grandma Alyn could cure an ague by applying a poultice to a clay figure of the sufferer, or (the whispers went) kill a goat with a pin stuck through a figurine. But, magic or not, Hawk's trick worked; and at heart Rantor was a practical man, not a religious one. If it worked, his creed said, then use it.

It was Hawk's genius that turned the resonator into a directional beacon. The metal shield, mounted on a track on the upper deck, a little wagon rolling in rails around a circle, pushed this way and that by a laughing gang of Hawk's most ardent apprentices (who were, almost by definition, the most incompetent sailors on board). When the shield was in line between the resonator and the lightning generator, the generator could blast away for all it was worth, and not a spark would be seen in the resonator. But displace the shield to one side, and the sparks appeared. Metal blocked the resonant corpuscles. Why, even Hawk could not say (nor could he fathom the strange way in which, the further they got from the castle, the more it seemed that the sparks in the resonator were *strongest* when the metal shield was on the *far* side of the resonator from the lightning generator). The discovery had been an accident, and Hawk had lost interest in it once it had been made to work – and once he had failed to explain it. But its value had been obvious to the Navigator, well versed in his craft and in the mathematics of trigonometry.

With a tried and tested navigation beacon to point their way home, and a sound ship under them, the crew of *Far Trader* were the first people to sail far out of sight of the Archipelago and yet expect to return home safely. They were following a course from which nobody had ever returned, and even the most ardent of Hawk's followers, Rantor guessed, probably gave thanks each morning that they had not fallen off the edge of the world in the night time. As the days had added up, and then the fivedays in their turn, it had not escaped his notice that a little crowd of casual observers would gather just before the Sun cast the nightglow aside, ready to check that there was still open sea ahead. Each day, the result had been the same. One moment, straining like the others to see beyond the bowsprit in the nightglow; the next, the reassuring return of the Sun, blazing out from its accustomed position at the zenith and lighting the ocean ahead. Always, open ocean, as far as the eye could see. Although he would admit it to no man, Rantor himself felt a flow of relief each morning when the ritual was safely accomplished.

Sparks had brought them here – beyond, far beyond, the point where unbelievers said the edge of the world must be. The priests who taught that the world was an infinite plane seemed to be vindicated with every day that passed. And yet, by bringing them here, sparks were responsible for Hawk's heretical new ideas, that cut away the foundations of a lifetime of belief from beneath the Navigator. Some nights before, in the cool of the afterdeck, Hawk had explained his vision to the Navigator.


'Well, Hawk.' The Navigator had been in a mellow mood, happy, as ever, to be at sea – in spite of his worries concerning the outcome of the mission. 'Two days since we had a spark out of that resonator of yours. And yet, I believe I might find my way back to the Three Islands after all.' He gestured to the misty nebulosity glowing low in the sky behind the ship. 'We may need your toy when we are closer to home, and the light fades. But by then, I have no doubt, you will come to our aid, eh?'

The Hawk was in a more reflective mood, unwilling to respond in kind to the bantering tone. 'You can use the glow as a beacon, Navigator, but I don't understand it. This far from land, all the torches in all the islands of the Archipelago could not produce a light bright enough for us to steer by. And that is no torchlight. It is too pale, and blue. If the air above the islands shines by night, why did we never notice, we who have spent all our lives in the Archipelago?'

'Hawk questions!' Rantor laughed. 'Why and how are no concerns of mine. Perhaps God sent the glow to guide wandering sailormen. All I care is that your sparks have brought us far enough out to sea for the lights in the sky to be made plain – both astern and,' he pointed, 'ahead. I'll never doubt you again, Hawk. The lights in the sky *are* other islands – other worlds – and *Far Trader* will live up to her name. We will all be rich, and famous, when we return to Lord Kyper's domain!'

'But why and how, my good Navigator, concern me greatly. How do the lights in the sky shine? And, most pressing in my mind at present, why are they above our heads? Always, we have to look up to the lights. Does that not make you wonder, with your training in geometry and navigation?'

Rantor frowned, his mood broken. 'The inner sphere? But it is a logical absurdity.'

'That rather depends on your point of view.'

The Hawk, it seemed, was getting around to what had been worrying him. He leaned forward, ticking items off on his fingers to emphasise the logic of his argument. Rantor noticed, with some amusement, that even Hawk now braced himself with legs wide apart, like a true sailorman, swaying gently with the roll of the ship as it glided over the sea under half sail in the light breeze. The wake behind seemed to glow with a life of its own, marking their arrow-straight course through the night. All was well with the ship, but Hawk's words removed some of the sense of well-being.

'We know that the Sun is always at the zenith, viewed from anywhere in the Archipelago, or even, we see now, from outside. A line of sight to the Sun is always perpendicular to the surface of the world. Parallel lines meet only at infinity, so the Sun, we are taught, must be infinitely far away, and the world is an infinite flat plane. Unless –'

'Unless the world is really the inner surface of a sphere, with the Sun at the centre. Yes, yes. But that is absurd. The priests teach us that only to *demonstrate* its absurdity – the law of the absurd alternative. Two possible solutions to a puzzle, but one is absurd, so the other must be true. If we live on the inner surface of a sphere, why doesn't all the water slop down to the bottom and drown us? If the Sun isn't infinitely far away, why doesn't it fall down and burn us? Come, Hawk, you'll have to do better than that.'

'What is absurd, Navigator, depends, as I say, on your point of view. The priests are honest men, but they have only a limited view, confined to one Archipelago. Now we have travelled further – further than any man who has lived and returned to tell the tale. And we see behind us a glow, a glow that can *only* mark the Archipelago – though, I admit we don't know how, or why – and that glow rises in the sky behind us as we advance. We see a glow ahead, that I will stake my life marks another Archipelago, dropping down the sky to meet us as we advance. And we see the Sun, just as at home, vertically above our heads. We *must* be moving over the inner sphere. From our point of view, the law of the absurd alternative tells us that it is *impossible* for the world to be flat. And that means that the Sun *is* only a finite distance above our heads. If I had means to measure the distance we have travelled from the Archipelago, then all I would have to do is measure the angle to that light in the sky behind us and I could tell you just how far above us the Sun sits – how far it is to the centre of the sphere.'

Instinctively, the Navigator, though scarcely a religious man, made the sign to ward off evil. 'And what keeps it there, floating above us while all other things fall to the surface of the world? What keeps an ocean of water poised like a wave above our heads, instead of flooding to the bottom of the sphere?'

The Hawk smiled. Rantor recognised the grin, and began to wonder what he was letting himself in for this time.

'Ah, Navigator. I have an idea about that. I thought perhaps – tomorrow if there is not too much wind – you might permit me to carry out a few simple tests.'

It had not, in fact, happened the next day. Strong winds, fair for their course, had blown them on for four days, while the night-time glow in the sky ahead, where Hawk had staked his life they would find another Archipelago, dropped down and dimmed into insignificance. Even under reduced sail, the *Far Trader* had ripped through the water, heeling to the wind until the lee rail dipped into each rolling wave as it lifted beneath them. Bryon had done well. Over the preceding fivedays, his crew of half-trained volunteers, still wet behind the ears when they had left the Three Islands, might not have become the best sailors in the Archipelago, but they were no longer fumbling incompetents.

Rantor remembered with pleasure the feel of the deck alive beneath his feet, and the spray stinging sharp against his cheek. The sailors had a saying that there was no such thing as bad weather – the only bad day for sailing was when there was no weather at all, in a flat calm. Give them wind, and a good ship, and they would voyage anywhere to find a profit for their Lord and a bonus for themselves. Another day at that pace, and they would be among the islands, if islands they were; Hawk had begged for permission to carry out his fire raising before then, but neither Rantor nor Captain Bryon would relent until the wind dropped.

Now, though, Hawk had his chance, almost as if the wind had dropped in response to his entreaties. At least half the crew thought Hawk was a wizard anyway, and this happy coincidence (Rantor told himself he was sure it *was* a coincidence) would do his reputation no harm. The Navigator knew that it was worth giving the Hawk his head, within reason, and it was better for him to get this current madness out of his system before they arrived in a strange island, where Hawk's talent for observation could prove invaluable to the traders. There would be plenty for all to do, tomorrow, or the next day …

Rantor's reverie was broken by a cry from the masthead lookout.

'Land! Land on the port bow!'

He leaped into the shrouds, and, shading his eyes against the Sun, looked out across the sea. After the winds of the past few days, the ocean was still heaving in a long swell, but he automatically adjusted his balance to the swaying rhythm. At the height of the roll, as the bow lifted, and hung, momentarily, before plunging back down into the trough, he caught a glimpse of something that might have been the top of an island. Damn the lookout! If land was visible from the deck already, he should have seen it long ago, from his vantage point. But, Rantor realised, like everyone else on the ship the lookout had been more engrossed in Hawk's antics than in his own duties. Damn the Hawk!

He opened his mouth to curse the lookout aloud, but closed it again. Bryon had appeared as if by magic at Rantor's side; it was the Captain's job to discipline the crew, and it was also, to some extent, Rantor's fault for permitting the distraction, when he knew they were approaching land. There was no need for words between them; both he and the Captain knew the situation.

'Douse that fire! All hands!'

The thunder of feet on the planking of the deck broke the silence that had followed the lookout's cry.

Bryon turned to Rantor. 'An outlying island. The new archipelago must still be a day's sailing away, but there are no ships to be seen. No harm has been done.'

The words were scarcely out of the Captain's lips when they were contradicted by events.

'Birds! Two great birds, ahead!'

As if to atone for his previous failure, the lookout had spotted something totally unexpected. They were still too far from land to expect to see birds. Yet there were two dots in the sky, between the ship and the strange island. They could only be birds, but the lookout had done well to spot them.

Rantor felt a thrill of anticipation. Birds meant that the land was alive. Where there were birds, there would be plants – and maybe people. *This* was what the *Far Trader's* voyage was all about. Hawk's toys, and his philosophising, were all very well in their place. But they could not compare to the prospect of discovering new lands, for the first time in the history of the Archipelago. If nothing else, they could replenish their diminished supplies, provisioning the ship for further explorations. And at best – who knew what the inhabitants of the new islands might have to trade?

In response to shouted orders from the Captain, the ship had altered course towards the lone island, and, with all sail now set, she was heeling slightly even in the fading breeze. Rantor shifted his position, maintaining balance without thinking. His eyes still peered intently at the scene ahead. There was something odd about those birds. Either they were much closer than he had thought, or they were *very* big, and still some distance away. Why did their wings not flap? They seemed curiously stiff, gliding through the air with outstretched wings. The glideagles back home soared that way, in the updrafts of wind along the cliff tops; but they never held their wings quite so straight for so long – certainly not out in the middle of the sea, where there were no updrafts. And whatever they were, those two birds *were* coming out to sea, towards the *Far Trader*.

Hawk joined them on the afterdeck. He seemed entirely oblivious to the new developments, and was chattering away excitedly, as much to himself as to anyone else.

'A great success! I believe I have the answer. Did you see how pieces of paper float upward in the heat, even when they are not on fire themselves? It all seems quite clear to me. Like attracts like, that is obvious – a law of similarities. Hot things are drawn to the Sun, and rise upwards. Cold things, of course, are repelled from the Sun, uniformly in all directions, and spread out evenly over the surface of the inner sphere. Which is why all the water doesn't slop down and drown the Islands. What will the priests make of this, eh?

'But the cold things repel the Sun, with equal but opposite strength, and push it to the centre of the inner sphere! If we could weigh the brazier, it would surely be lighter when the coals are glowing red, although it has too much inherent weight ever to float in the air. But the paper is so light, that even warm air, rising to greet the Sun, can carry it along. Ah, Navigator, this is a great day – and one you will remember. I think I can put land and sea breezes at your disposal, now I have this new perspective on things. It's all to do with the law of similarities. Hot air, moving to greet the Sun …'

'Not now, Hawk.' The Navigator's firm command cut off the flow of unheeded talk. 'What do you make of those birds? A little big, do you not think? Are they a danger?'

Even as Hawk looked up, taking notice of what was going on for the first time, a new cry came from the lookout.

'Men! Not birds! Flying men! Men with wings!'

Several of the crew made the sign to ward off evil. The older hands turned to the Captain for orders. Hawk, attention well and truly caught, ran the length of the deck and scrambled up into the rigging, staring forward. As the ship rolled, he lost his grip with one hand, and swayed out over the heaving waters; but he kept his eyes fixed on the fliers as he scrabbled for a secure hold. Rantor had the feeling that even if Hawk fell to his death he would spend the fall observing his surroundings and thinking about what it all meant.

'Prepare for boarders!' The Captain, as ever, thought first for his ship. 'Men or birds, they don't come aboard the *Far Trader* without my invitation, lads!'

The rough humour turned the mood of the crew away from thoughts of black magic. They had the best Captain in the Archipelago, *and* the best Navigator – and they had their own secret weapon, the Hawk.

The two swooping figures split up to pass either side of the ship, as crossbowmen hurriedly took up positions by the rail. Hawk slid down a rope, and scurried back, keeping pace with the fliers.

'Men indeed, Captain,' he panted. 'Not birds. Ordinary men like us. See the harness that fastens them to the wings. But see how they fly – like eagles.'

The two fliers had indeed soared high over the ship, having used the momentum of their dive, as they crossed the stern and turned back to pass the vessel, to lift them higher. But not quite like eagles. Their wings did not flap, and now they were sinking, slowly, towards the waves.

'I think not, Hawk.' Rantor had grasped their difficulty. 'These eagles will never regain the land. How they rose so high in the sky, I know not. Perhaps it was the attraction of the Sun, eh? A wonderful trick for a lookout – but they should have stayed closer to home. Now they are sinking lower. We may have two passengers for you, Captain – and wet passengers, at that.'

Suddenly, one of the fliers, now only a few span above their heads, veered to his right, towards the ship, losing height as he did so. The small group on the afterdeck flung themselves flat as his intentions became clear. For a moment, it looked as if he would succeed in landing on the deck. Then, the left wing snagged a standing line, part of the permanent rigging. There was a snap, and the whole wing crumpled, while the flier himself was jerked around and crashed heavily into the rail. Bryon and Rantor, with two crew members, rushed to his aid; Hawk moved with equal speed, but ignored the man and poked gently at the broken wing, no more than a delicate framework of wood covered with fine silk. It had scarcely more substance than the wing of a butterfly – and yet it had carried a man high above their heads, and brought him all the way here from the island ahead. A strange looking man, he was dressed in what would have been loose trousers, except for the thongs binding them tight around his legs, and a jerkin that left his arms bare. He was beardless – that was almost unheard of back on the Islands – and met Rantor's gaze steadily with blue eyes, not brown. A man for all that, who bled like any mortal man.

A splash alongside, accompanied by a slightly inaccurate cry of 'Man overboard!', announced that the other butterfly had come to the end of its flight. Bryon left the others attending to the injured flier – his arm seemed to be broken, and he was only semi-conscious.

'Get a line to him, then!'

In response to the man overboard cry, the helmsman had immediately hove to, and the flier, already disentangled from his wings, was struggling in the heaving water alongside. The wind had been dropping during all the activity, and in spite of its headway the ship was still comfortably close enough for a line to be heaved to the swimmer. He soon stood, panting, on the main deck. Rantor went to greet him, only to be taken aback by the flier's words.

'I hope you fools are worth the trouble.' The accent was peculiar, but intelligible. 'My wings lost, because your idiot crew were too busy saving me to think about them; Bah-lee's wings probably smashed beyond repair. And all because you weren't prepared to receive us properly! Don't you know the Code? Someone will have to pay for this mess!'

'We hardly expected such visitors, ah,' the Navigator decided to be tactful, 'Lord. Indeed, we have never seen such wonders as men that fly.'

'I am no Lord.' The visitor was looking about him. 'But where are you from? There is no ship like this in the Nations. All these ropes, and poles. And such a mess of sails. Where are your oars? Why is there no clear deck for fliers to land on?'

'We have oars – when we need them.' The Navigator looked at Bryon, and nodded.

The Captain took the hint. The weakening breeze was getting them nowhere now, and it began to look like a good idea to make land as soon as possible. A few quiet commands, and the ship was bustling with activity as sails were taken in, and, to the accompaniment of good natured complaints from the men who would have to heave on them, oars were unshipped. The flier, drying in the warm Sun, watched with obvious interest. The men labouring at the sweeps held so much fascination that, Rantor surmised, this was not the kind of oarsmanship he was used to. Irritated at the flier's manner, he tried, once again, to gain his attention.

'As I said, we have never seen men that fly.'

This time, the flier took it in. His attention jerked back to Rantor.

'Never seen fliers? Then you are strange fish indeed, and

*211*

King Rotono-ga will surely regard you as a catch worth even the cost of two sets of wings! Keep on this course, and I will take you in to harbour.'

Rantor frowned. He objected to being regarded as a catch. It was a long time since anyone had given *him* orders. But he had every intention of taking the ship into harbour – not just for supplies, but for the secret of the flying wings. And he never objected to the help of a local pilot. If this ill-mannered passenger wanted to think he was in charge, it was best to allow him that illusion, for now.

How could they have been so stupid! Rantor fumed inwardly. Six days of inaction. A standoff. The representatives of this cursed King Rotono-ga still demanded that the ship – the whole ship! – be given up in compensation for the loss of two sets of wings that they blamed on Rantor. They could take it by force, of course, here in the harbour; though Rantor would burn the vessel first, and had made sure they knew it. Or they could starve the *Far Trader*'s crew into submission, eventually. That, he thought with grim satisfaction, might take longer than they expected, and he would still burn the ship before they got their hands on it. Rantor had bought time, he hoped, by giving the impression that their supplies were all but exhausted, and he had repeatedly asked for more, without success. That should encourage this King and his men to play the waiting game, at least for a while. But could anything about them be predicted, when the idiots refused to trade?

Maybe they were not such idiots. They held all the best cards, with *Far Trader* in harbour, under the watchful eyes of the King's men. Eventually, the crew would be forced to beg for supplies, or try to sail off – and how could you sail off unobserved, even if you could sneak or fight your way out of harbour, when the King had fliers who could scan the seas for a sight of you from above? In the long haul, *Far Trader* could outpace any rowing galley. But if the rowboats knew where she was, and enough of them gave chase promptly, they could quickly catch her,

He had been a fool to lead them into this mess. He should have anchored off shore, and negotiated at arm's length. But even then, with those damned fliers, the locals would have been at an advantage. In any skirmish, it would be easy to keep them off the ship's decks – but that would not suffice. A few daredevils, landing in the rigging and cutting it, and the ship would be lost, disabled, while the rowboats came alongside at their leisure. *Far Trader's* clumsy sweeps, useful though they were for getting in and out of harbour, were no match for purpose-built galleys.

Still, he *had* been a fool to imagine that the whole wide world would be like the Archipelago, only bigger. Back there, there were always rival factions, shifting coalitions among the different groups of islands, so a good trader could play one off against the other, and find some way to turn things to his advantage. But here – he could still hardly believe it: a single, big island, isolated in the sea with everyone owing allegiance to a single ruler. There were no factions for him to set one against the other. No real ships, just those glorified rowboats – which was why they were so eager to lay hands on *Far Trader*, now that they had seen the possibilities she represented. The big mountain in the middle of the island made overland travel difficult, but the rowboats managed quite well plying around the coast. There were enough experienced sailors here to make copies of *Far Trader* and to sail them, and Rantor shivered at the thought of what they might do if let loose in the Archipelago. And who could have imagined the fliers – everything hinged on that.

'Navigator.'

'Hawk! I was contemplating your advice. Trying to find the right viewpoint to tackle the problem of how we get out of here.'

'I may be able to help.'

'Your lightning generator won't get us out of this harbour, friend.'

'No.' Hawk gripped the Navigator's shoulder, and

crouched close by his chair, keeping his voice low. 'But if we were at anchor, halfway round the island from here, and if there was a good strong land breeze blowing, and if I could guarantee no fliers could follow you for – oh, half a day, or so – what might your instructions to the Captain be?'

'Cut the cable. Run. With a head start, and no fliers to interfere with the sails, we could hold the rowboats off until they tire.' Rantor's eyes were, suddenly, alight with interest. 'But can it be done, Hawk? Do you really have a plan?'

'Oh yes, Navigator. I have a plan. And I have a secret worth far more to these people than the *Far Trader*. I can show them how to fly at night, and in the first light of morning, when, as you must have observed, their beautiful butterflies must stay on the ground.'

The Navigator sat back, with a sigh. 'A wonderful secret, indeed, my friend. But if you think this will pay for our release, you are sadly mistaken. This King of theirs will take your secret, and keep us, and our ship, into the bargain.'

'But I *cannot* stay here, Navigator. *We* cannot stay here. I have work to do – the theory of similarities has such interesting implications. I *must* have somewhere to work properly again.'

Rantor's hope was quickly fading. The Hawk, he remembered, had come to the Three Islands from a far distant part of the Archipelago. He owed no true allegiance to the Duke; all he wanted was a benefactor who would allow him his experiments. Even the precious ship meant nothing to him, except that it was a rather inconvenient platform for those studies. Yet, Rantor counted him as friend and believed the feeling was reciprocated. If not through allegiance to the Duke, then surely out of that friendship, Hawk would not simply slip away with his new secret and offer his services to the King?

'We go together, Hawk; or not at all. I'll not abandon *one* of those under my command.'

Hawk ignored, or failed to notice, the hard edge that had entered Rantor's voice.

'To be sure. Of course.' He was losing himself in his dreamworld again, muttering almost inaudibly as he went over complex plans in his head. 'Even a King must have his secrets, and my secret is so powerful that it cannot be revealed near the prying eyes of the town. Some distance away, around that headland yonder, would be appropriate. And the ship must be on hand, to ferry my equipment – they won't think that is odd, all the transport here goes by sea.' He stopped, and looked earnestly at Rantor again, as if a doubt had just occurred to him.

'Ah, Navigator, I will need rather a *lot* of equipment. It might be best if you were to explain this to the Captain.'

Rantor had got into the habit of trusting the Hawk. It was a habit he could not bring himself to break, although he vowed to himself that if this were some trick he would not rest until the trickster paid.

'The Captain will surely be in accord. Even if the fliers pursue us, it will be better to go down fighting, in the open sea, than to starve here in harbour. At night, with just a few guards to overpower, and the land breeze ...' he shrugged. 'Well, we won't win, but they'll know they've been in a fight.'

He stopped short. 'Where will you be, Hawk? How can we slip our cable and flee, if you are ashore, demonstrating some flim-flammery to the King's men?'

The Hawk's familiar grin returned. 'Flim-flammery, Navigator? Have you so little faith? Oh no. My tricks, as you well know, always work. But this one may not work out in the way that other people anticipate. All you have to do is wait a little while off shore, to collect me before you set full sail. I assure you, there will be no fliers to hinder your escape. It all has to do, you see, with the attraction of similarities and the repulsion of opposites.'

Try though he might, that was all the information Rantor could extract from his farsighted friend; that, and a list of essential equipment for hoodwinking the King's men that made no sense at all. Captain Bryon only agreed to the assault on his ship's stores on the strength of Rantor's own solemn vow that the result would be, at least, to get the ship out of this damned harbour.

Hawk was tired. It had seemed like a brilliant move on the Navigator's part, insisting so firmly that he could not possibly let his Hawk go into the midst of the islanders unescorted that, of course, Rho-gan, the King's man, had insisted even more firmly – and from a position of inarguable strength – that nobody except the Hawk was to leave the ship. Hostages, instead, were offered against the Hawk's safe return. Even now, Bah-lee, his arm in splints, sat in the Captain's cabin on board the *Far Trader*, guarded by the crew. The ship, in turn, was watched over by more of the King's men, in their 'rowboats'.

There was no point in worrying about it now, but if it had not been essential for Rantor's bluff to succeed, Hawk would have welcomed the presence of someone he could really trust, here to help him with the labour of setting everything up. It had been a long and lonely haul from the beach, almost a thousand paces; uphill and inland. The spot seemed almost perfect, and the sea breeze that still blew fitfully on their backs as they manhandled the materials upward had almost died away. The pyre was already well alight.

'Rho-gan!' The islander turned at the Hawk's call. 'Now the wind is dropping, we can begin. Get them to build the fire higher, and to keep the neck of the skysail above the rising smoke.'

'As you command, O Hawk.' Rho-gan was used to giving orders, not to taking them; but he seemed to prefer to amuse himself with mock-obsequious obedience rather than to allow the situation to upset him. This fitted well with Hawk's instructions from the Navigator – escape, by all means, and demonstrate that the crew of the *Far Trader* (and, by implication, the people of the Archipelago) were not to be trifled with; but leave the way open for trade, on more equal terms, later. There was no point in being too secretive about what he was up to, and it always calmed his nerves to explain things.

At Rho-gan's instruction, the men with the uncomfortable task of holding the circular mouth of the skysail over the fire had moved a little closer to the flames. The opening was supported on poles, above the fire itself, with each pole held by an uncomfortably hot man; and the neck of the device stretched on more poles from the mouth to the body of the skysail, swelling and stirring on the hillside above like a giant beast awakening from slumber.

'You see how the smoke and sparks rise in the warm air. This is a natural law, the repulsion of opposites. Hot things cannot abide the cold ground, and must rise up above it. My little skysail will do the same.'

'Little!' Rho-gan glanced at the billowing fabric, the remains of the ship's best fine weather sail, once flat against the slope of the hillside, but now beginning to take on a life of its own as heat from the pyre was directed into its gaping mouth. 'Why, twenty men could scarce encircle it with arms outstretched. But, no doubt, you have much bigger skysails, on your home island?'

'I have never flown one bigger myself.' Which was certainly true, thought Hawk; and, he hoped, sufficiently misleading for the islander to draw his own false impressions. 'It is nearly time for my demonstration. As an experienced flier yourself, perhaps you could help me with the harness. It is fortunate indeed that your wing-harness could be adapted to my needs; but the design is unfamiliar.'

They moved around the fire together. Even at ground level, the heat was intense. The skysail was almost rounded now, beginning to show signs of trying to lift off the ground, restrained by a wide net around which there were many strong ropes, held down by equally strong men.

It worked! Hawk tried to conceal his excitement. Of course it worked. He had known it would. But although the reality was still a thrill, he had to let them think this was all routine.

'Be careful not to let any sparks alight on the sail!' The nearest handler grunted something that might have been an acknowledgement. Hawk decided to leave well enough alone. He had plenty to worry about. Let them make sure the skysail was held in place above the rising air, being repelled from the cool ground as the laws of science dictated.

Rho-gan had the harness ready. Hawk, glad of his small stature, slipped it around his shoulders and looked down as the islander fastened the straps securely about his chest. Above his head, the leather harness was joined to ropes that were threaded around the broad mouth of the skysail. It all seemed secure – too secure, for what he had in mind.

'If I should descend a little abruptly, Rho-gan, I might need to wriggle out of this with some haste, before the skysail falls on my head and smothers me.'

The islander nodded. 'A real problem – should you rise more than a few span above the ground.' Was Rho-gan mocking him? No matter; mocking or not, he was explaining what Hawk needed to know. And the less faith he had in the skysail, the bigger the element of surprise that would help Hawk on his way.

'This knot here can be released by a tug, so –' he demonstrated, then began re-fastening the harness '– but it is best not to tug it when you are floating far above *our* heads!'

Hawk grinned. He could not help but like this man. Maybe they would meet again. There was much he would like to learn about the flying wings of the islanders. But timing was all important, now. He had instructed the Navigator to make his move when the fire began to die down, as it would as soon as he was safely on his way and the enthusiastic arsonists he had recruited ceased flinging wood onto the blaze. He felt a tug at his shoulders, and the hair rose on the back of his neck. He had never doubted the device would work, but this was a little different from his usual experiments. This time, he was experimenting on *himself*.

He looked up. The skysail was almost over his head, held to one side by the ropes, trapping the rising heat from the fire.

The ropes to his harness were stretched almost tight. He had to go, and trust the land breeze to appear on schedule. In his mind, he knew it would; but his stomach seemed to be trying to disagree with his mind.

Rho-gan was smiling at him. 'Well, Hawk. Time to live up to your name. A man is not a real man, I always say, without his wings. Your skysail is not my idea of flying. Dangling on a piece of string, unable to steer a course. But I have to admit that my wings would never get me aloft this night, while your skysail seems just as reluctant to have contact with the ground as you foretold. If it takes you higher than I can jump, I'll make you an honorary member of the fliers' guild tomorrow.'

I may not be able to steer a course, thought Hawk, but if it goes where I plan, you'll never get the chance. He smiled in return, with genuine warmth. He hoped Rho-gan would carry no blame for what was about to happen.

'Ready.'

Rho-gan took up the cry. 'Our Hawk is ready to fly! Release the bird!'

Well-disciplined, the men on one side of the network of ropes holding down the skysail released their grip, allowing it to slide out from under the mesh, and rise above the fire. Jerked sideways, Hawk began to run, then stumbled; for a moment, he thought he was being dragged into the fire. Then, with a bound, the sail was free of the netting and rose upwards at a giddy pace. His boots barely brushed the flames, and he was aloft, floating in a warm column of air, soundlessly, like a bird.

Time, he knew, was short. Soon, the heat in the skysail would be dissipated, escaping and vanishing into the sky as it was repelled by the cool surface below. As the skysail cooled, then, in accordance with the law of attraction of similars, it would descend gently (he hoped) back to the ground. But it was no use landing back where he had started. Everything depended on the land breeze, the night wind that *always* blew off from the shore to the sea, from every island, the Navigator had assured Hawk, that he had ever encountered.

Hawk knew why it did so, now. Air warmed by the Sun's action by day was drawn towards the heat of the Sun by the attraction of similars. That was why these island fliers could soar so high on their wings, during the heat of the day. The rising air lifted them up. Naturally, since the land was higher up than the sea, it felt the effect more strongly, so the rising air moved up over the sides of the mountain, reaching for the Sun.

At night, the pattern was reversed. The air above became cool when the Sun went dark at night. Cool air was attracted back down to the cool surface below, and that attraction was stronger on the high slopes of the mountain. Cold air fell down the mountainside and blew out to sea, as the land breeze.

No wing flier could leave the ground when the land breeze blew; he could fly upward only in rising air, in the heat of the day. Now the Hawk could fly upward even in cold air – simply by making his own warmth! Once he was aloft, though, on this occasion he needed the cold air, falling down the mountainside, to push him out to sea and back to the *Far Trader*. But nothing was happening! He could feel no breeze at all!

Alarmed, Hawk looked down between his boots. He was far above the tallest trees, twenty, thirty – perhaps fifty – span above the ground. The fire was no longer there! Twisting in his harness, Hawk caught sight of it, well to one side. As he watched, it seemed to drift away. He *was* moving! And towards the sea!

Cries from below broke into his thoughts.

'Hawk! Skysailer! How far do you plan to travel?'

He laughed. All was well. The opportunity was irresistible.

'All the way, Rho-gan! All the way back to my ship! And by the time your fliers can rise on their wings, we will be far, far away!'

Rantor himself led the attack, as soon as he judged that the fire on the hill was beginning to die down. He wanted to be in the thick of things, exercising a restraining influence. It was essential that none of the honour guard for their hostage should be killed; he wanted no excuse for continuing bad blood between the Archipelago and this island. The guards, though, were under no such restraint, and although they were fighting on unfamiliar territory this gave them an advantage. But they *must* be overpowered before the two rowing galleys, surely already alerted by the sounds of the scuffle, could take action.

Short clubs had disposed of several of the guards – Rantor only hoped they had not been wielded with too much enthusiasm – and he noted, grimly, that at least three of his own men were down, wounded seriously. But the swordsman in front of him was no novice, and it was all he could do to keep him at bay, while trying to manoeuvre the man into a position where one of the sailors could get in a clear blow at him. The sword flicked in low, stabbing at Rantor's groin; he danced sideways, deflecting the blade with a flick of his wrist, and gave way again. Dammit, this man was *good*; where were his helpers?

Suddenly, the *Far Trader* lurched, as the cable was cut and her head began to swing in the breeze. Rantor adjusted easily to the sway; his opponent, clearly a landsman, was caught off balance. Seeing an opening, Rantor lunged forward, aiming to disable his sword arm. To his horror, as the ship heaved his opponent stumbled into the strike. Desperately, at the last moment Rantor managed to lift the point of his blade, which struck high in the man's right shoulder, instead of penetrating deep into his chest. As the wounded man tried to switch the sword to his left hand, two of the crew swung from the rigging, taking him from behind. He sank to his knees, clearly in pain and losing blood fast; but not, Rantor prayed, mortally wounded.

He looked around. The fight was over, and the ship was under way. But there were more problems yet to be faced. Grunting an acknowledgement to his helpers, he ran back to the afterdeck, absently cleaning the sword on his cloak as he went.

'Steady.' Captain Bryon's quiet command travelled the length of the now silent ship. One of the guard boats was swinging round, under all oars, as if making to board. The other stood off for the moment, 'Now! Hard to port; in oars!'

Swept forward by the press of sails, even with all oars inboard, *Far Trader's* manoeuvre caught the galley crew, used only to fighting their own kind, off guard. Sliding down the side of the smaller vessel, *Far Trader* neatly snapped off every oar in turn, leaving the rowboat helpless, at least for the time being. Under the Captain's orders, *Far Trader* turned back onto course, heading directly out to sea, but under reduced sail. The other galley paced them easily, at a safe distance, hailing across the gap between the two vessels.

'*Far Trader!* Your hostage will be forfeit!'

Bryon looked at the Navigator, who nodded. The Captain hailed back.

'He must take his chance! But we have some passengers here who would like to join you. We will give them a boat.'

The Captain played out his scene, dawdling along, ostensibly in order to give the prisoners a chance to disembark, and carefully briefed crewmen took as long as possible over the job. All the while, anxious eyes, including those of the Navigator, scanned astern – for any sign of pursuit, or of the Hawk's skysail. Could it really work? A man – even the Hawk – was so much bigger than a scrap of paper. Would he even try to get back, or did he plan to stay on the Island, with a new benefactor? For all Rantor knew, another double hand of galleys might be ready for them, just out to sea, waiting to spring a trap.

'I see him! Twenty points on the starboard quarter!'

The Navigator looked to his left. A white blob, shining in the faint light of the nightglow, scarcely a mast's height above the water. And falling fast.

'A crown piece for that man!' The Captain's voice rang clear. 'Cut that boat free! Oars! In sail.'

Spinning almost in its own length, the *Far Trader* surged towards the rapidly sinking skysail. Suddenly, the skysail lifted once again, but as it did so a telltale splash beneath it told its own story. The Hawk had dropped free, into the water, abandoning his strange craft.

Surprised once again by this new turn of events, the remaining guardship was a full two lengths behind as a brawny sailor, supported by two of his mates, scooped a dripping Hawk through a rowing port while the vessel was still underway. At last, the Captain gave orders for full sail, and the ship heeled under the press of canvas, catching the full strength of the land breeze, as it turned onto its proper course, while the Hawk emerged, dripping, onto the afterdeck.

'So, Hawk.' Bryon turned his attention away, briefly, from the task of screwing the last measure of speed out of his ship. 'Where's my best light weather sail, when I need it, eh?'

Rantor laughed at the expression that crossed Hawk's face. 'Never fear, Hawk. You are worth more to us than a sail.' He clapped his friend on the shoulder, doubly relieved that the Hawk had indeed been true to his word. 'But that skysailing trick of yours.' He shook his head. 'Something to see. A man floating in the air.'

Hawk grinned. 'You should have seen me earlier, Navigator. At least a hundred span high. But it falls so quickly; it can never really compete with the wings of the islanders. A useless toy, now that the element of surprise is gone.'

'That may not be so.' The quiet voice drew their attention to a forgotten figure, standing awkwardly, one arm stiff, by the rail.

'Bah-lee – why didn't you leave with the others?'

He gave a lopsided shrug. 'Our King, my uncle,' he smiled at the little stir his words caused, 'may have underestimated you travellers. I don't understand the Hawk's trick, but I know its value. If one of those skysails

223

could lift a man and his wings, he could cut loose and be in flight with great ease. The King is no fool, and will value this gift far more than the ship which has so skillfully evaded his grasp.'

'Fine words.' Bryon's expression was sour. 'I'll not return to your island, though, for all your fine words.'

Bah-lee was unmoved.

'Our score, I think, is even. It would be safe to return. But you, I understand, are traders, not in the business of offering gifts, even to great kings. Unless I am mistaken, for all your own fine words I believe that this was your Hawk's first flight. An impressive display. In return for the gift of the skysail, perhaps I can educate your Hawk in the skills of the flying wings, that he may fully live up to his name. And then, maybe, you and your people would know that we are civilised, businesslike folk.'

'We welcome your offer, Bah-lee.' Rantor placed his hand on the flier's good shoulder, in a gesture of friendship. 'But we still have no intention of returning to harbour in your island just yet.'

The islander smiled. 'I am not sure how welcome I would be myself, just now, after having been fooled so completely. And I would like to learn of these other islands you speak of. My uncle instructed me to gain such information from you as I could, and how better to do so than by joining in your voyaging? Then, when we return, I may have enough value to atone for past errors – while you will have an emissary able to approach the King through, ah, the proper channels.'

Other islands. The words took away all thought of the pursuit, already lagging behind them. Together, the sailors and their guest turned to face out to sea. It was still dark. The nightglow, concentrated around the land, was behind them. Ahead, as their eyes adjusted to the gloom, they could pick out, faintly, other patches of light. Lights in the sky which, they now knew, must be other islands, other archipelagoes – other worlds, with their own strange customs. Next time, the Navigator vowed to himself, they would be prepared – for strange habits, new devices, and different points of view.

He turned back to the islander. 'And the Hawk may yet have something to teach you, Bah-lee. You are welcome to join us on our voyage; but it may take more time than you anticipate. If it is in my power, we will return you to your island, I promise –' He turned back to the rail, gazing out into the darkness, imagining the bowl of the inner sphere, with *Far Trader* crawling over it. Would the repulsion of opposites really hold them safely pressed against that bowl even while they crept over the top of the Sun? There was only one way to find out. Softly, he finished the sentence:

'– but we are travelling the long way around.'

# DIFFERENT CITIES

*by*
*Simon D. Ings*

Simon D. Ings has an English degree from King's College, London, where he almost met Garry Kilworth. His first story appeared in *Other Edens 3*, and he has also been published in *Interzone*. He currently lives in Bradford, with two bass guitars that he cannot play, and is 'gratefully unemployed'. This is believed to mean that he is writing full-time.

A man plummeted through the shaft. I gripped the rust-pitted Pavilion rail and watched him. His descent was surprisingly swift and soon he was lost in the darkness.

The dread this sight fastened upon my childish heart has never left me. I remember, I sank to my knees and stared hypnotised into the chasm, and wondered whether the man, free now from our precise sodium light, would diffuse in the unlimited darkness.

My mother's hand closed over my shoulder. I started with shock and gripped tighter the rail before me. The texture of rust and crumbling paint became to me then a little world, my trembling heart its centre.

Gently, the Pavilion attendants prised me away from the rail, and my mother's hand took me home.

The vicarage stood at the end of a long avenue of copper trees. When it rained the trees quoted scripture from little mouths high up in the branches.

In the front parlour sat my father. He was composing a letter. I told him what I had seen. He closed his eyes a moment and made the sign of the circle over his breast, damning the soul of the falling man to eternal, excruciating, existential suffering.

An hour after we returned from evening service a messenger called for my father. I was in my room, copying (badly) an intricate map of the level. I heard the front door close. I stood up and went to the window. My father, huddled up in his great-coat – its steel-blue finish blackened by orange nightlights – was headed down the street towards the centre of the town. The messenger followed at a discreet distance. When they were both lost to sight I looked out over the

229

modest roofs of the neighbouring houses to the lights and ribbons of colour that were the streets and buildings of home. Behind the last line of buildings lay the shaft.

The shaft connected this our level with innumerable others, which stretched in sequence both above and below us. Each level was inhabited by a different community, and they were separated from each other by mile upon mile of intervening, unlit shaft.

I turned from the window and went to my shelves and picked out a book. It was a devotional work. I was permitted no other books. I settled on my bed to read and await my father's return. I was awoken by two sets of footsteps on the metal road. Our front gate creaked. I heard a woman's voice.

Hurriedly I got off the bed, straightened my clothes and ran my fingers through my hair. I opened the door and ran down the stairs to the hall. Next to my father stood a woman, maybe forty years old. She wore wantonly tight trousers and a suggestive vinyl jacket.

Her right hand was bare, her left was gauntleted. Over her shoulder she carried a thick belt to which were clipped several unfamiliar devices.

I knew instantly that she was a walker. There could be no other explanation for her appearance. I completed my descent of the stairs in a more sober and adult fashion. My father looked me over, nodded curt approval, then pecked my mother solemnly on the cheek in greeting. 'This is my family,' he said.

The walker nodded and smiled. She was very confident. She looked perfectly at ease. She walked over to my mother and extended her hand. My mother shook it, gingerly; 'Leuran,' she said.

The stranger did not offer her name.

The walker approached me. We shook hands. Her grip was firm. Her accent was strong and awkward-sounding: 'My name is Lilith.'

'Alynn,' I murmured, somewhat intimidated by her off-level forwardness.

My father explained: 'Lilith arrived here this evening from the upper level. She wishes to rest. I have offered to billet her. She is our guest for so long as she wishes to stay.'

There followed an uneasy silence. Mother and I knew full well that my father was not a strong man. No other member of the council would have deigned to billet such a traveller. My father's good nature had once again been prevailed upon.

The Church's attitude to walkers was, to say the least, ambivalent. Walkers were romantic, charismatic figures. It was said they corrupted the young. More than one youth from this level had run away never to return as a direct result of such a visit as this.

What was worse, walkers were heretics. They searched the shaft for clues as to its construction. This implied that its purpose and design were open to understanding – a clear heresy.

Who decided on the billetting of walkers? My father's liberal proclivities had made enemies on the council. Perhaps they hoped that Lilith's stay at our house would embarrass my father.

I ate little of our evening meal. I was fascinated by Lilith the explorer. She used her right hand to eat. Her left was held out of sight upon her lap. I had been placed opposite her and I gazed at her all the time. Too often I caught her eye, and then cast my gaze down to my full plate, embarrassed.

Lilith picked up her wine glass and brushed her hair from her face with her left hand. The wrist was scarred and twisted.

'How did that happen?' I blurted. It was a silly, tactless question. The walker glanced at her shattered hand dispassionately.

'Please excuse my son,' my father intoned, solemnly. There was in my mind no doubt that there was some wild and daring exploit connected with her crippled hand. My father would never approve of my hearing it.

231

To my great, though appropriately concealed, pleasure, Lilith ignored him. 'It was a long time ago. Some levels aren't so charitable to walkers as yours. Some fix spikes to the ladders. I trod on one. It didn't penetrate my boot, but it pitched me off the rail. I grabbed for the rung, but missed, impaled myself – it was just as well. I could never have gripped hard enough to stop my fall.'

Lilith shrugged, and returned to her food. I wondered at what she said, and could not make head or tail of it. The pieces did not fit together – literally! Perhaps she was lying. The prospect excited me; how I longed for intrigue to colour my grey existence!

I asked hesitantly this time, 'How many levels did you climb through today?'

My father gave me a cool stare but said nothing. As a rule he tolerated my forwardness and never confiscated my tongue in front of guests.

Lilith smiled. 'Just one. It's the most I can travel in a day.'

My mother asked her, 'What were your impressions of the upper level?'

Lilith paused a moment, adjusting to our more parochial vision of the world. 'They reacted less kindly to my visit,' she replied. 'Apparently a walker broke into their holy places.'

An eidetic image rode before my eyes. I saw once more that man plummet down the shaft. When this disturbing reverie released me I found that somehow my father had got himself tangled in a one-sided debate with Lilith concerning 'sanctity of place'.

A cold, custardy dessert followed the main course. My heart sank. Invariably, my father ate this on the nights his parts came to my bed. I wondered if he was conscious of this, and whether my mother recognised the significance of trifle.

'How long do you think you will stay on this level?' my father asked, amenably enough.

'I am looking to settle here for a time.'

'What of the levels?' I asked, disappointed in the romantic figure I had assumed her to be.

The walker smiled and shook her head. 'A walker will climb for maybe ten, twenty years. But not without rest.'

My parents laughed indulgently. 'And what,' my father said, 'do you hope to find at the end of your walking?'

'Nothing,' Lilith replied, candidly. 'Another level like this one, I suppose. I once believed there was a bottom to the shaft. Of course, I don't believe that any more. I travel only to find a home. No great quests.'

My idealised image of her shattered. She was not as I imagined a walker should be. My bitterness was like a physical pain. I was silent for the rest of the meal.

That night I put a blanket under the gap in the door but still my father's organ of increase found its way into my room, and my bed. I opened my legs, spat on my fingers and lubricated the place so it did not hurt me. There must be a loose floorboard somewhere, I supposed, by which it gained entrance.

I drew my legs up further and in spite of myself I became erect and not long afterward attained orgasm. Semen splashed my sparsely-haired pubis like rain from some alien place.

Lilith renounced walking on several occasions and this, coupled with her unexpected (and, as far as I was concerned, thoroughly damning) interest in my father's church activities, brought her into greater favour and acceptance within our household.

It was the time of the Quarterly Assizes. My father was prosecuting counsel for many serious cases. Lilith attended some of these with me. The charges we heard were the staple sort – Vandalism, Destruction of Gifts, and so on. For the wrecking of an electrical substation a man was sentenced to life imprisonment. It was a deserved punishment, for it had taken the Council of Bishops many months to phrase the correct prayer before they were given a new one through the cornucopia. We were also invited by my father to attend the execution of a young priestess who had hit a prayerboard in rage. She had destroyed many of its functions by this behaviour. Prayer-boards were holy, 'ears of the machine', and were not replaceable through the cornucopia.

It was a sorry little affair. No one had the stomach for it. The ones who did not weep wore grim and determined expressions.

Lilith said nothing. There was no emotion on her face. I was left with the impression that she had witnessed this or similar procedures many times before, and the thought excited me.

Three weeks after her arrival Lilith applied for rights of residence. These were granted. My father insisted that she remain our guest until she found a permanent home.

Lilith accompanied me on my weekly outing to the shaft. My mother's ears bobbed along behind us for a while, trailing wisps of waxy glue. I was not concerned. I knew this was the day my mother did her most arduous housework. Sure enough, her ears went back home before the clocks struck Nothing.

The Pavilion lay to the right of the main thoroughfare but Lilith led me to a side street. This narrowed to a pot-holed alley, at the end of which stood a tall, rusted gate. Beyond it there was empty space. In the distance, on the other side of the shaft, I could make out the bright, horizontal band that was the opposite side of the level. Lilith led me down the alley to the iron gate. We gazed between the bars. The shaft was a mile in diameter. Across that distance I could make out the buildings opposite us, which likewise bordered on the shaft.

I craned my neck up to view the disorientating mirror-image of the shaft gaping above me.

'Come with me,' Lilith said and she brought out from the pocket of her trousers a strange, sharp instrument, like the fleshscrew my father used for baptism.

234

The gate was mounted on two massive hinges, hammered deep into the brickwork. It was secured by a sturdy padlock. Lilith took hold of the padlock with her gloved left hand, and with her right forced the probe into the keyhole. The lock came free. She chucked it carelessly to the ground. My heart raced. She could be whipped for that – I could be beaten for not trying to stop her! I stared about me in a panic, looking for eyes.

She noticed my expression. 'What's the matter?'

I was speechless with horror at her wanton vandalism. I could do nothing but shake my head.

She tugged at the gate. With difficulty she wrenched it open. There was a ladder below us. Lilith set foot upon it and beckoned me.

'No,' I said.

'Why not?'

'It's wrong.'

'It's not wrong. I've spent years on the ladders. It's not wrong.'

'It's leaving the level,' I said, panic closing my throat round each syllable. My knees were shaking. Any moment my legs might give way and run off, leaving me stranded here.

'We're not leaving the level,' she replied in a soothing, rather patronising fashion I recognised from my school teachers. It both calmed and angered me. 'We're just going to take a quick walk. So you can see the shaft from the inside. You want that, don't you? Most children do.'

'I'm not a child,' I said, childishly.

'Afraid of falling?' Her look was ironic – she was mocking me!

'No,' I (rep)lied.

'Then there's nothing to fear. You'll be safe. I'll look after you.' When I didn't respond she pouted and said, 'I thought you'd be pleased.'

'I can't,' I said desperately, 'my father –'

She subjected me to a most withering look and pushed past me, out of the alley. I followed.

235

Lilith was disappointed and angry. We crossed the thoroughfare to the Pavilion. Lilith stared at its exterior for some time, then snorted mirthlessly and said something I did not catch. We approached the turnstiles and she pressed two small coins into the slot. We passed through the barrier. The air was still. The multifarious sounds of the level at work dizzied me with their clarity and strangeness.

We were alone here. Lilith turned to me. 'You think shaft walking is unholy.'

She meant it as a question – an unfair one, to ask a boy whose life was the continual pull of opposite and equal forces: of youthful enthusiasm and puritan upbringing. I could not answer. Walkers *were* unpure; I had been brought up to believe this. Formerly, I could keep separate the romantic vision from the cold, religious reality. No longer. I shrugged and turned away from her. 'You've stopped shaft walking,' I said – a gauche gesture at conciliation.

She replied, 'I'm not what I seem, Alynn. I'm not of this place.' She grasped me by my shoulders and stared earnestly through me, as if trying to see inside me to some essential core midway through my skull. 'Once upon a time a very strange and powerful being, not human, visited us. Because it was not human, it did not realise what we were, and was about to tread on us, as we tread on dust. We tried to talk to it, establish a place where we could meet. This shaft is that place. But it mistook what we were trying to do, and thought we were attacking it. So it leeched power from what we built. That's why you've forgotten everything. That's why your bodies can be taken apart and rebuilt. Things here are tending to simple forms.'

'So what are you?'

Lilith grinned. 'Different. Complete. I'm from outside this place, come to repair it, get it working again.' Her grin faded. She was silent for a while. It was as if she was returning from a very private place inside her own head. 'I've journeyed a long way from this other place, this outside, to save you. But I can't do it alone. I need you, Alynn. We communicate, you and I. You must work through me, use my powers to break open this prison.'

It was all so confused in my head I felt like weeping. 'I don't know any of this,' I cried, and went to stare at the distant city-scape. 'I don't understand what you're trying to do, and I don't see how I can work through you. I don't know how.'

What misery filled my heart! How much I had longed for her to take an interest in me, and now, when she said she needed me – *needed* me! – it was for some terrible, heterodox rite I could neither understand nor countenance. My innocent breast shook with loathing. What pit of darkness did Lilith's fair form conceal?

Lilith turned me and pressed her hands to my cheeks. There was great compassion in her expression and it disarmed some of my revulsion. And, in spite of everything, I thrilled at her touch.

Then, as if my doubt and confusion had sparked some apocalyptic disintegration of the world's fabric, the buildings screamed. It was closing time.

A tense silence hung over us while we walked home.

That night my cheeks still held the imprint of her hands. I felt the touch of her fingers on my flesh, and scrub and scratch as I might the sensation did not leave me. As I grew weary, so the touch grew stronger, as if her ghostly fingers had entered the secret places of my skull, and when I slept, strange visions filled me.

I imagined that Lilith met me as I came out of school. She grabbed me. Her hands were covered in ichor and the cold liquid dribbled down my neck where she gripped my collar. Nausea buffeted me and I wailed with terror. She manhandled me down the thoroughfare. No one stopped us. The harder I screamed, the further people drew away. They were fearful of violence, of trouble, of confrontation in any form, and when I cursed the passers-by for their cowardice and their refusal, they treated me to looks of the most withering repugnance, assuming perhaps that I was some mad boy and Lilith was an elder sister or nurse, bearing me back to the cell from which I had escaped.

My cries of terror redoubled when we came to the alley – the alley which ended in the shaft. The gate was still open. We ran pell-mell towards it, then braked sharply. She turned to me. She was grinning. It was a cold, determined expression. 'Let's see what you can do,' she said, grabbed my arm, and flung me towards the drop, followed and pushed, and we plunged, hand in hand, into the mile-wide, endless, unlit shaft, leaving level, leaving home and friends and school and sanity, leaving everything, everything behind I ever knew or cared to know, and for many hours I wept, curled into a foetal ball, and Lilith's arms tightly encircled about me could bring me no comfort.

Not long after, something grey and ragged fluttered past us. We could hear fabric snap in the wind of its descent and called out in case we had stumbled upon another unfortunate. There was no response to our cries. As we neared the next level we were able to view our companion clearly, some fifty feet below us. The skeleton was wrapped in rags. Scraps of grey sacking quivered in its slipstream like battle-weary pennants.

The network of old bone offered the air little resistance and by the time we plummeted past the next level the corpse was lost to sight. Not long after this a terrible suspicion filled me. What had that person died from? Cold? Thirst? Hunger? Why had Lilith brought me along? Was I food? Perhaps she believed that by taking a living larder with her, she could survive longer than others who from despair or accident fell into the shaft. Would my flesh keep her alive long enough to reach the bottom of this (bottomless) space – and thereby achieve some messy apotheosis?

These paranoid speculations were followed by purely fantastical ones. Perhaps we were to mate together, I conjectured, so our offspring could continue the fall. Generation after generation would swell and people the shaft; a dust-grimed, falling race would consume the blackness, people it, build in it. They will live in aerodynamically sculpted houses, I thought to myself, and guide themselves by ropes from one building to another. Lines and hawsers will be their streets. A long central line will connect the upper and lower reaches of the community, and a system of weights and counterweights will convey goods and passengers from one part to another. Some mechanism will be devised whereby the rate of fall can be regulated, the community will make stops *en route*, take on passengers and deposit emigres, barter and talk, and, for a fee, build lifting devices to enable levels (however many lie along the length of the parked community) to maintain communication with each other when the community drops again.

I awoke in a room fashioned out of metal, which had been painted many bright colours. Geometrical shapes twisted the eye when I stared at the walls. I blinked and left the bed and found myself floating up to the ceiling. I kicked about in a panic.

There was a hideous clanging at the other end of the room and the squeal of a hatch. Lilith entered, pulled herself down on to the bed and held herself there by gripping the bedclothes. She looked up at me. 'Alynn,' she said, 'have you any idea what you've done?'

There was excitement in her voice. I could tell she was happy. I too felt good – rested after a long sleep. 'Ah, no,' I replied, abashed.

'Then follow me.' She took my hand and guided me to the hatch. I peered out and what I saw terrified me. Teardrop houses hung all about the rushing shaft. They were held together at an even distance by huge iron gantries, and in the distance I saw that these stressed architectures ended in huge metal pseudopodia, which were drawn back the merest fraction from the sides of the shaft.

Along the gantries ran brightly lit cars and wagons, their

smoked glass windscreens adding a bottle-green sheen to the faces and clothes of their drivers.

Winged craft dropped through the scooped, skeletal structures, then climbed, extending wings of tensile plastic to increase their air resistance and so slow their rate of fall relative to that of the community itself.

Braking the community was slow and noisy. There was nothing we could do in the meantime but bear the quakes and tortured-metal cacophony as best we could. By the time it was over, we were exhausted, and fell asleep on the bed almost immediately.


I awoke in my bedroom. All was as it had been. Dream and Reality danced a gavotte in my abdomen and finally righted themselves.

The strangeness of the vision was shocking. I wondered if it had a special significance. I directed my trembling hands to my groin, and sure enough my penis had disappeared. I lay back under the sheets and quivered expectantly. This was a fine night for me, a special night. Somewhere a woman had a visitor and on the morrow that woman would be my wife! How happy I was now of my room's secret breach! Had the room been secure, my errant prick's frustrated bumpings and thumpings would have awoken my parents (who were unbearably light sleepers) and there would have been a terrible fuss, and father would have sent for a suitable mate instantly, and the whole event would have become characterised by the kind of soulless, sordid institutionalism which had filled my life in this house for too long. Wickedly, I wondered if it was visiting my mother. It would then be my right to pretend to my father's estate; for one orgiastic moment, I indulged my most unfilial fantasies.

I sat up and waited for the morning, then, in spite of myself, I grew curious with the strange puckering where the organ had been attached. I explored it with my fingers, and snuggled further under the covers to keep warm during my probings, and the heat of the bedclothes, the late hour, and my own excitement sent me to sleep again in a matter of minutes. My last waking thoughts were of the events of the morrow. First, the town cryer with his Lost and Found bulletin, then the return of my organ, ribboned in pink and blue and white by my future bride's own hands, the Blessing, the Exchange of Vital Organs, the presentation of the family's handsomely bound Spares Manual by my mother, who would weep, as was customary for mothers.

Breakfast passed in silence. I held my peace and waited with baited breath for the cryer. Through the window I saw him take his customary place at the corner of the street and hail his news and – oh horror! No mention of my organ! It had not been returned! It was lost, and with it all hope of escape from my father's parts!

No doubt my appearance belied something of my mood, but my parents saw fit not to comment upon it – not, at least, while Lilith sat with us at the table.

As soon as I decently could I excused myself and went up to my bedroom. Had it escaped at all, I wondered? Or had it somehow become snared in the room itself, or in the mysterious conduit by which my father's organ was wont to enter? I found no loose floorboard, no copulative part – and it was time for me to go to school. Dispirited, I packed my bag and settled my mind as best I could towards the double period of Chastisement that began my day.

Lilith was waiting for me at the bottom of the stairs. I passed her without a murmur. She called after me, softly, so as not to let my parents hear. I turned, curious. 'By the look of you this morning,' she said, 'I suppose this is yours,' and she reached into her pocket and, with a look of withering disdain, held out between thumb and forefinger my flaccid organ. She dropped the grey and wrinkled mass into my outstretched hand, then sauntered past me out into the street.

Oh, the cruel woman. What a torture of shame and indignity. To be so abused, to be spurned in such a fashion – it was unheard of! Did she not know the rituals, the significances? Did she not know how to behave? Of course she did! I was not so naive that I could not face the enormity of her spite. She knew well enough what was expected of her. My father had taught her much about the customs and mores of our level.

*Why* had she refused me? Was I repugnant to her in some fashion? Self doubt set in, and I did badly in class. During lunch break, I hid myself away in the boys' toilets and masturbated furiously. It was the only sexual act I have ever performed which was motivated by hurt pride. May I never perform another.

The next morning Lilith could not be found. Her shaft-walking equipment was still in her room, however, so it was assumed that she had not left the level.

My father spent most of the day sitting eyeless in his favourite hide chair, while his orbs patrolled the level for his errant charge. They returned for luncheon, and it was then that he called me to him and asked me what had occurred between Lilith and me the previous day. I replied truthfully.

We heard nothing that day.

Early the next morning someone hammered on the front door. There was a muted exchange, then my father climbed back up the stairs to change. My mother complained and my father snapped at her to be quiet. Then, more slowly, he descended the stairs and the front door closed.

I tried to sleep, could not. I tried to read, but the religious fare with which my father had provided me hardly suited the moment.

It was not until after breakfast that my father, pale and tired, came home. He announced: 'Lilith was imprisoned early this morning.' He sat down heavily in his chair at the head of the table. 'She broke into the church. She stole a prayer-board.'

I stared at him in stunned, horrified silence. My mother, never the most stable of women, fell into hysterics, tore off her own head, and beat the sink with it. I left the room, took my coat off its peg and walked out into the street. I paced about the road for many minutes, absorbed in confusion and unhappiness. Eventually my father, his voice stern and cold, summoned me inside.

I obeyed.

It took much pleading and my mother's intercession for my father to allow me to speak to Lilith alone. I was shown into her cell. I dropped my heavy shopping bag and unpacked the gifts of food I had brought for her. She thanked me, but there was no warmth to her voice. While we talked I avoided her gaze and spoke stumblingly. I was not sure whether I hated her or pitied her. The truth was I loved her, as any sheltered boy would love a walker, but I was grievously hurt and could not believe but that somehow it was my own fault.

'You're a good dreamer,' she said.

'You bewitched me,' I breathed.

She shook her head. 'You bewitched yourself. I was merely the channel for your dreams.'

Her words filled me with fear. 'Did you – did we – *change* things?'

Lilith shrugged. 'I can't tell. I stole the prayerboard to find out, but they caught me before I could figure how to work it. Tell me,' she added, 'what will happen to me?'

I bowed my head. 'They will burn you,' I replied.

She remained calm. She said, 'You told the Reverend about the other day. The padlock and your prick.'

'I had no choice,' I replied, querulous.

'He's added that to his charge list. You know that? Vandalism and Abstention from Sexual Congress.'

I knew nothing of this last charge and gazed at her, dumbfounded.

'You're quite a daddy's boy, you know that?'

So that was it! It was hard to hide a smile of triumph. I knew now why she had spurned me. She had misunderstood me through and through. I would show her I was no daddy's boy!

From my jacket pocket, I drew out my father's baptismal fleshscrew.

She started back. 'Alynn?'

I laughed easily. 'Don't be afraid.' I approached her.

'What is it?' Her voice shook.

I held the fleshscrew out towards her. 'Escape,' I replied. Could she not understand my plan? Strange, indeed. Her imprisonment must have slowed and depressed her more than her manner revealed. 'You shall teach me to walk the shafts,' I told her. 'I'm not afraid, now. I'll undo you and carry the bits out in my bag, then we shall be free.'

Her voice was very low and barely sane. 'Alynn,' she hissed, 'I'm not like you. I told you that.'

'Trust me,' I urged her, and stepped forward.

She put her hands over her face and screamed. 'Alynn! I'm complete!'

Such a foolish, hysterical outburst. She would get her rescuer arrested. The time for talk was over. I grappled with her and plunged the screw deep into the soft part of her throat.

A foul red sewage burst from the puncture and hosed my face. I started back in surprise. Lilith fell to the ground, quivering. Her fingers scored the flagstones of the cell, painting them with carmine stripes as her nails tore. My mechanics classes had never prepared me for this, and I wondered with growing panic how I would ever put her back together. What strange lubricant *was* that? I wiped the red exudate from my face and licked crusty residue from my lips. The taste bloomed in my mouth, memories strange to me made reply, and I knew the truth.

The sentence for my bungled crime was death. My father's influence saved me. They mangled me instead. When I recovered I joined the seminary.

Ever after my abortive rescue of Lilith, my father viewed me with suspicion. He feared that I had been permanently corrupted by Lilith's stay. His eyes rarely left me for fear that I would once more fall into bad company.

But contrary to my father's expectations I followed to the

letter his advice and direction and in due course I entered the priesthood. My work was unexceptional but consistent, and in time I attained the rank of reverend.

Today I too, like my father before me, pray for windows, fingers, titles, lamps, internal organs, scissors – for such is my allotted task.

My private studies are more delicate. Did we change things? Did she win? I have not yet found a record of the place we shaped, but I keep faith with Lilith's purpose.

At night I hear the distant, barely perceptible screech of brakes. Strange breezes chill me. The air tastes different – metal on metal.

Our different city plumbs the blackness, filling and reshaping it.

One day it will spool through this place.

Perhaps it will redeem me.

# THE CAIRENE PURSE

*by*

*Michael Moorcock*

Michael Moorcock was educated in a fiction factory and soon promoted to an editor. He took over the magazine *New Worlds* in 1964 – and sf has never been the same since. Amongst his trophies are the Nebula, the Guardian Fiction Award, the World Fantasy Award and the John W. Campbell Memorial Award; but he is still waiting for the BSFA Award he was almost given in 1967. His next books will be *Jerusalem Commands*, the third Pyat novel, *Revenge of the Rose*, the 28th Elric novel, and the collection *Lunching with the Antichrist*. He is currently working with the illustrator Mike Foreman on a tale set in 1920s Morocco, *Where the Dead Meet*. The following is his first novella since 'The Great Rock & Roll Swindle' – which was published as a newspaper and lasted as long.

# 1 HER FIRST FOND HOPE OF EDEN BLIGHTED

On the edge of the Nile's fertile shadow, pyramids merged with the desert and seemed from the air almost two-dimensional in the steady light of late morning. Spreading now beyond the town of Giza, Cairo's forty million people threatened to engulf, with their old automobiles, discarded electronics and every dusty non-degradable of the modern world, the grandiose tombs of their ancestors.

Though Cairo, like Calcutta, was a monument to the enduring survival of our race, I was glad to leave. I had spent only as much time as I needed, seeking information about my archaeologist sister and discovering that everyone in the academic community thought she had returned to England at least a year ago. The noise had begun to seem as tangible as the haze of sand which hung over the crowded motorways, now a mass of moving flesh, of camels, donkeys, horses, mules and humans hauling every variety of vehicle and cargo, with the occasional official electric car or, even rarer, petrol-driven truck.

I suppose it had been a tribute to my imagined status that I had been given a place on a plane, rather than having to take the river or the weekly train to Aswan. Through the porthole of the little VW8 everything but the Nile and its verdant borders were the colours of sand, each shade and texture of which still held meaning for the nomad Arab, the Bedouin who had conquered the First Kingdom and would conquer several others down the millennia. In the past only the Ptolmies, turning their backs on the Nile and the Sahara, ever truly lost the sources of Egypt's power.

My main reason for accepting the assignment was personal rather than professional. My sister had not written for some months and her letters before that had been disconnected, hinting at some sort of emotional disturbance, perhaps in connection with the dig on which I knew she had been working. An employee of UNEC, I had limited authority in Egypt and did not expect to discover any great mysteries at Lake Nasser, which continued to be the cause of unusual weather. The dam's builders somewhat typically had refused to anticipate this. They had also been warned by our people in the 1950s that the New High Dam would eventually so poison the river with bilharzia that anyone using its water would die. The rain, some of it acid, had had predictable effects, flooding quarries and washing away towns. The local Nubians had long-since been evicted from their valleys to make way for the lake. Their new settlements, traditionally built, had not withstood the altered environment, so the government had thrown up concrete shells for them. The road to Aswan from the airport was lined with bleak, half-built structures of rusted metal girders and cinder blocks. Today's Egyptians paid a high price for regulated water.

From the airport my horse-drawn taxi crossed the old English dam with its sluices and gigantic gauges, a Victorian engineer's dream of mechanical efficiency, and began the last lap of the journey into town. Aswan, wretched as much of it is, has a magic few Nile settlements now possess, rising from the East Bank to dominate the coppery blue waters and glinting granite islands of the wide river where white-sailed feluccas cruise gracefully back and forth, ferrying tourists and townspeople between the two sides. The heights, massive grey boulders, are commanded by a beautiful park full of old eucalyptus, poplars and monkey-puzzle trees. Above this, the stately Edwardian glory of Cook's Cataract Hotel is a marvellous example of balconied and shuttered rococco British orientalism at its finest.

The further up river one goes the poorer Aswan becomes,

though even here the clapboard and corrugated iron, the asbestos sheeting and crumbling mud walls are dominated by a splendid hill-top mosque in the grand Turkish style. I had asked to be billeted at a modest hotel in the middle of town, near the Souk. From the outside, the Hotel Osiris, with its pale pink and green pseudo-neon, reminded me of those backstreet Marseilles hotels where once you could take your partner for a few francs an hour. It had the same romantic attraction, the same impossible promises. I found that, once within its tiny fly-thick lobby – actually the communal hallway leading directly to the courtyard – I was as lost to its appeal as any pop to his lid. I had discovered a temporary spiritual home.

The Osiris, though scarcely more than a bed and breakfast place by London standards, boasted four or five porters, all of them eager to take my bag to the rooms assigned me by a Hindu lady at the desk. I let one carry my canvas grip up two flights of dirty stairs to a little tiled, run-down apartment looking into the building's central well where two exhausted dogs, still coupled, panted on their sides in the heat. Giving him a five-pound note, I asked my porter on the off-chance if he had heard of an Englishwoman called Noone or Pappenheim living in Aswan. My sister had used the *poste restante* and, when I had last been here, there were few Europeans permanently living in town. He regretted that he could not help. He would ask his brother, who had been in Aswan several months. Evidently, now that I had as it were paid for the information in advance he felt obliged to me. The *bakshish* custom is usually neither one of bribery nor begging in any European sense, but has a fair amount to do with smooth social intercourse. There is always, with legitimate *bakshish*, an exchange. Some measure of mutual respect is also usual. Most Arabs place considerable emphasis on good manners and are not always tolerant of European coarseness.

I had last been in Egypt long before the great economic convulsion following that chain-reaction of destruction or near-exhaustion of so many resources. Then Aswan had been the final port of call for the millions of tourists who cruised the Nile from dawn to dusk, the sound of their dance music, the smell of their barbecues, drifting over fields and mud villages which had remained unchanged for five thousand years.

In the 80s and 90s of the last century Aswan had possessed, among others, a Hilton, a Sheraton, Ritz-Carlton and a Holiday Inn, but now the luckiest local families had requisitioned the hotels and only the State-owned Cataract remained, a place of pilgrimage for every wealthy enthusiast of 1930s detective stories or autobiographies of the 20th century famous. Here, during wartime, secret meetings had been held and mysterious bargains struck between unlikely participants. Today on the water below the terrace some tourists still sailed, the Israelis and the Saudis on their own elegant schoomers, while other boats carried mixtures of Americans, Italians and Germans, French, English, Swedes, Spaniards, Japanese and Hungarians, their women dressed and painted like pagan temptresses of the local soap-operas, displaying their bodies naked on the sundecks of vast slow-moving windliners the size of an earlier era's ocean-going ships, serving to remind every decent Moslem exactly what the road to Hell looked like. No 18th century English satirist could have provided a better image.

As an officer of the UN's Conservation and Preservation Department I knew all too well how little of Egypt's monuments were still visible, how few existed in any recognisable state. Human erosion, the dam raising the water-table, the volume of garbage casually dumped in the river, the activities of archaeologists and others, of tourists encouraged in their millions to visit the great sites and bring their hard currency, the two-year Arabian war, all had created a situation where those monuments still existing were banned to everyone but the desperate restorers. Meanwhile replicas had been made by the Disney Corporation and located in distant desert settlements surrounded by vacation towns, artificial trees and vast swimming pools, built by French and German experts and named 'Rameses City', 'Land of the Gods' or 'Tutankhamen World'. I was sure that this was why my sister had been secretive about her team's discoveries, why it was important to try to avoid the circumstances which now made Abu Simbel little more than a memory of two great engineering miracles.

When I had washed and changed I left the Osiris and strolled through busy evening alleys in the direction of the corniche, the restored Victorian riverfront promenade which reminded me more than anywhere of the old ocean boulevard at Yalta. Without her earlier weight of tourists, Aswan had developed a lazy, decayed glamour. The foodstalls, the fake antiquities, the flimsy headdresses and *gelabeas* sold as traditional costume, the souvenir shops and postcard stands, the 'cafeterias' offering 'Creme Teas' and 'Mix Grile', were still patronised by a few plump Poles and tomato-coloured English who had been replaced in the main by smaller numbers of blond East Africans, Swedes and Nigerians affecting the styles and mannerisms of thirty or forty years earlier and drawn here, I had heard, by a Holy Man on the outskirts of Aswan who taught a peculiar mixture of orthodox Sunni Islam and his own brand of mysticism which accepted the creeds of Jews and Christians as well as the existence of other planetary populations, and spoke of a 'pure' form of Islam practised in other parts of the galaxy.

Aswan's latter-day hippies, wearing the fashions of my own youthful parents, gave me a queer feeling at first, for although Egypt offers several experiences akin to time-travel, these images of recent history, perhaps of a happier period altogether, were somehow more incongruous than a broken down VW, for instance, being dragged behind a disgusted camel. There was a greater preponderance of charm-sellers and fortune-tellers than I remembered, together with blank-eyed European men and women, some of them with babies or young children, who begged me for drug-money on the street. With the rise of Islamic-Humanism, the so-called Arab Enlightenment, coupled to the increasing power of North Africa and the Middle East in world politics, the drug laws, introduced originally to placate foreign tour operators and their governments, had been relaxed or formally abolished. Aswan, I had heard, was now some kind of Mecca for privileged youngsters and visionary artists, much as Haight Ashbury or Ladbroke Grove had been in the 1960s. Romanticism of that heady, exaggerated, rather mystical variety was once again loose in the world and the comforts it offered seemed to me almost like devilish temptations. But I was of that puritanical, judgemental generation which had rejected the abstractions of its parents in favour of more realistic, as we saw it, attitudes. A good many of us had virtually rejected the entire Western Enlightenment itself and retreated into a kind of liberal mediaevalism not incompatible with large parts of the Arab world. In my own circles I was considered something of a radical.

I had to admit however that I found these new Aswanians attractive. In many ways I envied them. They had never known a time when Arabia had not been a major power. They came here as equals with everyone and were accepted cheerfully by the Nubians who treated them with the respect due to richer pilgrims and potential converts to the divine revelation of Islam.

Again in common with my generation, I was of a secular disposition and saw only damaging, enslaving darkness in any religion. We had even rejected the received wisdoms of Freud, Jung, Marx and their followers and embraced instead a political creed which had as its basis the eminent likelihood of ecological disaster and the slight possibility of an economic miracle. They called us the Anaemic Generation now; a decade or more that was out of step with the progress of history as it was presently interpreted. It suited me to know that I was an anachronism; it afforded me a special kind of security. Very few people took me seriously.

An Egyptian army officer marched past me as I crossed to the river-side of the corniche to look down at the half-completed stairways, the crumbling, poorly-mixed concrete and the piles of rat-infested rubble which the Korean engineers, who had put in the lowest tender for the work, had still neither repaired nor cleared. The officer glanced at me as if he recognised me but then went past, looking, with his neatly-trimmed moustache and rigid shoulders, for all the world like a World War Two English Guards captain. Even his uniform was in the English style. I suppose Romans coming to 5th century Britain after some lapse of time would have been equally impressed to see a Celt striding through the streets of Londinium, impeccable in a slightly antiquated Centurion's kit. The whole casual story of the human race seemed to be represented in the town as I paused to look at the hulks of converted pleasure boats, home to swarms of Nubian families impoverished by the altered climate and the shift of tourism towards the Total Egypt Experience found in the comfort of Fort Sadat and New Memphis. Despite the piles of filthy garbage along the shore, Aswan had acquired the pleasant, nostalgic qualities of unfashionable British resorts like Morecombe or Yarmouth, a local population careless of most strangers save sometimes for the money they brought.

About halfway along the corniche I stopped at a little café and sat down on a cane chair, ordering mint tea from a proprietor whose ancient tarboosh might have escaped from the costume department of a touring production of *Death on the Nile*. He addressed me as '*effendi*' and his chosen brand of English seemed developed from old British war movies. Like me, I thought, he was out of step with the times. When he brought the tea I told him to keep the change from a pound and again on the off-chance asked after my sister. I was surprised by the enthusiasm of his response. He knew the name Pappenheim and was approving when I told him of our relationship. 'She is very good,' he said. 'A tip-top gentlewoman. But now, I think, she is unwell. It is hard to see the justice of it.'

Pleased and a little alarmed, I asked if he knew where she lived.

'She lived in *Sharri al Sahahaldeen*, just off the *Sharri al Souk*.' He pointed with his thumb back into town. 'But that was more than a year ago. Oh, she is very well known here in Aswan. The poor people like her immensely. They call her *Saidneh Duukturah*.'

'Doctor?' My sister had only rudimentary medical training. Her doctorate had been in archaeology. 'She treats the sick?'

'Well, not so much any more. Now only if the hospitals refuse help. The Bisharim, in particular, love her. You know those nomads. They trust your sister only. But she moved from Sahahaldeen Street after some trouble. I heard she went to the English House over on the West Bank, but I'm not so sure. Perhaps you should ask the Bisharim.' He raised his hand in welcome to a small man in a dark blue *gelabea* who walked briskly into the darkness of the shop's interior. 'A customer.' From his pocket he took a cut-throat razor. '*Naharak sa'id*,' he called and, adopting the swagger of the expert barber, waved farewell to me and entered his shop.

'*Fi amani 'llah*.' Picking up my hat I crossed to a rank where the usual two or three ill-used horses stood between the shafts of battered broughams, still the commonest form of taxi in Aswan. I approached the first driver, who stood flicking at flies with his ragged whip while he smoked a cigarette and chatted with his fellows. He wore an American sailor's hat, a faded T-shirt advertising some Russian artpopper, a pair of traditional baggy trousers exposing ulcerated calves and on his feet pink and black Roos. From the state of his legs I guessed he had retained the habit, against all current warnings, of wading into the Nile to urinate. I asked him to take me first to the dam's administration office where, for courtesy's sake, I presented myself and made an appointment with my old aquaintance Georges Abidos, the Chief Press Officer, who had been called out to the northern end of the lake. His secretary said he was looking forward to seeing me tomorrow and handed me a welcoming note. I then asked the calash-driver if he knew the Bisharim camp on the outskirts of town. I had heard that in recent years the tribe had returned to its traditional sites. He was contemptuous. 'Oh, yes, sir. The barbarians are still with us!' I told him I would give him another ten pounds to take me there and back. He made to bargain but then accepted, shrugging and gesturing for me to get back in his carriage. I guessed he was maintaining some kind of face for himself. In my travels I had grown used to all kinds of mysterious body-language, frequently far harder to interpret than any spoken tongue.

We trotted back to town and jogged beside a river strewn with old plastic water-bottles, with all the miscellaneous filth from the boats that no legislation appeared able to limit, past flaking quasi-French facades still bearing the crests of Farouk and his ancestors and each now occupied by twenty or thirty families whose washing hung over the elaborate iron balconies and carved stone sphinxes like bunting celebrating some joyous national holiday. We passed convents and churches, mosques and graveyards, shanteys, monuments, little clumps of palm-trees sheltering donkeys and boys from a sun which as noon approached grew steadily more intense.

We went by the English holiday villas where hippies nowadays congregated; we passed the burned-out shells of warehouses and storerooms, victims of some forgotten riot, the stained walls sprayed with the emerald-coloured ankh of the Green Jihad, and eventually, turning inland again, reached the old Moslem necropolis, almost a mile long and half-a-mile across, surrounded by a low, mud wall and filled with every shape and size of stone or sarcophagus. Beyond this, further up the hill, I made out clumps of palms and the dark woollen tents of the Bisharim.

My driver reined in his horse some distance from the camp, beside a gate into the graveyard. 'I will wait for you here,' he said significantly.

## 2 AH, WHENCE, AND WHITHER FLOWN AGAIN, WHO KNOWS?

The nomad camp, showing so few outward signs of Western influence, had the kind of self-contained dignity which city Arabs frequently manage to recreate in their homes and yet which is not immediately noticed by those visitors merely disgusted by, for instance, Cairo's squalor.

Sheikh Khamet ben Achmet was the patriarch of this particular clan. They had come in a month ago, he said, from the Sudan, to trade horses and camels. They all knew my sister but she had disappeared. He employed a slow, classical Arabic which was easy for me to understand and in which I could easily respond. 'God has perhaps directed thy sister towards another vocation,' he suggested gently. 'It was only a short time since she would visit us whenever we put down our tents here. She had a particularly efficient cure for infections of the eye, but it was the women who went to her, chiefly.' He looked at me with quiet amusement. 'The best type of Englishwoman, as we say. Sometimes God sends us His beneficence in strange forms.'

'Thou has no knowledge of her present dwelling?' I sipped the coffee a servant brought us. I was glad to be in the cool tent. Outside it was now at least 35°. There was little danger of freak rain today. He looked up at me from his ironic grey eyes. 'No,' he said. 'She always visits us. When we needed her we would send messages to the Copt's house. You know, the carpenter who lives on the street leading from the great mosque to the souk.'

I did not know him, I said.

'He is as gold-haired as thou. They nickname him The German, but I know he is a Copt from Alexandria. I think he is called Iskander. I know that he is easily found.'

'Thou knowest my sister was an archaeologist?' I was a little hesitant.

'Indeed, I do! We discussed all manner of ancient things together and she had the courtesy to say that I was at least as informative as the great Egyptian Museum in Cairo!' He was amused by what he perceived as elegant flattery. My sister, if I still knew her, had done no more than state her direct opinion.

It would have been ill-mannered of me to have left as soon as I had the information I sought, so I spent two further hours answering the Sheikh's questions about current American and European politics. I was not surprised that he was well-informed. I had seen his short-wave radio (doubtless full of *piles noires*) standing on the ivory-inlaid chest on the far side of the tent. I was also unsurprised by his interpretations of what he had learned. They were neither cynical nor unintelligent, but they were characteristic of certain desert Arabs who see everything in terms of power and opportunity and simply cannot grasp the reverence for political institutions we have in the West. For a few minutes I foolishly tried to re-educate him until it became clear I must give offence. Recalling my old rules, I accepted his terms. As a result we parted friends. Any South African apologist for apartheid could not have been more approving of my good manners.

When I got up to leave, the old man took my arm and wished me God's grace and help in finding my sister. 'She was associated with Jews.' He spoke significantly. 'Those who did not like her said that she was a witch. And it is true that two of my women saw her consorting with the spell-seller from the Souk. The one called Lallah Zenobia. The black woman. Thou and I art men of the world and understand that it is superstitious folly. But thou knowest how women are. And they are often,' he added in an even lower tone, 'susceptible to Yehudim flattery and lies.'

It was by no means the first time I had to accept such

sentiments from the mouth of one who was otherwise hospitality, tolerance and kindness personified. To persuade a desert Arab that Jews are not in direct and regular touch with Satan and all His minions is still no easier than persuading a Dixie Baptist that the doors of a Catholic Church are not necessarily a direct gateway to Hell. One is dealing with powerful survival myths which only direct experience will disprove. In such circumstances I never mention my mother's family. I said I would visit Iskander the Carpenter. At this point a braying, bellowing and snorting chorus grew so loud I could barely hear his elaborate goodbyes. The stock was being beaten back from the water. As I emerged from the tent I saw my driver in the distance. He was sitting on the wall of the cemetery feinting with his whip at the boys and girls who flowed like a tide around him, daring one another to run within his range.


## 3 CRYSTAL TO THE WIZARD EYE

I had no difficulty in discovering Iskander the Carpenter. He was a slight man wearing a pair of faded denim overalls. Sanding off a barley-sugar chairleg, he sat just inside his workshop, which was open to the street and displayed an entire suite of baroque bedroom and living room furniture he had almost completed. He chose to speak in French. 'It is for a couple getting married this weekend. At least they are spending their money on furniture rather than the wedding itself!' He put down his chairleg and shook my hand. He was fair-skinned and blond, as Sheikh Achmet had said, though I could not have taken him for anything but Egyptian. His features could have come straight from the Egyptian Museum's clay statue displays of ancient tradespeople. He might have been a foreman on a Middle Kingdom site. He turned up a chair which still had to have the upholstery over its horsehair seat, indicated that I should sit and sent his son to get us a couple of bottles of Pyramid beer.

'Of course I know Saidneh Duukturah. She was my friend. That one,' he pointed to his disappearing boy, 'owes his life to her. He was poisoned. She treated him. He is well. It is true I knew where she lived and would get messages to her. But for a year or more she went away from us. Until recently she was staying at the English House. There are many rumours. Most of them are simply stupid. She is no witch. She was a woman blessed by God with the healing touch. The other woman, now, is undoubtably a witch. My wife heard that your sister fell in love and went to the Somalin, Zenobia, for a philtre. Certainly, by chance, my wife saw her handing Zenobia a heavy purse. A Cairene purse, she was sure.'

'I do not know what that is.' I moved further into the shade. Outside, Aswan had fallen into a doze as the population closed its shutters until mid-afternoon. The yellow walls of the houses were now almost blistering to the touch.

'A purse of money, that's all. It used to mean a bag of gold. About twenty sovereigns. That is what a witch demands for a very powerful spell. Something very valuable, my friend.'

'My sister was buying a charm from a spell-seller?'

'A powerful one, yes. That negress has been involved with the police more than once. She was suspected of killing a rival suitor at the behest of another, of being responsible for the death of a man who was owed over a thousand pounds by another man. Now, if your sister was disposed to witchcraft, why would she go to a witch and pay her a healthy sum for a job she could as readily do herself?'

I agreed it was unlikely my sister was a witch. I asked how the matter had come to official attention.

'The police went to see her, I think. My wife's friend – friend no more – gossiped. They arrested Zenobia, then let your sister go. You should visit the *mamur* at the *markaz*, the police department. The *mamur* here is a very just man. He never accepts money unless he can do whatever it is he promises. His name is Inspector el-Bayoumi. If anyone knows where your sister is living in Aswan he probably will.'

By the time I had discussed the affairs of the day and thanked the carpenter for the beer, it was already cooler and I walked down to the *Sharri el Souk* which was beginning to open for business again, filling with women in black lacy *milayum* which barely revealed the vivid colours of their house dresses beneath, clutching bright plastic shopping bags and going about their weekend buying. Because it was Friday afternoon the butchers were displaying their calves' heads and bullock tails, their sheep's hearts and heads, their divided carcasses, all protected from an unforgiving sun by the thick coating of black flies which also covered the fish and offal on other stalls. Sellers of turkeys, pigeons and chickens took water in their mouths to force between the beaks of their wares so that they would not dehydrate before they were sold, and seemed to be kissing, tenderly, each one. Cheerful greengrocers called out the virtues of their squash, mangoes, potatoes or green beans. Gas lorries, electro-scoots, bicycles and a few official cars moved in slow competition with rickshaws, donkeys, mules or camels through alleys where, every so often, a bright sign would advertise in English the virtues of unobtainable Panasonic televisions or Braun refrigerators and others would, almost pathetically, alert the passerby to the Color Xerox machine or Your Local Fax Office. Like every similar souk in the Arab world, the tools and artefacts of the centuries were crowded side by side and functioning in perfect compatability. Aswan had adapted, far more readily and more cheerfully, to modern energy restraints than had London, for instance, where it had taken an Act of Parliament to reintroduce the public horse trough.

I made my way to the northern end of the street where the police station, the *markaz*, resembling an old British garrison, was guarded by two boys in serge khaki who were armed with the Lee Enfield 303s with which Lawrence had armed his men for the Desert War and which had, then, been an Arab's prized possession. Now it was unlikely any reliable ammunition existed for these antiques. I understood only the crack militia was allowed to sport the old Kalashnikovs or M16s issued to regular infantry. With the end of international arms trading, almost any well-made gun was valuable, if only as status.

I had no appointment and was informed by the bright young civilian woman on the duty desk that Inspector el-Bayoumi would be back from New Town, the concrete development near the airport, in about an hour. I gave my name, my business, and said I would be back at about five-thirty. Courteously she assured me that the Inspector would await me.

## 4 HER HEART ALL EARS AND EYES, LIPS CATCHING THE AVALANCHE OF THE GOLDEN GHOST

I had forgotten how much time one had to spend on enquiries of this kind. I returned to my apartment to find an envelope pushed under my door. It was not, as I had hoped, from my sister, but a letter welcoming me to Aswan, a short personal note from my friend Georges, a list of appointments with various engineers and officials, some misleading publicity about the dam, consisting mainly of impressive photographs, a variety of press releases stressing the plans for 'an even better dam' and so on. I went out again having glanced at them. I was obsessed with all the mysteries with which I had been presented in a single day. How had my sister metamorphosed from a dedicated archaeologist to some kind of local Mother Theresa?

Disturbed by my own speculations I forced myself to think about the next day's work when I would be discussing methods of reducing pollution in all its varieties and rebuilding the dam to allow silt down to the arable areas. The signs of serious 'redesertisation', as ugly official jargon termed it, were now found everywhere in the Nile valley. In other words, the Aswan Dam was now seriously contributing to ecological damage as well as helping to wipe out our most important links with the remote past. I could not believe how intelligent scientists, who were not those industrial developers motivated only by greed, failed to accept the dreadful psychic damage being done to people whose whole identities were bound up with a particular and very specific landscape. My own identity, for instance, was profoundly linked to a small Oxfordshire village which had remained unchanged for hundreds of years after successfully resisting developers wanting to surround it with high quality modern properties instead of its existing beeches and oaks.

Few Egyptians were in such comfortable circumstances or could make any choice but the one promising the most immediate benefit, yet they had the same understanding of their tribal homes and what values they represented, and still resisted all attempts to force them to lose their traditional clothes, language and attitudes and make them modern citizens of their semi-democratic society. Unfortunately, this attitude also extended to a dam now much older than many of its staff and never at any time an engineering miracle. UNEC had plans for a replacement. Currently they and the Rajhidi government were arguing over the amounts each would contribute. Happily, that was not my problem.

With a slightly clearer head, I walked to the Post Office on the corner of Abdel el Taheer street. Though almost fifty years had passed since the First Revolution, the building still bore the outlines of earlier royal insignia. The elaborate cast-ironwork on doors and windows was of that 'Oriental' pattern exported from the foundries of Birmingham to adorn official buildings throughout the Empire east of Gibraltar. Even by the 1970s the stuff was still available from stock, during the brief period after the death of Britain's imperial age and before the birth of that now much-despised and admittedly reckless Thatcher period known ironically as 'the Second Empire', the period which had shaped my own expectations of life as well as those of uncounted millions of my fellows, the period in which my uncle had died, a soldier in the Falklands cause.

I entered the main door's cool archway and walked through dusty shafts of light to a tiled counter where I asked to speak to the Post Master. After a moment's wait I was shown into his little gloomy mahogany office, its massive fan constantly stirring piles of documents which moved like a perpetually unsettled flight of doves. A small, handsome Arab entered and closed the door carefully behind him. His neat, Abraham Lincoln beard suggested religious devotion. I told him that my name was Pappenheim and I was expecting mail. I handed him an envelope I had already prepared. On the outside was my name and occupation. Inside was the conventional 'purse' – actually another envelope containing a few pounds. I said I would appreciate his personal interest in my mail and hoped he could ensure it was available to me the moment it arrived. Absently, he took the envelope and put it in his trouser pocket. He had brightened at the sound of my name. 'Are you related to that woman of virtue whom we know here in Aswan?' He spoke measured, cultured Arabic with the soft accents of Upper Egypt.

'My sister.' I was trying to locate her, I said. Perhaps her mail was delivered here?

'It has not been collected, Si Pappenheim, for several months. Yet she has been seen in Aswan recently. There was a small scandal. I understand that El Haj Sheikh Ibrahim Abu Halil intervened. Have you asked him about your sister?'

'Is he the governor?'

He laughed. Clearly the idea of the governor intervening on behalf of an ordinary member of the public amused him. 'No. Sheikh Abu Halil is the gentleman so many come to Aswan to see these days. He is the great Sufi now. We are blessed in this. God sends us everything that is good, even the rain. So much more grows and blooms. People journey to us from all over the world. Here, God has chosen to reveal a glimpse of Paradise.'

I was impressed by his optimism. I told him I would go to see Sheikh Abu Halil as soon as possible. Meanwhile I had an appointment with the police chief. At this his face grew a little uncertain, but his only response was some conventional greeting concerning Allah's good offices.

Police Inspector el-Bayoumi was one of those suave career officers produced by the new academies. His manners were perfect, his hospitality generous and discreet, and when I had replied to his question, telling him where I had been born in England, he confessed affectionate familiarity with another nearby Cotswold village. Together, we deplored the damage tourism had done to the environment and confessed it to be a major problem in both our countries, which depended considerably on the very visitors who contributed to the erosion. He sighed. 'I think the human race has rather foolishly cancelled many of its options.'

Since he preferred to speak it, I replied in English. 'Perhaps our imaginative resources are becoming as scarce as our physical ones?'

'There has been a kind of psychic withering,' he agreed. 'And its worst symptom, in my view, Mr Pappenheim, is found in the religious and political fundamentalism to which so many subscribe. As if, by some sort of sympathetic magic, the old, simpler days will return. We live in complicated times with complicated problems. It's a sad fact that they require sophisticated solutions.'

I admitted I had been schooled in many of those fundamentalist notions and sometimes found them difficult to resist. We chatted about this for a while. Coffee was brought, together with a selection of delicious *gurrahiya* pastries, whose secret the Egyptians inherited from the Turks, and we talked for another half-hour, during which time we took each other's measure and agreed the world would be a better place if civilised people like ourselves were allowed a greater voice. Whereupon, in that sometimes abrupt change of tone Arabs have, which can mislead

Europeans into thinking they have somehow given offence, Inspector el-Bayoumi asked what he could do for me.

'I'm looking for my sister. She's an economic archaeologist who came here two and a half years ago with the Burbank College Project. It was an international team. Only about half were from California and those returned the next year, after the big earthquake. Most of them, of course, had lost relatives. My sister stayed on with the remaining members.' I did not mention her talk of a wonderful discovery out in the Western Sahara. Their sonavids had picked up a New Kingdom temple complex almost perfectly preserved but buried some hundred feet under the sand. My sister had been very excited about it. It was at least on a par with the discovery of the Tutankhamen treasures and probably of far greater historical importance. She and the team kept the discovery quiet, of course, especially since so many known monuments had suffered. Naturally, there were some conflicts of interest. There was little she could tell me in a letter and most of that was a bit vague, making reference to personal or childhood incidents whose relevance escaped me. I added delicately. 'You know about the discovery, naturally.'

He smiled as he shook his handsome head. 'No, Mr Pappenheim, I don't. I think an elaborate dig would not escape my notice.' He paused, asking me if he might smoke. I told him I was allergic to cigarette smoke and he put his case away. Regretfully, he said: 'I should tell you that your sister is a little disturbed. She was arrested by us about a year ago. There was something we had to follow up. An outbreak of black magic amongst the local people. We don't take such things very seriously until it's possible to detect a cult growing. Then we have to move to break it up as best we can. Such things are not a serious problem in London, but for a policeman in Aswan they are fairly important. We arrested a known witch, a Somali woman they call Madame Zenobia, and with her an Englishwoman, also rumoured to be practising. That was your sister, Mr Pappenheim. She was deranged and had to be given a sedative. Eventually, we decided against charging her and released her into the custody of Lady Roper.'

'The Consul's wife?'

'He's the Honorary Consul here in Aswan now. They have a large house on the West Bank, not far from the Ali Khan's tomb. You can't see it from this side. It is our miracle. Locally, it's called the English House. More recently they've called it the Rose House. You'll find no mysteries there!'

'That's where my sister's staying?'

'No longer. She left Aswan for a while. When she came back she joined the community around Sheikh Abu Halil and I understand her to be living in the old holiday villas on the Edfu road, near the race course. I'll gladly put a man to work on the matter. We tend not to pursue people too much in Aswan. Your sister is a good woman. An honest woman. I hope she has recovered herself.'

Thanking him I said I hoped my search would not involve the time of a hardworking police officer. I got up to leave. 'And what happened to Madame Zenobia?'

'Oh, the courts were pretty lenient. She got a year, doing quarry work for the Restoration Department in Cairo. She was a fit woman. She'll be even fitter now. Hard labour is a wonderful cure for neurosis! And far more socially useful than concocting love potions or aborting cattle.'

He sounded like my old headmaster. As an afterthought, I said, 'I gather Sheikh Abu Halil took an interest in my sister's case.'

He flashed me a look of intelligent humour. 'Yes, he did. He is much respected here. Your sister is a healer. The Sufi is a healer. He sometimes makes an accurate prophecy. He has a following all over the world, I believe.'

I appreciated his attempt at a neutral tone, given his evident distaste for matters psychic and mystical. We shared, I think, a similar outlook.

I found myself asking him another question. 'What was the evidence against my sister, Inspector?'

He had hoped I would not raise the matter, but was prepared for it. 'Well,' he began slowly, 'for instance, we had a witness who saw her passing a large bag of money to the woman. The assumption was that she was paying for a spell. A powerful one. A love philtre, possibly, but it was also said that she wanted a man dead. He was the only other member of her team who had remained behind. There was some suggestion, Mr Pappenheim,' he paused again, 'that he made her pregnant. But this was all the wildest gossip. He did in fact die of a heart attack shortly after the reported incident. Sometimes we must treat such cases as murder. But we only had circumstantial evidence. The man was a drug addict and apparently had tried to force your sister to give him money. There was just a hint of blackmail involved in the case, you see. These are all, of course, the interpretations of a policeman. Maybe the man had been an ex-lover, no more. Maybe she wanted him to love her again?'

'It wasn't Noone, was it?'

'It was not her estranged husband. He is, I believe, still in New Zealand.'

'You really think she got tangled up in black magic?'

'When confused, men turn to war and women to magic. She was not, as the Marrakshim say, with the caravan.' He was just a little sardonic now. 'But she was adamant that she did not wish to go home.'

'What did she tell you?'

'She denied employing the witch. She claimed the Somali woman was her only friend. Otherwise she said little. But her manner was all the time distracted, as if she imagined herself to be surrounded by invisible witnesses. We were not unsympathetic. The psychiatrist from the German hospital came to see her. Your sister is a saintly woman who helped the poor and the sick and asked for no reward. She enriched us. We were trying to help her, you know.'

He had lost his insouciance altogether now and spoke with controlled passion. 'It could be that your sister had an ordinary breakdown. Too much excitement in her work, too much sun. Caring too much for the hardships of others. She tried to cure the whole town's ills and that task is impossible for any individual. Her burden was too heavy. You could see it written in every line of her face, every movement of her body. We wanted her to recover. Some suspected she was in the witch's power, but in my own view she carried a personal weight of guilt, perhaps. Probably pointlessly, too. You know how women are. They are kinder, more feeling creatures than men.'

## 5 THE SEASONS OF HOME – AYE, NOW THEY ARE REMEMBERED!

That evening, while there was still light, I took the felucca across the Nile, to the West Bank. The ferryman, clambering down from his high mast where he had been reefing his sail, directed me through the village to a dirt road winding up the hillside a hundred yards or so from the almost austere resting place of the Ali Khan. 'You will see it,' he assured me. 'But get a boy.'

There were a couple of dozen children waiting for me on the quay. I selected a bright looking lad of about ten. He wore a ragged Japanese T-shirt with the inscription I LOVE SEX WAX, a pair of cut-off jeans and Adidas trainers. In spite of the firmness with which I singled him out, we were followed by the rest of the children all the way to the edge of the village. I had a couple of packs of old electronic watches which I handed out, to a pantomime of disappointment from the older children. Watches had ceased to be fashionable currency since I had last been in Aswan. Now, from their requests, I learned it was 'real' fountain pens. They showed me a couple of Sheaffers some tourist had already exchanged for their services as guides and companions of the road.

I had no fountain pen for the boy who took me to the top of the hill and pointed down into the little valley where, amongst the sand and the rocks, had been erected a large two-storey house, as solidly Edwardian as any early twentieth century vicarage. Astonishingly, it was planted with cedars, firs and other hardy trees shading a garden to rival anything I had ever seen in Oxfordshire. There were dozens of varieties of roses, of every possible shade, as well as hollyhocks, snapdragons, foxgloves, marigolds and all the flowers one might find in an English July garden. A peculiar wall about a metre high surrounded the entire mirage and I guessed that it disguised some kind of extraordinarily expensive watering and sheltering apparatus which had allowed the owners to do the impossible and bring a little bit of rural England to Upper Egypt. The grounds covered several acres. I saw some stables, a garage, and a woman on the front lawn. She was seated in a faded deckchair watching a fiche-reader or a video which she rested in her left hand. With her right hand she took a glorious drink from the little table beside her and sipped through the straw. As I drew nearer, my vision was obscured by the trees and the wall, but I guessed she was about sixty-five, dressed in a thoroughly unfashionable Marks and Ashley smock, a man's trilby hat and a pair of rubber-tyre sandals. She looked up as I reached the gate and called 'good afternoon'. Happy with cash, my boy departed.

'Lady Roper?'

She had a quick, intelligent, swarthy face, her curls all grey beneath the hat, her long hands expressive even when still. 'I'm Diana Roper.'

'My name's Paul Pappenheim. I'm Beatrice's brother.'

'The engineer!' She was full of welcome. 'My goodness, you know, I think Bea could foretell the future. She *said* you'd be turning up here about now.'

'I wrote and told her!' I was laughing as the woman unlocked the gate and let me in. 'I knew about this job months ago.'

'You're here on business.'

'I'm going through the rituals of sorting out a better dam

and trying to do something about the climactic changes. I got sent because I know a couple of people here – and because I asked to come. But there's little real point to my being here.'

'You don't sound very hopeful, Mr Pappenheim.' She led me towards the back of the house, to a white wrought-iron conservatory which was a relatively recent addition to the place and must have been erected by some forgotten imperial dignitary of the last century.

'I'm always hopeful that people will see reason, Lady Roper.'

We went into the sweet-smelling ante-room, whose glass had been treated so that it could admit only a certain amount of light, or indeed reflect all the light to perform some needed function elsewhere. Despite its ancient appearance, I guessed the house to be using up-to-date EE technologies and to be completely self-sufficient. 'What an extraordinary garden,' I said.

'Imported Kent clay.' She offered me a white basket chair. 'With a fair bit of Kenyan topsoil, I understand. We didn't have it done. We got it all dirt cheap. It takes such a long time to travel anywhere these days most people don't want the place. It belonged to one of the Fayeds, before they all went off to Malaysia. But have you looked carefully at our roses, Mr Pappenheim? They have a sad air to them, a sense of someone departed, someone mourned. Each bush was planted for a dead relative, they say.' Her voice grew distant. 'Of course, the new rain has helped enormously. I've survived because I know the rules. Women frequently find their intuition very useful in times of social unrest. But things are better now, aren't they? We simply refuse to learn. We refuse to learn.'

Grinning as if enjoying a game, a Nubian girl of about sixteen brought us a tray of English cakes and a pot of Assam tea. I wondered how I had lost the thread of Lady Roper's conversation.

'We do our best,' I said, letting the girl take tongs to an

éclair and with a flourish pop it on my plate. 'I believe Bea lived here for a while.'

'My husband took quite a fancy to her. As did I. She was a sweetie. And so bright. Is that a family trait? Yes, we shared a great deal. It was a luxury for me, you know, to have such company. Not many people have been privileged as she and I were privileged.' She nodded with gentle mystery, her eyes in the past. 'We were friends of your uncle. That was the funny thing we found out. All at Cambridge together in the late sixties. We thought conservation an important subject *then*. What? Fifty years ago, almost? Such a jolly boy. He joined up for extremely complicated reasons, we felt. Did you know why?'

I had never really wondered. My picture of my mother's brother was of the kind of person who would decide on a military career, but evidently they had not known that man at all. Finding this disturbing, I attempted to return to my subject. 'I was too young to know him. My sister was more curious than I. Did she seem neurotic to you, while she was here?'

'On the contrary. She was the sanest of all of us. Sound as a bell upstairs, as Bernie always said. Sharp intelligence. But, of course, she had been there, you see. And could confirm everything we had been able to piece together at this end.'

'You're referring to the site they discovered?'

'That, of course, was crucial. Especially at the early stages. Yes, the site was extraordinary. We went out to see it with her, Bernie and I. What a mind-blower, Paul! Amazing experience. Even the small portion they had excavated. Four mechanical sifters just sucking the sand gradually away. It would have taken years in the old days. Unfortunately three of the operators left after the earthquake and the sifters were recalled for some crucial rescue work over in Sinai. And then, of course, everything changed.'

'I'm not sure I'm …'

'After the ship came and took Bea.'

'A ship? On the Nile?'

She frowned at me for a moment and then her tone changed to one of distant friendliness. 'You'll probably want a word with Bernie. You'll find him in his playroom. Nadja will take you. And I'm here if you need to know anything.'

She glanced away, through the glass walls of the conservatory and was at once lost in melancholy reflection of the roses and their guardian trees.


## 6 THE SMOKE ALONG THE TRACK

A tape of some antique radio programme was playing as I knocked on the oak door and was admitted by a white-haired old man wearing a pair of overalls and a check shirt, with carpet slippers on his feet. His skin had the healthy sheen of a sun-baked reptile and his blue eyes were brilliant with trust. I was shocked enough to remain where I was, even as he beckoned me in. He turned down his stereo, a replica of some even older audio contraption, and stood proudly to display a room full of books and toys. One wall was lined with glass shelves on which miniature armies battled amidst a wealth of tiny trees and buildings. 'You don't look much like a potential playmate!' His eyes strayed towards the brilliant jackets of his books.

'And you're not entirely convincing as Mr Dick, sir.' I stood near the books, which were all well-ordered, and admired his illustrated Dickens. The temperature in the room was, I guessed, thoroughly controlled. Should the power fail for just a few hours the desert would fade and modify this room as if it had been a photograph left for an hour in the sun.

My retort seemed to please him. He grinned and came forward. 'I'm Bernie Roper. While I have no immediate enemies, I enjoy in this room the bliss of endless childhood. I have my lead soldiers, my bears and rabbits, my model farm, and I read widely. *Treasure Island* is very good, as are the "William" books, and Edgar Rice Burroughs and, as you say, Charles Dickens, though he's a bit on the scarey side sometimes. E. Nesbit and H. G. Wells and Shaw. I enjoy so much. For music I have the very best of *Children's Favourites* from the BBC – a mixture of comic songs, Gilbert and Sullivan, *Puff the Magic Dragon*, *The Laughing Policeman*, popular classics and light opera. Flanders and Swann, Danny Kaye, *Sparky's Magic Piano*, *Peter and the Wolf* and *Song of the South*. Do you know any of those? But I'm a silly chap! You're far too young. They'd even scrapped *Children's Hour* before you were born. Oh, dear. Never to enjoy *Larry the Lamb* or Norman and Henry Bones, the Boy Detectives! Oh!' he exclaimed with a knowing grin, 'Calamity!' Then he returned his attention to his toys for a moment. 'You think I should carry more responsibility?'

'No.' I had always admired him as a diplomat. He deserved the kind of retirement that suited him.

'I feel sorry for the children,' he said. 'The pleasures of childhood are denied to more and more of them as their numbers increase. Rajhid and Abu Halil are no real solution, are they? We who remember the Revolution had hoped to have turned the desert green by now. I plan to die here, Mr –?'

'My name's Pappenheim. I'm Bea's brother.'

'My boy! Thank goodness I offered an explanation. I'm not nearly as eccentric as I look! "Because I could not stop for Death, He kindly stopped for me. We shared a carriage, just we two, and Immortality." Emily Dickinson, I believe. But I could also be misremembering. "The child is Father to the Man", you know. And the lost childhood of Judas. Did you read all those poems at school?'

'I was probably too young again,' I said. 'We didn't do poetry as such.'

'I'm so sorry. All computer studies nowadays, I suppose.'

'Not all, sir.' The old fashioned courtesy surprised us both. Sir Bernard acted as one cheated and I almost apologised. Yet it was probably the first time I had used the form of address without irony. I had, I realised, wanted to show respect. Sir Bernard had come to the same understanding. 'Oh, well. You're a kind boy. But you'll forgive me, I hope, if I return to my preferred world.'

'I'm looking for my sister, Sir Bernard. Actually, I'm pretty worried about her.'

Without irritation, he sighed. 'She was a sweet woman. It was terrible. And nobody believing her.'

'Believing what, Sir Bernard?'

'About the spaceship, you know. But that's Di's field, really. Not my area of enthusiasm at all. I like to make time stand still. We each have a different way of dealing with the fact of our own mortality, don't we?' He strolled to one of his displays and picked up a charging 17th Lancer. 'Into the Valley of Death rode the six hundred.'

'Thank you for seeing me, Sir Bernard.'

'Not at all, Paul. She talked about you. I liked her. I think you'll find her either attending Abu Halil's peculiar gymnasium or at the holiday homes. Where those Kenyan girls and boys are now living.'

'Thank you. Goodbye, sir.'

'Bye, bye!' Humming some stirring air, the former Director General of the United Nations hovered, contented, over his miniature Death or Glory Boys.

# 7 ANOTHER RELAY IN THE CHAIN OF FIRE

Lady Roper had remained in her conservatory. She rose as I entered. 'Was Bernie able to help?'

'I could be narrowing things down.' I was anxious to get back to the East Bank before dark. 'Thank you for your kindness. I tried to find a phone number for you.'

'We're not on the phone, lovie. We don't need one.'

'Sir Bernard mentioned a spaceship.' I was not looking forward to her reply.

'Oh, dear, yes,' she said 'The flying saucer people. I think one day they will bring us peace, don't you? I mean one way or another. This is better than death for me, at any rate, Paul. But perhaps they have a purpose for us. Perhaps an unpleasant one. I don't think anybody would rule that out. What could we do if that were the case? Introduce a spy? That has not proved a successful strategy. We know that much, sadly. It's as if all that's left of Time is here. A few shreds from a few ages.'

Again I was completely nonplussed and said nothing.

'I think you share Sir B's streak of pessimism. Or realism is it?'

'Well, we're rather different, actually ...' I began to feel foolish.

'He was happier as Ambassador, you know. Before the UN And then we were both content to retire here. We'd always loved it. The Fayeds had us out here lots of times, for those odd parties. We were much younger. You probably think we're both barking mad.' When I produced an awkward reply she was sympathetic. 'There *is* something happening here. It's a *centre*. You can feel it everywhere. It's an ideal place. Possibly we shall be the ones left to witness the birth of the New Age.'

At that moment all I wished to do was save my sister from that atmosphere of half-baked mysticism and desperate faith, to get her back to the relative reality of London and a doctor who would know what was wrong with her and be able to treat it.

'Bea was never happier than when she was in Aswan, you know,' said Lady Roper.

'She wrote and told me as much.'

'Perhaps she risked a bit more than was wise. We all admire her for it. What I don't understand is why she was so thick with Lallah Zenobia. The woman's psychic, of course, but very unsophisticated.'

'You heard about the witness? About the purse?'

'Naturally.'

'And you, too, are sure it was a purse?'

'I suppose so. It's Cairo slang, isn't it, for a lot of money?

277

The way the Greeks always say "seven years" when they mean a long time has passed. Bernie's actually ill, you realise? He's coherent much of the time. A form of P.D. we were told. From the water when we were in Washington. He's determined to make the best of it. He's sweet, isn't he?'

'He's an impressive man. You don't miss England?'

She offered me her hand. 'Not a bit. You're always welcome to stay if you are bored over there. Or the carping materialism of the Old Country gets to you. Simplicity's the keynote at the Rose House. Bernie says the British have been sulking for years, like the Lost Boys deprived of their right to go a-hunting and a-pirating at will. I'm afraid, Paul, that we don't think very much of home any more.'


## 8  AND ALL THESE IN THEIR HELPLESS DAYS ...

The great Egyptian sun was dropping away to the horizon as in the company of some forty blue-cowled Islamic schoolgirls and a bird-catcher, I sailed back to the East. Reflected in the Nile the sky was the colour of blood and saffron against every tone of dusty blue; the rocks, houses and palms dark violet silhouettes, sparkling here and there as lamps were lit, signalling the start of Aswan's somewhat orderly nightlife. Near the landing stage I ate some *mulakhiya*, rice and an antique salad at Mahommeds' Cafeteria, drank some mint tea and went back to the Osiris, half expecting to find that my sister had left word, but the Hindu woman had no messages and handed me my key with a quick smile of encouragement.

I slept poorly, kept awake by the constant cracking of a chemical 'equaliser' in the basement and the creak of the all-but-useless wind-generator on the roof. It was ironic that Aswan, so close to the source of enormous quantities of electricity, was as cruelly rationed as everyone.

I refused to believe that my sister, who was as sane as I was and twice as intelligent, had become entangled with a black magic flying saucer cult. Her only purpose for associating with such people would be curiosity, perhaps in pursuit of some anthropological research connected with her work. I was, however, puzzled by her secrecy. Clearly, she was deliberately hiding her whereabouts. I hoped that, when I returned the next day, I would know where she was.

My meetings were predictably amiable and inconsequential. I had arrived a little late, having failed to anticipate the levels of security at the dam. There were police, militia and security people everywhere, both on the dam itself and in all the offices and operations areas. I had to show my pass to eleven different people. The dam was under increased threat from at least three different organisations, the chief being Green Jihad. Our main meetings were held in a large, glass-walled room overlooking the lake. I was glad to meet so many staff, though we all knew that any decisions about the dam would not be made by us but by whomever triumphed in the Geneva negotiations. It was also good to discover that earlier attitudes towards the dam were changing slightly and new thinking was being done. Breakfasted and lunched, I next found myself guest of honour at a full-scale Egyptian dinner which must have taken everyone's rations for a month, involved several entertainments and lastly a good deal of noisy toasting, in cokes and grape juice, our various unadmired leaders.

At the Hotel Osiris, when I got back that night, there was no note for me so I decided next day to visit the old vacation villas before lunching as arranged at the Cataract with Georges Abidos, who had told me that he was retiring as Public Relations officer for the dam. I had a hunch that my sister was probably living with the neo-hippies. The following morning I ordered a calash to pick me up and sat on the board beside the skinny, cheerful driver as his equally thin horse picked her way slowly through busy Saturday streets until we were on the long, cracked concrete road with the railway yards on one side and the river on the other, flanked by dusty palms, which led past the five-storey

Moorish-style vacation complex, a tumble of typical tourist architecture of the kind once found all around the Mediterranean, Adriatic and parts of the Black and Red Seas. The white stucco was patchy and the turquoise trim on window-frames and doors was peeling, but the new inhabitants, who had occupied it when the Swedish owners finally abandoned it, had put their stamp on it. Originally the place had been designed for Club Med, but had never sustained the required turnover, even with its special energy dispensations, and had been sold several times over the past ten years. Now garishly-dressed young squatters from the wealthy African countries, from the Australias, North and South America, as well as Europe and the Far East, had covered the old complex with their sometimes impressive murals and decorative, computer-sprayed graffiti. I read a variety of slogans. LET THE BLOOD CONSUME THE FIRE, said one. THE TYGERS OF THE MIND RULE THE JUNGLE OF THE HEART, said another. I had no relish for such undisciplined nonsense and did not look forward to meeting the occupants of this bizarre New New Age fortress. Psychedelia, even in its historical context, had never attracted me.

As I dismounted from the calash I was greeted by a young woman energetically cleaning the old Club Med brass plate at the gate. She had those startling green eyes in a dark olive skin which one frequently comes across everywhere in Egypt and are commonly believed to be another inheritance from the Pharoanic past. Her reddish hair was braided with multi-coloured ribbons and she wore a long green silk smock which complemented her eyes.

'Hi!' Her manner was promiscuously friendly. 'I'm Lips. Which is short for Eclipse, to answer your question. Don't get the wrong idea. You're here to find a relative, right?' Her accent was Canadian with a trace of something else, possibly Ukrainian. 'What's your name?'

'Paul,' I said. 'My sister's called Bea. Are the only people who visit you trying to find relatives?'

'I just made an assumption from the way you look. I'm pretty good at sussing people out.' Then she made a noise of approving excitement. 'Bea Palestine, is it? She's famous here. She's a healer and an oracle. She's special.'

'Could you take me to her apartment?' I did my best not to show impatience with the girl's nonsense.

'Lips' answered me with a baffled smile. 'No. I mean, sure I could take you to one of her rooms. But she's not here now.'

'Do you know where she went?'

The girl was vaguely apologetic. 'Mercury? Wherever the ship goes.'

My irritation grew more intense. But I controlled myself. 'You've no idea when the ship gets back?'

'Now? Yesterday? There's so much time-bending involved. No. You just have to hope.'

I walked past her into the complex.


9 FAST CLOSING TOWARD THE UNDELIGHTED
   NIGHT …


By the time I had spoken to a dozen or so *enfants des fleurs* I had found myself a guide who introduced himself as Magic Mungo and wore brilliant face-paint beneath his straw hat. He had on an old pair of glitterjeans which whispered and flashed as he walked. His jacket announced in calligraphic Arabic phonetic English: THE NAME IS THE GAME. He was probably no older than thirteen. He asked me what I did and when I told him he said he, too, planned to become an engineer 'and bring back the power.' This amused me and restored my temper. 'And what will you do about the weather?' I asked.

'It's not the weather,' he told me, 'not Nature – it's the ships. And it's not the dam, or the lake, that's causing the storms and stuff. It's the Reens.'

I misheard him. I thought he was blaming the Greens.

Then I realised, belatedly, that he was expressing a popular notion amongst the New New Agers which by the time I had heard it several times more had actually begun to improve my mood. The Reens, the flying saucer people, were used by the hippies as an explanation for everything they couldn't understand. In rejecting Science, they had substituted only a banal myth. Essentially, I was being told that the Gods had taken my sister. In other words they did not know where she was. At last, after several further short but keen conversations, in various rug-strewn galleries and cushion-heavy chambers smelling strongly of kif, incense and patchouli, I met a somewhat older woman, with grey streaks in her long black hair and a face the colour and texture of well-preserved leather.

'This is Ayesha.' Mungo gulped comically. 'She-who-must-be-obeyed!' He ran to the woman who smiled a perfectly ordinary smile as she embraced him. 'We encourage their imaginations,' she said. 'They read books here and everything. Are you looking for Bea?'

Warily expecting more Reen talk, I admitted that I was trying to find my sister.

'She went back to Aswan. I think she was at the medrassah for a bit – you know, with the Sufi – but after that she returned to town. If she's not there, she's in the desert again. She goes there to meditate, I'm told. If she's not there, she's not anywhere. Around here, I mean.'

I was relieved by the straightforward nature of her answer. 'I'm greatly obliged. I thought you, too, were going to tell me she was taken into space by aliens!'

Ayesha joined in my amusement. 'Oh, no, of course not. That was more than a year ago!'


# 10 THOUGHTS OF TOO OLD A COLOUR NURSE MY BRAIN

I decided to have a note delivered to the Sufi, El Haj Ibrahim Abu Halil, telling him that I planned to visit him next day, then, with a little time to spare before my appointment, I strolled up the corniche, past the boat-ghetto at the upper end, and along the more fashionable stretches where some sporadic attempt was made to give the railings fresh coats of white paint and where a kiosk, closed since my first time here, advertised in bleached Latin type the *Daily Telegraph, Le Monde* and the *New York Herald-Tribune*. A few thin strands of white smoke rose from the villages on Elephantine Island, and from *Gazirat-al-Bustan*, Plantation Island, whose botanical gardens, begun by Lord Kitchener, had long since become a marvellously exotic jungle, came the laughter of the children and teenagers who habitually spent their free days there.

Outside the kiosk stood an old man holding a bunch of faded and ragged international newspapers under one arm and *El Misr* under the other. 'All today!' he called vigorously in English, much as a London coster shouted 'All fresh!' A professional cry rather than any sort of promise. I bought an *El Misr*, only a day old, and glanced at the headlines as I walked up to the park. There seemed nothing unusually alarming in the paper. Even the EC rate had not risen in the last month. As I tried to open the sheet a gust came off the river and the yellow-grey paper began to shred in my hands. It was low-density recyke, unbulked by the sophisticated methods of the West. Before I gave up and dumped the crumpled mess into the nearest reclamation bin I had glimpsed references to the UNEC conference in Madagascar and something about examples of mass hysteria in Old Paris and Bombay, where a group called *Reincarnation* was claiming its leader to be a newly-born John Lennon. There were now about as many reincarnated Lennons abroad as there had been freshly-risen Christs in the early Middle Ages.

I stopped in the park to watch the gardeners carefully tending the unsweet soil of the flower-beds, coaxing marigolds and nasturtiums to bloom at least for a few days in the winter, when the sun would not burn them immediately they emerged. The little municipal café was unchanged since British days and still served only icecreams, tea, coffee or soft-drinks, all of them made with non-rationed ingredients and all equally tasteless. Pigeons wandered hopelessly amongst the debris left by customers, occasionally pecking at a piece of wrapping or a sliver of *Sustenance* left behind by some poor devil who had been unable to force his stomach to accept the high-concentrate nutrients we had developed at UNEC for his benefit.

The Cataract's entrance was between pillars which, once stately, Egyptianate and unquestionably European, were now a little the worse for wear, though the gardens on both sides of the drive were heavy with freshly-planted flowers. Bougain-villeas of every brilliant variety covered walls behind avenues of palms leading to a main building the colour of Nile clay, its shutters and ironwork a dark, dignified green, the kind of colour Cook himself would have picked to represent the security and solid good service which established him as one of the Empire's noblest champions.

I walked into the great lobby cooled by massive carved mahogany punkahs worked on hidden ropes by screened boys. Egypt had had little trouble implementing many of the UN's mandatory energy-saving regulations. She had either carried on as always or had returned, perhaps even with relief, to the days before electricity and gas had become the necessi-ties rather than the luxuries of life.

I crossed the lobby to the wooden verandah where we were to lunch. Georges Abidos was already at our table by the rail looking directly over the empty swimming pool and, beyond that, to the river itself. He was drinking a cup of Lipton's tea and I remarked on it, pointing to the label on the string dangling from his tiny metal pot. 'Indeed!' he said. 'At ten pounds the pot why shouldn't the Cataract offer us Lipton's, at least!' He dropped his voice. 'Though my guess is the teabag has seen more than one customer through the day's heat. Would you like a cup?'

I refused. He hadn't, I said, exactly sold me on the idea. He laughed. He was a small, attractively ugly Greek from Alexandria. Since the flooding, he had been driven, like so many of his fellow citizens to seek work inland. At least half the city had not been thought worth saving as the sea-level had steadily risen to cover it.

'Can't you,' he asked, 'get your American friends to do something about this new embargo? One misses the cigarettes and I could dearly use a new John B.' He indicated his stained Planter's straw and then picked it up to show me the label on the mottled sweatband so that I might verify it was a genuine product of the Stetson Hat Co. of New Jersey. 'Size seven and a quarter. But don't get anything here. The Cairo fakes are very close. Very good. But they can't fake the finish, you see.'

'I'll remember,' I promised. I would send him a Stetson next time I was in the USA.

I felt we had actually conducted our main business before we sat down. The rest of the lunch would be a social affair with someone I had known both professionally and as a close personal acquaintance for many years.

As our mixed *hors d'oeuvres* arrived, Georges Abidos looked with a despairing movement of his mouth out towards the river. 'Well, Paul, have you solved any of our problems?'

'I doubt it,' I said. 'That's all going on in Majunga now. I'm wondering if my function isn't as some kind of minor smokescreen.'

'I thought you'd volunteered.'

'Only when they'd decided that one of us had to come. It was a good chance, I thought, to see how my sister was. I had spare relative allowance and lots of energy and travel owing, so I got her a flight out with me. It took forever! But I grew rather worried. The last note I had from her was three months ago and very disjointed. It didn't tell me anything. I'd guessed that her husband had turned up. It was something she said. That's about all I know which would frighten her that much. My mistake, it's emerged. Then I wondered if she'wasn't pregnant. I couldn't make head or tail of her letters. They weren't like her at all.'

'Women are a trial,' said Georges Abidos. 'My own sister

has divorced, I heard. But then,' as if to explain it, 'they moved to Kuwait.' He turned his eyes back to the river which seemed almost to obsess him. 'Look at the Nile. An open sewer running through a desert. What has Egypt done to deserve rescue? She gave the world the ancestors who first offered Nature a serious challenge. Should we be grateful for that? From Lake Nasser to Alexandria the river remains undrinkable and frequently unusable. She once replenished the Earth. Now, what with their fertilisers and sprays, she helps poison it.' It was as if all the doubts he had kept to himself as a publicity officer were now being allowed to emerge. 'I listen to Blue Danube Radio from Vienna. The English station there. It's so much more reliable than the World Service. We are still doing less than we could, they say, here in Egypt.'

The tables around us had begun to fill with Saudis and wealthy French people in fashionable silk shifts, and the noise level rose so that it was hard for me to hear my acquaintance's soft tones.

We discussed the changing nature of Aswan. He said he would be glad to get back to Cairo where he had a new job with the Antiquities Department raising money for specific restoration or reconstruction projects.

We had met at the re-opening of the Cairo Opera House in 1989, which had featured the Houston Opera Company's *Porgy and Bess*, but had never become more than casual friends, though we shared many musical tastes and he had an extraordinary knowledge of modern fiction in English. His enthusiasm was for the older writers like Gilchrist or DeLillo, who had been amongst my own favourites at College.

We were brought some wonderfully tasty Grönburgers and I remarked that the cuisine had improved since I was last here. 'French management,' he told me. 'They have one of the best teams outside of Paris. They all came from Nice after the troubles. Lucky for us. I might almost be tempted to stay! Oh, no! I could not. Even for that! Nubian music is an abomination!'

I told him about my sister, how I was unable to find her and how I was beginning to fear the worst. 'The police suggested she was mad.'

Georges was dismissive of this. 'A dangerous assumption at any time, Paul, but especially these days. And very difficult for us to define here, in Egypt, just as justice is at once a more brutal and a subtler instrument in our interpretation. We never accepted, thank God, the conventional wisdoms of psychiatry. And madness here, as elsewhere, is defined by the people in power, usually calling themselves the State. Tomorrow those power holders could be overthrown by a fresh dynasty and what was yesterday simple common sense today becomes irresponsible folly. So I do not like to make hasty judgements or pronounce readily on others' moral or mental condition – lest, indeed, we inadvertently condemn ourselves.' He paused. 'They say this was not so under the British, that it was fairer, more predictable. Only real trouble-makers and criminals went to jail. Now it isn't as bad as it was when I was a lad. Then anyone was liable to arrest. If it was better under the British, then that is our shame.' And he lowered his lips to his wineglass.

We had slipped, almost automatically, into discussing the old, familiar topics. 'It's sometimes argued,' I said, 'that the liberal democracies actually stopped the flow of history. A few hundred years earlier, as feudal states, we would have forcibly Christianised the whole of Islam and changed the entire nature of the planet's power struggle. Indeed, all the more childish struggles might have been well and truly over by now!'

'Or it might have gone the other way,' Georges suggested dryly, 'if the Moors had reconquered France and Northern Europe. After all, Islam did not bring the world to near-ruin. What has the European way achieved except the threat of death for all?'

I could not accept an argument which had already led to massive conversions to Islam amongst the youth of Europe, America and Democratic Africa, representing a sizeable proportion of the vote. This phenomenon had, admittedly, improved the tenor of world politics, but I still deplored it.

'Oh, you're so thoroughly out of step, my friend.' Georges Abidos smiled and patted my arm. 'The world's changing!'

'It'll die if we start resorting to mystical Islamic solutions.'

'Possibly.' He seemed unconcerned. I think he believed us unsaveable.

A little drunk, I let him take me back to the Osiris in a calash. He talked affectionately of our good times, of concerts and plays we had seen in the world's capitals before civilian flight had become so impossibly expensive, of the Gilbert and Sullivan season we had attended in Bangkok, of Wagner in Bayreuth and Britten in Glyndebourne. We hummed a snatch from *Iolanthe* before we parted.

When I got up to my room all the shutters had been drawn back to give the apartment the best of the light. I recognised the subtle perfume even as my sister came out of the bathroom to laugh aloud at my astonishment.


## 11 SAW LIFE TO BE A SEA GREEN DREAM

Beatrice had cut her auburn hair short and her skin was paler than I remembered. While her blue eyes and red lips remained striking, she had gained an extra beauty. I was overjoyed. This was the opposite of what I had feared to find.

As if she read my mind, she smiled. 'Were you expecting the Mad Woman of Aswan?' She wore a light blue cotton skirt and a darker blue shirt.

'You've never looked better.' I spoke the honest truth.

She took both my hands in hers and kissed me. 'I'm sorry I didn't write. It began to seem such a sham. I *couldn't* write for a while. I got your letters today, when I went to the post office. What a coincidence, I thought – my first sally into the real world and here comes good old Paul to help me. If anyone understands reality, you do.'

I was flattered and grinned in the way I had always

responded to her half-mocking praise. 'Well, I'm here to take you back to it, if you want to go. I've got a pass for you on the Cairo plane in four days' time, and from there we can go to Geneva or London or anywhere in the Community.'

'That's marvellous,' she said. She looked about my shabby sitting room with its cracked foam cushions, its stained tiles. 'Is this the best you get at your rank?'

'This is the best for any rank, these days. Most of us don't travel at all and certainly not by plane.'

'The schoomers are still going out of Alex, are they?'

'Oh, yes. To Genoa, some of them. Who has the time?'

'That's what I'd thought of, for me. But here you are! What a bit of luck!'

I was immensely relieved. 'Oh, Bea. I thought you might be dead – you know, or worse.'

'I was selfish not to keep you in touch, but for a while, of course, I couldn't. Then I was out there for so long ...'

'At your dig, you mean?'

She seemed momentarily surprised, as if she had not expected me to know about the dig. 'Yes, where the dig was. That's right. I can't remember what I said in my letters.'

'That you'd made a terrific discovery and that I must come out the first chance I got. Well, I did. This really was the first chance. Am I too late? Have they closed down the project completely? Are you out of funds?'

'Yes,' she smiled. 'You're too late, Paul. I'm awfully sorry. You must think I brought you on a wild goose chase.'

'Nonsense. That wasn't why I really came. Good Lord, Bea, I care a lot for you!' I stopped, a little ashamed. She was probably in a more delicate condition than she permitted me to see. 'And, anyway, I had some perks coming. It's lovely here, still, isn't it? If you ignore the rubbish tips. You know, and the sewage. And the Nile!' We laughed together. 'And the rain and the air,' she said. 'And the sunlight! Oh, Paul! What if this really is the future?'

She asked if I would like to take a drive with her beside the evening river and I agreed at once. I was her senior by a year but she had always been the leader, the initiator and I admired her as much as ever.

We went up past the ruins of the Best Western and the Ramada Inn, the only casualties of a shelling attack in '02, when the Green Jihad had attempted to hole the dam and six women had died. We stopped near the abandoned museum and bought a drink from the ice-stall. As I turned, looking out at the river, I saw the new moon, huge and orange, in the cloudless night. A few desultory mosquitoes hung around our heads and were easily fanned away as we continued up the corniche, looking out at the lights from the boats, the flares on the far side, the palms waving in the soft breeze from the North.

'I'm quitting my job,' she said. 'I resigned, in fact, months ago. I had a few things to clear up.'

'What will you do? Get something in London?'

'Well, I've my money. That was invested very sensibly by Jack before our problems started. Before we split up. And I can do freelance work.' Clearly, she was unwilling to discuss the details. 'I could go on living here.'

'Do you want to?'

'No,' she said. 'I hate it now. But is the rest of the world any better, Paul?'

'Oh, life's still a bit easier in England. And Italy's all right. And Scandinavia, of course, but that's closed off, as far as residency's concerned. The population's dropping quite nicely in Western Europe. Not everything's awful. The winters are easier.'

She nodded slowly as if she were carefully noting each observation. 'Well,' she said, 'anyway, I don't know about Aswan. I'm not sure there's much point in my leaving Egypt. I have a permanent visa, you know.'

'Why stay, Bea?'

'Oh, well,' she said, 'I suppose it feels like home. How's daddy? Is everything all right in Marrakesh?'

'Couldn't be better, I gather. He's having a wonderful time. You know how happy he always was there. And with the new government! Well, you can imagine.'

'And mother?'

'Still in London. She has a house to herself in West Hampstead. Don't ask me how. She's installed the latest EE generators and energy storers. She's got a TV set, a pet option and a gas licence. You know mother. She's always had the right contacts. She'll be glad to know you're OK.'

'Yes. That's good, too. I've been guilty of some awfully selfish behaviour, haven't I? Well, I'm putting all that behind me and getting on with my life.'

'You sound as if you've seen someone. About whatever it was. Have you been ill, Bea?'

'Oh, no. No. Not really.' She turned to reassure me with a quick smile and a hand out to mine, just as always. I nearly sang with relief. 'Emotional trouble, you know.'

'A boyfriend?'

'Well, yes, I suppose so. Anyway, it's over.'

'All the hippies told me you'd been abducted by a flying saucer!'

'Did they?'

I recognised her brave smile. 'What's wrong? I hadn't meant to be tactless.'

'You weren't. There are so many strange things happening around here. You can't blame people for getting superstitious, can you? After all, we say we've identified the causes, yet can do virtually nothing to find a cure.'

'Well, I must admit there's some truth in that. But there are still things we can do.'

'Of course there are. I didn't mean to be pessimistic, old Paul.' She punched me on the arm and told the driver to let his horse trot for a bit, to get us some air on our faces, since the wind had dropped so suddenly.

She told me she would come to see me at the same time tomorrow and perhaps after that we might go to her new flat. It was only a temporary place while she made up her mind. Why didn't I just go to her there? I said. Because, she said, it was in a maze. You couldn't get a calash through and even the schoolboys would sometimes mislead you by accident. Write it down, I suggested, but she refused with an even broader smile. 'You'll see I'm right. I'll take you there tomorrow. There's no mystery. Nothing deliberate.'

I went back into the damp, semi-darkness of the Osiris and climbed through black archways to my rooms.


## 13 YOU'LL FIND NO MIRRORS IN THAT COLD ABODE

I had meant to ask Beatrice about her experience with the Somali woman and the police, but her mood had swung so radically I had decided to keep the rest of the conversation as casual as possible. I went to bed at once more hopeful and more baffled than I had been before I left Cairo.

In the morning I took a cab to the religious academy, or *madrassah*, of the famous Sufi, El Haj Sheik Ibrahim Abu Halil, not because I now needed his help in finding my sister, but because I felt it would have been rude to cancel my visit without explanation. The *madrassah* was out near the old obelisk quarries. Characteristically Moslem, with a tower and a domed mosque, it was reached on foot or by donkey, up a winding, artificial track that had been there for at least two thousand years. I climbed to the top, feeling a little dizzy as I avoided looking directly down into the ancient quarry and saw that the place was built as a series of stone colonnades around a great courtyard with a fountain in it. The fountain, in accordance with the law, was silent.

The place was larger than I had expected and far more casual. People, many obviously drugged, of every age and race sat in groups or strolled around the cloisters. I asked a

pale young woman in an Islamic *burqa* where I might find
Sheikh Abu Halil. She told me to go to the office and led me
as far as a glass door through which I saw an ordinary business
layout of pens and paper, mechanical typewriters, acoustic
calculators and, impressively, an EMARGY console. I felt as if I
were prying. My first job, from which I had resigned, was as
an Energy Officer. Essentially the work involved too much
peeping-tomism and too little real progress.

A young black man in flared Mouwes and an Afghan jerkin
signalled for me to enter. I told him my business and he said,
'No problem, man.' He asked me to wait in a little room
furnished like something still found in any South London
dentist's. Even the magazines looked familiar and I did not
intend to waste my battery ration plugging in to one. A few
minutes later the young man returned and I was escorted
through antiseptic corridors to the Sufi's inner sanctum.

I had expected some rather austere sort of Holy Roller's
Executive Suite, and was a trifle shocked by the actuality
which resembled a scene from *The Arabian Nights*. The Sufi
was clearly not celibate, and was an epicurean rather than an
aescetic. He was also younger than I had expected. I guessed
he was no more than forty-five. Dressed in red silks of a
dozen shades, with a massive scarlet turban on his head, he
lay on cushions smoking from a silver and brass hookah while
behind him on rich, spangled divans, lolled half-a-dozen
young women, all of them veiled, all looking at me with frank,
if discreet, interest. I felt as if I should apologise for intruding
on someone's private sexual fantasy, but the Sufi grinned,
beckoned me in, then fell to laughing aloud as he stared into
my face. All this, of course, only increased my discomfort. I
could see no reason for his amusement.

'You think this a banal piece of play-acting?' He at once
became solicitious. 'Pardon me, *Herr Doktor*. I misunderstood
your expression for a moment. I thought you were an ·old
friend.' Now he was almost grave. 'How can I help you?'

'Originally,' I said, 'I was looking for my sister Beatrice. I
believe you know her.' Was this my sister's secret? Had she

involved herself with a charismatic charlatan to whom even I felt drawn? But the banality of it all! True madness, like true evil, I had been informed once, was always characterised by its banality.

'That's it, of course. Bea Porcupine was the name the young ones used. She is a very good friend of mine. Are you looking for her no longer, Dr Porcupine?'

I pointed out that Pappenheim was the family name. The hippies had not made an enormously imaginative leap.

'Oh, the children! Don't they love to play? They are blessed. Think how few of us in the world are allowed by God to play.'

'Thou art most tolerant indeed, sidhi.' I used my best classical Arabic, at which he gave me a look of considerable approval and addressed me in the same way.

'Doth God not teach us to tolerate, but not to imitate, all the ways of mankind? Are we to judge God, my compatriot?' He had done me the honour, in his own eyes, of addressing me as a coreligionist. When he smiled again his expression was one of benign happiness. 'Would you care for some coffee?' he asked in educated English. 'Some cakes and so on? Yes, of course.' And he clapped his hands, whispering instructions to the nearest woman who rose and left. I was so thoroughly discomforted by this outrageously old-fashioned sexism which, whatever their private practices, few sophisticated modern Arabs were willing to admit to, that I remained silent.

'And I trust that you in turn will tolerate my stupid self-indulgence,' he said. 'It is a whim of mine – and these young women – to lead the life of Haroun-el-Raschid, eh? Or the great chiefs who ruled in the days before the Prophet. We are all nostalgic for that, in Egypt. The past, you know, is our only escape. You don't begrudge it us, do you?'

I shook my head, although by training and temperament I could find no merit in his argument. 'These are changing times,' I said. 'Your past is crumbling away. It's difficult to tell good from evil or right from wrong, let alone shades of intellectual preference.'

'But I can tell you really do still think there are mechanical solutions to our ills.'

'Don't you, sidhi?'

'I do. I doubt though that they're much like a medical man's.'

'I'm an engineer, not a doctor of medicine.'

'Pardon me. It's my day for gaffs, eh? But we're all guilty of making the wrong assumptions sometimes. Let us open the shutters and enjoy some fresh air.' Another of the women went to fold back the tall wooden blinds and let shafts of sudden sunlight down upon the maroons, burgundies, dark pinks, bottle-greens and royal blues of that luxurious room. The women sank into the shadows and only Sheik Abu Halil remained with half his face in light, the other in shade, puffing on his pipe, his silks rippling as he moved a lazy hand. 'We are blessed with a marvellous view.'

From where we sat it was possible to see the Nile, with its white sails and flanking palms, on the far side of an expanse of glaring granite.

'My sister –' I began.

'A remarkable woman. A saint, without doubt. We have tried to help her, you know.'

'I believe you're responsible for getting her out of police custody, sidhi.'

'God has chosen her and has blessed her with unusual gifts. Dr Pappenheim, we are merely God's instruments. She has brought a little relief to the sick, a little consolation to the despairing.'

'She's coming home with me. In three days.'

'A great loss for Aswan. But perhaps she's more needed out there. Such sadness, you know. Such deep sadness.' I was not sure if he described my sister or the whole world. 'In Islam, you see,' an ironic twitch of the lip, 'we share our despair. It is a democracy of misery.' And he chuckled. 'This is blasphemy I know, in the West. Especially in America.'

'Well, in parts of the North maybe.' I smiled. My father was

295

from Mississippi and settled first in Morocco, then in England after he came out of the service. He said he missed the old, bitter-sweet character of the U.S. South. The New South, optimistic and, in his view, Yankified, no longer felt like home. He was more in his element in pre-Thatcher Britain. When she, too, began a programme of 'Yankification' of her own he retreated into fantasy, leaving my mother and going to live in a working class street in a run-down North Eastern town where he joined the Communist Party and demonstrated against closures in the mining, fishing and steel industries. My mother hated it when his name appeared in the papers or, worse in her view, when he wrote intemperate letters to the weekly journals or the heavy dailies. But Pappenheim was a contributor to *Marxism Today* and, later, *Red is Green* during his brief flirtation with Trotskyist Conservationism. He gave that up for anarcho-socialism and disappeared completely into the world of the abstract. He now wrote me letters describing the 'Moroccan experiment' as the greatest example of genuinely radical politics in action. I had never completely escaped the tyranny of his impossible ideals. This came back to me, there and then, perhaps because in some strange way I found this sufi as charming as I had once found my father. 'We say that misery loves company. Is that the same thing?' I felt I was in some kind of awful contest. 'Is that why she wanted to stay with you?'

'I knew her slightly before it all changed for her. Afterwards, I knew her better. She seemed very delicate. She came back to Aswan, then went out to the dig a couple more times, then back here. She was possessed of a terrible restlessness she would allow nobody here to address and which she consistently denied. She carried a burden, Dr Pappenheim.' He echoed the words of Inspector el-Bayoumi. 'But perhaps we, even we, shall never know what it was.'

She arrived at the Osiris only a minute or two late. She wore a one-piece worksuit and a kind of bush-hat with a veil. She also carried a briefcase which she displayed in some embarrassment. 'Habit, I suppose. I don't need the maps or the notes. I'm taking you into the desert, Paul. Is that OK?'

'We're not going to your place?'

'Not now.'

I changed into more suitable clothes and followed her down to the street. She had a calash waiting which took us to the edge of town, to a camel camp where, much to my dismay, we transferred to grumbling dromedaries. I had not ridden a camel for ten years, but mine proved fairly tractable once we were moving out over the sand.

I had forgotten the peace and the wonderful smell of the desert and it was not long before I had ceased to pay attention to the heat or the motion and had begun to enjoy a mesmeric panorama of dunes and old rock. My sister occasionally used a compass to keep course but sat her high saddle with the confidence of a seasoned drover. We picked up speed until the heat became too intense and we rested under an outcrop of red stone which offered the only shade. It was almost impossible to predict where one would find shade in the desert. A year ago this rock might have been completely invisible beneath the sand; in a few months it might be invisible again.

'The silence is seductive,' I said after a while.

My sister smiled. 'Well, it whispers to me, these days. But it is wonderful, isn't it? Here you have nothing but yourself, a chance to discover how much of your identity is your own and how much is actually society's. And the ego drifts away. One becomes a virgin beast.'

'Indeed!' I found this a little too fanciful for me. 'I'm just glad to be away from all that …'

'You're not nervous?'

'Of the desert?'

'Of getting lost. Nothing comes out here, ever, now. Nomads don't pass by and it's been years since a motor vehicle or plane was allowed to waste its ER on mere curiosity. If we died, we'd probably never be found.'

'This is a bit morbid, isn't it, Bea? It's only a few hours from Aswan, and the camels are healthy.'

'Yes.' She rose to put our food and water back into their saddlebags, causing a murmuring and an irritable shifting of the camels. We slept for a couple of hours. Bea wanted to be able to travel at night, when we would make better time under the almost full moon.

The desert at night will usually fill with the noises of the creatures who waken as soon as the sun is down, but the region we next entered seemed as lifeless as the Bical flats, though without their aching mood of desolation. The sand still rose around our camels' feet in silvery gasps and I wrapped myself in the other heavy woollen *gelabea* Beatrice had brought. We slept again, for two or three hours, before continuing on until it was almost dawn and the moon faint and fading in the sky.

'We used to have a gramophone and everything,' she said. 'We played those French songs mainly. The old ones. And a lot of classic Rai. It was a local collection someone had bought with the machine. You wouldn't believe the mood of camaraderie that was here, Paul. Like Woodstock must have been. We had quite a few young people with us – Egyptian and European mostly – and they all said the same. We felt privileged.'

'When did you start treating the sick?' I asked her.

'Treating? Scarcely that! I just helped out with my First Aid kit and whatever I could scrounge from a pharmacy. Most of the problems were easily treated, but not priorities as far as the hospitals are concerned. I did what I could whenever I was in Aswan. But the kits gradually got used and nothing more was sent. After the quake, things began to run down. The Burbank Foundation needed its resources for rebuilding at home.'

'But you still do it. Sometimes. You're a legend back there. Ben Achmet told me.'

'When I can, I help those nomads cure themselves, that's all. I was coming out here a lot. Then there was some trouble with the police.'

'They stopped you? Because of the Somali woman?'

'That didn't stop me.' She raised herself in her saddle suddenly. 'Look. Can you see the roof there? And the pillars?'

They lay in a shallow valley between two rocky cliffs and they looked in the half-light as if they had been built that very morning. The decorated columns and the massive flat roof were touched a pinkish gold by the rising sun and I could make out hieroglyphics, the blues and ochres of the Egyptian artist. The building, or series of buildings, covered a vast area. 'It's a city,' I said. I was still disbelieving. 'Or a huge temple. My God, Bea! No wonder you were knocked out by this!'

'It's not a city or a temple, in any sense *we* mean.' Though she must have seen it a hundred times, she was still admiring of the beautiful stones. 'There's nothing like it surviving anywhere else. No record of another. Even this is only briefly mentioned and, as always with Egyptians, dismissively as the work of earlier, less exalted leaders, in this case a monotheistic cult which attempted to set up its own God-king and, in failing, was thoroughly destroyed. Pragmatically, the winners in that contest re-dedicated the place to Sekhmet and then, for whatever reasons – probably economic – abandoned it altogether. There are none of the usual signs of later uses. By the end of Nyusere's reign no more was heard of it at all. Indeed, not much more was heard of Nubia for a long time. This region was never exactly the centre of Egyptian life.'

'It was a temple to Ra?'

'Ra, or a sun deity very much like him. The priest here was represented as a servant of the sun. We call the place Onu'us, after him.'

'Four thousand years ago? Are you sure this isn't one of

those new Dutch repros?' My joke sounded flat, even to me.

'Now you can see why we kept it dark, Paul. It was an observatory, a scientific centre, a laboratory, a library. A sort of university, really. Even the hieroglyphics are different. They tell all kinds of things about the people and the place. And, it had a couple of other functions.' Her enthusiasm died and she stopped, dismounting from her camel and shaking sand from her hat. Together we watched the dawn come up over the glittering roof. The pillars, shadowed now, stood only a few feet out of the sand, yet the brilliance of the colour was almost unbelievable. Here was the classic language of the 5th Dynasty, spare, accurate, clean. And it was obvious that the whole place had only recently been refilled. Elsewhere churned, powdery earth and overturned rock spoke of vigorous activity by the discovering team; there was also, on the plain which stretched away from the Southern ridge, a considerable area of fused sand. But even this was now covered by that desert tide which would soon bury again and preserve this uncanny relic.

'You tried to put the sand back?' I felt stupid and smiled at myself.

'It's all we could think of in the circumstances. Now it's far less visible than it was a month ago.'

'You sound very proprietorial.' I was amused that the mystery should prove to have so obvious a solution. My sister had simply become absorbed in her work. It was understandable that she should.

'I'm sorry,' she said. 'I must admit …'

For a moment, lost in the profound beauty of the vision, I did not realise she was crying. Just as I had as a little boy, I moved to comfort her, having no notion at all of the cause of her grief, but assuming, I suppose, that she was mourning the death of an important piece of research, the loss of her colleagues, the sheer disappointment at this unlucky end to a wonderful adventure. It was plain, too, that she was completely exhausted.

She drew towards me, smiling an apology. 'I want to tell

you everything, Paul. And only you. When I have, that'll be it. I'll never mention it again. I'll get on with some sort of life. I'm sick of myself at the moment.'

'Bea. You're very tired. Let's go home to Europe where I can coddle you for a bit.'

'Perhaps,' she said. She paused as the swiftly risen sun outlined sunken buildings and revealed more of a structure lying just below the surface, some dormant juggernaut.

'It's monstrous,' I said. 'It's the size of the large complex at Luxor. But this is different. All the curved walls, all the circles. Is that to do with sun worship?'

'Astronomy, anyway. We speculated, of course. When we first mapped it on the sonavids. This is the discovery to launch a thousand theories, most of them crackpot. You have to be careful. But it felt to us to be almost a contrary development to what was happening at roughly the same time around Abu Ghurab, although of course there were sun-cults there, too. But in Lower Egypt the gratification and celebration of the Self had reached terrible proportions. All those grandiose pyramids. This place had a mood to it. The more we sifted it out the more we felt it. Wandering amongst those light columns, those open courtyards, was marvellous. All the turquoises and reds and bright yellows. This had to be the centre of some ancient Enlightenment. Far better preserved than Philae, too. And no graffiti carved anywhere, no Christian or Moslem disfigurement. We all worked like maniacs. Chamber after chamber was opened. Gradually, of course, it dawned on us! You could have filled this place with academic people and it would have been a functioning settlement again, just as it was before some petty Pharoah or local governor decided to destroy it. We felt we were taking over from them after a gap of millennia. It gave some of us a weird sense of responsibility. We talked about it. They knew so much, Paul.'

'And so little,' I murmured. 'They only had limited information to work with, Bea …'

'Oh, I think we'd be grateful for their knowledge today.'

Her manner was controlled, as if she desperately tried to remember how she had once talked and behaved. 'Anyway, this is where it all happened. We thought at first we had an advantage. Nobody was bothering to come out to what was considered a very minor find and everyone involved was anxious not to let any government start interfering. It was a sort of sacred trust, if you like. We kept clearing. We weren't likely to be found. Unless we used the emergency radio nobody would waste an energy unit on coming out. Oddly, we found no monumental statuary at all, though the engineering was on a scale with anything from the 19th dynasty – not quite as sophisticated, maybe, but again far in advance of its own time.'

'How long did it take you to uncover it all?'

'We never did. We all swore to reveal nothing until a proper international preservation order could be obtained. This government is as desperate for cruise-schoomer dollars as anyone …'

I found myself interrupting her. 'This was all covered by hand, Bea?'

'No, no.' Again she was amused. 'No, the ship did that, mostly. When it brought me back.'

A sudden depression filled me. 'You mean a spaceship, do you?'

'Yes,' she said. 'A lot of people here know about them. And I told Di Roper, as well as some of the kids, and the Sufi. But nobody ever believes us – nobody from the real world, I mean. And that's why I wanted to tell you. You're still a real person, aren't you?'

'Bea – you could let me know everything in London. Once we're back in a more familiar environment. Can't we just enjoy this place for what it is? Enjoy the world for what it is?'

'It's not enjoyable for me, Paul.'

I moved away from her. 'I don't believe in spaceships.'

'You don't believe in much, do you?' Her tone was unusually cool.

I regretted offending her, yet I could not help respond. 'The nuts and bolts of keeping this ramshackle planet running somehow. That's what I believe in, Bea. I'm like that chap in the first version of *The African Queen*, only all he had to worry about was a World War and a little beam-engine. Bea, you were here alone and horribly over-tired. Surely ...?'

'Let me talk, Paul.' There was a note of aching despair in her voice which immediately silenced me and made me lower my head in assent.

We stood there, looking at the sunrise pouring light over that dusty red and brown landscape with its drowned architecture, and I listened to her recount the most disturbing and unlikely story I was ever to hear.

The remains of the team had gone into Aswan for various reasons and Bea was left alone with only a young Arab boy for company. Ali worked as a general servant and was as much part of the team as anyone else, with as much enthusiasm. 'He, too, understood the reasons for saying little about our work. Phil Springfield had already left to speak to some people in Washington and Professor al-Bayumi, no close relative of the inspector, was doing what he could in Cairo, though you can imagine the delicacy of his position. Well, one morning, when I was cleaning the dishes and Ali had put a record on the gramophone, this freak storm blew up. It caused a bit of panic, of course, though it was over in a minute or two. And when the sand settled again there was the ship – there, on that bluff. You can see where it came and went.'

The spaceship, she said, had been a bit like a flying saucer in that it was circular, with deep sides and glowing horizontal bands at regular intervals. 'It was more drum-shaped, though there were discs – I don't know, they weren't metal, but seemed like visible electricity, sort of protruding from it, half on the inside, half on the outside. Much of that moved from a kind of hazy gold into a kind of silver. There were other colours, too. And, I think, sounds.

It looked a bit like a kid's tambourine – opaque, sparkling surfaces top and bottom – like the vellum on a drum. And the sides went dark sometimes. Polished oak. The discs, the flange things, went scarlet. They were its main information sensors.'

'It was organic?'

'It was a bit. You'd really have to see it for yourself. Anyway, it stood there for a few minutes and then these figures came out. I thought they were test-pilots from that experimental field in Libya and they'd made an emergency landing. I was going to offer them a cup of tea when I realised they weren't human. They had dark bodies that weren't suits exactly but an extra body you wear over your own. Well, you've seen something like it. We all have. It's Akhenotan and Nefertiti. Those strange abdomens and elongated heads, their hermaphroditic quality. They spoke a form of very old-fashioned English. They apologised. They said they had had an instrument malfunction and had not expected to find anyone here. They were prepared to take us with them, if we wished to go. I gathered that these were standard procedures for them. We were both completely captivated by their beauty and the wonder of the event. I don't think Ali hesitated any more than I. I left a note for whomever returned, saying I'd had to leave in a hurry and didn't know when I'd be back. Then we went with them.'

'You didn't wonder about their motives?'

'Motives? Yes, Paul, I suppose hallucinations have motives. We weren't the only Earth-people ever to go. Anyway, I never regretted the decision. On the dark side of the Moon the main ship was waiting. That's shaped like a gigantic dung-beetle. You'll laugh when I tell you why. I still find it funny. They're furious because their bosses won't pay for less antiquated vessels. Earth's not a very important project. The ship was designed after one of the first organisms they brought back from Earth, to fit in with what they thought was a familiar form. Apparently their own planet has fewer species but many more different sizes of the

304

same creature. They haven't used the main ship to visit Earth since we began to develop sensitive detection equipment. Their time is different, anyway, and they still find our ways of measuring and recording it very hard to understand.'

'They took you to their planet?' I wanted her story to be over. I had heard enough to convince me that she was in need of immediate psychiatric help.

'Oh, no. They've never been there. Not the people I know. Others have been back, but we never communicated with them. They have an artificial environment on Mercury.' She paused, noticing my distress. 'Paul, you know me. I hated that von Daniken stuff. It was patently rubbish. Yet this was, well, horribly like it. Don't think I wasn't seriously considering I might have gone barmy. When people go mad, you know, they get such ordinary delusions. I suppose they reflect our current myths and apocrypha. I felt foolish at first. Then, of course, the reality grew so vivid, so absorbing, I forgot everything. I could not have run away, Paul. I just walked into it all and they let me. I'm not sure why, except they know things – even circumstances, if you follow me – and must have felt it was better to let me. They hadn't wanted to go underwater and they'd returned to an old location in the Sahara. They'd hoped to find some spares, I think. I know it sounds ridiculously prosaic.

'Well, they took us with them to their base. If I try to pronounce their language it somehow sounds so ugly. Yet it's beautiful. I think in their atmosphere it works. I can speak it Paul. They can speak our languages, too. But there's no need for them. Their home-planet's many light-years beyond the Solar System which is actually very different to Earth, except for some colours and smells, of course. Oh, it's so lovely there, at their base. Yet they complain all the time about how primitive it is and long for the comforts of home. You can imagine what it must be like.

'I became friends with a Reen. He was exquisitely beautiful. He wasn't really a he, either, but an androgyne or something similar. There's more than one type of fertilisation, involving several people, but not always. I was completely taken up with him. Maybe he wasn't so lovely to some human eyes, but he was to mine. He was golden-pale and looked rather negroid, I suppose, like one of those beautiful Masai carvings you see in Kenya, and his shape wasn't altogether manlike, either. His abdomen was permanently rounded – most of them are like that, though in the intermediary sex I think there's a special function. My lover was of that sex, yet he found it impossible to make me understand how he was different. Otherwise they have a biology not dissimilar to ours, with similar organs and so on. It was not hard for me to adapt. Their food is delicious, though they moan about that, too. It's sent from home. Where they can grow it properly. And they have extraordinary music. They have recordings of English TV and radio – and other kinds of recordings, too. Earth's an entire department, you see. Paul,' she paused, as if regretting the return of the memory, 'they have recordings of events. Like battles and ceremonies and architectural stuff. He – my lover – found me an open-air concert at which Mozart was playing. It was too much for me. An archaeologist, and I hadn't the nerve to look at the past as it actually was. I might have got round to it. I meant to. I'd planned to force myself, you know, when I settled down there.'

'Bea, don't you know how misanthropic and nuts that sounds?'

'They haven't been "helping" us or anything like that. It's an observation team. We're not the only planet they're keeping an eye on. They're academics and scientists like us.' She seemed to be making an effort to convince me and to repeat the litany of her own faith; whatever it was that she believed kept her sane. Yet the creatures she described, I was still convinced, were merely the inventions of an overtaxed, isolated mind. Perhaps she had been trapped somewhere underground?

'I could have worked there, you see. But I broke the rules.'

'You tried to escape?' Reluctantly I humoured her.

'Oh, no!' Her mind had turned backward again and I realised then that it was not any far-off interstellar world but her own planet that had taken her reason. I was suddenly full of sorrow.

'A flying saucer, Bea!' I hoped that my incredulity would bring her back to normality. She had been so ordinary, so matter-of-fact, when we had first met.

'Not really,' she said. 'The hippies call them Reens. They don't know very much about them, but they've made a cult of the whole thing. They've changed it. Fictionalised it. I can see why that would disturb you. They've turned it into a story for their own purposes. And Sheikh Abu Halil's done the same, really. We've had arguments. I can't stand the exploitation, Paul.'

'That's in the nature of a myth.' I spoke gently, feeling foolish and puny as I stood looking down on that marvellous construction. I wanted to leave, to return to Aswan, to get us back to Cairo and from there to the relative sanity of rural Oxfordshire, to the village where we had lived with our aunt during our happiest years. She nodded her head. 'That's why I stopped saying anything.

'You can't imagine how hurt I was at first, how urgent it seemed to talk about it. I still thought I was only being taught a lesson and they'd return for me. It must be how Eve felt when she realised God wasn't joking.' She smiled bitterly at her own naiveté, her eyes full of old pain. 'I was there for a long time, I thought, though when I got back it had only been a month or two and it emerged that nobody had ever returned here from Aswan. There had been that Green Jihad trouble and everyone was suddenly packed off back to Cairo and from there, after a while, to their respective homes. People assumed the same had happened to me. If only it had! But really Paul I wouldn't change it.'

I shook my head. 'I think you were born in the wrong age,

Bea. You should have been a priestess of Amon, maybe. Blessed by the Gods.'

'We asked them in to breakfast, Ali and me.' Shading her eyes against the sun, she raised her arm to point. 'Over there. We had a big tent we were using for everything while the others were away. Our visitors didn't think much of our C-Ral and offered us some of their own rations which were far tastier. It was just a scout, that ship. I met my lover later. He had a wonderful sense of irony. As he should, after a thousand years on the same shift.'

I could bear no more of this familiar modern apocrypha. 'Bea. Don't you think you just imagined it? After nobody returned, weren't you anxious? Weren't you disturbed?'

'They weren't away long enough. I didn't know they weren't coming back, Paul. I fell in love. That wasn't imagination. Gradually, we found ourselves unable to resist the mutual attraction. I suppose I regret that.' She offered me a sidelong glance I might have thought cunning in someone else. 'I don't blame you for not believing it. How can I prove I'm sane? Or that I was sane then?'

I was anxious to assure her of my continuing sympathy. 'You're not a liar, Bea. You never were.'

'But you think I'm crazy.' All at once her voice became more urgent. 'You know how terribly dull madness can be. How conventional most delusions are. You never think you could go mad like that. Then maybe it happens. The flying saucers come down and take you off to Venus, or paradise, where war and disease and atmospheric disintegration are long forgotten. You fall in love with a Venusian. Sexual intercourse is forbidden. You break the law. You're cast out of Paradise. You can't have a more familiar myth than that, can you, Paul?' Her tone was disturbing. I made a movement with my hand, perhaps to silence her.

'I loved him,' she said. 'And then I watched the future wither and fade before my eyes. I would have paid any price, done anything, to get back.'

That afternoon, as we returned to Aswan, I was full of

desperate, bewildered concern for a sister I knew to be in immediate need of professional help. 'We'll sort all this out,' I reassured her, 'maybe when we get to Geneva. We'll see Frank.'

'I'm sorry, Paul.' She spoke calmly. 'I'm not going back with you. I realised it earlier, when we were out at the site. I'll stay in Aswan, after all.'

I resisted the urge to turn away from her, and for a while I could not speak.

## 15 WHEREAT SERENE AND UNDEVOURED HE LAY ...

The flight was leaving in two days and there would be no other ticket for her. After she went off, filthy and withered from the heat, I rather selfishly used my whole outstanding water allowance and bathed for several hours as I tried to separate the truth from the fantasy. I thought how ripe the world was for Bea's revelation, how dangerous it might be. I was glad she planned to tell no one else, but would she keep to that decision? My impulse was to leave, to flee from the whole mess before Bea started telling me how she had become involved in black magic. I felt deeply sorry for her and I felt angry with her for not being the strong leader I had looked up to all my life. I knew it was my duty to get her back to Europe for expert attention.

'I'm not interested in proving what's true or false, Paul,' she had said after agreeing to meet me at the Osiris next morning. 'I just want you to *know*. Do you understand?'

Anxious not to upset her further, I had said that I did.

That same evening I went to find Inspector el-Bayoumi in his office. He put out his cigarette as I came in, shook hands and, his manner both affable and relaxed, offered me a comfortable leather chair. 'You've found your sister, Mr Pappenheim! That's excellent news.'

I handed him a 'purse' I had brought and told him, in the convoluted manner such occasions demand, that my sister was refusing to leave, that I had a ticket for her on a flight and that it was unlikely I would have a chance to return to Aswan in the near future. If he could find some reason to hold her and put her on the plane, I would be grateful.

With a sigh of regret – at my folly, perhaps – he handed back the envelope. 'I couldn't do it, Mr Pappenheim, without risking the peace of Aswan, which I have kept pretty successfully for some years. We have a lot of trouble with Green Jihad, you know. I am very short-staffed as a result. You must persuade her, Dr Pappenheim, or you must leave her here. I assure you, she is much loved and respected. She is a woman of considerable substance and will make her own decisions. I promise, however, to keep you informed.'

'By the mail packet? I thought you wanted me to get her out of here!'

'I had hoped you might *persuade* her, Mr Pappenheim.'

I apologised for my rudeness. 'I appreciate your concern, inspector.' I put the money back in my pocket and went out to the corniche, catching the first felucca across to the West Bank where this time I paid off my guides before I reached the English House.

The roses were still blooming around the great brick manor and Lady Roper was cutting some of them, laying them carefully in her basket. 'Really, Paul, I don't think you must worry, especially if she doesn't want to talk about her experiences. *We* all know she's telling the truth. Why don't you have a man to man with Bernie? There he is, in the kitchen.'

Through the window, Sir Bernard waved with his cocoa cup before making a hasty and rather obvious retreat.

# 16 YOUR FUNERAL BORES THEM WITH ITS BRILLIANT DOOM

Awaking at dawn the next morning I found it impossible to return to sleep. I got up and tried to make some notes but

310

writing down what my sister had told me somehow made it even more difficult to understand. I gave up. Putting on a cotton *gelabea* and some slippers I went down to the almost empty street and walked to the nearest corner café where I ordered tea and a couple of rolls. All the other little round tables were occupied and from the interior came the sound of a scratched Oum Kal Thoum record. The woman's angelic voice, singing the praises of God and the joys of love, reminded me of my schooldays in Fez, when I had lived with my father during his brief entrepreneurial period, before he had returned to England to become a Communist. Then Oum Kal Thoum had been almost a goddess in Egypt. Now she was as popular again, like so many of the old performers who had left a legacy of 78 rpms which could be played on spring-loaded gramophones or the new clockworks which could also play a delicate LP but which few Egyptians could afford. Most of the records were re-pressed from ancient masters purchased from Athenian studios which, fifty years earlier, had mysteriously manufactured most Arabic recordings. The quality of her voice came through the surface noise as purely as it had once sounded through fractured stereos or on crude pirate tapes in the days of licence and waste. *Inte el Hob*, wistful, celebratory, thoughtful, reminded me of the little crooked streets of Fez, the stink of the dyers and tanners, the extraordinary vividness of the colours, the pungent mint bales, the old men who loved to stand and declaim on the matters of the day with anyone who would listen, the smell of fresh saffron, of lavender carried on the backs of donkeys driven by little boys crying '*balek!*' and insulting, in the vocabulary of a professional soldier, anyone who refused to move aside for them. Life had been sweet then, with unlimited television and cheap air-travel, with any food you could afford and any drink freely available for a few dirhams, and every pleasure in the reach of the common person. The years of Easy, the years of Power, the paradise from which our lazy greed and hungry egos banished us to eternal punishment, to the limbo of the Age of Penury, for which we have only ourselves to blame! But Fez was good, then, in those good, old days.

A little more at peace with myself, I walked down to the river while the muezzin called the morning prayer and I might have been back in the Ottoman Empire, leading the simple, steady life of a small land-owner or a civil servant in the family of the Bey. The debris of the river, the ultimate irony of the Nile filling with all the bottles which had held the water needed because we had polluted the Nile, drew my attention. It was as if the water industry had hit upon a perfect means of charging people whatever they wanted for a drink of *eau naturelle*, while at the same time guaranteeing that the Nile could never again be a source of free water. All this further reinforced my assertion that we were not in the Golden Age those New New Aquarians so longed to recreate. We were in a present which had turned our planet into a single, squalid slum, where nothing beautiful could exist for long, unless in isolation, like Lady Roper's rose garden. We could not bring back the Golden Age. Indeed we were now paying the price of having enjoyed one.

I turned away from the river and went back to the café to find Sheikh Abu Halil sitting in the chair I had recently occupied. 'What a coincidence, Mr Pappenheim. How are you? How is your wonderful sister?' He spoke educated English.

I suspected for a moment that he knew more than he allowed but then I checked myself. My anxiety was turning into paranoia. This was no way to help my sister.

'I was killing time,' he said, 'before coming to see you. I didn't want to interrupt your beauty sleep or perhaps even your breakfast, but I guessed aright. You have the habits of Islam.' He was flattering me and this in itself was a display of friendship or, at least, affection.

'I've been looking at the rubbish in the river.' I shook his hand and sat down in the remaining chair. 'There aren't enough police to do anything about it, I suppose.'

'Always a matter of economics.' He was dressed very

differently today in a conservative light and dark blue *gelabea*, like an Alexandrian business man. On his head he wore a discreet, matching cap. 'You take your sister back today, I understand, Dr Pappenheim.'

'If she'll come.'

'She doesn't want to go?' The Sufi's eyelid twitched almost raffishly, suggesting to me that he had been awake most of the night. Had he spent that time with Bea?

'She's not sure now,' I said. 'She hates flying.'

'Oh, yes. Flying is a very difficult and unpleasant thing. I myself hate it and would not do it if I could.'

I felt he understood far more than that and I was in some way relieved. 'You couldn't persuade her of the wisdom of coming with me, I suppose, sidhi?'

'I have already told her what I think, Paul. I think she should go with you. She is unhappy here. Her burden is too much. But she would not and will not listen to me. I had hoped to congratulate you and wish you God Speed.'

'You're very kind.' I now believed him sincere.

'I love her, Paul.' He gave a great sigh and turned to look up at the sky. 'She's an angel! I think so. She will come to no harm from us.'

'Well –' I was once again at a loss. 'I love her too, sidhi. But does she want our love, I wonder?'

'You are wiser than I thought, Paul. Just so. Just so.' He ordered coffee and sweetac for us both. 'She knows only the habit of giving. She has never learned to receive. Not here, anyway. Especially from you.'

'She was always my best friend.' I said. 'A mother sometimes. An alter-ego. I want to get her to safety, Sheikh Abu Hilal.'

'Safety?' At this he seemed sceptical. 'It would be good for her to know the normality of family life. She has a husband.'

'He's in New Zealand. They split up. He hated what he called her "charity work".'

'If he was unsympathetic to her calling, that must be inevitable.'

313

'You really think she has a vocation?' The coffee came and the oversweetened breakfast cakes which he ate with considerable relish. 'We don't allow these at home. All those chemicals!' There was an element of self-mockery in his manner now that he was away from his *medrassah*. 'Yes. We think she has been called. We have many here who believe that of themselves, but most are self-deluding. Aswan is becoming a little over-stocked with mystics and wonder-workers. Eventually, I suppose, the fashion will change, as it did in Nepal, San Francisco or Essaouira. Your sister, however, is special to us. She is so sad, these days, Paul. There is a chance she might find happiness in London. She is spending too long in the desert.'

'Isn't that one of the habitual dangers of the professional mystic?' I asked him.

He responded with quiet good humour. 'Perhaps of the more old-fashioned type, like me. Did she ever tell you what she passed to Lallah Zenobia that night?'

'You mean the cause of her arrest? Wasn't it money? A purse. The police thought it was.'

'But if so, Paul, what was she buying?'

'Peace of mind, perhaps,' I said. I asked him if he really believed in people from space, and he said that he did, for he believed that God had created and populated the whole universe as He saw fit. 'By the way,' he said. 'Are you walking up towards the Cataract? There was some kind of riot near there an hour or so ago. The police were involved and some of the youngsters from the holiday villas. Just a peaceful demonstration, I'm sure. That would be nothing to do with your sister?'

I shook my head.

'You'll go back to England, will you, Dr Pappenheim?'

'Eventually,' I told him. 'The way I feel at the moment I might retire. I want to write a novel.'

'Oh, your father was a vicar, then?'

I was thoroughly puzzled by this remark. Again he began to laugh. 'I do apologise. I've always been struck by the curious fact that so much enduring English literature has sprung, as it were, from the loins of the minor clergy. I wish you luck, Dr Pappenheim, in whatever you choose to do. And I hope your sister decides to go with you tomorrow.' He kissed me three times on my face. 'You both need to discover your own peace. *Sabah el Kher.*'

'*Allah yisabbe'h Kum bil-Kher.*'

The holy man waved a dignified hand as he strolled down towards the corniche to find a calash.

By now the muezzin was calling the mid-morning prayer. I had been away from my hotel longer than planned. I went back through the crowds to the green and white entrance of the Osiris and climbed slowly to my room. It was not in my nature to force my sister to leave and I felt considerably ashamed of my attempt to persuade Inspector el-Bayoumi to extradite her. I could only pray that, in the course of the night, she had come to her senses. My impulse was to seek her out but I still did not know her address.

I spent the rest of the morning packing and making official notes until, at noon, she came through the archway, wearing a blue soft cotton dress and matching shawl. I hoped this was a sign she was preparing for the flight back to civilisation. 'You haven't eaten, have you?' she said.

She had booked a table on the Mut, a floating restaurant moored just below the Cataract. We boarded a thing resembling an Ottoman pleasure barge, all dark green trellises, scarlet fretwork and brass ornament, while inside it was more luxurious than the sufi's 'harem'. 'It's hardly used, of course, these days.' Bea said. 'Not enough rich people wintering in Aswan any more. But the atmosphere's nice still. You don't mind? It's not against your puritan nature, is it?'

'Only a little.' I was disturbed by her apparent normality. We might never have ridden into the desert together, never have talked about aliens and spaceships and Ancient Egyptian universities. I wondered, now, if she were not seriously schizophrenic.

'You do seem troubled, though.' She was interrupted by a large man in a dark yellow *gelabea* smelling wildly of garlic who embraced her with affectionate delight. 'Beatrice! My Beatrice!' We were introduced. Mustafa shook hands with me as he led us ecstatically to a huge, low table looking over the Nile, where the feluccas and great sailing barges full of holidaymakers came close enough to touch. We sat on massive brocaded foam cushions.

I could not overcome my depression. I was faced with a problem beyond my scope. 'You've decided to stay I take it?'

The major domo returned with two large glasses of Campari Soda. 'Compliments of the house.' It was an extraordinary piece of generosity. We saluted him with our glasses, then toasted each other.

'Yes.' She drew her hair over her collar and looked towards the water. 'For a while, anyway. I won't get into any more trouble, Paul, I promise. And I'm not the suicide type. That I'm absolutely sure about.'

'Good.' I would have someone come out to her as soon as possible, a psychiatrist contact in MEDAC who could provide a professional opinion.

'You'll tell me your address?'

'I'm moving. Tomorrow. I'll stay with the Ropers if they'll have me. Any mail care of them will be forwarded. I'm not being deliberately mysterious, dear, I promise. I'm going to write. And meanwhile, I've decided to tell you the whole of it. I want you to remember it, perhaps put it into some kind of shape that I can't. It's important to me that it's recorded. Do you promise?'

I could only promise that I would make all the notes possible.

'Well, there's actually not much else.'

I was relieved to know I would not for long have to suffer those miserably banal inventions.

'I fell in love, you see.'

'Yes, you told me. With a spaceman.'

'We knew it was absolutely forbidden to make love. But

we couldn't help ourselves. I mean, with all his self-discipline he was as attracted to me as I was to him. It was important, Paul.'

I did my best to give her my full attention while she repeated much of what she had already told me in the desert. There was a kind of Biblical rhythm to her voice. 'So they threw me out. I never saw my lover again. I never saw his home again. They brought me back and left me where they had found me. Our tents were gone and everything was obviously abandoned. They let their engines blow more sand over the site. Well, I got to Aswan eventually. I found water and food and it wasn't too hard. I'm not sure why I came here. I didn't know then that I was pregnant. I don't think I knew you could get pregnant. There isn't a large literature on sexual congress with semi-males of the alien persuasion. You'd probably find him bizarre, but for me it was like making love to an angel. All the time. It was virtually our whole existence. Oh, Paul!' She pulled at her collar. She smoothed the table-cloth between her knife and fork. 'Well, he was wonderful and he thought I was wonderful. Maybe that's *why* they forbid it. The way they'd forbid a powerful habit-forming stimulant. Do you know I just this second thought of that?'

'That's why you were returned here?' I was still having difficulty following her narrative.

'Didn't I say? Yes. Well, I went to stay with the Ropers for a bit, then I stayed in the commune and then the *medrassah*, but I kept going out to the site. I was hoping they'd relent, you see. I'd have done almost anything to get taken back, Paul.'

'To escape from here, you mean?'

'To be with him. That's all. I was – I am – so lonely. Nobody could describe the void.'

I was silent, suddenly aware of her terrible vulnerability, still convinced she had been the victim of some terrible deception.

'You're wondering about the child,' she said. She put her

hand on mine where I fingered the salt. 'He was born too early. He lived for eight days. I had him at Lallah Zenobia's. You see, I couldn't tell what he would look like. She was better prepared, I thought. She even blessed him when he was born so that his soul might go to heaven. He was tiny and frail and beautiful. His father's colouring and eyes. My face, I think, mostly. He would have been a *wunderkind*, I shouldn't be surprised. Paul ...' Her voice became a whisper. 'It was like giving birth to the Messiah.'

With great ceremony, our meal arrived. It was a traditional Egyptian *meze* and it was more and better food than either of us had seen in years. Yet we hardly ate.

'I took him back to the site.' She looked out across the water again. 'I'd got everything ready. I had some hope his father would come to see him. Nobody came. Perhaps it needed that third sex to give him the strength? I waited, but there was not, as the kids say, a Reen to be seen.' This attempt at humour was hideous. I took firm hold of her hands. The tears in her eyes were barely restrained.

'He died.' She released her hands and looked for something in her bag. I thought for a frightening moment she was going to produce a photograph. 'Eight days. He couldn't seem to get enough nourishment from what I was feeding him. He needed that – whatever it was he should have had.' She took a piece of linen from her bag and wiped her hands and neck. 'You're thinking I should have taken him to the hospital. But this is Egypt, Paul, where people are still arrested for witchcraft and here was clear evidence of my having had congress with an *ifrit*. Who would believe my story? I was aware of what I was doing. I'd never expected the baby to live or, when he did live, to look the way he did. The torso was sort of pear-shaped and there were several embryonic limbs. He was astonishingly lovely. I think he belonged to his father's world. I wish they had come for him. It wasn't fair that he should die.'

I turned my attention to the passing boats and controlled my own urge to weep. I was hoping she would stop, for she was, by continuing, hurting herself. But, obsessively, she went on. 'Yes, Paul. I could have gone to Europe as soon as I knew I was pregnant and I would have done if I'd had a hint of what was coming, but my instincts told me he would not live or, if he did live, it would be because his father returned for him. I don't think that was self-deception. Anyway, when he was dead I wasn't sure what to do. I hadn't made any plans. Lallah Zenobia was wonderful to me. She said she would dispose of the body properly and with respect. I couldn't bear to have some future archaeologist digging him up. You know, I've always hated that. Especially with children. So I went to her lean-to in Shantytown. I had him wrapped in a shawl – Mother's lovely old Persian shawl – and inside a beautiful inlaid box. I put the box in a leather bag and took it to her.'

'That was the Cairene Purse? Or did you give her money, too?'

'Money had nothing to do with it. Do the police still think I was paying her? I offered Zenobia money but she refused. "Just pray for us all," was what she said. I've been doing it every night since. The Lord's prayer for everyone. It's the only prayer I know. I learnt it at one of my schools.'

'Zenobia went to prison. Didn't you try to tell them she was helping you?'

'There was no point in mentioning the baby, Paul. That would have constituted another crime, I'm sure. She was as good as her word. He was never found. She made him safe somewhere. A little funeral boat on the river late at night, away from all the witnesses, maybe. And they would have found him if she had been deceiving me, Paul. She got him home somehow.'

Dumb with sadness, I could only reach out and stroke her arms and hands, reach for her unhappy face.

We ate so as not to offend our host, but without appetite. Above the river the sun was at its zenith and Aswan experienced the familiar, unrelenting light of an African afternoon.

319

She looked out at the river with its day's flow of debris, the plastic jars, the used sanitary towels, the paper and filth left behind by tourists and residents alike.

With a deep, uneven sigh, she shook her head, folded her arms under her breasts and leaned back in the engulfing foam.

All the *fhouls* and the marinated salads, the *ruqaq* and the meats lay cold before us as, from his shadows, the proprietor observed us with discreet concern.

There came a cry from outside. A boy perched high on the single mast of his boat, his white *gelabea* tangling with his sail so that he seemed all of a piece with the vessel, waved to friends on the shore and pointed into the sky. One of our last herons circled overhead for a moment and then flew steadily south, into what had been the Sudan.

My sister's slender body was moved for a moment by some small, profound anguish.

'He could not have lived here.'

Aswan, Egypt, Oct/Nov 1988
Oxford, England, Jul/Aug 1989
Porto Andratx, Majorca, Sept 1989

Chapter Quotes:
1 Hood; 2 Khayyam Fitzgerald; 3 AE; 4 Dylan Thomas; 5 Wheldrake; 6 Yokum; 7 Aeschylus MacNiece; 8 Vachel Lindsay; 9 F. Thompson; 10 Peake; 11 Treece; 12 Duffy; 13 Nye; 14 C.D. Lewis; 15 E. St. V. Millay; 16 Nye.